Heart Eternal

Heart-Glow Volume III

Heart Eternal

Heart-Glow Volume III

SHEILAH R CRAFT

STARLIGHT BOOKS

STARLIGHT BOOKS

Cover photograph taken by Sheilah R Craft. The doll in the cover photograph represents King Eric II, Angilia's and Matthew's son. Based on the author's description, Monica Kohnke customized the doll to resemble King Eric II. Front piece photograph taken by Laurie Lenz, and is used with permission. The doll in the front piece photograph represents Angilia, who was customized by Laurie Lenz. The dolls were manufactured by the Tonner Doll Company. The author does not have any business affiliations with Tonner Doll Company, Monica K. Star Dolls, or ANGELS Doll Studio.

This novel is registered with the United States Library of Congress.

First Starlight Books edition March 2014

ISBN-13: 978-0615834429

ISBN-10: 0615834426

ACKNOWLEDGMENTS

More than anyone else, I thank God, literally, for blessing me with the characters and stories that populate the Heart-Glow novel series. These are more than gifts of some mythical Muse. These characters are gifts from God. I know that without God, I would not be able to write these novels. He gave life to them within me. He alone provides the physical and mental strength needed to carry me through the emotionally-toiling work of crafting the saga of the DeBruce Martineau dynasty.

I must thank the characters themselves, who are so alive and real. I feel them, their essence—their souls—around me constantly. They fill my waking and sleeping dreams, practically my every moment. They exist in me and with me, internally and externally. They were born in my soul, and I do love them immensely. Writing their story—past, present, and future—takes me through the depth and breadth of human emotions and experiences. At rare times I bemoan that, for I often feel drained, as if I have gone through those experiences personally. I have. I do. My heart, soul, and blood imprint these novels. I admit that I am deeply invested in these characters and what happens to them. I care intensely.

That care and love apparently translate for the readers who tell me that they, too, love the characters: Angilia, Eric, Patrick, Matthew, Dr. Taylor, Katherine, Alejandro, Juanita, and Eduardo. I did not know when I wrote the first novel, Heart-Glow, in 2012, how readers would respond, or if they even would respond. I am grateful to the loyal readers who share my devotion to these characters. Without them, this family saga would, for all intents and purposes, remain silent.

Some readers remain more involved than others. Laurie Lenz of ANGELS Doll Studio continues to bring the characters to life, just as she did Angilia, Eric, Matthew, Juanita, Alejandro, and Mitchell. Laurie has created Angilia as she appears in this novel. Now that everyone knows Angilia's heavenly past, how appropriate that she have a slightly more ethereal appearance, as if surrounded by a halo. Laurie captured that perfectly, as you can see in the front piece photograph, which depicts the ethereal Angilia in a photograph taken by Laurie. Laurie's web site is at laurielenzdollstudio.com/index

Monica Kohnke, whose work can be seen at monicakstardolls.blogspot.com, brought Prince Eric de Valdavia to life. Angilia's and Matthew's son, who was born near the end of the second novel, <u>First Love Never Dies</u>, grows to manhood in this novel. Monica made him resemble his grandfather, King Eric, yet managed to give him that unique quality that allows his personality to shine forth. He graces the front cover, bridging the gap between the past and the future perfectly, as the heir to the Kingdom of Valdavia should.

In the cover picture, King Eric II wears the coronation outfit, robe, and crown worn by every Valdavian King since the first, King Christophe, in 1331. The outfit and robe are one-of-a-kind pieces that were made by Louise Goldsborough-Bird, couturier and owner of Angelique Miniatures. Louise's exquisite work can be seen on her web site at angeliqueminiatures.co.uk

Gratitude goes to Bonnie Whicher, ace photographer and the inspiration for the character of Bonnie Glaser. Bonnie provided valuable information about Tavares, Florida, where she lives. Bonnie owns Bonnie Whicher Photography, and her work can be viewed on her website at bonniewhicherphotography.com

As always, I thank my family for allowing me the time and space necessary in order to write this novel. Other aspects of life were neglected during the process, yet they rarely complained. They put up with not seeing me for long stretches, knowing that writing a book demands time and energy. They also know that with four more novels remaining in the series that this pattern will continue for another two or three years.

DEDICATED TO E.A.P.--

THANK YOU FOR THE PERFECT TITLE

--AND THE INSIRATION FOR KING ERIC I

AND I GIVE UNTO THEM ETERNAL LIFE;

AND THEY SHALL NEVER PERISH.

--JOHN 10:28

CHAPTER 1

Angilia stood in the doorway of her father's suite and watched him leaf through a stack of papers at his desk as the sun began to tint the morning sky. Suddenly, Eric tossed the papers on the desk and turned to face his daughter with a beaming smile and those always-remarkable turquoise eyes. Those world-famous eyes sparkled with love and joy as he looked at his beloved daughter, whose own turquoise eyes shone with that familiar look of love that had first branded his heart over 52 years earlier, on the day his brother Patrick died.

"Happy birthday, Daddy," Angilia said, and went to hug her father. "I love you so very much, more than I have before, yet less than I will in the future. As immense as my love for you is, it increases moment by moment. I love you, my magnificent father." Angilia held him close to her, her tears wetting his suit jacket.

"I love you, my beautiful daughter Angilia. You continue to awe and inspire me, baby. That's what today is about. I know you never intended to plant the seed in my brain 17 years ago, but your sermon about King David making his son Solomon his co-monarch truly inspired me. I got the idea to make you my co-monarch then, and I knew I would when the time was right. You were so very young then, and I knew you and Matthew would marry fairly soon and start your family. I wanted you to enjoy your life and have the time to do the things important to you.

"I never expected the years that followed to be quite so full and amazing, Angel, but in retrospect, I am glad I waited for this. God sure had more important plans for you, didn't he?" Eric grinned, referring to her books—especially her memoir—as well as her recordings, worldwide tours, and speaking engagements with Patrick.

"I never could have predicted any of that, Daddy. God planned it all perfectly, though, and the past 17 years have been amazing, even at the turbulent moments. Despite the close calls and the sad times, our lives are truly blessed and just as God wants them to be, aren't they, Daddy?" Angilia's smile reflected her never-wavering faith, and Eric smiled in return.

"Yes, they are, Angilia. I am certain that I am the most blessed man ever created by God. All of you fill my life with so much love and joy. It began with Mother and Father, Grandfather and Grandmother, and Patrick. Marisol, my only love, made my life so rich and glorious, even if our time together was brief. Papa and Mamá and Eduardo, of course, are so important, and then Matthew, Mitchell, and Katherine brought even more love to my life. And Eric, our precious prince. How can he be eight years old already?" Eric giggled. "Angilia, you will always be the miracle of my life and my most treasured gift. In 75 years, I have received many wonderful and special gifts, especially those from you, Angel. God gave me the most precious gift of all when he ordained me as your father." Tears filled Eric's eyes, as well as Angilia's.

The tears trickled from Angilia's eyes as she looked up at her father. "The even greater gift is the eternity we shall spend together, Daddy. Our family reunion in Heaven will be quite grand and jubilant, for we will never part again. The day I do die will not be sad, because I will be with God and our family for all time. Seeing Mommy eight years ago when she came as Abuelo's Spirit Guide was a true gift from God. I look forward to meeting her, talking with her, and just being with her. Knowing that she, Abuelo, Abuela, and Grandmother will be waiting for me, with all of my ancestors, Tim, and Mr. Brennan is a happy, peaceful thought."

"You are so wise, my Angel, and so right. When God decides that my life on earth is over, I will not be sad. I will not necessarily want to leave all of you, but I know you will join me when God sends for you. You're right, death itself is not sad. The only pang will be in saying goodbye for a while. I love my life here with all of you in Valdavia, of course I do, but I look forward to being with everyone else again, too. Eight years ago when Mommy came to us, I knew then how glorious it will be when we go to Heaven. I can only try to imagine the beauty, peace, and love there, Angel," Eric said with a smile and a wistful look.

"Daddy, this is the perfect moment to give you my birthday gift. Do you remember at my wedding reception when Uncle Patrick gave me something from Michael and told me to open it privately in my room later?" Angilia asked him. Eric nodded and smiled at the memory. "I opened it when Matthew and I were in our sitting room that night, and it literally took my breath away. For 13 years, Matthew and I have found peace and comfort in Michael's blessed gift.

"I never showed you or told you about Michael's gift before, because that night the idea came into my head to give it to you when the time is right. I shared that with Matthew when we were on our honeymoon, and he agreed that this is the perfect gift for you. On our anniversaries this year, I knew I would give it to you today, Daddy. Matthew and I spent hours looking at it last night, so happy and warm. I want you to have this, Daddy, and to find the same joy, peace, and comfort from it that Matthew and I have enjoyed."

Angilia pulled a gold chain from under her dress and over her neck, and held the pendant in her hand. "Open your hand, Daddy," she softly told him, and when he did, she placed the necklace in his palm, curled his fingers over it, and kissed his hand. "I can think of nothing else I would rather give you today."

Eric unexpectedly felt his heart pounding furiously, and he looked at Angilia's love-filled eyes as he wondered what amazing treasure she just handed him. Eric smiled at her, took a deep breath, and slowly unfurled his fingers. As Matthew had on his wedding night, Eric looked at the pendant curiously, unsure just what it was. To Eric, it resembled a large, exotic marble suspended in a gold frame, much like the antique globe that had been in the palace sitting room for centuries. It looked like a miniature of King Philippe's 1379 coronation gift from King Charles V of France. "Is it a replica of Philippe's globe?"

"No, Daddy. Look closely. Look into the globe," Angilia whispered, knowing that the sight would take him by surprise as it had her. Still, it would fill his heart with wonder, love, and gratitude, as it had filled her heart and Matthew's heart. She felt her own heart dizzily pounding as Eric lifted the globe and peered into its core. Marisol! His wife! Eric watched his wife walk amongst flowers, and although her back was to him, Eric recognized his Marisol instantly. Suddenly, he saw her turn and smile at him. Literally. He saw himself clasp her hand and dance her into an embrace. They kissed, looking as they had in the early 1990s when they had married. Eric was nearly blinded by his tears, but he saw them smile and hold open their arms. Their beautiful daughter Angilia ran to them, hugged and kissed them, and looked happier than ever. Eric breathlessly watched the three of them walk arm-in-arm upon a gold road, with beautiful flowers surrounding them. He watched Angilia smile and hold open her arms for Matthew, who swept her into a hug. He watched the four of them sit amongst the flowers, smiling, talking, laughing, together. Eric stood rigid as he watched the phenomenal scene several times.

"Angilia, baby, this is a miracle," Eric said as his voice cracked through his emotional tears. "Despite everything you and Patrick shared with me about Heaven, trying to imagine my life there with Marisol was impossible. Michael, God's Warrior, gave you this on your wedding day, which was also my and Marisol's anniversary and Mother's Day. He knew what this meant to you, baby. I know what this means to you, to Matthew, and to me."

Eric pulled his daughter to him and held her close. "I can never thank you enough for sharing this with me, Angel. What a blessed start to this blessed day. I can never let you give this to me. It was meant for you," Eric said as he reached to place it over Angilia's head.

She gently took hold of her father's hands and smiled through her own emotional tears. "I want you to have this, Daddy.

No one deserves this more than you. I have kept this with me constantly. I have kept Mommy with me constantly for the past 13 years. She has brought me comfort, hope, truth, and love for those 13 years. I want you to have that, Daddy. Wear this under your shirt, next to your heart, and you will feel Mommy with you always. She is your one true love, your first and only love, and you should have this now, Daddy." Angilia stood on the toes of her left leg and slid the chain over her father's head, around his neck. She kissed his cheek. "God allowed Michael to give us this miraculous gift. Happy birthday, Daddy."

"I know how blessed I am to see and to wear this, Angel. I will wear it for the rest of my life. After that, I want you to wear it again. At the right time, you will give this to Eric. This pendant will be our family's holy relic for all generations to come," Eric prophesied, kissed Angilia, and went down to breakfast with her before that morning's church service.

§§§§§

Eric, Patrick, Angilia, Prince Eric, and Matthew greeted the congregation alongside Reverend Hutchins that morning for a very special Saturday morning Service of Thanksgiving on King Eric's 75th birthday. As they arrived at the church, everyone wished both King Eric and Prince Eric a happy birthday. The entire country celebrated their beloved King's birthday that day. "Happy birthday, Sir. Happy birthday, Eric. Good morning, Princess darling. Hello, Matthew."

"Thank you, Billy," Eric said and his grandson echoed. Eric smiled at Billy, now a 27-year-old college graduate working as a senior executive at Valmondois' most successful time management company. Billy thrived in his role as facilitator trainer, providing professionals the skills and tools they needed in order to maximize their time, goals, decisions, and scheduling. He watched as Billy kissed Angilia's hand as he had done most of his life.

Angilia smiled as she watched the several hundred members of the congregation wish her father and her son happy birthday. Her close friends Nicole and William arrived with their daughter Yvonne, who was now seven years old and her mother's veritable twin. They all wished King Eric a happy birthday. Yvonne curtsied to King Eric, and then much to everyone's delight, curtsied to Prince Eric, who was just seven months older than she and her closet friend. Prince Eric smiled, bowed, and kissed Yvonne's hand. Nicole and Angilia smiled at one another, constantly amazed and charmed by their darling children.

Before the Royal Family entered the church for the service, Darlene and Scott breathlessly arrived, apologizing for their lateness. "I'm sorry. I had to finish my surprise for this afternoon," Darlene said, referring to her homemade gift for the double birthday party for Eric and Eric that afternoon. Prince Eric and Yvonne looked at one another and giggled, as both were well aware of Darlene's enthusiastic admiration of King Eric. Scott greeted everyone and led his wife of three years to their seats before the service began. Nicole, William, and Yvonne followed them, leaving the Royal Family to follow Reverend Hutchins into the church.

Reverend Hutchins took his place at the pulpit, and began the day's service as he began every service, with a prayer. The congregation stood in unison and bowed their heads as the prayer began. "Dear God, We thank you for your abundant and loving blessings upon each of us and upon Valdavia. Our nation remains unfettered by most of the woes and ills which plague many of our fellow nations. Valdavians remain free from poverty, unrest, wars, hunger, financial and employment depressions, and malcontent. We, the citizens of Valdavia, know how blessed and fortunate we are and have been since the nation's founding 698 years ago. The Kings of Valdavia in succession have put us and our needs foremost. We know our King Eric is a benevolent, compassionate man who does not take his birthright for granted. Rather, he sees it as his duty to consistently place our needs before all else. Going forward, through this 21st century, we know that we and Valdavia are under the leadership of a King and a future Queen whom you, God, saw fit to ordain as our monarchs. We humbly thank you for your continued blessings and for the life of King Eric on this, his 75th birthday. Amen."

The congregation echoed the Amen, and took their seats for the sermon. Other than Reverend Hutchins and those in the Royal Family and household, no one else knew in advance the purpose behind the day's sermon. Reverend Hutchins reminded everyone watching the live broadcast of the service across Valdavia—and the world—of God's ordination of King David and his son, Solomon. "David, a man eternally renowned for his wisdom, knew that his son was equally wise and ordained, and when David knew he needed a co-monarch he wisely proclaimed his son King Solomon. The two men co-ruled Israel, beginning when Solomon was in his early 20s. When David died, he departed this world knowing that Israel was under the reign of the best possible King. Like his father, Solomon was wise and godly, ruling Israel with prayer and under God's divine law. Valdavia is blessed with a King and a future Queen who are similarly wise and godly." Reverend Hutchins bowed to Eric, who stood and walked to the pulpit, a parchment scroll in his hand.

"Thank you, Reverend Hutchins," Eric smiled at his minister and friend. "Like Solomon, I was blessed with a wonderful and wise father and teacher, from whom I learned so very much about what it means to lead this country with compassion and prayer. In many ways, I have had a co-monarch since the day I assumed this title and role. God has guided me, assisted me, and taught me constantly every day over the past 37 years. I could never do this without Him, nor do I want to. God blesses me immensely, and for that I am eternally grateful.

"God's greatest blessing and gift to me is and always will be my daughter Angilia. She is the light, joy, and love of my life. My daughter is my strength and my inspiration and my greatest teacher. From Angilia, I learn so very much about life, love, faith, eternity, and courage. More than anyone I know, Angilia lives a godly life, a life built upon faith, prayer, and obedience. She is truly a divine blessing to me, to Valdavia, and to the world. All of you know that very well. God created Angilia to be Queen of Valdavia. I have known that in my heart since before her birth.

"Today, as Reverend Hutchins mentioned, is my 75th birthday. On this three-quarters-of-a-century mark in my life, the time is right and sanctified to fulfill the inspiration I received, albeit unintentionally, from my daughter during her 2012 Father's Day sermon. With Reverend Hutchins' blessing, I am deeply honored to read this Royal Proclamation to all of you, my fellow Valdavians.

Royal Proclamation

By

King Eric de Valdavia

Whereas Her Royal Highness Princess Consort Angilia, Duchesse de Valmondois provides consistently wise counsel and support to the King;

Whereas Her Royal Highness tirelessly increases her foundations, patronages, and endless work for the betterment of all Valdavians' lives, the country's educational systems, the arts, and overall wellbeing of Valdavia;

Whereas Her Royal Highness humbly and courageously follows God's will in all she does, I hereby issue this Royal Proclamation.

On this 17ᵗʰ day of November 2029, I, King Eric de Valdavia, do decree upon Her Royal Highness the title of Her Majesty Queen Angilia de Valdavia. From this moment onward, Angilia remains my co-monarch of Valdavia. Her Majesty and I shall henceforth share the duties of the monarchy.

Her Majesty Queen Angilia de Valdavia will be Coronated formally as co-monarch on the 3ʳᵈ day of January 2030.

Signed: King Eric R

Dated: 17 November 2029

My heart is so full of love, gratitude, joy, and peace knowing that my daughter is our Queen. Angilia and I shall work together henceforth to maintain Valdavia's strength, security, and tranquility."

In Christ Church Valmondois, members of the congregation openly praised God for such a magnificent blessing. They had long known how ordained Angilia was, and they recognized how bountifully they were blessed to have her as their Queen. Across Valdavia, those watching the live feed of the service echoed the praise and thanksgiving as they rejoiced in unison. Simultaneously, people across the globe watched in stunned amazement, never expecting Angilia to become Queen before her father's death.

"Both Angilia and I have always felt so honored to live in this wonderful country with all of you and to work on your behalf. I know I speak for both of us when I say that we are truly blessed by God to serve you. You fill our lives with love, joy, and purpose. You give us so very much, and for that we thank you and God," Eric concluded before he returned to his seat.

The congregation stood to sing one of Angilia's favorite hymns, "Where No One Stands Alone." Prince Eric held his mother's hand as he sang, fighting the tears of love and happiness that threatened to spill from his eyes. Angilia smiled down at her son, the boy destined to lead Valdavia after she and her father departed earth. Prince Eric smiled up at her in return, his turquoise eyes so full of love and wonder.

Angilia pondered whether Prince Eric ever remembered his past in the Unborn Children Sphere, where they had met long ago. She had seen him there as the man he would be in a few decades, a man in his late 40s. Perhaps that is when her son would become King Eric II de Valdavia. The thought filled her heart and soul with immense love and peace. Prince Eric was so much like his grandfather, already empathetic, compassionate, and benevolent. Angilia knew, deep in her soul, that her son would be a King much like his beloved, respected grandfather. Valdavia was indeed truly blessed to have King Eric and Prince Eric.

"On this day of celebration, let us remember foremost from whom we receive our blessings. Our King and our Queen are sanctified by God. He created Eric and Angilia to be Valdavia's King and Queen, and how fitting that their reign mirrors that of David and Solomon, God's sanctified Kings of Israel. Let us pray," Reverend Hutchins commanded.

Every Valdavian watching bowed their heads simultaneously to offer prayers of praise, thanksgiving, and joy. "Dear God, We, the citizens of Valdavia, thank you for ordaining King Eric and Queen Angilia our monarchs. Their Majesties lead us with your laws and commandments guiding their every thought, decision, and act. They not only put our needs and concerns before their own, but they show us by example what it means to live a life of obedience to you, God. We ask you, dear God, to continue to watch over them with your loving compassion as they do your bidding on earth. Amen."

The congregation joyfully echoed the Amen, never expecting the Proclamation—and a new Queen—that day. The traditional receiving line instantly became a thanksgiving session overflowing with tears, prayers, hugs, kisses, and joyfulness. Angilia's friends encircled her in a collective embrace as they congratulated her. Darlene burst into tears, typically overcome by her emotions. "This is so awesome, Angilia," Shannon said as Darlene wept, a comment repeated by the rest of the friends.

"No one deserves these honors and blessings more than you do, Angilia. I am so proud to call you my friend," Nicole smiled through her tears. Darlene grabbed Angilia in a hug as she sobbed loudly—quite loudly. Others began to look at her, wondering what was wrong with Darlene this time. Scott kissed Angilia's cheek and told everyone he and Darlene would see them later at the birthday party. He quickly shepherded his crying wife to their car.

Soon, the other friends left as well, with their own promises to arrive early for the joint party. Eric, Roger, and Patrick talked with those who had gone to high school with them, all of whom were invited to the party, not to bring presents but to spend the afternoon together in friendship. Reverend Hutchins was counted among them, even though he had been three years ahead of Eric and Roger. Samuel Hutchins had been a supportive, kind friend to them most of their lives. All of their former classmates promised to attend, all still pleasantly stunned by Eric's Proclamation.

The Royal party left the church with Reverend Hutchins' blessings and his promise to share their joy that afternoon. When they all walked down the steps, they were immediately surrounded by cameras, microphones, and a herd of reporters. From where had they come so suddenly? Eric wondered aloud. Angilia smiled and slipped her arm around her father's waist. "They started arriving yesterday to cover your birthday," she smiled up at him.

"What a waste of resources," Eric claimed, his face betraying his unadulterated surprise. "People have birthdays every day."

"Sure they do, but the world's most popular King has his 75th birthday only once," Katherine added, her brown eyes impishly smiling at Eric, who appeared even more handsome than ever with a bit more grey in his raven hair.

Eric blushed in response, just as dozens of cameras flashed in their faces. Patrick, Eric, Angilia, Prince Eric, and Matthew led the Royal group on the short walk home, much to the photographers' pleasure. Several of them screamed "Your Majesty," which Angilia presumed meant her father. After a moment, Prince Eric gently tugged his mother's hand, and said, "They mean you, Mommy. They want you to look at the cameras."

Angilia giggled and smiled gleefully at the photographers, who stumbled while they simultaneously walked backwards, jostled for the best angles, and snapped hundreds of pictures. She smiled up at her father, her eternal love for him clearly evident on her radiant face. Eric returned her smile, elated that his precious daughter was his co-monarch. Marisol had been his Queen Consort from 15 September 1992 until 23 October 1995—just three years. She had planned to do so very much. She wanted to establish foundations and charities. Marisol wanted to help the people of Valdavia who had welcomed her so kindly and enthusiastically when she had arrived as Prince Eric's future fiancée. They loved her, because Eric loved her.

Eric often speculated about everything that his wife would have accomplished had her destiny been different. He could never remain sad for long, though, when he looked at their daughter and all that she had accomplished in 33 years. Eric glowed when he realized how very much more Angilia would do in the decades that followed.

At that moment, a woman holding a crying baby approached Angilia, and Angilia smiled at her. "Your Majesty, forgive me for intruding, but I would like to ask you and your uncle a favor. An honor, actually. Would you bless my baby by praying for him? Please? It would mean so much to me to know that he is protected by your prayers. I know you can intervene with God for Nick and make him well again. I know you can. Please."

Angilia was stunned, and while she glanced at her Uncle Patrick, the woman placed her son in Angilia's arms. The boy stopped crying instantly, and his mother began weeping. Angilia motioned for Patrick to step closer, and he did so, placing his hands on the baby. Angilia and Patrick closed their eyes and softly prayed for the baby's divine protection and love. As they did, the gathered photographers took hundreds of photographs. A few news cameras captured the entire scene, which hit the airwaves and Internet almost immediately.

The crowd that had surrounded and followed the Royal party quickly grew as word spread of the miracle in progress. Patrick and Angilia concluded their prayer with a joint "Amen," upon which the baby boy laughed and reached for Angilia. She kissed his forehead tenderly, and returned him to his grateful mother's arms.

"Thank you. You have no idea what this means to me. Nick has cried almost nonstop for three weeks. He doesn't sleep, and he has been just miserable. None of the doctors could figure out why. All of the tests they did came back negative. My husband and I were at the end of our hope. Last night as I tried to rock Nick to sleep, and he just kept crying, I remembered your book. I had to come to you, Your Majesty. I'm sorry for barging in on your special day, but you have no idea how grateful I am to you both. God bless you," the woman said and kissed Angilia's and Patrick's hands.

Even when cameras and people surrounded him, baby Nick did not cry or panic. Nick's exhausted mother made her way home while everyone else stood, processing what they had witnessed. Matthew smiled and kissed Angilia's cheek, and just as the Royal party began walking, they were forced to stop again. Many people who had followed them knelt in prayer before them. They praised Angilia and Patrick as genuine saints, knowing they had witnessed a miracle.

When people began kissing Angilia's and Patrick's feet, Angilia looked at her father helplessly. Roger understood well how people felt, but he also knew how uncomfortable this was for Angilia. He quickly and quietly called Reverend Hutchins, who arrived within minutes. Reverend Hutchins stood between Patrick and Angilia, his arms around their shoulders, planning to address the crowd. However, when people saw their minister with Patrick and Angilia, approving of them, they took that as a sign of God's confirmation of the Prince's and the Queen's divinity. Rather than quell the praise and prayers, Reverend Hutchins' appearance merely increased the fervor.

Despite his efforts to silence the crowd, Reverend Hutchins' words were unheard or ignored. In exasperation, Eric raised his voice and demanded peoples' attention. "Thank you all for greeting us on this very special day. We deeply appreciate your blessings and well wishes. I can never say enough how much we love you all and how honored we are to serve you. You fill our lives with such light and love. Today is among the happiest, most blessed days of my life for several reasons. One important reason is my amazing grandson Eric, who celebrates his eighth birthday today. In fact, we have a birthday party to finish preparing, so for now, if you will excuse us, we must return home. Thank you all," Eric said with his charmingly dimpled smile.

"Thank you. We do love you," Angilia reiterated, her own smile reflecting her joy.

Reverend Hutchins walked to the palace with them, past a throng of elated well-wishers on the mall. Angilia and Eric posed briefly for pictures before thanking everyone and entering the foyer. "What an auspicious start to your queenship, Angilia. As unnerving as that may have felt, I find it encouraging. People recognize you as an agent of God, my dear, and as such, you can do so much good for people on his behalf. People love you, trust you, and follow you. God knew what he was doing when he made you Eric's heir."

"Thank you, Reverend Hutchins. I will always do whatever God wants me to do. It does feel odd to have people fall at my feet, though. I'm just me. I'm not a saint at all, not by any stretch."

"They see God working through you, my dear. They see you as a soldier of God. You are their direct link to God, Angilia, much the way I and other ministers are. You and Patrick always keep the focus on God, not on yourselves. Unlike ministers, you two are truly heavenly beings, and that does set you apart from all other people."

"I know. I'm not used to all of this sort of attention, though. As long as it's about worshipping God, not me, that's fine. When some of them began to pray to me and to Patrick, instead of to God, that was very uncomfortable for us," Angilia admitted, looking up at her uncle. Patrick agreed with his niece.

"I know, dear. But I expect that's rather normal when people witness what appears to be a miracle," Reverend Hutchins advised. "Just continue your work as usual. That's what you should and will do, both of you. Well, I best return to the rectory and dress more appropriately for today's birthday celebration," he smiled and walked back to his small home behind the church.

"Speaking of which, I better make sure things are in order," Roger said and went to check with Chef Antoine.

"Why don't we also dress more appropriately for our party?" Eric winked at his grandson, and then hoisted him for a piggy-back ride up the staircase to their third-floor suites. Angilia smiled up at Matthew, her love and joy boundless.

§§§§§

Eric, Angilia, Prince Eric, and Matthew greeted the party guests at the front door, while hundreds of well-wishers shouted their greetings to the Royal Family. Paparazzi took pictures as each guest arrived, much to their amusement or discomfort. By 1:00, everyone was seated comfortably around the dining table for a festive lunch, which began with Prince Eric's grace.

Antoine and his protégé son, Anthony, served the first course, Eric's favorite tomato and basil soup. The main course consisted of Angilia's favorite, Juanita's delicious couscous-stuffed green peppers. Desert was the huge birthday cake that awaited Eric and Eric in the sitting room, where everyone gathered moments after lunch ended.

Both King Eric and Prince Eric had requested that their friends not bring gifts. On this birthday in particular, they had everything they treasured. Their beloved Angilia was their Queen, and their friends and family surrounded them with love. Eric and Eric stood side by side, their arms around one another, and blew out the twin heart-shaped candles simultaneously. Everyone applauded, and Yvonne charmed everyone by kissing Prince Eric's cheek.

The no-gifts request was ignored by Darlene, who presented King Eric with a huge tin of what she persistently—but mistakenly—claimed were his favorite cookies. Eric graciously thanked Darlene, and nearly made a near-fatal faux pas by lifting her hand to kiss it. Mitchell cleared his throat to warn Eric not to, lest Darlene crumble into a dead faint. Without missing a beat, Eric gallantly bowed over her hand instead, and she turned bright red. Yvonne and Prince Eric tried to stifle their giggles, as did Roger, who still found Darlene's infatuation of Eric rather humorous.

Nonetheless, everyone truly enjoyed the camaraderie and love through dinner, after which the guests began heading home for the night. They all promised to see one another at the next morning's church service. The family and friends went to the third floor, where everyone hugged before entering their respective suites.

"My Angel is the most magnificent Queen this world will ever know. I love you so very much," Eduardo said through his tears as he held his niece close. He kissed her cheek before he went to his suite.

Katherine and Mitchell hugged and kissed their family, as well, realizing they had known Eric and Angilia for nearly 18 years now. How much they loved them. Katherine dabbed at her tears as she kissed her precious grandson and wished him a happy birthday for the last time before she and Mitchell went downstairs and to their home on the palace grounds.

Eric, Matthew, Angilia, Prince Eric, and Patrick hugged and prayed together before ending this most ecstatic and historic of days. Patrick flashed his characteristic peace sign and returned to Heaven. Eric smiled, and then hugged his son-in-law. Tears yet again filled his eyes as he hugged his beautiful daughter Angilia. He then turned to his grandson. "Come on, my little man, let's get ourselves in bed now," Eric winked to his grandson. "We're another year older now, and this has been the most spectacular birthday ever."

"I agree, Grandfather. It's official now. My Mommy is the Queen. I'm so happy she became Queen on our birthday." Prince Eric hugged his Mommy, and Angilia held him close to her for several moments.

She bent and kissed his cheek, and he kissed hers. "I love you so very much, Eric."

"I love you so very much I bet it wouldn't fit in all of Heaven," Prince Eric declared. Angilia smiled up at her father and Matthew, all of them recalling what she had shared with them before Prince Eric was born. Angilia's and Prince Eric's love was forged in Heaven, long before either of them was born.

Eric went with his grandson to tuck him in bed. He did so often, and always on their shared birthday. Angilia turned and hugged her husband as very happy tears trickled from her eyes.

§§§§

17 November 2029

Today was extraordinary. My magnificent father turned 75 years old. My precious son turned 8 years old. To say I love them barely touches how I truly feel. Mundane words can never capture or explain what I feel. I do love them, yet what I feel is so much more than that. They are my soul. They fill and own my heart. Without them, I would never exist, nor would I want to exist without them. Who I am is all because of them, only them. Daddy and Eric are my soul. God created me for and because of them.

Uncle Patrick shared today with us, which made every moment far more extraordinary. He is so very special and cherished to me. He has been since that moment I came for him in 1977. We bonded instantly. Uncle Patrick was my second friend. Matthew was my first. They both remain so very important in my life. Every day when I look at my husband, I recall that magical time we shared in the Unborn Children Sphere. Now we share every moment of this life. We will share every moment of eternity! What an indescribable blessing!

This summer, while we all spent a week at our country house, Daddy told me that he wanted to make me his co-monarch, the Queen. I was so stunned. I never expected or anticipated any of that. He explained that he first thought of our being co-monarchs during the 2012 Father's Day service. He said he wanted to do this, and that he had prayed about this a lot. He waited until Eric was old enough to comprehend everything, and for Matthew, Eric, and me to have several years as a family before the duties and responsibilities of queenship entered my life.

I prayed about this, too, and that night as I sat on the tree swing praying, Michael came to me! He took my hand and told me that God wanted me to become Queen. This was part of my destiny. That is all I needed to know. The next day, I shared this with Daddy, and the happiness in his eyes sent my joy into the stratosphere.

Daddy told me he wanted to make the official Royal Proclamation on his 75th birthday, which was so appropriate and symbolic. When we learned that there would be a Service of Thanksgiving on Daddy's birthday, he and Reverend Hutchins agreed that the announcement should be made during the Service of Thanksgiving, given that God had sanctioned and ordained all of this. That is what did happen this morning.

I always knew I would become Queen someday of course. That was supposed to happen many years from now when God takes Daddy to Heaven. That is what I expected. I have watched, listened to, and learned from Daddy all of my earthly life. I knew I would be ready to carry on when the time came. I am ready to work alongside Daddy now, and so very honored to do so.

Eric is learning from Daddy—and from me—as he subsumes what we do. Eric II will be such a marvelous King, I have every certainty. He is so kind, thoughtful, and benevolent—like Daddy. Eric will place the citizens of Valdavia foremost.

We are all so incredibly blessed and loved. Thank you for your love and blessings, God.

§§§§

"Happy birthday, Your Majesty."

Angilia smiled at Matthew as he leaned on his elbow, looking at her with his love-filled amber eyes. "Thank you, Your Royal

Highness." She leaned up, kissed him, and giggled when he pulled her closer. He kissed her passionately, thanking God that his exquisite wife was healthy, happy, and in his arms.

"Oh, Angilia, I do love you so very much," Matthew softly said through his tears.

"I love you so very much, too, Mommy," they heard Prince Eric say outside their bedroom. "May I come in?"

"Of course," Matthew responded, and Prince Eric all but ran to Angilia's side of the bed and hugged her.

"Happy birthday, Mommy," Prince Eric said against her. He stood straight and handed her a gift bag. "Open it, Mommy."

Angilia smiled and dutifully pulled the contents from the bag. Tears stung her eyes when she saw an envelope with *"Mommy"* written on the front—a birthday letter from Prince Eric, the first he had written her. "Read that later," he requested, and she promised him she would.

A small box wrapped in pink demanded her attention, and she carefully removed the paper. Angilia unlatched the black velvet box and gasped when she saw a gold charm for the charm bracelet her band members had given her on her 16th birthday in 2012. Someone gave her a charm every year, each charm very special and personal. Few of them, though, touched her heart as much as this one from her little boy.

"Oh, Eric, this is so beautiful," Angilia managed to say before tears overcame her. She pulled her son to her, while Matthew looked at them with unadulterated love reflected on his face.

Eric stepped into the room at that moment, his own gift and letter for Angilia in his hand. The scene set his emotions aflame as well, and he felt tears fill his eyes as he leaned against the door frame. "Someone beat me, I see," he softly said with a smile. Angilia held a hand toward her father, and he sat on the edge of the bed facing her. Eric kissed her cheek and Prince Eric's head.

"I received my charm bracelet and first charms 18 years ago, and since then you have all filled the bracelet with lovely charms. Eric just gave me the 25th charm," Angilia said, and held the velvet box for her father and Matthew to see. Both of them smiled, knowing what the charm represented for Angilia. "Isn't it gorgeous?"

"Yes, Angel, it really is. What a wonderful charm for your bracelet," Eric smiled. "You are very thoughtful, Eric," he added, as he hugged his grandson.

"I want to attach this to the bracelet. I'd like to wear the bracelet today, Daddy. I will symbolically have everyone important to me right there with me. Would that be all right, considering the traditions and formalities of the ceremony?"

Her turquoise eyes stunned Eric, as always, with their depths, and he felt that familiar all-consuming love fill him. "Of course it's all right, Angilia. What a beautiful thought. Is the bracelet in your jewel box?" Angilia nodded, and he went to her wardrobe and removed the bracelet from the carved jewelry box he had given her, filled with her mother's and grandmother's pieces, also on her 16th birthday.

Eric held the bracelet as he sat again on the bed, looking at the 24 charms. Angilia handed the Archangel Michael charm to her son. "I want you to attach Michael where you think he should be," she told him. Prince Eric took the bracelet from his grandfather and found just the spot he wanted. He opened the lobster clasp and placed the Michael charm between the gold carved heart from his grandfather and Marisol's purity ring that Angilia had worn until her wedding day. Prince Eric handed the bracelet back to his grandfather, who felt tears fill his eyes yet again.

The four of them spent an hour looking at the various charms, remembering those who had given them to Angilia. "This is the crucifix from Abuela," Matthew said with a smile, recalling the Christmas of 2015 when Angilia had opened the box.

"And here is the love charm from Abuelo the last Christmas he spent with us in 2020," Eric softly said.

"I love them so much," Angilia said as she fingered the charms. "I know Abuelo and Abuela will be with us today. So will Mommy, Grandmother, Grandfather, Great-grandfather, and Mr. Brennan. I remember that last birthday he shared with me, the day our engagement was announced." Angilia fingered a charm as she spoke. "He gave me this beautiful enamel butterfly, because he remembered how much I adored his earliest memory story. So many people and memories are part of this bracelet, including our miracle son," Angilia smiled at Matthew. "I have to wear this bracelet today."

"Today is extremely beautiful, Angel. It will also be very busy. We need to get down to breakfast soon, but I want to give you this first," Eric said and handed her a present and an envelope. His birthday letters always warmed her. She gently traced her name, written on the front of the envelope in her father's elegant script.

Angilia smiled at her father and told him, "I have two very special letters today." She held up Prince Eric's letter, and placed both letters on her bedside table. "I will read them both after breakfast," she promised them.

Eric smiled at his grandson and squeezed Prince Eric's shoulder in appreciation. His heart soared knowing that young Eric already carried forward his personal tradition of writing birthday letters to Angilia. She knew what he felt, for the same thought had entered her heart earlier. Angilia kissed her father's cheek, sharing his emotions.

She removed the wrapping paper from her father's gift, lifted the lid on another velvet jewel case, and instantly grabbed him in a hug. She could no longer keep her tears away, and Eric held her close to him while she cried. "I love you and Mommy so much," Angilia said through her tears.

"We love you more than you know, baby," Eric managed to whisper. "I know Mommy wants you to have this and to wear this today."

"I am so proud to wear this, Daddy. I have seen it so many times in yours and Mommy's coronation portraits. It's so gorgeous and special, and I love you for sharing this with me and entrusting this to me. Mommy's brooch will make today even more emotional and personal."

Prince Eric understood how important his grandfather's gift to Angilia was and how his mother felt. He had never met his maternal grandmother, of course, but he knew her and he loved her. Marisol was alive and well-known to Prince Eric, because his family made her part of their everyday moments.

Angilia put her arms around Matthew and her son, forming a circle of love. "I love you, each of you, so very much. I hope you know and feel that. I am so blessed by you, and I thank God every morning and every night for each of you. I doubt I could do anything I do were you not in my life and my heart. Thank you for loving me, supporting me, helping me, and teaching me. You are my life."

"You are my life, too, Mommy. I love you and Daddy, Grandfather, Grandpa and Grandma. I love Roger, Daniel, and Susan. I feel like I am surrounded by so much love. I am so blessed." Prince Eric pulled his mother into a hug and kiss, then his grandfather, and then he walked around the bed to his father. Each of them felt surrounded by love, and they each knew how true Prince Eric's statement was: they were so blessed.

§§§§

January 3, 2029

Dearest Mommy,

Happy birthday! I love your birthdays, because they mean that you are with me for another year. That makes me very thankful to God, because I love you so very much. I love you more than anyone, which doesn't mean that I don't love everyone else. It's just that you are the biggest part of my soul. Everyone else is part of my soul, too, but you are there more than anyone else. You and I are like you and Grandfather.

I am so happy that you are the Queen, Mommy. I love watching you work, and I love how you do everything you do. You are the coolest Queen and the coolest and best Mommy in the whole world. I know you are.

I know that if Grandfather had not made you his co-monarch that I would not see a coronation for a very long time. I know how very special today is for the world. We have studied the past coronations in school this year, which is really fun, because the Kings of Valdavia are our ancestors. I know how blessed I am, because not many people in the world can say that. I feel like I am living through history every day, and I guess I am. You and Grandfather are King and Queen, and Daddy is the first Duc de Valmondois. I know that I will be the next King de Valdavia. That is how it's meant to be, I know that. I just don't want it to happen for a very, very long time, Mommy. It's not that I am afraid to be King, but I just love you and Grandfather too much, and I love having you here every day. I know that's not wrong, because love is never wrong.

I will watch your coronation today, and I will remember every second. Tonight, I will write it all in my diary so that a very long time from now our descendants will read it and know how proud I am of you and how much I love you, Mommy.

With all my heart,

Your Son Eric

§§§§

3 January 2029

My Beautiful Daughter Angilia,

My heart and my soul are so full of love, respect, and admiration for you, my Angel. My little girl celebrates her birthday and her coronation today. I have no words that can adequately say what I do feel today.

I am immeasurably happy that you, Angilia, are my Queen. You take my breath away. In less than two months, you have done so much—you created two new foundations, you were elected President of the School Board, and you executed your first law. I always knew you would be a hard-working, tireless, level-headed, and compassionate Queen, and you indeed are. Every day, I thank God for the gift of you. You bless me and surround me with such love every moment.

However many years God has left for me to stay here on earth, I will remain in awe of you. I am so honored to work with you, to learn from you, and to have your undying love. You have mine, you know that.

Today, as you take the Oaths, know, too, that all of the Kings who preceded us will stand with you as I will. You are their legacy and you are my legacy. Love fills us and encompasses us, Angilia, our love for each other, and the love that streams down to us from our ancestors. Love is our legacy, and that will live on through our precious Eric and carry forward to his children and grandchildren and all succeeding generations.

I love you so incredibly much, my beautiful daughter Angilia.

Eternally Yours,

Daddy

§§§§

"Oh, Angilia, this is such a glorious day," Susan said, tears evident in her choked voice, as she styled Angilia's trademark long hair simply by pulling the sides back into a diamond barrette. "You are so beautiful, my dear. You look more peaceful lately."

"I am, Susan. Everything is truly as perfect as possible. I have never felt as happy or content before. My life seems almost too good to be true, even to me. I love you all so much. You are such a beautiful friend to me, Susan. Thank you for everything, especially your friendship." Angilia stood and hugged Susan as they prepared for the coronation.

"Can anyone join the hug?" Katherine asked as she entered Angilia's wardrobe. Angilia and Susan held open their arms, welcoming her. Angilia kissed her mother-in-law and told Katherine how much she loved her. "I love you, too, dear girl. I came to ask if I can help you get ready. Mitchell is helping Matthew and Eric across the hall in Eric's room."

"Of course. We'll help Angilia into her gown, and then attach the train, jewels, and finally the robe. I have a steam iron here if we need to press anything, too," Susan explained. "Speaking of which, we need to get you into the slip and the gown."

Angilia removed her robe, revealing pretty, demure lacy lingerie. Susan held the slip, and Katherine held Angilia's arm while she stepped in to the white silk slip. Susan fastened the slip, and then removed the linen bag from Angilia's white satin and lace coronation gown. Katherine gasped at her first sight of the gown. "That is one of the most beautiful gowns I have ever seen."

"Thank you," Angilia smiled and opened her jewelry box. She reverently removed the diamond brooch that Eric had made for Marisol to wear on their coronation day. Angilia pinned it to the left shoulder of her gown, and smiled seeing her beloved mother's brooch glistening on her own coronation gown.

Susan removed the gown from its white velvet hanger and held it for Angilia to step into. Susan and Katherine pulled it up, over Angilia's hips and arms, and then fastened the three dozen pearl buttons down the back. Susan smoothed the lace and satin, and then removed the white satin pumps from their box. Angilia slipped her feet into her shoes, and then Susan removed the train from its linen garment bag. She and Katherine attached it to the gown, and finally Susan fastened the white pleated cummerbund around Angilia's tiny waist.

Angilia took her tiara from its velvet case, and Susan helped her place it atop her head. The diamonds gleamed in the vanity mirror lights, appearing rather halo-like. She next put on a pair of her grandmother's diamond earrings. Susan and Katherine looked in loving admiration at Angilia, this young lady who handled every pressure and task with grace and calm.

"You are so gorgeous," Katherine cried and grabbed tissues quickly. "Oh, poo, here I am crying again. Susan, we seem to cry an awful lot," she managed to giggle.

"I know. Life here is so full of emotions that I just can't help it," Susan admitted. "You are beautiful, my dear. It's not just the pretty gown. It's everything about you. You do seem to glow more now."

Roger had removed the coronation robe from the Throne Room vault, along with the Coronation Crown and jewels, and had them prepared for the ceremony. Now the robe was waiting for Angilia to put it on. They had timed their preparations so they would be ready no earlier than 15 minutes before the first carriage left the palace. Matthew came in at that moment, debonair in a morning suit, and stopped mid-step when he saw his Angilia, angelic in her white gown. His eyes brimming with tears, he walked to her and kissed her tenderly. Katherine and Susan began sobbing again, just as Eric and Prince Eric entered the bedroom.

"Why are Grandma and Susan crying?" young Eric asked, looking both confused and concerned.

Eric bit back his laughter and patted his grandson's back. "Because they are very happy," he simply said.

"Oh," Prince Eric replied. "May I give Mommy a kiss, too, before we all have to leave for the church?"

Angilia smiled at Matthew, and held her arms open for her son. She bent to kiss him, and Prince Eric pulled her into a close hug. "I love you, Mommy. You look like an angel in that white gown. I mean, like the angels we see in pictures."

"Thank you, darling. I actually wore a white gown when I lived in Heaven." She looked up at her father. "It was the same one I wore that first day we saw each other."

"I remember, Angel. I will always remember. I knew you were an angel before I knew the truth about you," Eric said through a teary-eyed smile.

"So did I," Patrick suddenly said, and put an arm around his brother's shoulders. "Angilia made everything all right."

"Looks like a family reunion," Mitchell joked as he and Eduardo entered to gather Katherine for the first carriage. "Hey, why don't we ask Bonnie to take a family picture before we leave?" Eduardo called her, and soon Bonnie rushed in with a camera. Everyone stood close together, including Susan, Roger, and Daniel, for the first of many portraits that day.

"All right, we have to get Angilia in her robe, and then everyone will be ready," Roger said. Eric lifted the purple velvet and ermine heirloom robe over his daughter's shoulders and secured it in place. Mitchell, Katherine, and Eduardo hugged her and even dabbed tears as Roger directed them to the first of three carriages in the procession.

"I just have to put on my charm bracelet," Angilia smiled and walked to her jewelry box to remove her very personal piece. Eric gently took it and clasped it around his daughter's right wrist. He kissed her hand and breathed deeply, knowing that all was right and perfect in their lives. Angilia had been created to become Valdavia's first hereditary Queen, and Eric felt such reverence knowing that she was.

Before she had to leave, Susan handed Angilia her bouquet, which had been designed just for Angilia's coronation according to her wishes. Four flowers, all of them white, mingled in what resembled a chaste bridal bouquet: chrysanthemum, Eric's birth month flower; lily, Marisol's birth month flower; carnation, Angilia's birth month flower; and lily of the valley, the flower long called Mary's Tears and associated with Christ's Crucifixion. Eric understood the personal and symbolic importance of the four flowers and the color white. He kissed her hand in gratitude, put on his uniform hat and gloves, and prepared for their glorious yet solemn day.

Roger rushed back in at that moment to marshal Susan, Daniel, and Bonnie for the second carriage. Angilia wanted the four of them to have equal status on this most special of days. They were, after all, far more than staff members; they were true friends, lifelong friends. They deserved the public recognition. Angilia hugged and thanked her friends as they left to enter their carriage for the ride to the church.

Ten minutes later, the final carriage made its way to the courtyard accompanied by the exhilarated cheers of thousands of people crowding the streets and mall. King Eric and Queen Angilia sat on one seat facing forward, while Duc Matthew—as people fondly called him—Prince Eric, and Prince Patrick sat across from them. They were showered with white rose petals and streamers, much to their delight, and escorted on their journey by screams, cheers, and applause.

The Coronation Carriage, which was led by Starlight and driven by Joseph, took the same route through Valmondois that Eric's and Angilia's carriage had taken on her wedding day. That gave a greater number of people a chance to see them that day, a day on which their beloved Queen took the official Oaths and wore the same Coronation robe and crown worn by every King de Valdavia from the first, Christophe, to the current, Eric.

Prince Eric did indeed attentively take in the sights and sounds along the route, and he just as frequently watched his grandfather and mother, making mental note of every detail. He already understood the historic purpose and importance of the diaries they each kept. Prince Eric knew that years after his death, his descendants would read his diaries and learn from him. The history through which he lived was daily recorded in his diaries, and he never took for granted his responsibility in recording that history for future generations.

When the carriage stopped in front of the church, the exultant cheers of the several thousand spectators tightly crammed in Valmondois—many of whom watched the entire ceremony on large screens that had been placed throughout the country—deafened the Royal Family and forced Franklin and Laurie to cease talking as they broadcast the ceremony. Mike and Tony, acting as footmen—their guns concealed as a precaution—opened the carriage door. Matthew stepped out, assisted his son, and then Patrick alighted.

Eric stood, eliciting more intense cheers, and stepped down. He waved at everyone before he took Angilia's hand and helped her down the carriage steps. Mike and Tony held her coronation robe until she and Eric were far enough up the church steps that it did not drag the ground. As they had on her wedding day, the King and Queen turned at the top of the stairs, waved to those gathered, and smiled for a few moments.

She did look like a bride to those watching, her white gown and train intentionally bridal. The Coronation Ceremony was in two parts, the first being the Christian Ceremony in the church. During that ceremony, led by Reverend Hutchins, Angilia would take the Religious Oath to uphold God's law and to govern according to divine commandment. Later that day, she would participate in the Constitutional Ceremony, led by King Eric, and take the Monarch's Oath. That portion of the Coronation Ceremony was conducted in the Throne Room.

The Christian ceremony began with the military trumpeters announcing the King's and the Queen's arrival with a fanfare. Angilia blew a kiss to the crowds, and then linked arms with her father and entered the nave. There, they were greeted by Reverend Hutchins, who prayed with them before he began the procession up the aisle. Eric removed his military cap and placed it under his left arm as he and his daughter made their way down the aisle. As they slowly walked, Eric recalled his own coronation and his walk behind Reverend Hutchins with his Queen Consort Marisol beside him. What a bittersweet day that had been, knowing he was now King because his father had died. Despite the solemnity of the day and the ceremony, Eric knew he was ready to assume the title and duties, for he had learned from the best teacher, his father.

Now his daughter walked with him on her journey to take the official Oaths and to be crowned Queen de Valdavia. Eric's smile reflected his joy, peace, and love that day, and all who sat in Christ Church Valmondois and watched the ceremony around the world could almost literally feel Eric's emotions. Angilia nodded to their friends and neighbors who filled the church, including her producer and band, as well as to the various crowned heads and leaders of state who attended the ceremony. She even gently nudged her father's arm when she heard Darlene sobbing, and Eric acknowledged with a gentle squeeze of her hand.

Angilia noticed her son standing between Matthew and Patrick, watching her and Eric intently, and knowing he would record every detail in his diary. Prince Eric smiled at her as she and Eric stepped closer, and she smiled with love when he bowed to his grandfather the King. Angilia felt her father's hand tighten on hers, and she knew that he, too, felt such a glowing surge of love in his soul. Eric handed his cap and gloves to Roger, who would return them when Eric and Angilia began the recessional after the ceremony.

A moment later, Eric and Angilia stood at the altar, and Reverend Hutchins turned to face them. The pulpit he used every Sunday had been moved, and in a place of prominence on the altar was the Coronation Throne that had been gifted to King Christophe de Valdavia by King Philippe VI de France for the first Valdavian coronation on November 17, 1331. The same Coronation Throne had been used by every King de Valdavia since then, and now by the first Queen de Valdavia. The gold throne had been moved under the protection of armed guards, from the Throne Room vault to the church very early that morning, along with the crown, sceptre, orb and ring.

King Eric escorted Queen Angilia to the throne, and arranged her long robe so that it cascaded before her. He smiled at her just before he rose and stood beside the throne. At that moment, the Coronation Ceremony began in earnest, as Reverend Hutchins presented the Monarch for the acceptance of the congregation. "Sirs and Ladies, I hereby present to you, the citizens of Valdavia, your indisputable Queen. Wherefore all you who are gathered this day to witness Her Majesty's coronation, are you willing to publicly accept Angilia Erica Charity DeBruce Martineau Taylor as your Queen?"

The congregation stood and answered in unison, "We are." When Reverend Hutchins nodded in acknowledgment of their response, he turned toward Angilia, who stood from the throne. She curtseyed to the congregation, an act that confirmed that she was their servant, not merely their monarch. Angilia took her seat on the throne again, and then the congregation followed suit and sat down.

Reverend Hutchins faced Angilia for the Religious Oath. "Your Majesty, will you to the utmost of your power uphold and maintain the Laws of God and the absolute profession of the Gospel? Will you to the utmost of your power uphold and preserve the doctrine of the Church, its worship, and government? And will you preserve the Christian foundation upon which Valdavia was founded in 1331 and has dwelt upon consistently since that time?"

Angilia's voice was gentle yet firm when she gave her response. "All of this I promise to do. The things which I have beforehand promised, I will perform and uphold. All of this I vow, so help me God."

A clergy from Cathédrale Notre-Dame de Paris stepped forward and bowed before Angilia. He presented her with a Bible, contained in a specially carved box made of olive wood from Jerusalem. Angilia showed her appreciation by bowing her head and kissing his hand. The clergy bowed and resumed his stance on the far right of the altar. Angilia handed the box to Reverend Hutchins, who walked to the ritual table and placed the Bible alongside the anointing oil he would use momentarily.

While Reverend Hutchins prepared the white linen garment for the anointing, Eric removed Angilia's diamond tiara and handed it to a matron who stood nearby to assist. Angilia then stood, and Eric removed the Coronation Robe from Angilia and likewise handed it carefully to the matron. Eric turned to take the anointing garment from Reverend Hutchins, and he slipped it over Angilia's gown and fastened it in the back.

Angilia knelt on a gold velvet kneeler in front of the Coronation Throne, looking to some people like Saint Joan d'Arc in her simple, chaste garment, her eyes closed, and her hands folded in prayer before her. Reverend Hutchins stood facing her, dipped his thumb in the oil, and placed the oil on each of her hands. He again dipped his thumb in the small container, and placed a bit of oil on her head. Once more, he dipped his thumb, and finally placed the oil over her heart. "In the name of God the Father, God the Holy Spirit, and God the Son, I hereby anoint our most reverent Queen Angilia de Valdavia." Angilia and Reverend Hutchins briefly clasped hands and prayed together.

He assisted Angilia in standing, and Eric removed the anointing garment, replaced the Coronation Robe and attached it to her shoulders, and once again arranged the robe before her as she resumed her seat upon the Coronation Throne. The matron appeared again, ready to hand the Crown Jewels to Reverend Hutchins for the climax of the ceremony.

"Your Majesty, I present to you the Orb of Jesus," Reverend Hutchins said as he placed a crystal sphere, surmounted by a gold and pearl cross, into Angilia's left hand. The Orb represented Jesus' rule over the world.

"Your Majesty, I place upon your finger this gold ring symbolizing your marriage to the nation of Valdavia," Reverend Hutchins proclaimed. He lifted Angilia's right hand and placed the gold band upon her ring finger, which he then bent to kiss in reverence and obedience.

"Your Majesty, I present to you the Sceptre of Wisdom," Reverend Hutchins stated, and placed the tall gold sceptre into Angilia's right hand.

As Angilia held the Orb of Jesus and the Sceptre of Wisdom, Reverend Hutchins took the Coronation Crown from the matron. He stood before Angilia, held the Crown above her, and slowly lowered it onto her head. At that second, the congregation—and thousands of people on the streets of Valdavia and across the globe—joyously cried, "God Bless the Queen."

The Homage to the Queen concluded the Religious Ceremony. The first to pay homage to Angilia was Reverend Hutchins, who would be followed by her family and members of the Royal household. Finally, in the one break with tradition at Angilia's express request, a citizen of Valdavia would step forward to pay homage. This person would represent every Valdavian citizen and the bond between Angilia and her fellow Valdavians.

"I, Reverend Samuel Hutchins of Christ Church Valmondois, will remain faithful and obedient, unto God and unto you, and faith and obedience shall bear unto you, our Sovereign Lady, Queen de Valdavia, and unto your heir and successors according to God's Holy Law. So help me God." Reverend Hutchins bent to kiss Angilia's cheeks before stepping to the left side of the altar.

Eric stepped before his daughter and knelt on one knee to pay his homage next. "I, King Eric de Valdavia, remain faithful and loyal unto you, and vow to walk alongside you all the days of my life. I furthermore vow to serve you and to support you in every step you take or decision you make. Alongside you, I will maintain my faith in and obedience to God, so that we co-reign over Valdavia according to God's Holy Law. So help me God." Only Angilia saw the love and the tears shining in her father's eyes as he spoke. Eric rose before her and kissed her cheeks, as he had done so often, and whispered in her ear as he did so. "I love you so very much, my beautiful daughter Angilia." She whispered her love for him before he stood and resumed his stance alongside the Throne.

Matthew walked to the altar and knelt on one knee before Angilia, and she saw tears shining in his luminous eyes. "I, Matthew, Duc de Valmondois, vow to give you my trust, faith, and loyalty all of the days of my life. I vow to support you and stand with you in all that you do. With you, I will remain obedient to God and live according to God's Holy Law. So help me God." Matthew bent over her knees briefly in prayer, and then kissed both of her cheeks. As Eric had done, Matthew whispered in her ear before he returned to the pew. "I love you, my Angilia."

As soon as Matthew was seated, Prince Eric stood and walked to his mother. He, too, knelt before her, and he placed his hand over her right hand, which utterly charmed everyone watching. "I, Prince Eric de Valdavia, do swear an oath to God that I will stay loyal and faithful to you as long as I live. I promise to do all that I can do to support you, to help you, and to honor you. As your servant and your heir, I promise to live according to God's Holy Law so that I remain your rightful heir and so that we shall live together for all eternity. So help me God." Katherine, Susan, Bonnie, Yvonne, Nicole, and Darlene sobbed, feeling Eric's love for his mother. Angilia felt tears in her eyes, and when Eric stood and kissed her cheeks, she kissed his, too. "I love you, Mommy," he whispered through his own tears before he returned to his seat.

Angilia could not help but smile when her precious Uncle Patrick stood, wearing his Army plebe uniform. She had only seen pictures of him in uniform, and she was thrilled to see him so dashing and handsome. He had long ago told her that he had wanted to be a career soldier, and he had just begun to fulfill that dream when he died. Eric noticed his brother wink at Angilia as Patrick knelt before her, and Eric's heart swelled with love.

"I, Prince Patrick de Valdavia, do solemnly vow to offer you my loyalty and allegiance for all eternity. I bequeath you my unwavering support and fellowship. We shall together remain always obedient and faithful to God for all eternity and live according to God's Holy Law. So help me God." Patrick prayed as he knelt, and then he kissed her cheeks. He placed his right hand tenderly over her left cheek, a break with traditional Homage protocol which no one truly minded. "I love you so, Little One," he smiled, and then returned to the pew and put his arm around his grandnephew.

Eduardo briefly hugged Patrick; the two men shared a close bond as Angilia's only uncles. Tears unashamedly slid down Eduardo's cheeks when he knelt in front of his angelic niece. "I, Eduardo Alejandro Martínez, do for all of my life, pledge my faith, trust, and loyalty to you. I promise to you all of the support I can offer to you. I promise to remain obedient to you and to God, and to live the remainder of my life according to God's Holy Law. So help me God." Eduardo stood, leaned down, and said, "I love you, my Angel." He kissed both of her cheeks and returned to his seat next to Patrick, who patted Eduardo's shoulder.

Mitchell next approached the throne, and knelt in front of his daughter-in-law. "I, Dr. Mitchell Taylor, do hereby pledge my loyalty and faith to you and to God. I offer you my full support and obedience for as long as I shall live. Under your guidance, I vow to live and to serve according to God's Holy Law. So help me God." Mitchell stood, grasped her shoulders in his firm yet gentle hands, and kissed both of Angilia's cheeks. Before he stepped away, he tenderly squeezed her shoulders, his way of telling her without words how much he loved her.

Mitchell likewise squeezed Katherine's hand as she stood to pay homage to Angilia. Katherine looked into Angilia's eyes as she spoke. "I, Mrs. Katherine Taylor, give you all of my trust and loyalty for the rest of my days on earth. I vow to do all that I can to assist you and to support you. Your wisdom and leadership I vow to adhere to, just as I promise to live the rest of my life according to God's Holy Law. So help me God." Katherine could not stop tears from sliding down her cheeks as she kissed Angilia's cheeks, and Angilia whispered, "I love you" in her mother-in-law's ear. Katherine dabbed her eyes while she managed to make her way to her seat, where Mitchell put his arm around her shoulders.

Roger took a deep breath and knelt before Angilia, as all who paid homage did that day. "I, Roger Rocard, give to you, my Queen, my undying loyalty, support, and gratitude. I vow to willingly follow your wise counsel and to remain faithful and obedient to God for the remainder of my life. I vow to do all in my power to assist you. My promise is to live my life according to God's Holy Law. So help me God." Roger stood and kissed her cheeks, and while close to her ear he whispered, "You are remarkable, Angilia." With tears filling his eyes, Roger rather quickly returned to his seat beside Daniel.

Daniel patted Roger's back just before he stepped forward and knelt in front of the Throne. Daniel tried to look into Angilia's eyes, but that was far too emotional for him. Instead, he looked above her eyes at the crown, praying to maintain his composure for his homage to his best friend's daughter. "I, Daniel Sein, do pledge to you my complete loyalty and obedience. I vow to do all in my capacity to support you and to assist you. So that I may be the best servant possible, I promise to live my life according to God's Holy Law. So help me God." Daniel stood, but closed his eyes as he kissed Angilia's cheeks. He dared not speak, for the tears were far too overwhelming, and it took every ounce of his willpower not to cry before Eric and Angilia, his King and Queen.

Susan knew she, too, would struggle not to cry during her homage to the Queen she had known from the moment of Angilia's birth. Susan knelt, and she did look at Angilia as she spoke. Tears trickled from Susan's eyes. "I, Susan Pierce, forevermore give you my undying loyalty and obedience. I promise to you to do all that I humanly can to support and to assist you. I promise to remain a servant of yours and of God's, and I vow to live according to God's Holy Law for as long as I live. So help me God." Tears did fall down Susan's cheeks as she stood and kissed Angilia's cheeks, and Angilia whispered in Susan's ear. "I love you, Susan. Thank you for everything."

Bonnie finally stood, knelt before Angilia, and looked into the eyes of the young woman who had orchestrated her and Eduardo's freedom with one sincere letter in 2012. "I, Bonnie Glaser, do forevermore pledge to you all of my loyalty, support, obedience, and appreciation. I am honored to serve you, and pledge to do all in my power to support you however I am able. I vow to live according to God's Holy Law. So help me God." Bonnie stood, unable and unwilling to quench her tears, and she hugged Angilia in gratitude before kissing both of her cheeks.

By then, many people around the world were crying, too, as the emotions became palpable. One last person remained to pay homage to Queen Angilia, and he stepped forward with a heart and a soul full of love and honor. Angilia nodded as he knelt before her. He surprised her and everyone else by kneeling low to the ground and kissing the hem of her gown. He then looked into her eyes, as he had done frequently over the years, and smiled. "I, William Panning, do become your liege man of life and limb, and of earthly worship. I will bear unto you faith and truth every day of my life. I am truly honored to pledge to you my troth. For you, my Queen de Valdavia, I will live and die. I promise to remain obedient to Your Majesty. I promise to live according to God's Holy Law. So help me God." Billy stood and bent to kiss Angilia's cheeks. He next bowed to her, and then to Eric, and returned to his seat in the pews.

Angilia stood, still holding the Sceptre of Wisdom and the Orb of Jesus, and curtseyed to Valdavia's citizens once more as a symbol of her service to them. She then turned to face her father, and she curtseyed to him, something that had not been scripted. She wanted to show him and the world that she would always remain obedient to her King. Following her heartfelt curtsey, Eric swallowed his tears and bowed to his Queen, showing the world his reverence for and obedience to her.

Eric and Angilia prepared to begin their slow, steady walk along the red-carpeted aisle. Just as they stepped down from the altar, the congregation stood and sang the Valdavian National Anthem. Eric took his cap and gloves from Roger and held them under his arm until he and Angilia neared the huge double doors. He there put on his cap and gloves, and then two soldiers opened the doors. People got their first glimpse of Their Majesties at that moment, and when Angilia stepped into the sunlight, she again curtseyed to all of those who filled the space near the church.

Eric held her right elbow as they walked down the stairs, with Matthew, Prince Eric, and Patrick several paces behind. Mike and Tony quickly alighted from the carriage as it pulled in front of the church, and assisted Angilia into her seat. They carefully lifted and arranged the Coronation Robe around her feet, and then held the door for Eric to climb up and sit beside his daughter. Moments later, to never-ending cheers, Patrick, Prince Eric, and Matthew climbed into the carriage and sat across from Angilia and Eric. Patrick smiled across to his niece, overjoyed and grateful that everything was just as God had planned.

"Mommy, you are so beautiful. I am so happy, and I love you," Prince Eric said, echoing the thoughts that Patrick, Matthew, and Eric each felt at that moment.

Angilia handed the Sceptre of Wisdom to her father and held out her arm for her son. Prince Eric stood and hugged her, which sent the crowd's raptured cheers into a state of passion. Prince Eric kissed her and took his seat before the carriage pulled away. Angilia waved to the crowds, and then took the Sceptre from her father's hand and smiled at him.

People cheered, bowed or curtseyed, and threw rose petals as the carriage traveled slowly through Valmondois. One young woman in the crowd frantically screamed for Patrick, and he acknowledged her with a wave and that charming slanted smile of his. She was so ecstatic to receive his attention that she broke through the police barricade and ran to the carriage. She seized hold, trying to open the door and get in, and Angilia yelled for Joseph to stop so that the woman was not dragged under the carriage. Tony and Mike jumped from the back of the carriage and grabbed her several seconds after she forced the door open and seized Patrick's leg, pulling on him. They finally pried her loose, despite Patrick being dragged from the carriage by her adrenaline-fueled strength. She was handcuffed by a police officer, the whole time crying and screaming her love for Patrick.

"Are you all right?" Matthew asked Patrick before the carriage resumed its journey. Eric helped his brother back into his seat, himself horrified at what had happened.

"Yeah, sure, I'm fine. That was trippy, though," Patrick smiled. "I'm sorry, Little One."

"Don't be sorry, just be alert and safe. I warned you and Daddy years ago about this sort of attention," Angilia reminded him.

Mitchell, Katherine, and Eduardo watched the scene in horror from their carriage, relieved when the young woman was handcuffed and taken away by police officers. Mitchell actually had to use smelling salts on Katherine when she passed out against him. They had seen exuberant fans before, but they had never seen a member of the Royal Family attacked in such a manner.

Patrick realized that everyone stood stunned and horrified along the route, silent and unmoving, and he waved and loudly shouted, "I'm okay. Everyone's fine. Let's get on with the party." The cheers and applause resounded in response, and Angilia giggled. So did Prince Eric, who leaned across his granduncle to wave at everyone. Patrick lifted Prince Eric onto his lap, and Angilia beamed at the sight. What a spectacular miracle to have Patrick with them on this extraordinary day.

§§§§

Once everyone returned to the palace, they rallied around Patrick, aghast at the aggressive incident. Patrick reassured them that he was fine. "I can't get hurt. I'm a soul manifestation of my physical body, so I don't have flesh and bones the way you do or I used to. I was just worried that someone else would get hurt. Or that she'd ruin my uniform. I don't think I could replace this uniform, you know. I got this in 1976, so I'm pretty sure plebe uniforms don't look like this anymore."

Roger rolled his eyes, as did Eric. "Patrick, really, a uniform can be replaced. I'm just grateful she didn't or couldn't hurt you. You did handle the crowds well, though, considering they were scared immobile," Eric commented.

"It sure looked like she was mauling you, like a lion with its prey," Katherine declared, and held Mitchell's arm again.

Patrick giggled. "Nah. At least you know the next time not to let it scare you."

"The next time? I don't think I can stand a next time," Katherine said. "I need to pull myself together. Come on, Mitchell," she demanded and led him to a third floor suite so she could relax and freshen before the Constitutional Ceremony began soon. Everyone else followed suit, and gathered at the Throne Room on the fifth floor 15 minutes later. Reverend Hutchins and Billy were also present, as they had participated in the Christian Ceremony earlier. Angilia's friends, including Sam and the band, were invited, too, and everyone stood reverently at attention when Eric and Angilia entered together.

Angilia still wore her white gown, the Coronation Robe, the Coronation Crown, and the gold ring, and she still held the Sceptre of Wisdom and the Orb of Jesus. Eric now wore his Monarch's Robe over his military uniform, as well as his diadem. Darlene audibly gasped at the sight of King Eric, and Angilia bit back her giggle and subtly nudged her father's elbow. Mitchell heard, too, and prayed silently that he did not have to revive her with smelling salts that day during the ceremony. One incident that day was one too many.

Eric and Angilia stood below the thrones, at the bottom of the steps that led to them, and smiled at one another. Unveiled for the first time since his coronation as King and Marisol's as Queen Consort, both thrones awaited the King and the Queen. The last person to sit upon the Queen's Throne had been Angilia's mother. Both Eric and Angilia felt her spirit hover near them, and they bowed their heads together in silent prayer.

Eric took the Orb of Jesus and the Sceptre of Wisdom from Angilia and placed them on an altar across from the thrones. He picked up a worn Bible and held it in his palms. Angilia placed her left hand upon the Bible and her right hand up, prepared to take the Monarch's Oath.

"Your Majesty Queen Angilia de Valdavia, will you to your power and wisdom cause Law and Justice, in Mercy, to be executed in all of your actions and judgments? Will you execute Law and Justice that are in the interest of and betterment of the citizens of Valdavia?" King Eric asked Queen Angilia the questions which formed the centuries-old Monarch's Oath.

Angilia stared up into her father's eyes and confidently replied, "I will, Your Majesty King Eric de Valdavia."

Eric bowed, held her right hand, and kissed the gold band that Reverend Hutchins had placed there during the Christian Ceremony. Angilia curtseyed, and likewise lifted and kissed her father's right hand. Eric smiled, removed the gold band from her right hand, and placed the ring on the altar alongside the Bible.

"Your Majesty, you have been officially coronated Queen de Valdavia. I shall now remove the Coronation Crown," Eric stated, and lifted the heavy crown from her head. Eric placed the Coronation Crown on the altar and unlatched a black velvet box. He stood before Angilia, holding his first gift for her. "I now place upon your head the diadem of Her Majesty Queen Angilia de Valdavia." Angilia saw the most beautiful diamond diadem in her father's hands seconds before he gently placed it atop her head.

Eric smiled at her, and said, "I shall now remove the Coronation Robe." He unfastened the Coronation Robe and carefully placed it on the altar. He opened a linen garment bag and removed his next gift for Angilia. As he stood before her, he held behind her the crimson velvet and ermine Queen's Robe he had ordered made just for her, ready to fasten it around her shoulders. "I now place upon you the Queen's Robe of Her Majesty Queen Angilia de Valdavia." Her Royal Monogram was embroidered in gold near the bottom of the robe, a script *A* underneath a crown.

Angilia looked at her father with the utmost love and solemnity, and she felt nothing but love surround and fill her. Eric linked his right arm with her left arm, and they climbed the stairs to their thrones. Simultaneously, they turned and stood before the thrones for one minute. Eric kissed his daughter's cheek, and they took their seats upon their thrones. Their robes trailing down the stairs and their diadems gleaming, King Eric and Queen Angilia appeared truly regal and beautiful before God, their family, and their friends.

Bonnie had taken pictures throughout the day, and now she took the official portrait of Eric and Angilia as the co-monarchs of Valdavia. Only one member of the media had been allowed in the

Throne Room. Franklin Sydney had been invited, and given exclusive privilege to witness and even to film the Constitutional Ceremony. The legal agreement he and Carol, the Press Secretary, had signed, stated that Franklin's network could broadcast the ceremony only once, on the evening of the event. He would also be the first to reveal the official Coronation Portraits to the world. After Bonnie took portraits of Eric and Angilia together and alone, she took family portraits, the most charming of which was Prince Eric kissing his mother's cheek while she glowed.

Reverend Hutchins closed the ceremony with a prayer, and then Eric and Angilia mingled with their family and friends for an hour. Billy approached Angilia. "Thank you for granting me such a wondrous honor today, Your Majesty. I can't call you Princess darling anymore. You are my Queen. I meant every word of my homage, I really did. If you ever need anything, I will be here for you. I promise you that."

"Oh, Billy, you made me so happy today by taking part in the ceremony. I could think of no one else I wanted for that role. Thank you," Angilia said and kissed his cheek as she had done so often when he was a child. Now that he was a man, he loved her and respected her more than he had imagined possible. Angilia was his friend and his Queen.

Angilia's friends bowed, curtseyed, hugged, kissed, and congratulated her. Darlene's eyes were huge in awe, and she soon gasped the reason to them. "King Eric is so incredibly gorgeous, more than ever. God help me, but he is more handsome than ever." Scott rolled his eyes at his wife's undying enchantment, but he knew that, at this point, it was there to stay. "And Prince Patrick. I may burn in Hell for even thinking it, but he is amazing! I can't blame that woman for wanting him."

"Good grief, Darlene, really. Patrick is an angel, after all," Shannon whispered.

"I know. That makes him all the more attractive, don't you think?"

"Darlene, gain control of yourself before the banquet. You really don't want to choke or faint here today," Nicole warned her.

Scott actually asked Mitchell for a smelling salt capsule before the banquet began, just as a precaution. Thankfully, he did not need it that day, for the banquet went smoothly.

The Royal Family and friends gathered in the ballroom for a grand Coronation Banquet to celebrate Angilia's official coronation. Eduardo, Patrick, and Matthew offered toasts in honor of Angilia. Prince Eric, though, unintentionally stole the spotlight with his emotional toast to his mother, which left everyone in tears. "Your Majesty Queen Angilia, I offer you my sincere congratulations today. I am honored to call you my Queen and to be your obedient servant. More than that, I am blessed to call you Mommy and to be your ever-loving and devoted son. God Bless the Queen."

§§§§

January 3, 2030

Today, Mommy was coronated as Queen Angilia de Valdavia. I love her so extremely much! She is everything to me, always and forever.

Grandfather, Mommy, Daddy, Uncle Patrick, and I rode in the carriage together to and from the church for the Christian Ceremony this morning. She was especially beautiful today. She was glowing. She wore a white satin and lace gown that really made her look like the angel she is, although some people said she looked like a bride. Mommy said she wanted her gown to resemble a wedding gown, because she was symbolically marrying Valdavia during the ceremony. That was very beautiful for her to do, to show the importance of the symbolism of the ceremony so much throughout today. She also wore the charm bracelet her band gave her on her 16th birthday, with the Archangel Michael charm I gave her this morning. She carried all of us with her today. That was very beautiful to see, too. She wore Grandmother's coronation brooch from 1992, which Grandfather gave to Grandmother the day they were coronated. Grandfather gave it to Mommy this morning, and by wearing the brooch on her gown above her heart, she carried Grandmother with her today. I know what that means to her and to Grandfather. There was so much about today that made my heart swell with love.

We all got to write our own homages to Mommy, which we spoke to her at the end of the Christian Ceremony. I think we all got emotional. We all love Mommy so much. She is much more than our Queen.

Grandfather led the Constitutional Ceremony in the throne room this afternoon, and everyone saw how much he loves Mommy and how much she loves him. Daddy says that Grandfather's and Mommy's love is unique, and I know he's right. I can see it and even feel it. I love them both.

Grandfather surprised Mommy with a diadem and robe he had made just for her as Queen. When they sat next to each other on their thrones, I thought I would burst. They almost didn't look human. They were so beautiful and glowing.

Speaking of being human, it's a good thing that Uncle Patrick isn't human, but an angel. He was dragged from the carriage today on our way home! Some lady actually attacked the carriage and forced her way in and grabbed Uncle Patrick! I was scared, and Daddy actually held me tight. Grandfather held onto Mommy, because she tried to go to Uncle Patrick. Mike and Tony are pretty big men with lots of muscles, and they had a hard time getting that woman off of Uncle Patrick. That was crazy! I've never seen anything like that before. People get excited when they see Grandfather, Mommy, Daddy, Patrick, and even me, but I've never seen someone kind of attack one of us. Grandma was upset by it, and I can see why. If he were human, Uncle Patrick would have been hurt by that woman. Geez.

I have no idea when I will be coronated King, but I hope it is when I am very old. I want Mommy to stay here with us for a very long time. I would miss her if God took her to Heaven anytime soon. Mommy says it's normal to feel that, because she feels that way about Grandfather. We know we will be together in Heaven forever, but that doesn't mean I won't miss them until I am in Heaven. I just want them here with me for a long, long time. I hope you understand that God, and that you aren't upset about the way I feel. I love my family, and I love you. I just pray that you protect my family, and I know you will.

CHAPTER 2

Angilia and Katherine returned home from a Light Within board meeting at 12:45, in time for lunch with everyone in the dining room. Anthony served lunch at 1:00, while Antoine prepared everything in the sitting room. Angilia smiled at Matthew, knowing that Mitchell and Katherine would enjoy their surprise anniversary party. Matthew had invited a few of his parents' closest friends from Oxford, who were actually enjoying lunch in the kitchen so as not to spoil the surprise. They quietly went to the sitting room before Mitchell, Katherine, and the rest of the Royal party finished eating.

When everyone finished, Eric stood, smiled, and suggested they move to the sitting room for desert. Angilia took the elevator, and she hurried as best as she could to catch up with everyone before Mitchell and Katherine entered the room. When they did, Katherine began weeping at the collective "Happy anniversary" greeting. Then she and Mitchell saw their friends, and they looked as surprised and happy as they felt. Angilia and Matthew smiled and hugged at the happiness that permeated the room. "They are so lovely, Matthew. I am so glad that their friends could come."

"So am I," Matthew smiled. "Mom and Dad are pretty special. I'm glad they're my parents," he added and pulled his wife closer.

After everyone mingled and chatted for a while, Katherine and Mitchell cut the first piece of the anniversary cake and fed one another small bites, just as they had done at their wedding reception in 1984. Everyone found the gesture enchanting, and Bonnie captured the moment in a photograph that she later framed and presented to them. Antoine then cut pieces of cake for everyone, and they settled comfortably on sofas and chairs while they nibbled the delicious cake and continued talking.

Angilia suddenly asked her parents-in-law, "When, where, and how did you two meet? I'd adore hearing the story."

Katherine's smile broadened immediately. "Oh, we met in 1982 at John Radcliffe Hospital where Mitchell was a doctor. I was the new medical records clerk, and on my first day there, this doctor came in and said he needed a patient's chart immediately. I wanted to locate the chart right away and make a good first impression, which I am so glad I did. That was the first time a doctor asked me to pull a chart, and I happened to be the only one in the department at that moment. I was so nervous that I nearly toppled a file cabinet and dropped the chart. That would have been a disaster, because I didn't want to appear incompetent in front of this doctor."

"What she didn't know," Mitchell said with a wink, "is that I waited until the other staff had left the department so I would get the new girl to pull the chart for me. What she also didn't know is that the patient's appointment was more than an hour later. As soon as Katherine handed me the chart, another clerk returned and told Katherine she could go on her lunch break then. I really timed it perfectly, because I told her—I didn't ask her—that I would go to lunch with her."

"So of course I was even more flustered," Katherine admitted with a blush. "'*I thought you had a patient, Dr. Taylor,*' I told him, looking at his name badge. He told me he did—more than one hour later! I knew what he was up to, and I am pretty sure I barely ate lunch. I was never that unnerved before!"

"She got over it, though," Mitchell smiled. "We had lunch every day we possibly could. Katherine and I dated for a couple of years and married on this date in 1984. Matthew was born a little more than two years later, and Katherine decided to quit her job when she began her maternity leave. She became a stay-at-home wife and mother, although things were far from normal, as Eric well understands. Matthew ended up in college and medical school quite young, so that's when Katherine started volunteering."

"I had to fill my time productively somehow," she added. "I decided not to get a regular job, first so my schedule could be more flexible for anything that came up, and second because we really didn't need the money. I didn't do a whole lot, just various things. It was fun, and I felt like I helped people. That's why I just adore working with Angilia. Light Within has really flourished, and I am so proud of what we do."

"I could never do it without you," Angilia told her, and stood to hug Katherine and then Mitchell. "That is such a sweet story. You know I have to write that in the family book tonight," Angilia said, referring to a huge blank book in which she had written various family stories and anecdotes since she was a child. She did write Katherine's and Mitchell's love story in the book, preserving it for all future generations of their family.

§§§§

"Mom is so excited about today, darling. She's really psyched about having a girl's day out with just you and her. You should have heard her last night," Matthew giggled as he and Angilia finished getting ready for breakfast.

"I'm excited, too, my dear. It's been a long time since Katherine and I have spent a day together with no meetings, no one else, no agenda. We're not even sure where we'll go or what we'll do. That's such a wonderful feeling," Angilia smiled while she slid her feet into white tasseled loafers.

Matthew smiled at her. Angilia wore skinny jeans and a red-and-white striped nautical t-shirt with her loafers. "You look like a high school student. I feel like I did when you were 16, like I'm committing a mortal sin just for looking at you," he admitted and grinned as he pulled her to him. "Almost." He kissed her passionately, feeling his love for his wife overwhelm him.

"Oh, Matthew, you are my love. That's such a sweet thing to say, but I hardly look like a teenager anymore. I'm an old married lady of 34 now," she jested, kissed him, and pulled him behind her to the elevator, where they continued kissing.

"Still on the honeymoon, I see," Eric greeted them with a smile as he passed the elevator just as the door opened on the first floor. Matthew and Angilia giggled, and she leaned up to kiss her father on the cheek. They entered the dining room together, enjoying a jovial, laughter-filled meal with their family and friends.

An hour after breakfast, Katherine hugged and kissed Mitchell, Matthew, Eric, and Prince Eric before she and Angilia left for the day. Angilia and Matthew kissed several times in their suite after Angilia freshened, and then she found her son and her father downstairs. She bent to hug and kiss her son, who held her close. "I love you so much, Mommy. Have a wonderful time today with Grandma, and you can tell me all about it over dinner."

Angilia giggled, kissed him again, and said, "I promise, Eric." She stood and hugged her father close, breathing deeply, enjoying the familiar scent of his cologne. Eric kissed her forehead and smiled at her. "Eric is right. You and Katherine just enjoy your day together. You both deserve a day of relaxing fun together. I want to hear all about it, too, when you both get home."

"So do I," Mitchell said, and hugged his daughter-in-law before she joined Katherine at the patio door. The ladies smiled, waved, and walked to the garage, where they settled in Katherine's car and set out for their spontaneous day of shopping, lunch, and girl time. They very rarely had such moments when they could literally do whatever they wanted whenever they wanted, and they intended to create a memorable day.

Katherine drove to a small town several miles from Valmondois, where she parked the car on the main street near a block of shops. She and Angilia linked arms, strolled along the sidewalks window shopping, and suddenly decided to enter a boutique. Inside, Angilia selected a cute pink cotton sweater that she could dress up or wear casually. Katherine gushed over a dress, tried it on, modeled it for Angilia, and bought it, as well as matching pumps and handbag.

"Oh, look, a gift shop," Angilia said after they left the boutique. "Do you mind if we go in?" Katherine of course did not mind, so they placed their bags in the car trunk and crossed the street. Angilia immediately picked up a carved cedar box. "I want to get this for Eric. It's the perfect treasure box for him, where he can put all of his special little things."

"That's such a sweet idea, Angilia. Every boy needs a treasure box," Katherine said and hugged Angilia. Something caught her attention, and she went across the store and picked it up. "And this is perfect for Mitchell," Katherine giggled. She held up a golf lover's gift basket, and Angilia laughed delightfully and agreed with Katherine.

"That really is perfect for Dr. Taylor." Angilia, too, spotted something on the self behind Katherine, and she reached for it. "I have to get this for Matthew," she softly said while she looked at a coffee table book of Henri Matisse's works. "Matthew really enjoys Matisse's work." Katherine put an arm around Angilia and kissed her cheek.

The two women browsed through the store, and Angilia found gifts for Eduardo, Susan, Roger, Daniel, Joseph, Antoine, and even her beloved Starlight. For her palomino, she bought a new blue saddle blanket. Finally, she stopped in front of a crystal box and gently ran her finger along its edge. Engraved on the lid was a silhouette of a father and daughter and the fifth Commandment: *Honour thy father and thy mother: that thy days may be long upon the land which the Lord thy God giveth thee. Exodus 20:12* "I am getting this for Daddy," she whispered through tears. Katherine patted her back, and they paid for their items and placed them in the car trunk.

"Where do we go next?" Katherine asked. "Where else has little boutiques and stores where we can find pretty clothes and trinkets?" Angilia mentioned another town a few miles away, so the ladies bought cups of herbal tea to drink on their drive. Just under an hour later, Katherine parked near the shops and restaurants there, and then she and Angilia purchased a few more dresses, sweaters, and accessories at a smart little boutique.

After they placed those bags in the car trunk, Katherine said she was hungry, and they agreed on a French restaurant for a late lunch. Everyone recognized Angilia throughout the day, although they realized that she was with her mother-in-law and did not intrude. Some people did take pictures, but for the most part Katherine and Angilia enjoyed relative privacy on their off-duty day.

They lingered over lunch and desert, relishing the chance to talk woman-to-woman and create an even tighter bond. "Matthew's birthday is in three months, and I know there's still plenty of time, but I was thinking about something special for the two of you that week. September 30 is on a Monday, and I know you plan your schedule far in advance, so I wanted to throw this by you now.

"I thought it would be wonderful to arrange a trip to Greece for you and Matthew, where you could celebrate his birthday, visit all of the historic sights, and take in all of the ancient works of art. I know he would get a thrill from that. What do you think, my dear?"

"Oh, Katherine, that would be a dream for Matthew," Angilia said and placed her hands over Katherine's. "I know he would cherish every second."

"Good, then it's settled. I was pretty sure you'd think so, too, so I have already made hotel reservations and arranged museum passes. I even talked to Eric before I went too far with this, and you two are using one of his planes for the trip. Everything is planned. We just have to keep it all from Matthew until a few days before you leave. We can alert Susan, Roger, and Daniel when we get home, and they can avoid scheduling any events for you and Matthew that week. Oh, I am so happy!" Katherine lifted Angilia's hands and kissed them, her smile proving her happiness. Angilia returned the smile, enjoying Katherine's joy.

Soon, they paid the bill and decided to head home. Katherine drove more leisurely than normal, and she and Angilia chatted and laughed as they traveled. Later that afternoon, as they neared Valmondois, they realized they were practically alone on the street. Few other cars were visible, which enabled them to hear the birds singing in the nearby trees.

"It's so peaceful here, isn't it? So relaxing and tranquil. We need to do this more often, Angilia. I really, truly enjoyed today alone with you. Thank you, my dear." Katherine smiled and briefly glanced at Angilia.

"Oh, Katherine, today was so wonderful. I am so grateful we spent the day together away from work, proposals, and board meetings. We needed this just to refresh our souls. I love you, Katherine."

"Oh, Angilia, I love you, too." Katherine's smile suddenly and unexpectedly vanished, and Angilia watched in horror as Katherine sat immobile. The car swerved, heading toward an embankment, and Angilia quickly leaned across Katherine, grabbed the steering wheel, and stopped the car from plunging down the embankment.

Angilia turned her attention to Katherine and felt for a pulse. She could not feel one, and she began to reach for her purse so she could get her phone and call for help. At that moment, Katherine's body jerked and flailed, and the car began to move very fast. Angilia could not get Katherine's foot off of the gas pedal. Angilia was viciously thrown against the passenger door. Mere seconds later Angilia felt the dashboard slam into her and the passenger's side of the car smash into a tree.

Angilia gasped for air and managed to whisper Katherine's name. She saw her mother-in-law slumped over. Katherine's eyes were open, but she was not breathing. "Katherine, please, you have to breathe. Please Katherine."

Angilia could not move her right arm, as it was tightly wedged against the twisted metal of the car door. She managed to use her left hand to fumble and locate her phone. Before she could call her father, though, Angilia saw a man appear, a man who seemed to be in his 60s. He wore an RAF uniform from the 1960s, and he looked at Angilia with sadness. She had not seen Katherine's soul manifest and look at her in concern, then motion for her father to stay and help Angilia. Angilia never knew that even in death Katherine's major concern was for her daughter-in-law.

"Little One! I'm here. I'm going to get you out of the car." Patrick stood next to the passenger's side of the car, his own face frantic. The RAF soldier moved to Patrick's side and put his hands on Patrick's arms.

"We can't risk moving her. We need to get help," the man insisted.

"I need to call Daddy," Angilia weakly said, and dialed his cell phone number.

Eric recognized her ring tone and answered on the first ring, feeling inexplicably scared. Before he could say anything, he heard her soft, gasping voice say, "Daddy help."

"Where are you, baby?" Eric urgently asked. Roger suddenly stood from his seat next to Eric's desk, alert and afraid. "Angilia, just tell me where you are."

"How can I tell Matthew?" she replied, crying. "How can I tell him and Dr. Taylor?"

"You have to tell me where you are!" Eric was standing, too, more scared than he had felt since he saw his daughter shot in the heart. "Angilia!"

"Eric, you need to hurry. Get an ambulance here now," Patrick suddenly said. He had taken the phone from his niece, knowing they needed to get help on the scene immediately. "They had an accident. They're on Turnier Road, 30 miles from the Valmondois turnoff, near that little nature preserve with all the trees. Just hurry."

"Stay on the phone with Roger while I call the ambulance," Eric said, passed his cell phone to Roger, and called the ambulance from his desk phone. While Eric told the dispatcher what he knew, Patrick told Roger that Katherine was dead.

Eric hung up, grabbed his phone from Roger, and told him to get Mitchell and Matthew to the garage quickly. Eric ran at lightning speed, yelled for the guard to unlock the gates, started his car, and pulled it out of the garage, ready to leave. Scared, frantic, and confused, Mitchell and Matthew quickly jumped into the car with Roger, Matthew holding his medical bag. Eric sped through the gates, shocking the people gathered on the mall.

Patrick stayed on the phone with Eric, trying to keep his brother calm yet informed. Angilia begged for the phone, and Eric suddenly heard her weak voice urgently tell him, "Please, please be careful, Daddy. You have to be careful."

"I will, baby," Eric promised her, tears choking him.

Matthew reached for the phone, pleading to talk to his wife, and Eric could not help but cry when he gave the phone to his son-in-law. Matthew's mother was dead and his wife was injured. *Dear God*, Eric prayed, *please take care of my little girl.* At that moment, he heard Matthew say, "Ginny, how is she?" Ginny? Mr. Brennan's nurse? How did she get there?

Matthew quickly told everyone that Ginny saw the accident and stopped, not knowing it was Angilia and Katherine. Matthew listened, his heart sinking when Ginny said she thought Angilia might have a punctured lung due to her rapid, shallow, and raspy breathing. Matthew never asked about his mother, for he knew that she was dead. Ginny had never mentioned Katherine, and neither had Eric. Angilia had only whispered how sorry she was and that she loved him. Matthew knew that his mom was dead. His dad did not know. Mitchell would know soon, though.

Matthew peppered Ginny with questions, getting a grasp of Angilia's condition, as well as of how she was trapped in the car. He wanted to mentally estimate her injuries so he could begin treating her as soon as he arrived and the emergency crew freed her from the car. Ginny told him that the team had arrived and were assessing the accident so they could safely remove Angilia. The ambulance arrived moments later, and an EMT placed an oxygen mask on Angilia.

Matthew once more shared the information with everyone, but stayed on the phone with Ginny until Eric arrived and parked near the scene. Eric rushed to Katherine's car, and Ginny held onto his arms while he talked to his daughter and let her know he was there. Angilia looked up at him, nodded slightly, and began to cry when she saw Matthew and Mitchell approach. "It's going to be all right, Angel. It will be. God's in control here, baby. Just focus on that." His heart ached, though, at the immensity of what had happened. He looked at Katherine, and he could not fathom what it must have been like for both her and Angilia.

Two EMTs opened the driver's door, lifted Katherine's body onto a stretcher, and turned their full focus onto Angilia. One EMT climbed into the back seat and positioned himself directly behind Angilia, where he could hold onto her and keep her as immobile and stabilized as possible. Another EMT sat in the driver's seat, covered Angilia with a wool blanket, and protected her body with a metal shield.

The emergency crew made everyone move away from the car until they cut through the metal and lifted the roof of the car away. The emergency crew began by removing all of the car windows and the trunk lid. They worked rapidly, carefully, and safely to make sure Angilia was more accessible to the doctors as quickly as possible. They prepared the roof removal by using spreaders to crush the bars that attached the roof to the car, and then another crew member used powerful cutters to slice through the metal.

It felt like hours to her family, but it took minutes for the crew to cut through all of the bars. The crew lifted the roof forward, folding it onto the hood of the car. Even though they dared not move the car itself and risk injuring Angilia further, Matthew, Mitchell, and the EMTs had access to Angilia. Matthew stepped around his mother's body, scrambled into the driver's seat, and kissed his wife's cheek.

"I'm here, darling. We're going to take care of you now. We'll get you out of here soon, but I just want to examine you first. I love you," Matthew said while he removed items from his medical bag. He listened to her breathing, to her lungs, and he was certain that Ginny was right—Angilia seemed to have a punctured right lung. Matthew very carefully felt her ribs and established that three were broken. A broken rib had apparently punctured her lung.

Matthew noticed a large black bruise on Angilia's right shoulder, and he cut her t-shirt sleeve open carefully. Mitchell climbed behind Angilia's seat, next to the EMT, and helped Matthew determine that she had a dislocated shoulder and most likely a fractured collar bone. Matthew examined her legs the best he could, and did not ascertain any fractures. Mitchell quickly cleaned and wrapped a gash on Angilia's right arm.

Matthew and Mitchell assisted an EMT slide a longboard behind Angilia, carefully slide her onto the board, and very slowly lift the longboard while keeping her immobile. The three men lifted her from the car, and placed the longboard onto a gurney. Matthew then cut her shirt off so that he could more closely examine her. She had numerous contusions, scrapes, and cuts, at least three broken ribs, a collapsed lung, a dislocated shoulder, and a fractured collar bone.

Matthew inserted an IV and told his father to get blood and saline solution attached. Matthew could not know what, if any, internal injuries his wife had until they took scans, so they quickly placed her in the ambulance. Eric, Matthew, Mitchell, and Ginny sat in the ambulance with her, continuing to treat her wounds as best they could until they arrived at the hospital.

Eric and Matthew looked at one another, their eyes revealing their heartbreak and fear. That morning, they could not have known that this day of fun and friendship would end so tragically for Katherine and Angilia.

§§§§

Matthew and Mitchell could only afford to allow Eric a moment with Angilia before they had to rush her to imaging for scans. Matthew knew ribs were fractured and a lung collapsed based on his examination and her symptoms. He and Mitchell had seen enough of both injuries to not need x-rays; as they knew, fractured ribs often did not appear on x-rays. Instead, they were more concerned about possible internal damage.

Angilia's images were rushed, and soon Matthew and Mitchell studied Angilia's organs. Mitchell saw his son collapse into a chair and cover his face with his hands. "Matthew?"

"I was so terrified of something like this. We can treat everything else, but Angilia's heart is bruised. We have to get the chest tube and antibiotics in her now. Her heart isn't strong enough to support her body right now. We need to get more oxygen into her. Come on." Matthew rushed to Angilia's treatment room and explained what he was doing as he did it, like he had done in the ambulance in 2012.

"Darling, I need to insert a chest tube so it can suction the air out of your right lung." Ginny assisted Matthew, and she sanitized the incision location, and then gave Angilia a hypodermic of local anesthesia. Matthew made an incision, inserted the tube between the lung and chest wall, and attached a suction devise. "This will remove the air slowly, darling, so your lung can begin to heal. Okay?"

Angilia nodded and reached her left hand toward him. Matthew held her hand and kissed it, and then explained that they would give her an antibiotic intravenously to prevent an infection. Ginny prepared and attached the medicine to her IV.

"You have three fractured ribs, Angilia, and they will heal on their own over time. We never tape or bind fractured ribs, even though that might help the pain, because that restricts breathing. We'll do what we can to reduce the pain, though, I promise." Matthew had left the oxygen mask on her, so she could only nod at him to let him know she understood.

"I'm sure you feel the pain where you are injured, sweetie, so you know your right shoulder needs attention. There are actually two issues there, but we can only treat one right now. Your right shoulder is dislocated, but there is no way we can reposition it until the other issue is resolved. Your clavicle is fractured. We have to address that before we can even think about forcing your shoulder into position." He looked at her with such pain on his face, and Angilia prayed she could undo the accident and make everything all right.

She pulled off the oxygen mask with her left hand, and she refused to let him put it back. "I'm okay, Matthew. You don't have to stay here. Eric needs you. He's going to be scared. I'm so sorry," Angilia said as she gasped for each breath and began to cry, which caused her pain to escalate.

"There is nothing to feel sorry about, darling. You are my wife, and of course I need to be here. I want to be here with you. We'll take care of Eric. Right now, we want and need to take care of you. Everything's going to be all right, I promise." Matthew kissed her lips, replaced the oxygen mask, and told Ginny to give her a seven milligram dose of morphine. He dared not risk a higher dose with her heart contusion.

"Dad, Ginny, take care of the cuts and scrapes, please." Ginny nodded her head and gathered the suture supplies. "I'm going to talk to Eric, darling, and once we get you settled in your private room, he and Patrick can come in. I'll be back soon." Angilia held up her left hand and signed *I love you*, as she had done to Eric after her emergency surgery years earlier. Matthew said he loved her, too, and quickly left the room before he cried.

Matthew leaned against the wall outside her door, tears attempting to overtake him, but he forced himself to remain focused on treating his wife over all else. Everything else could wait. His mother was dead. Matthew could not help his mother. He had to help his wife. He stood straight and went to the private room where Eric, Patrick, and Roger waited. Eric immediately stood when Matthew entered.

"Matthew?"

"Angilia's getting some stiches for her cuts right now. She's got some serious injuries that Dad and I are treating and will keep monitoring constantly. She's alert and talking, which means she's her willful self and removes the oxygen mask so she can talk. That's always a positive sign." Matthew smiled at Eric, although both men had tears flooding their eyes.

Eric stepped to Matthew and hugged him tight, understanding how horrifically devastating the afternoon was for him. "I'll be okay. I will. There's nothing I can do for Mom now, and I do know she's fine where she is. I just want to take care of Angilia." Matthew dried his eyes. "I know you saw her shoulder on the scene. The shoulder is dislocated, but we can't do anything about that anytime soon." He saw the flash of fear in Eric's eyes. "Her right collar bone is fractured. We've called in an orthopedic shoulder specialist, and he will advise us on the best treatment. Hopefully a special sling will be enough, rather than surgery to place screws or a plate to hold the bones together. I don't want her to face surgery unless there's no other option. I'll talk all of this over with that doctor when he arrives and has a chance to evaluate her shoulder."

Matthew took a deep breath. "That's not all. The impact fractured three of her ribs on the right side, and one of them caused a punctured lung that collapsed. I've inserted a chest tube that will slowly remove the air in her chest wall, and that will help that wound to heal on its own. The ribs will heal without any procedures, too. It all just takes some time. Pain management is the best way to keep her calm and comfortable so that her body can heal. I also have an IV antibiotic going that will prevent any lung infections.

"I pretty much ascertained all of this on the scene by examination, her symptoms, and lots of prior experience. What I didn't know is if there was any internal damage. There is one issue, and I am going to watch that like hawk. The dashboard hit her about here," Matthew said, and placed a hand just below his sternum. "Angilia's heart is bruised, but there is no bleeding or trauma. The main concern I have is potential swelling, so I have ordered a portable CT scanner in her private room. I do plan to take a scan every hour so that I can see what her heart looks like and stay on top of this. I have to. There is no way I'll allow even the remotest chance. The good news is that there is no swelling so far, and in heart trauma that usually occurs early. So this is more a precaution than anything. I had Ginny give her a small dose of morphine for the pain, but I refuse to give her too much. We know she can get through this pain, no matter how much it kills us to watch her suffer."

Matthew began crying, and Eric again pulled his son-in-law to him. Eric held him, fighting his own tears as Matthew cried. Eric knew Matthew had to cry and release his emotions. He had been in that place before, and he understood Matthew's competing emotions. Marisol died three months before Angilia's birth, and was buried the day after Angilia's birth. The happiest event of Eric's life—Angilia's birth—was tied to the saddest—Marisol's death. Eric knew the internal struggle Matthew fought that afternoon.

§§§§

Matthew, Mitchell, and Ginny moved Angilia's bed to her private hospital room. Matthew took a heart CT scan before he let Eric in, as he did not want to upset his father-in-law. Matthew saw the dark contusion, and he felt nauseous seeing the pain his wife felt. Angilia hid her pain from him and Mitchell, more concerned about their pain and grief than her own pain. She was so strong and compassionate, and it took every ounce of Matthew's strength not to crumble under the weight of what his wife did for him.

"Ginny, please prepare seven milligrams of morphine for Angilia. We'll give her a small dose every three hours." Ginny nodded and soon injected the morphine into the IV lumen, and then gently patted Angilia's left arm. "I'm going to go get your dad and Patrick. I don't want you to talk too much, though. You need to conserve your energy and get some sleep tonight. Okay?" he told her, kissed her cheek, and went to the private waiting room.

Minutes later, Eric went to her left side, leaned down, kissed her cheek, and swallowed his tears. "I love you, my beautiful daughter Angilia. I love you."

Patrick held her left hand. "I love you, Little One."

"I love you, Daddy, Uncle Patrick. I'm so sorry."

"You just get some sleep, baby. Let your body heal. Patrick and I are staying right here," Eric said and sat in a chair beside her bed, his hand stroking her hair and soothing her to sleep.

§§§§

Prince Eric finished his homework in his sitting room, and then looked at the clock. It was very close to dinner time. *Grandma and Mommy should be home soon.* He knew that his mother would come to see him when she got home, so he stretched out on the floor and opened the Internet browser on his handheld computer. The news headlines appeared, and Prince Eric stared at the screen in disbelief.

He read the story, he watched the video report, but he could not believe any of it. The man said Katherine was dead and Angilia was seriously injured. Prince Eric ran downstairs, out the front door, and screamed for the guard to open the gates. The people gathered on the mall began crying, realizing that Prince Eric had just learned about the accident. Valdavian networks refused to broadcast the news, wanting to respect the family until King Eric or someone on his behalf issued a formal statement. That respect obviously did not extend to other media services, and now Prince Eric had to inadvertently learn about his grandmother and mother in the cruelest way.

Susan herself had received the news moments earlier, and she ran after Prince Eric when she heard him screaming and crying. "I need to go to Mommy!" he yelled through his tears.

"We will, Eric. Come on," Susan assured him and held his hand as they went to the garage and got in her car. Susan drove to the hospital, and both she and Eric sat rigid and quiet until they entered the hospital and were told where Angilia's room was. Susan still held Prince Eric's hand as they took the elevator to the fifth floor. When the elevator door opened, Prince Eric broke free from Susan's grasp and ran toward the pulmonary intensive care unit.

"Eric." Angilia murmured her son's name and woke from her sleep, frantic and alarmed. Matthew held her still. "Eric. He's in distress. I need to get to him."

"Susan and Daniel are home with him," Matthew said, but Angilia's breathing grew more labored.

Eric leaned close and said he would go home and check on Prince Eric. "No, I'll go," Patrick said and stood. "You stay here. I'll take care of him, Little One." Angilia nodded, thanked her uncle, and looked at her father and Matthew helplessly. She felt her son's fear as if it were tangible.

Patrick walked quickly down the hall, and saw his grandnephew running toward him. Patrick knelt, stopped Prince Eric, and picked him up. The boy was terrified, Patrick could feel it. What had he heard? Patrick sat on a sofa against a wall nearby, and held Prince Eric on his lap.

"Is it true that Grandma is dead?" Prince Eric asked Patrick. Susan caught up and sat near them.

"Yes, it is, Eric."

"Oh. Then I'm grateful that I told her how much I love her before she and Mommy left this morning," Eric said. Susan covered her mouth with a hand to stifle her sobs.

"Yeah, she knows, buddy. She knows, and she's all right now," Patrick reassured Eric, who was experiencing his first death.

"Mommy? The man just said that Mommy is very seriously hurt. What does that mean? I want to see my Mommy."

"You will soon, I promise. I'll take you in her room, but I have to tell you a few things first. She is hurt, Eric. When you go in, don't hug her and don't touch her right side or right arm. Your Mommy was pretty banged up, so she's very sore," Patrick explained.

"She will be all right. Won't she?"

"Yeah, but it will take some time for her to heal. She's gonna need our help until she does heal, just like we promised her in our homages at her coronation."

"I do promise. I'll do anything for my Mommy. Take me to her now, Uncle Patrick." Patrick nodded, took Prince Eric's hand, and motioned for Susan to follow. She knew Angilia needed to rest and stay calm, so she said she would visit another day. She promised to stay there, though, in case someone needed anything.

Patrick quietly opened Angilia's door. "I'm back, with a special visitor. He was on his way here when I shanghaied him for a bit." Prince Eric went to his father first, and hugged him tight. Prince Eric knew his Daddy was sad. So was his Grandpa, and he went to Mitchell next and hugged him. Prince Eric did not have to say anything to either man. Both knew what young Eric felt.

Finally, Prince Eric walked to the left side of Angilia's bed and held her hand. He looked at her for several seconds, knowing she was hurt but thankful she was alive. "I love you, Mommy."

"I love you, Eric. Come here," Angilia said, and Prince Eric stepped closer to her. She put her left arm around him, and he tenderly kissed her left cheek. Angilia kissed the top of his head. Prince Eric sat next to his Grandfather, and held his mother's hand until she fell asleep again. Eventually, he fell asleep, too, so Patrick picked him up, placed him on the couch in her room, covered him, and stayed near him. That is what Angilia would want.

§§§§§

The next day, the shoulder specialist arrived, examined Angilia, and evaluated the scans. Dr. Ransing concluded that the fracture of Angilia's collar bone would not properly fuse itself independent of intervention. He advised a titanium plate, which would remain in place permanently and provide lifelong stability and support. That is what Matthew had dreaded hearing.

Matthew and Dr. Ransing talked for a few hours, and Matthew made it clear that general anesthetic was far too dangerous for Angilia. Dr. Ransing was aghast at the thought of performing any surgery without general anesthetic, although Matthew finally made him understand that it would cause Angilia's heart to stop and result in cardiac arrest. Matthew was adamant and refused to jeopardize Angilia's life.

The two doctors entered Angilia's room, said they needed to discuss something with her, and Angilia understood that her son should not be present. "Uncle Patrick, please take Eric for lunch." When her son said he wanted to stay, she insisted, so Prince Eric kissed her and left with Patrick.

Angilia's father was horrified at the thought of surgery without anesthetic, but Eric also knew the fatal dangers of anesthesia for his daughter. What could they do to set her shoulder and keep her safe? The fairly heated discussion between Matthew,

Mitchell, Eric, and Dr. Ransing went on for almost an hour before Angilia got their attention. She looked at Dr. Ransing and asked point blank, "Is this absolutely necessary?"

"Yes, Your Majesty, it is. The fracture is not a clean break, and the bone will not reunite on its own. A titanium plate really is the best option. Besides, while I am in there, I can reposition your shoulder back in place and take care of both injuries at once. That will ultimately cause far less trauma for you and get your healing started much quicker."

"Then do it. I can get through this, I know I can. I've gotten though worse," she said, struggling to breathe, and winked at Roger. "Matthew will be there, won't you? I'll just look at you and keep my mind off of everything else. I just want to get this over with as soon as possible and get our lives back to normal. I'm so sorry for causing us to miss church today. Happy Father's Day, my magnificent Daddy. I love you."

§§§§

The following morning, before her surgery, Angilia promised her father and her son that she would be fine and would focus on them while she held Matthew's hand. Both of them stayed strong for her, though neither could imagine the pain she would feel. Angilia reassured them, and then looked at Roger. He knew she had endured far worse in 2012, and he knew she had told only him about that surgery.

"You are so brave, Mommy. I love you so much, and I am so happy that God made you my Mommy."

"Oh, Eric, I love you more than life. I promise I'll see you as soon as Dr. Ransing is done," Angilia said and kissed his cheek. "I love you, Daddy," she said and reached for him. He leaned close to her, kissed her cheek, and told her he loved her. "Dr. Taylor," she gasped and held out her left hand to him. "I love you."

Mitchell held her hand, smiled at her, kissed her forehead, and told her, "You just get well, dear. That's the only thing that matters. You know how much we love you. Don't worry about Eric. I'm spending some time with him while Dr. Ransing and

Matthew take care of you." Angilia kissed his cheek and thanked him.

"Uncle Patrick." He came to her, leaned down, and put his face close to his niece's. "Please pray with me." Patrick and Angilia closed their eyes, held hands, and Patrick prayed to God for Angilia's safekeeping during surgery.

"I'm going to be beside you today, too, Little One. You'll have Matthew and me there to keep your mind off of everything else. Heck, if anyone can refocus your mind, I can. I've always been able to do that. Right?" She nodded, smiled, and kissed his cheek in gratitude. Eric pulled his brother into a grateful hug. He knew Angilia would come through this, no matter how painful or horrifying it seemed.

§§§§§

While Matthew held her hand and monitored her heart, Patrick sang to her. Angilia forced herself into another place both mentally and physically, looking only at her husband and her uncle. She consciously disregarded Dr. Ransing's and the nurses' comments, the sounds of the surgical tools, and the pain. She had to.

Dr. Ransing looked at Matthew, his eyes expressing his complete amazement. Angilia never moved during the surgery. She never moaned or cried. She seemed to be in another zone, on another plane. Prince Eric was right—she was very brave. She was also glad that Prince Eric was spending this time with his Grandpa, who needed love and family more than ever.

Matthew, Eric, and Patrick knew what Mitchell and Prince Eric were doing during Angilia's surgery. Many years earlier, Katherine had made her wishes known to her husband and later to her son. When she died, Katherine wanted to be cremated. She did not want a funeral. After the autopsy, Mitchell and Matthew took a few moments to say their private goodbyes before Katherine's body was placed in the crematory. Mitchell later carried his wife's urn and placed it in Matthew's hospital locker for safekeeping.

Mitchell explained Grandma's wishes to Prince Eric moments after Angilia was taken to surgery. "I think Grandma will really enjoy it if we both take her urn to the Royal Vault at the church. The two of us can have our own private memorial service for her. You can pick the spot for her final resting place. That will really make Grandma so happy, Eric. It will make me happy. Is that all right with you?"

"You know, when Uncle Patrick told me it was true about Grandma, I said I'm grateful I told her I love her before she left that morning. I am. I do love her, always. I love you, Grandpa, always. Yes, I'd like to do this with you for Grandma." Prince Eric hugged Mitchell, and held his Grandma's urn while Mitchell drove them to the church.

There, Prince Eric looked around the large Vault and selected a niche. "Will Grandma like it here?" he asked Mitchell.

Mitchell looked at the spot Prince Eric had chosen. Above the niche was an ancient mosaic tile depicting a little dark-haired boy reaching up to a female angel. "This is perfect, Eric. Would you like to place Grandma's urn there?"

Prince Eric nodded and tenderly placed Katherine's urn in the niche. He then reached for Mitchell's hand and tearfully said, "I love you, Grandma. Someday, I will see you again."

§§§§

Eric wrote the official statement announcing Katherine's death while most everyone except Roger was out of the room. He texted it to his Press Secretary, Carol, for immediate release.

10 June 2030

With the utmost sadness, I confirm the automobile accident that occurred two days ago, on 8 June 2030. Her Majesty Queen Angilia de Valdavia is recovering in the hospital.

Mrs. Katherine Taylor, my dear friend and mother of Matthew, Duc de Valmondois, died in the accident. We all love Katherine immensely, and we will miss her joyousness, friendship, and kindness every day. Words can never express the sorrow in not having Katherine here, although we rejoice that she is safe in the loving arms of God.

In keeping to Katherine's wishes, there will not be a funeral, although a memorial service will be held in the future as a celebration of her life.

My family and I thank you for your prayers, cards, and flowers. We do ask that our privacy is respected at this time.

King Eric R

§§§§§

Angilia was released two weeks after the surgery, on June 24, and she walked from the hospital between her father and her husband, wearing a figure eight brace and a sling with her loose black cotton dress. Matthew held her left arm, and Eric placed his hand on her back. Prince Eric and Mitchell held hands as they walked alongside Matthew. Patrick stayed beside his brother. Angilia briefly waved to everyone with her left hand, and smiled at their cheers, applause, and shouts of blessings.

Matthew and Mitchell carefully helped her into the Rolls Royce, chosen for its spaciousness. The men settled in, and Roger drove everyone to the church, much to Angilia's relief. Mitchell and Prince Eric had told her about Katherine's wishes and private ceremony, and she regretted that Matthew could not have been there with his father and his son. Mitchell also told Angilia who the RAF soldier was who appeared when Katherine died—her father. Angilia was grateful that Katherine's father was her Spirit Guide.

Angilia wanted to visit the Royal Vault to pay her respects, and Matthew reluctantly agreed. Angilia held Matthew's hand and kissed him when they entered the Vault and stood before Katherine's resting place. Angilia bowed her head and prayed, and stunned everyone when she softly said she was sorry. Mitchell stood in front of his daughter-in-law, looked into her eyes, and told her the truth.

"Angilia, dear, you did nothing wrong. Katherine suffered a fatal stroke while she was driving. Even if the EMTs or a doctor were on the scene when it happened, no one could have done anything. Katherine died instantly. What caused the crash was postmortem spasm, which sometimes occurs after a traumatic death. You did not cause the accident by talking to her while she drove, my dear."

"Dad's right, darling. This would have happened at that moment no matter what Mom was doing or where she was. Her last words were that she loves you. Carry that in your heart always, Angilia. That is the beautiful moment," Matthew added and kissed his wife.

"Grandpa and Daddy are right, Mommy. We told Grandma we love her that day, and she went to Heaven knowing and feeling that. You can't blame yourself for the accident, Mommy. Please."

"Thank you, Eric darling. Matthew, you are so strong and wise. Dr. Taylor, you are remarkable. I love you all. This is the perfect place for Katherine, isn't it? The little boy and the angel look like Eric and his Grandma. We'll miss you, Katherine, but we will join you in Heaven someday."

SSSS

That afternoon, Angilia asked that the shopping bags from June 8 be brought to her in the sitting room. Roger gently patted her cheek and went to get them and to call everyone to the sitting room at her request. Joseph and Antoine were somewhat surprised to be included, and fought their tears when she handed them the gifts she had bought them. "Please give this to Starlight for me and tell him I'll visit him as soon as I can," Angilia told Joseph when she handed him the blue saddle blanket. He promised her he would.

She gave Susan, Roger, Daniel, and Eduardo their gifts, which had been well wrapped and protected in the trunk of the car. Angilia called her son to her next, and he sat on the edge of the chaise lounge facing her. "Eric, I thought you'd like this box for all of your extra special little things," Angilia said and handed the carved cedar box to him.

"I do, Mommy. I'm going to start by putting the cards and letters all of you have given to me in here," he said and kissed both of her cheeks. "Thank you, Mommy."

"Matthew, I saw this and thought of you instantly," she smiled and motioned to the large Matisse book on the table beside her seat. Matthew picked it up and giggled, thanked her, and kissed her for quite a few seconds. The first gift she had given him in 2012 was an art book, as well. Angilia certainly knew what he enjoyed.

A large bag next to the chaise lounge contained Katherine's gift to Mitchell, and Angilia motioned for him to come to her. "Dr. Taylor, Katherine found just the ideal gift for you. It's all by itself in that large bag."

Mitchell laughed when he pulled out a not-so-miniature golf bag filled with sundry treats and golf accessories. "Absolutely! Well, Eric, my boy, looks like we are well stocked for our next golf game. We'll have to make sure we go again soon." Prince Eric smiled at his Grandpa, already looking forward to spending the day with him.

"Dr. Taylor, Katherine bought some other things, too."

"Don't tell me. Clothes. She loved buying clothes." Mitchell picked up the bags, looked inside, and suddenly stood. "Susan, you and Katherine wore the same size, she said. Here, you take these and put them to good use." Susan hugged and kissed Mitchell, thanked him, and took the boutique bags with tears in her eyes. Mitchell kissed Angilia's cheek in gratitude.

"Daddy, yours is last but never least. I just had to get this for you," she said and handed him the crystal box that the clerk had wrapped in cotton and tissue paper and placed in a sturdy cardboard box. Eric finally unwrapped the crystal box and stared at it for a few moments in silence. How much it reminded him of her 2012 Father's Day Sermon. Eric silently thanked God for his precious daughter.

"Oh, Angel, this is so very special and meaningful. Thank you." Eric kissed her cheeks, forehead, and nose, smiled, and said, "I love you, my beautiful daughter Angilia."

§§§§

September 19, 2030

Grandpa's birthday was today. He is 80 now. It's his first birthday without Grandma, too. That had to be hard for him.

We had a party for him this evening, and Daddy invited Grandpa's Oxford friends again, just because they mean a lot to him, too. It was a very fun day, and we all laughed, which is nice. Grandpa really enjoyed the party.

This morning, though, just Grandpa and I went golfing! No one else, just the two of us. That was extra special. It's not that I love golf. I enjoy it, but I don't love it. I love Grandpa. It's all about being with Grandpa. I love him. I want to make him happy, and I want to spend time with him. I could tell he was happy today when we were at the golf course together. That's all that matters.

Daddy's birthday is later this month, and he and Mommy are going to Greece. That is Grandma's birthday gift to Daddy. She told Mommy about it the day of the accident. Grandma wanted to do something special for Daddy that he would always remember. He will. I'll miss Mommy and Daddy, but I think it's cool that they can go on vacation after everything that happened this summer. They deserve some time away from all of the work and people. I love them both, and I know Daddy will take very good care of Mommy while they're in Greece. She will take care of Daddy, too. It will be his first birthday without his mother. That's rough, so I want Daddy to enjoy this trip because it is from Grandma.

It's been a fun but long day, and I'm tired. Good night, God.

§§§§§

Matthew barely opened his eyes as he awoke from a deep sleep, and was pleasantly startled wide awake by Angilia's kiss. "Happy birthday, my love," she said with a smile.

"It is now," he giggled and pulled her close for a more passionate kiss. "Let's have breakfast in bed. I feel like cuddling with my wife."

Angilia laughed in her charming way, and Matthew ordered breakfast. They cuddled, kissed, and caressed one another long after they fed each other breakfast. Finally, they showered, dressed, and took a taxi to the area around Greece's ancient Corinth. Mike accompanied them, but as he had on their honeymoon, he kept a distance so as to give them privacy.

They explored the sights for a time, and then sat while Matthew sketched wonders he never thought he would see up close. He even asked Angilia to sit amongst some ruins so he could sketch her, and in her long white dress, she resembled a goddess. Mike snapped a picture and sent it to Eric and Mitchell, letting them see how happy Angilia and Matthew were on their vacation.

In the early afternoon, they bought some fruit, cheese, and grape juice at a market, and found a rather secluded spot amidst some column ruins, where they could sit and eat lunch uninterrupted. Mike sat nearby, always alert, eating a sandwich. Angilia softly sang to Matthew, an enchanting song that made his heart flutter. For a brief millisecond, he felt he had been there with her before.

Angilia noticed the flash of memory in his eyes and smiled. "You do remember, Matthew."

"Remember what?"

"Being together in the Unborn Children Sphere. I sang that song to you there a very long time ago. Something in you remembers, my love, and once in a while a latent memory is triggered."

"Your song was very familiar. I've never really felt déjà vu before, but I did while you sang. It was just the briefest flurry of a memory, but it was there. Oh, darling, this really is the most amazing birthday of all," Matthew smiled and kissed her.

"When your mother told me what she planned for your birthday, I knew you would enjoy Greece. Katherine knew you would, and she was so thrilled to plan this for you."

"For us. She planned this for us, and I am so grateful she did. Mom's last gift to me is the most meaningful gift she gave to me. I will remember every moment of our week in Greece forever.

This is far too important and special to ever forget. You are here with me, and Mom is watching our happiness from Heaven."

§§§§§

"Today is going to be long and emotional, Daddy. Are you going to be all right?" Prince Eric asked Matthew while he finished dressing for the Father's Day church service.

Matthew smiled down at his son. "Yeah, I'll be fine, Eric. The Father's Day sermon is a chance for me to honor both Grandpa and Grandfather."

"And you," Prince Eric quickly added, which made Matthew laugh and hug his son.

"All fathers," Matthew corrected. "This afternoon will be a little bit sad but mostly fun and happy, I think. That's what Grandma would want. She doesn't want us to be sad and to cry, because she is just fine. Right?"

"Right. I learned a lot about Heaven not just from the Bible and Reverend Hutchins, but mostly from Mommy and Uncle Patrick. It's the most amazing place. I know Grandma loves it there. I miss her, but someday I'll be with her again."

"Yes, you will. We all will," Matthew smiled, took his son's hand, and joined Angilia to leave for church with the others.

§§§§§

Matthew spoke from his heart that morning, paying tribute to his father and his father-in-law in his sermon. "My father's strength encouraged me during those early years when my life accelerated at such a pace that I sometimes thought of giving up. Then I returned home from college or medical school and watched my father, always calm and level-headed even in the most severe crises. He was my role model, and I wanted to emulate him and honor him in my work. If I can believe his biased comments to me, I have done so," Matthew smiled.

"My father-in-law has such a pillar of faith and conviction that struck me from the beginning, four years before he actually became my father-in-law. He reminded me how important faith and prayer are every step through life. When I was mired in fear and doubt, he showed me the power of prayer. He showed me how to turn everything over to God, which has saved my soul many times over the past 19 years.

"Without these two strong, honorable men to teach, guide, and help me, I would have faltered long ago. I would not be here, living my dreams, were it not for them. They are proof that fathers do know best and deserve our love, respect, and praise."

§§§§§

That afternoon, the Royal party returned to Christ Church Valmondois for the Celebration of Mrs. Katherine Margaret Trumball Taylor's Life. The memorial service was open to the public, and the family was touched that the pews quickly filled, with dozens of friends and neighbors standing wherever space permitted. Angilia, Matthew, Mitchell, Prince Eric, King Eric, Eduardo, Susan, Daniel, and Roger mingled with everyone until the service began with King Eric's welcome.

"I first met Katherine when her son Matthew, who was Angilia's cardiologist, decided to leave his job and become Angilia's personal doctor. Mitchell called his wife to Angilia's hospital room so Katherine could hear her son's plans and begin to see what Mitchell and I had already seen. Katherine instantly realized that Matthew loved Angilia and wanted to be closer to her. What also happened is that her maternal affections drew her to Angilia, and thus Katherine entered our lives forevermore.

"Katherine brought her love of life, her energy, her laughter, and her tears to us, and she was easy to love. I haven't met anyone who knew her, even briefly, who didn't fall in love with her. She was that rare person who never judged anyone and who accepted each person without question or pause. She didn't have to agree with you to love you. Katherine was a beautiful person, inside and outside, and I am honored to have known her and to have shared our lives."

Mitchell told the story of how he and Katherine met and how he staged the whole thing just so he could get to know her. "See, I knew what I wanted, and I made sure I got her," he said to much laughter. "I could tell she was smitten with me, too, so I doubt I had much of a battle on my hands. Our wedding day was happy, because I got the girl of my dreams."

Matthew joined his father at the pulpit and quickly added, "It's a good thing, too, or I wouldn't be here. Mom really was wonderful, because she helped me settle in and be comfortable with myself in those early years when things moved too quickly for me. She also kept me grounded and never let any of it go to my head. She made sure I wasn't treated differently just because I skipped grades in school. I still had to do my chores, believe it or not.

"I remember one weekend, I was researching cell regeneration for a medical class, and she came to my room and told me to mow the lawn. She did me a huge favor, because my instinct was to use my college demands as an excuse. She just told me that college never exempted anyone from other work or duties, and she was right. Her refusal to put me on some pedestal, combined with Dad's example, taught me to be the man I am today, and I can never thank her—thank them both—enough for that." Mitchell dabbed a tear from his eye, and Matthew hugged him.

Matthew then mentioned that, "Mom laughed and cried a lot. She cried far more than she laughed. She was an emotional crier. She cried over sappy movies and novels, something someone said to her, and pretty much everything that happened to me. My major life events were christened with her tears. Graduations, jobs, leaving Oxford, engagement, marriage, Eric's birth, art exhibits, overseas trips and returning home from those trips. Mom got teased for her crying sometimes, but her tears showed how much she cared and felt. Not everyone has the capacity to express their feelings, and that is one of the greatest gifts Mom gave to us. Mom found her soul mate in Susan. The two of them realized they shared this propensity for crying, and it forged a close friendship that Mom treasured. Thank you, Susan."

Matthew held his arms open for Susan, and she walked to him in a tearful hug. "See, I told you," Matthew joked, eliciting much laughter. "She's crying."

"Yes, I am, and it's all your fault," Susan said and dried her eyes on a handkerchief. Mitchell noticed that Susan wore one of the dresses that Katherine had bought one year ago to the day, a dress she had never gotten to wear. Angilia had noticed, too, and she knew that Matthew also appreciated Susan's unspoken tribute to his mother.

Susan spoke about her friend with some laughter and lots of emotional tears. Daniel and Roger followed, and both spoke of Katherine's kindness, sense of humor, and boundless energy. "I also remember how very much she adored Miss Yost, and how her week assisting in Miss Yost's classroom really made her part of the community and led to her getting more involved with charities," Roger said.

That seemed the perfect opening for a young woman in the middle of the church to stand and ask to speak. "I had to come today. I remember Mrs. Taylor very well, even though it was 19 years ago that she visited Miss Yost's classroom. Your Royal Highness," she said to Matthew, "I don't expect you to remember me, but I was one of Miss Yost's students that year, and I honestly had so much fun that week. Mrs. Taylor made everything so exciting, because she changed things up and put her stamp on the same routine we had to do every day. I remember the first day when you and she were nervous and weren't sure what to do, but you did it anyway and had fun with it. You both helped me learn that even when something seems embarrassing or uncomfortable, I don't have to take it to heart and take myself so seriously. I just want to thank you and Mrs. Taylor for that, Sir."

Matthew was amazed at how many of those students, now adults, stood to speak of how joyfully they remembered his mother. Board members from Light Within spoke of Katherine's intellect, kindness, and unending desire to help people. People she had helped through her volunteering also praised Katherine's compassion and positivity.

Prince Eric stood on the altar with his family and friends, and as Matthew had that morning, spoke from his heart. "My Grandma is very special to me. She always will be. We loved each other, and we told each other that one year ago today. The last thing we told each other is how much we love each other. I'm really happy in my heart that we did, because I know she went to Heaven filled with love. That means so much to me to know that.

"Grandma wasn't afraid to get on her hands and knees and play with me when I was little. She bought me this astronaut play set for my fifth birthday, and right there at the party, in her new dress, she sat on the floor and played with me. That doesn't seem like much, but it is. She always put me and everyone else first before herself. She showed us how much she loves us. That's how I remember my Grandma."

Many people felt tears fill their eyes, and some, especially Susan, cried. Matthew hugged his son, and Angilia knelt to kiss him. "That is so beautiful, Eric. I am so in awe of you, my little man."

"I love you, Mommy. I'm in awe of you, too," Prince Eric said and kissed her cheek. Matthew handed Angilia his handkerchief, as that moment affected Angilia deeply.

"Katherine and I became fast friends," Angilia began. "She helped to take care of me and my father after my surgery in 2012. She was security, comfort, and normalcy at the time I needed those most. Our families forged an eternal bond that year, and I know how blessed I am to have Katherine and Dr. Taylor in my life. Katherine was more than my mother-in-law. She was my friend and supporter.

"I am so grateful that we shared friendship, laughter, joy, and love one year ago. That last day together was glorious and special. That's what we said to one another moments before the accident, actually. I have to echo my son Eric. The very last thing Katherine and I said to one another, seconds before the accident, is that we love each other. Eric is right. That is a blessing. Love was the last thing Katherine heard and the last thing she felt. Love is the gift she leaves with all of us. There is no greater gift."

§§§§

Two weeks later, the Royal Family and Reverend Hutchins greeted the parishioners as they arrived for the Mother's Day service. Reverend Hutchins began the service with a prayer, a hymn, and a lesson on the blessed gift God gave us all in our mothers. When he finished, Reverend Hutchins bowed, and Prince Eric stood, walked to the pulpit, and smiled at his mother.

"Mothers are God's greatest gift to us, for without them we obviously would not exist. More than that, though, is what our mothers do for us. They don't just give life to us. They give everything to us. They do everything for us. They give all of themselves for us and to us. Mothers don't have to do all that they do. They do it all because they do love us.

"I watched my mother's 2012 Mother's Day sermon many times, and what she says about Grandmother is true about her. My mother is the Queen of Valdavia, but she is my mother above all else. No matter what else she has on her agenda, I come first. She never tells me to wait. When she does come home from meetings or events, the first thing she does is help me with my homework and talk to me about my day. She lets me know how much she loves me by what she does for me.

"My mother made her love for me clear before I was born. She risked her life during her pregnancy with me, and she fought to keep us both healthy so that I could live. She knows that God has a plan for me, and she made sure I am alive to fulfill that plan. Nothing could ever prove her love for me more than that.

"My mother has many jobs and titles. Her most important job is motherhood, and her most important title is Mommy. My mother is the epitome of what God intended all mothers to be, and I am so blessed by God to call her Mommy."

Eric held his daughter's hand as tears slid from her eyes and she hugged her precious son. Angilia smiled at her father, now understanding how he felt when she surprised him with her sermon on Father's Day 2012. Angilia offered a silent prayer of thanksgiving to God for her family, knowing indeed how incredibly blessed she was.

§§§§

That afternoon, the Royal Family gathered at the Musée National de Valdavia for a very special portrait unveiling. Muriel Laperen, Director of the Musée, performed her final Royal event before her retirement in July. As always, the unveiling was a ticketed event, with 100 percent of the proceeds donated to charity. Matthew wanted the proceeds donated to the Light Within Foundation, since his mother had been closely involved with the foundation.

"Welcome, ladies and gentlemen, to the installation of a very special portrait to the Royal Portrait Gallery. We at the Musée are so honored to add this portrait to the Gallery, because it pays tribute to and portrays someone much loved by all of us in Valdavia. I welcome to the podium Her Majesty." Ms. Laperen curtseyed when Angilia stepped to the podium.

"Thank you, Ms. Laperen, not only for your introduction, but for your years of hard work and dedication. We all thank you and wish you all the best." The audience, led by Eric and Matthew, stood and applauded Ms. Laperen, much to her surprise. "Today is Mother's Day, the perfect day for my husband to unveil this portrait of his mother, Mrs. Katherine Taylor. Katherine's loving kindness gleamed in her brown eyes, and Matthew captured that impeccably in this portrait. I am so very happy that Katherine's portrait joins the family portraits here. Matthew, please unveil your portrait of your beautiful mother."

Matthew smiled and walked to the gold cord, which he pulled to reveal a lifelike portrait of his mother. Katherine looked as she always had, with her blonde hair braided and styled, her brown eyes shining, her mouth smiling, and her love of life evident. The audience stood in approving cheers, happy to see the Duc's mother so honored.

"Ladies and gentlemen, Matthew has one more surprise for you," Angilia said, to Eric's and Mitchell's astonishment. The two men wondered what Matthew and Angilia had planned. Prince Eric beamed, and they realized that he was in on the secret. He was the first one to stand and cheer when Matthew unveiled a portrait of his father. The audience soon followed.

"My father-in-law, Dr. Mitchell Taylor," Angilia gleefully announced, and was thrilled by the expression of love in his eyes when he looked at Matthew, Prince Eric, and her. They wanted to show him how much they treasured him, and decided his portrait should be placed next to his wife's and unveiled at the same time. Mitchell hugged them, surprised but elated that he and Katherine were immortalized for all eternity with their family.

Eric walked to the podium and shared his happiness with everyone there. "Ladies and gentlemen, this was a complete surprise to Mitchell and to me. Angilia, Matthew, and Prince Eric kept their secret well. I am so honored to have portraits of Mitchell and Katherine join the Royal Portrait Gallery, where they rightfully belong. I had mentioned to Matthew and Angilia two years ago that portraits of Dr. and Mrs. Taylor should be installed on their 50th wedding anniversary. How very appropriate that they are installed on this beautiful Mother's Day."

§§§§§

"Happy anniversary, darling," Matthew softly said and kissed his wife just as she woke from her dreams that morning.

Angilia returned his kiss, put her arms around him, and said, "Happy anniversary, my love. I do love you so very much, Matthew. I never knew I would feel such love and happiness until I met you again."

Matthew giggled. "We are happy. Our love lives in Eric. That is such a miracle, Angilia. A beautiful miracle."

"Yes, he is. So are you. My life is a blessing and a miracle, Matthew. You are my love, my one and only love. I now understand better the love Mommy and Daddy have, a love greater than any force."

Matthew and Angilia held one another and kissed, interrupted by a knock on their bedroom door. "May I come in?"

"Of course, Eric," Angilia said with a smile.

Prince Eric went to his father and hugged him, and then went to Angilia and kissed her. "Happy anniversary, Mommy and Daddy," he said with a huge smile. "Here." He handed Angilia a wrapped gift and a card. She gave the gift to Matthew to open, and she opened the card and read it. She showed it to Matthew, who felt joy at seeing his son's handwritten *Happy Anniversary—I love you, Mommy and Daddy—Your Loving Son Eric—26 June 2031*

Matthew tore the paper from the gift and felt love surge through him at the sight. He handed it to his wife with a smile, knowing she would forever treasure this gift. Angilia gasped when she saw a recent portrait of Prince Eric—at the age of nine—that looked so very like the drawing she had done of him when she was five and that depicted him in his late 40s. She had drawn him from her detailed memory of meeting him in the Unborn Children Sphere. Yes, his features were younger, but so similar.

"I wanted to give you something special, so I asked Bonnie to take my picture as your anniversary gift," Eric explained.

"This is far more special than you know, my handsome son. I love you eternally," Angilia said and held him close to her. Matthew pulled Prince Eric onto the bed between them, and the three held each other, surrounded one another with love, and thanked God for their miraculous and blessed lives.

CHAPTER 3

Roger ran up to Angilia just as she finished freshening after lunch and neared the elevator. She smiled up at him, reminded of the first time she had seen him the day she was born. "Are you in a hurry? I wanted to throw something by you, Princess." Roger stomped his foot in frustration. "I did it again. I still call you Princess, when I shouldn't."

"Oh, Roger, you know I don't mind," she told him and placed her hand on his arm. "You've called me that since I was born. It's not about the title. That's your pet name for me, Roger, and I've always enjoyed your calling me that. Please don't stop now." She leaned up and kissed his cheek. "Is anything wrong?"

"No. I'm planning to take your dad to lunch tomorrow, with Daniel, as a surprise treat. He's been working so hard on that new energy bill that he deserves some time out of the office. There's a new Indian restaurant over in Albian, and I made reservations there. But now I'm wondering if Eric will like it there. It's not what he usually eats. You know him better than anyone. What do you think?"

"It's ideal, Roger, really. Daddy mentioned it a week and a half ago, actually, and said he'd like to go there sometime. You couldn't have made a better choice." Angilia's brow suddenly furrowed as she watched Roger clutch his left arm. She pulled her phone from her slacks pocket to call Matthew, who was at the coffee shop across from the mall getting Mitchell's favorite cookies, when Roger fell forward against her. Angilia held him, and as she had in 2019, she loosened his tie and unbuttoned his shirt. Roger collapsed to the floor, taking Angilia with him. She cradled his head on her lap while she called Matthew. She yelled for her father and Daniel, who ran from Eric's suite, where he was getting ready for a meeting. Eric knelt next to one of his two best friends.

Roger grasped Eric's hand tightly, and looked at his best and longest friend with sadness on his face. His words were raspy, breathless, and slurred when he spoke to Eric. "I'm so glad I met you, Eric. You are the brother I never had. I'm not ready to leave you guys yet, but God says I am."

"You know I love you, buddy. You and I shared everything. And then Daniel joined us. We are the Three Musketeers. Remember? That's what you called us."

"Yeah, and we always will be, Roger," Daniel said, his hand on Roger's head.

"Always," Roger gasped. "I suppose I have to wear that tunic now, don't I, Princess?" Roger weakly smiled at Angilia. "I love you."

"I love you, Roger," Angilia told him and kissed his cheek. Just then Matthew ran from their suite with his medical bag and dropped to his knees. At the same moment, Angilia saw a man standing beside her, looking down at Roger with a smile.

"Roger, do you see him?" Roger nodded once and tried to smile. Matthew listened to Roger's heart, knowing he was dying. He tried to place a nitroglycerine tablet in Roger's mouth, but Roger brushed it aside.

"I'm okay now. Dad is here," Roger barely managed to say. He smiled at Eric, and died surrounded by his friends who loved him.

Angilia saw his soul manifest and walk away with his father. Before they disappeared, Roger turned and winked at Angilia. Eric,

Daniel, and Matthew saw her wink back. Matthew recorded Roger's death at 1:23 on the afternoon of August 22, 2031 at the age of 79.

§§§§

"I miss Roger, Angilia," Eric admitted with a touch of sadness. He and Angilia sat alone at the table in the watch tower.

Angilia placed her hand over her father's hand as the warm summer air wafted around them. "I know, Daddy. We all do. It's not the same without him here. It can never be the same. That is sad. It's difficult to accept. Death isn't sad, but adjusting to not having him here is sad."

"I knew Roger longer than anyone else, really, since before I started school. His family attended Christ Church Valmondois, and we became friends there. Roger was beside me for darn near everything, especially once he started working for Father. Roger was at the charity dinner in Spain when Marisol and I fell in love at first sight. He was beside me when you were born. He was always here to help me, to comfort me, to share everything. His friendship never wavered. We never once got angry with one another or had an argument. I don't know if any other people can claim that about their best friends."

"I seriously doubt so," Angilia said. "Roger was one of the first people I saw when I was born. I've never known life without Roger. It's very hard to take in that he isn't here anymore, Daddy."

Eric held her hand in both of his, and watched the birds fly to and from tree branches. Finally he said, "Roger and I came here after Father's death, more to take a reprieve from all of the external demands that pelted us. I was the new King, my father had just died, Mother was grief-stricken, and I just needed a little while to process it all, to make sense of it all. Roger stayed beside me, always a friend. Yet he never skipped a beat in dealing with everything that had to get done. He allowed me time to grieve and to assume my new duties. Roger made that period as painless and seamless as humanly possible. Roger was my rock."

"He knew that, Daddy. The eulogy this morning was so beautiful. We know Roger and Patrick were listening and watching.

81

I felt them there. It was Patrick who really eased Roger's fears of death after his first heart attack. Roger came to me with lots of questions, and I was honest with him. I didn't really help him, so I called for Uncle Patrick. He really made all the difference."

"Roger saw Patrick die. He was there with us that day. Roger told me you talked to him. You did help him, Angel. He said you were so strong, stronger than any of us ever knew. He said it was after the shooting. I saw your strength. I was beside you every second except therapy after the shooting."

"No, not every second. I never told you or anyone except Roger, and I only told him to help him see how I got through that trauma by focusing on you and Eric. I hoped he'd find someone or something he could really zone in on," Angilia confessed to her father.

"When wasn't I with you?" Eric asked, and then suddenly recalled when. "Your surgery. I was in that exam room that afternoon and night."

Angilia told her father what she had told Roger, about how she had regained consciousness during that surgery. She revealed everything she had heard, felt, and sensed. Eric was stunned, sickened, and horrified, more than Roger had been. "Oh, Angilia, my darling. You are extraordinary. Now I understand what you meant last year when you said you had been through worse than the shoulder surgery without anesthesia." Eric held her close for several minutes. "You are the strongest, bravest person. You truly are my miracle, Angilia."

"It's all due to you, Daddy. That's what I told Roger. He believed that, because he loves you, too. In fact, he was planning a surprise for you. That's what we were discussing when he had the heart attack. He wanted to do something special for his best friend with Daniel, too, of course. I'd like to do it on his behalf. Shall we get Daniel and go?"

Eric smiled and texted Daniel to meet them in the garage. To Eric's genuine and pleasant surprise, Angilia drove them to the Indian restaurant in Albian. Eric, Daniel, and Angilia enjoyed their food, their love, and their memories of Roger. They lifted their glasses of mineral water and toasted Roger with love and gratitude.

SSSSS

Angilia stood with other parents near the grade school exit one sunny mid-September afternoon. Prince Eric came out, chatting with a group of friends. His smile filled Angilia's heart with joy when he saw her, rather than his security officer, Nathan.

"Mommy!" Prince Eric hugged her. "Is Nathan okay? He always picks me up."

"He's fine. He's at the car waiting. Let's go," Angilia smiled, looking collegiate in her jeans, white t-shirt, sweater, and loafers. Prince Eric and Angilia held hands and walked to her familiar pink car. Prince Eric placed his backpack on the floor behind his seat and greeted Nathan, who stood beside the car.

The three of them got in, fastened their seatbelts, and Angilia began driving. Eric looked surprised when she turned in the opposite direction of the palace. "Where are we going, Mommy?"

"We are spending the afternoon together. It's Friday, and you don't have to go to school tomorrow, so we have all afternoon to ourselves. I have a very special surprise for you," Angilia teased with a huge smile.

"What? What is it?" Prince Eric asked, his own smile and eyes huge.

"You'll find out when we get there. It wouldn't be a surprise if I told you now."

Two hours later, Angilia turned onto a dirt road and finally parked near a huge horse stable and paddock. Prince Eric looked confused. "Why are we at horse stables? We have beautiful horses at home."

Angilia smiled and said, "You'll see. Come on." A man wearing blue jeans, denim shirt, and cowboy boots smiled when he approached them and greeted her.

83

"It's been a long time, Your Majesty. I will never forget your 10th birthday when your father brought you here to select your horse. You and Starlight fell in love at first sight. You even had his name immediately. I'm always thrilled when I see a picture of the two of you. How is he?"

"Thank you, Mr. Holt. Starlight is still the same, very active and healthy. I don't always ride him as vigorously as I used to, though, more to prevent joint and bone stress. He is my beautiful boy, as always."

"I see you've brought Prince Eric to visit the horses," Mr. Holt said with a wink. "Aren't you nine years old now?" he asked Eric.

"It's nice to meet you, Sir. Yes, I am nine, almost 10," Prince Eric replied.

"Almost the same age your mother was when she got Starlight."

"Eric, would you like to visit Mr. Holt's horses and select your horse?" Angilia asked him with a smile.

The boy's eyes gleamed, and he grabbed his mother in a huge hug. "Oh, yes, Mommy! Thank you!"

Mr. Holt guided Prince Eric through the first stable, and smiled when the boy stopped at the stall of a Morgan colt. Angilia watched her son pet the colt's muzzle and neck and saw the horse stomp a hoof in happiness. She knew her son had found his horse.

"I like him. I think he likes me. I want him to be my horse, Mommy," Prince Eric said with the happiest of smiles.

"I like him, too, Eric. He's yours, darling. Mr. Holt is actually going to drive him home in a trailer this afternoon. You can introduce him to Starlight and Midnight."

"Will you take my first picture with him now?" he asked Angilia. Mr. Holt led the colt from his stall and into the paddock, and there he lifted Prince Eric onto the horse. Angilia took Prince Eric's first picture with his colt.

Mr. Holt already had the saddle, blankets, bridle, and other supplies Prince Eric's colt would need loaded into his truck. Prince Eric hugged his horse before Mr. Holt led him to the trailer. "I'll see you at home soon, Rocket," Prince Eric said and petted his new friend. "Thank you so much, Mommy. He's just wonderful."

"I'm so happy for you and for Rocket," Angilia smiled.

That evening, they returned home, with Mr. Holt following, and Prince Eric immediately ran to the stable as soon as Angilia parked in the garage. Eric, Mitchell, Matthew, and Eduardo came outside, curious to see Prince Eric's new horse. Eric put his arm around Angilia as they all walked to the stable. He recalled her instant love for Starlight, a love that was mutual and spectacular. Angilia had told him that she wanted her son to experience that kind of relationship with a horse.

Angilia described Prince Eric's instant connection to Rocket, and confirmed that her son and Rocket had bonded instantly, just as she and Starlight had. By the time they arrived at the paddock, young Eric was walking Rocket, getting him familiar with his new home. They all watched his glee, especially when Angilia brought Starlight out to meet his new friend. Angilia and her son smiled joyously when the two horses seemed to be talking.

Eric went into the stable and brought his Midnight outside, as well, even though the horse was elderly and not ridden any more. Eric loved his horse, and he still exercised and visited him frequently. The veterinarian had told him that Midnight probably would not live more than another six months, so Eric made sure that Midnight was comfortable, happy, and loved. He always had, but Eric was especially cognizant of Midnight's comfort and care now that he was elderly and in need of special attention.

Angilia had known Midnight most of her life, just as she had known Roger. She knew Midnight's death would be another sad occasion for her and her father. The death of someone you love, even if that someone is a horse, is always sad, Angilia knew, despite the promise of eternal life. She hugged her precious father, anticipating the sadness ahead, all the while enjoying the happiness of the present.

ഗഗഗഗഗ

After a school board meeting, Angilia returned to the office she shared with her father. She greeted him with a kiss before opening the calendar on her computer and entering the date and time of the next school board meeting. "You seem very pensive, Daddy. Is anything wrong?"

"No, Angel, nothing's wrong. I need to hire another personal assistant, though. It just feels strange, almost wrong, to think about that, though. Father hired Roger to replace his personal assistant, and I never considered replacing Roger. Roger held that job for 54 years. That's incredible. I will never replace Roger, but I do need someone to take over that job."

"I'm so sorry, Daddy," Angilia said and stood behind his chair, putting her hands on his shoulders. "Is there anything I can do?"

"Yes, actually," Eric replied. "I called Billy this morning and spoke with him for almost 45 minutes. I don't want him to take time away from his job, so he is coming here on Saturday. We need to discuss my job offer to him, and I'd like you to be here for that discussion."

Angilia stepped from behind her father and faced him. "You want Billy to become your personal assistant? How exciting! I know he enjoys his job, but he always wanted to work for you."

Eric giggled. "You. He wanted to be your dragon slayer. He is very interested, and we talked enough so that he understands what his duties would encompass. He's known us most of his life, and he even shadowed Roger for a week when he was in college. He never let go of his interest in working here, so he was at the forefront of my mind when I had to start finding someone."

"That's why he went into time management, you know. He does enjoy his job, but it really gave him more experience and knowledge so he could be ready if an opportunity presented itself.

86

He talked to me about all of this while he was still in high school," Angilia informed her father.

"I don't want to force him into this, but it seems that I found the perfect person," Eric smiled.

§§§§

Two days later, Billy arrived at Eric's and Angilia's office for their discussion. After their greetings, they sat, enjoyed tea, and talked comfortably.

"Billy, I know you learned a lot from Roger when you shadowed him that week. What do you remember most from that week?" Eric asked.

"From the beginning, I keyed in on how calm and in control Roger remained, even when several things were happening at once. He never seemed stressed or flustered by it all. That first morning, he had three important phone calls at the same time, and he went back and forth between them rather than keeping anyone on hold for a long period or playing phone tag. He kept the callers straight in his mind and answered their questions completely instead of just giving quick answers to end the calls. While he was on the phone, he had an unscheduled guest, whom he greeted while he was dealing with the three calls. He knew how to multi-task well.

"As soon as the guest left, Roger immediately printed the agenda and proposal for your meeting, gathered and organized necessary files, and accompanied you to the meeting. During the meeting, he took notes, and afterwards he scheduled appointments in your calendar. He stayed on top of everything so that you could focus on what you needed to do.

"That week actually taught me about time management. That's why I entered that field in the first place. Time management is all about how to take care of everything in your life, not just work, so that you maximize the time available. The bonus for Roger is that he was helping his best friend," Billy stated.

Eric cleared his throat of impending tears and looked at Billy. Eric's desk phone rang at that moment, and buttons lit up indicating two incoming calls at the same time. "Excuse me."

"May I?" Billy asked. Eric nodded, and watched Billy take charge and address both calls simultaneously, as Eric had seen Roger do at least once every day for many years. Billy even scheduled an energy council meeting to further discuss Eric's energy law. Eric was impressed that Billy went straight to Eric's computer calendar, noticed a time conflict, and requested a later start time for the meeting. Billy was careful in not scheduling the meetings back-to-back. Billy quickly handled the next caller, a reporter who requested Eric's thoughts on the political upheaval in Iran. "If His Majesty finds it necessary for him to comment on the events in Iran, he will issue a statement through his Press Office," Billy calmly and firmly replied. Billy hung up and returned to his seat across from Eric's desk.

"Billy, do you want to be my Personal Assistant? I do prefer that my Personal Assistant live in the palace so that he is always available. Is that all right for you?"

"Yes, Sir, I do," Billy said, remaining calm despite his complete elation. "Living here is fine with me, yes."

"Wonderful. Are you able to begin on Monday, September 29?" Eric asked, wanting to give Billy time to organize his life.

"Yes, Sir, I am."

"You will have Roger's office across the hall. Your suite will be prepared, also, and you can begin moving your personal belongings there next week. I will prepare your employment contract, and you may sign it next week, as well. Let me know when you want to do that, and I will have everything you need ready for you so that your transition and move will be as smooth as possible." Eric stood, as did Angilia and Billy. "Thank you for coming today, on your day off. The nice thing is that you know most everyone here, so hopefully you will feel at home here as soon as you move in." Eric extended his hand, and Billy reciprocated in a handshake.

"Thank you so much for inviting me. I am so honored that you trust me and want me to work for you. I really did learn from the best, Sir." Billy turned to Angilia and bowed over her hand. "Thank you for everything."

"I'll go downstairs with you, Billy," she said, and they took the elevator to the first floor. Angilia walked to the garage with him. "I'm so happy for you, Billy."

"Thank you. This is a dream come true for me, literally, you know that. I meant it when I said I will do whatever I can to help you, all of you. You and your family mean so much to me."

"Thank you, Billy. That's mutual, I hope you know that," Angilia said and hugged him.

§§§§

3 January 2032

My Beautiful Daughter Angilia,

You are far more amazing than I ever realized, my darling daughter. Your strength, courage, faith, and love awe and stun my soul. The past two years proved your strength to me unequivocally, Angilia.

I thought I saw how strong and brave you really are 20 years ago. You risked your priceless life for my life. I still feel such reverence for you and your truly selfless willingness to die so that I could live. Your love for me pushed you to ignore the most gut-wrenching pain and to fight like a warrior so that you could protect me. Learning all that you had endured and kept secret from me— and everyone else—magnified my respect for you. My tiny little girl suffered so, in silence and fear, for me.

When you faced that brutal surgery nearly two years ago, I admit that I was terrified and sickened. But I had seen your strength, and I had faith that you would come through despite the pain. I had no idea that day just how strong you really are, Angilia.

What you told me the day of Roger's funeral horrified me. It also made my love and respect for you skyrocket to Heaven's furthest reaches. Just when I thought you could not surprise or amaze me more than you already have in your remarkable life, you did so that day.

You showed me more than once that you love me more than life. You can never know how your love fills me, buoys me, and gives me strength. You are not just my heart-glow. You, my beloved and beautiful daughter Angilia, are my hero.

I love you far more than I ever imagined it possible for one person to love another,

Daddy

§§§§§

8 March 2032

Yesterday, Daddy, Matthew, Eric, and I flew to Oxford for the annual Eric DeBruce Scholarship for Musical Excellence at the University of Oxford. Today marked the 20th anniversary of the first Scholarship Ceremony.

I remember vividly every second of that first ceremony. How Daddy charmed and awed everyone! That was the very first time he sang in public. From that moment, his singing career skyrocketed!

Today, the ceremony ran as always, with a discussion/question-and-answer session and then a short concert. The band! Tim, John, Greg, and Joe are amazingly kind, talented, and loyal. I know that they will not do this for too many more years. Like everyone, they deserve time for themselves, their families, and their other interests. They have been performing most of their lives, and as a band with Tom and then me since 1971. When they do retire, I will miss them so much, of course I will, but our love and friendship will bind us for all time. We will never stop getting together—I won't let that happen. They are too important to me.

Daddy may be 77 now, but is he ever still a heartthrob! He still has no idea how talented and remarkable he is, which only adds to his appeal and charm. Uncle Patrick made a brief appearance, too, which sent the audience into a frenzy unlike any other. Daddy and I asked him to sing the last song with us, and he simply manifested right there between us on the stage. We're so used to that, but no one else really is, so that alone caused a near riot. We had a blast, and this actually gave me the idea that we should do a trio album. Daddy and I have recorded duets; so have Uncle Patrick and I. The three of us have sung together occasionally, and now we need to record together. I will discuss this with them tomorrow.

This year's scholarship recipient is a young flautist who began her studies at Oxford this past term. Tashina Spears was so happy to win, and she gave a very sweet speech. What was really gratifying is how she reacted when she met Daddy. Tashina is 21, so she said she's heard Daddy's songs her whole life. That is so awesome!! She cried when she shook his hand, which I totally understand. Meeting someone you have admired for many years is very emotional.

I am so thrilled that Matthew and Eric were here to witness this and to experience seeing Daddy perform outside of Valdavia. The love people have for him across the world never surprises me, but it fills me with joy. Eric remarked that his Grandfather is the biggest star ever! I, of course, agree with my son. ☺

20 years. What blessings we have received in those 20 years! Thank you God!

§§§§

"Uncle Eduardo, can you please come help me in the sitting room? Everyone else is busy, and I need something that I can't reach. I hate to bother you, but you're the only one I can ask." Angilia called her uncle from the sitting room, knowing he had gone for a walk on the grounds.

"Sure, no problem. It'll take me a few minutes to get there, Angel," he happily replied. Nothing was too much for his niece.

Finally, she heard him coming and made sure everything was ready. He opened the door, only to receive a shock. "Happy birthday, Eduardo!" several people loudly greeted him. Eduardo looked around, stunned to see so many people, including the other eight Gulf War hostages who had been rescued with him and Bonnie.

They gathered for a group hug, into which they soon pulled Angilia. Eduardo asked Matthew to take a picture of them all together, realizing that, at their ages, this was probably the last time all of them would be together. Matthew and Mitchell recalled Eduardo's homecoming, and the first time they had seen the ten former hostages together at Eric's 20th Jubilee. Now, 20 years later, they were reunited.

Angilia had arranged their trips and hotel rooms in Valmondois so as to maintain the birthday surprise for Eduardo. Even Bonnie did not know they were coming until everyone gathered in the sitting room for the party. Everybody chatted and mingled for quite a while as people caught up and shared family pictures.

Finally, Eduardo blew out the heart-shaped candle on his cake and cut the first piece, which he handed to Angilia. The laughter and conversation lasted for a couple of hours, until Angilia brought a box to Eduardo. The card was signed by Angilia, Matthew, and Prince Eric. Eduardo unwrapped the box, only to feel confused to see a safari outfit inside. Angilia giggled, and told her father to give his gift to Eduardo next so everything would make more sense.

Eric hugged his brother-in-law and handed him a thick envelope. Inside were hotel reservations in Kenya. Eduardo was more stunned than since the soldiers had come to rescue the hostages. "Are you kidding? Kenya? I've always wanted to go there, but it just never happened. I've thought about it, and I even considered arranging the trip. I don't know what to say."

"You don't have to say anything, Eduardo. Just enjoy your trip," Eric smiled.

"You need to take lots of pictures, so you'll need this," Bonnie said and gave him a professional camera with several lenses for wildlife snaps.

"You're a writer, so we thought you could use this," Bill Sturgis said on behalf of the former hostages. Eduardo opened a handmade leather journal, in which he would record his experiences, thoughts, and feelings during his dream-come-true journey through Kenya.

Eduardo turned to Angilia and pulled her close. "You set this in motion, Angel. I mentioned Kenya to you, and you got everyone together on this. Thank you, my remarkable niece. I do love you so very much."

"I love you, Uncle Eduardo. I hope you know how much."

Susan and Bonnie dried their tears, and everyone went to the dining room for a dinner that nourished their bodies and their souls. The love and friendship surrounded them and confirmed that time and space did not dampen the strong bonds they had forged. Eduardo said several prayers of thanksgiving that evening as he sat engulfed in the loving warmth of his family and friends on his 75th birthday.

§§§§§

Angilia double checked her calendar for April 14 to confirm that she had no scheduled appointments or meetings for the rest of the day, and then told Susan that she was going to the stable. Midnight had become weaker over the past couple of weeks, and she knew his death was imminent. She did not want him to be alone when he died. Eric regretted having to leave for a meeting, wanting instead to spend time with his horse.

Joseph was looking in on Midnight when Angilia entered, and his sorrowful smile told her that Midnight's condition was worse. "He is trying to stand, and I don't think he understands why he can't. Poor Midnight doesn't understand that things are not the same for him anymore. I've been here a lot today, just letting him know I'm here."

"Thank you, Joseph. I know he appreciates that. I want to see our other two boys before I sit with Midnight," Angilia said and grabbed some sugar cubes. She entered Starlight's stall, hugged him, told him how much she loved him, and promised him she would ride him soon. She gave him a few sugar cubes, and he kissed her cheek.

She patted his forehead, closed his stall, and went to Rocket's stall. She hugged him, too, rubbed his ears—which he always liked—and treated him to some sugar cubes before she told him Eric would probably come for a visit after school. He seemed to understand, which made her smile. She needed a smile.

She entered Midnight's stall, and Joseph helped her to the floor beside the handsome horse. She leaned down and kissed Midnight's forehead, stoked his neck, and talked to him. She stayed beside him for hours, petting him, talking to him, and singing to him. By mid-afternoon, Midnight's breathing was labored, and she knew he was beginning to die.

Angilia kept talking and singing to Midnight, and even cushioned his head on her lap. Eric came into the stable close to 3:30, and the sight of Angilia soothing Midnight in his last hours really got to him. He had managed to keep his emotions under control throughout the day, despite thinking of his horse constantly and wondering how he was.

Angilia looked up at her father, and he sat next to her in the stall. He, too, stroked Midnight and talked to him, retelling the day he first saw the stallion and bought him on the spot. He had not intended to buy a horse, but Midnight instantly changed his mind. He had bought Midnight when Angilia was two years old and Midnight was four. At 38 years old, Midnight had outlived his breed's lifespan, and for that Eric was grateful.

"Daddy, I remember the first time I rode a horse. You held me as you walked Midnight around the paddock, and I laughed the whole time. That was such a glorious experience. Midnight is such a wonderful horse, and you cared for him so well. Your care and love extended his life, and he knows that, I am sure he does. Horses are very intelligent and intuitive. He knows how much you love him. He loves you, too."

As if to prove his love, Midnight looked up at his master and rubbed Eric's hand with his muzzle. Angilia put her arm around her father, as they both felt Midnight gasp and then stop breathing. A few moments later, he moaned as his lungs completely stopped working, and then Angilia felt his heart stop. Midnight died in their embrace just as Prince Eric ran into the stable to visit Rocket.

Seeing his mother and grandfather with Midnight drew him into the stall. He knew Midnight was dead, and he knew that made his grandfather and mother sad. Prince Eric hugged his grandfather. "Midnight was a handsome horse, Grandfather. He was a good horse. I'm so sorry."

Eric hugged his grandson tight, knowing the boy had inherited Angilia's sensitive and empathetic soul. "I'm going to miss him, I won't lie. But he gave me so much joy and a lifetime of memories. I'll hold onto that for the rest of my life."

Angilia put her head on her father's shoulder and her hand on her son's cheek. "You know, there are a lot of animals in Heaven. I'm sure we'll see Midnight again someday, Daddy and Eric. Then you can ride him forever."

"Does that mean Rocket will be in Heaven, too? I can ride him for all time, Mommy?"

"Yes, Eric, you can. Love and life are eternal," Angilia said with a teary-eyed smile.

§§§§

Angilia drove from the Light Within offices to the coffee shop across from the mall, where she and Nicole met for lunch. Angilia hugged her friend, and they talked happily, ordered salads and lemonade, and enjoyed the breeze that kept the summer heat away. Finally, Angilia revealed why she had asked Nicole to meet with her.

"Yvonne's birthday is in three weeks. Do you and William have any special plans for that day?"

"Nothing concrete yet. We thought we'd invite her friends over for a party, but we haven't planned anything extravagant. Eric is invited, of course."

"Well, I was wondering if she'd like to have her party at our place. We can have games and tents set up in the back, and anything else she wants."

"You mean have her party at the palace? Are you serious, Angilia? Yvonne would just love that! But are you sure? It won't cause any problems?" Nicole asked, amazed and delighted.

"Of course not. I talked it over with Daddy and Matthew, and they think it will be nice to have Eric, Yvonne, and their friends there for the day. We can plan the menu and cake with Antoine and Anthony, mail the invitations, and anything you want. This is going to be so much fun!" Angilia gushed, reminding Nicole of the 16-year-old who told the girls some family stories on Halloween 2012.

"Thank you so much, Angilia! Can you believe it's been 20 years since we met? I was just remembering that slumber party. Poor Darlene fainted every time your father looked at her. Oh my gosh, was that ever uncomfortable."

Angilia giggled. "It was, but mostly for my father. He's still not used to the admiration he receives every time he goes somewhere."

"Speaking of admiration," Nicole softly said when a young girl approached and stood next to Angilia.

Angilia turned and smiled at the little girl, who was holding a pretty Cairn terrier. "Hello, sweetheart. What a darling little dog. He looks just like Dorothy's Toto," Angilia said to the girl, and noticed that she looked rather sad.

"That's his name, Toto. Queen Angilia, I need you to heal him. Please. Will you touch him and pray for him so he will get well?"

"Oh, darling, of course I will pray for Toto. I can't heal him, though, as much as I wish I could," Angilia told the girl.

"Yes, you can. You performed miracles before. Please heal Toto. He is very sick, and the vet says he'll die soon. Please help him," the girl said and began to cry.

Angilia pulled her close, and promised her she would pray to God to heal Toto. The girl placed Toto in Angilia's lap, and Angilia held the little dog in her arms. "You are a cutie, Toto. What's wrong with him?"

"He has kidney failure, and he hasn't eaten in a long time, more than two weeks. He doesn't drink water. The vet says it's 'cause everything tastes really bad, and Toto's body can't process food and water. We take him a few times a week to get his nutrients through a tube. He used to run and play all the time. Now he can't even stand on his own. I'll show you."

The girl took Toto and gently placed him on the ground. His legs collapsed under him. She pulled one of his favorite treats from her pocket, and he ignored it. "See. He can't do anything anymore. I don't want him to be sick and die. Please."

Angilia picked up Toto, and he lay his head on her left shoulder while she stroked his back. Other diners watched the girl and her dog, heartbroken by the scene. They watched in respectful silence while Angilia closed her eyes and prayed for Toto's healing, all the while running her hand up and down his back. She felt Toto tremble, and wondered if he were getting ill.

Suddenly, Toto barked, wagged his tail, and licked Angilia's face. "Toto!" the girl said happily, and reached for him. Toto practically jumped into her arms, and the girl looked expectantly at Angilia. She gently sat Toto on the ground, and he walked over to Angilia and stood on his hind legs. "Give him this," the girl said, and handed Angilia a dog treat. Toto took it, ate it, and barked again.

"You did it! You healed Toto! Thank you, Queen Angilia! Thank you!" The girl flung herself at Angilia and hugged her. "I knew you could save him. You are the realest angel there is. I have to go show the vet," she said, picked up Toto, and ran off. "I love you, Queen Angilia! My name is Elizabeth. Thank you!"

Nicole sat stunned by the miracle she had seen. Everyone else who had witnessed the miracle stood and applauded. Angilia stood, too, and motioned for everyone to stop. "I didn't do anything except pray for God to heal Toto. If Toto is healed, God did it, and I am grateful for that. Thank you."

Nicole hugged Angilia before they left the coffee shop. "Even if God did heal the dog, your prayer is what got his attention. You just keep doing wonders, girl. Thank you for Yvonne's party. I'll call you soon."

§§§§

June 16 was a lovely summer day for Yvonne's birthday party. Yvonne followed her best friend Prince Eric's example and requested that her friends did not have to bring her gifts. She just wanted them to have fun and enjoy the day with her. Nicole, William, and Yvonne came to the palace one hour before the party guests began arriving, and Prince Eric got permission to take her to the stable for a short visit with Rocket.

The guests were shown to the patio, where tables and chairs awaited the adults. The children began playing on the spacious lawn, and laughter soon filled the air. Yvonne and Prince Eric happily greeted each of their friends as they arrived. One girl, though, said she wanted to talk to Queen Angilia first, and Prince Eric wondered why. He watched as the girl motioned for her mother to hurry, and was surprised to see a dog on a leash.

The girl took the leash and unbuckled it. Angilia was suddenly astonished to feel a dog pawing at her leg. "Toto!" She picked him up, and noticed Elizabeth watching with a huge smile. "Elizabeth. It's so nice to see you again. It looks like Toto is doing well. Is he responding to treatments now? What did the vet say?"

"Toto doesn't need any treatments. The vet said he is fine. You know that. You saw him. You saved him. You healed Toto."

By then, everyone stood silently watching and listening, including the adults, Prince Eric, Yvonne, and Elizabeth's friends. They were shocked to see Toto; he had been nearly dead when they had last seen him. Nicole, though, smiled, knowing what had happened and how Angilia had somehow cured Toto.

Elizabeth's mother, Mrs. West, approached Angilia and curtseyed to her and to Eric. "Queen Angilia, Elizabeth surprised us all three weeks ago when she called us from the vet's office and told us that the vet said Toto's kidney failure seemed to have disappeared. My husband and I went to the vet's office and couldn't believe we were looking at the same dog we had seen just a short time earlier. Elizabeth told us what you did, and if it had been anyone else we wouldn't have believed it, I have to say. But we know about you. You cured Elizabeth's dog! You performed a miracle, Your Majesty. We can never thank you enough for that." She kissed Angilia's hand.

"I am so grateful that Toto is healthy, but all I did was pray. God healed Toto," Angilia gently insisted.

"God had a hand in it, yes, but you did it. Elizabeth said you kept stroking Toto's back. Your touch cured him."

Angilia started to protest, but Mrs. West flabbergasted Eric by grabbing him in a hug and proclaiming, "You, Sir, sired a saint."

Patrick manifested beside his brother at that moment and placed his hands on Mrs. West's shoulders. "Mrs. West, we rejoice in Toto's healing. God works many miracles every day, and he often works through people. Isn't God wondrous?" Patrick asked her, steering her attention away from Eric and Angilia.

"Yes, yes he is, of course he is," Mrs. West mumbled, shocked to see the famous angel standing before her. She regained enough of her senses to thank everyone and take Toto's leash. She turned to Elizabeth and told her to behave and have fun.

Thankfully, Yvonne motioned for Elizabeth to join the games, and the girls ran off. Eric looked and felt dazed. "I'm sorry, Daddy," Angilia said. "I held Toto and prayed for his recovery. That's all. I never expected any of this."

"It's not your fault, Angilia. Mrs. West certainly threw me a zinger. Did she really say that?"

Daniel could no longer restrain his giggle. "*You sired a saint,*" he repeated. "I haven't heard that word in a long time, since Shakespeare class in college."

"Good grief," Eric said, and apologized to the parents and guests gathered on the patio. "Your prayers are very powerful, darling," he said and hugged his daughter.

"More than you realize," Patrick very softly said.

§§§§

Angilia called Sam, John, Tim, Greg, and Joe and asked if they could come to Valmondois in a few days. When they all said they would, she arranged to send one of Eric's planes to pick them up. The five men lived in various parts of the United States, and she knew they always enjoyed traveling together. They had done so for so long with Tom Greenfield that life on the road became normal and comfortable for them.

She missed Tom, and sat reliving memories for a while. Had it really been 21 years since the plane crash that killed Tom? She smiled as she recalled that first meeting in the courtyard when she was six years old. Tom and Tim were in Valmondois for a concert, and they were viewing the palace when they heard her playing the guitar and singing a song Tom had written many years earlier. She had heard it many times, because Eric owned several of Tom's albums and played them often.

She remembered Tom's and Tim's long shaggy hair, battle-scarred blue jeans, and brightly-colored shirts. Their expressions when she came down from the tower were priceless—they stared down at her as she carried her guitar, which was almost larger than she was. That little girl had been singing Tom's song? From that moment, Tom was her most ardent fan and supporter other than her father, who was as unprepared for her singing career as she.

Thirty years later, she, Eric, and Patrick were ready to record their trio album. She had written some songs for the album, Patrick had selected some he wanted to sing, and Eric had totally surprised her by bringing his 1989 diary to her. He showed her a poem he had written in the very early morning of July 10—hours after he and Marisol had met. Angilia had never seen any of her father's poems before, and she asked him how many others he was hiding away.

Eric giggled and said, "None. This is the only poem I've ever written. Patrick's poems gave me the courage to ask you to put this to music for me. What do you think?"

"I think this is beautiful, romantic, and perfect. I can hear it in my head," she said, grabbed his hand, and went to the music room with him. She played the melody on the piano, wrote the sheet music, and handed it to her father. He asked her to sing it so he could put the melody with the words, and he smiled, knowing she had complemented his poem perfectly. Eric sang it through once, and declared that would be his solo for the album.

All of the songs were ready, just waiting for the band to arrive and learn them. They were spending the week of June 21 at the palace, and Angilia knew her father's song would carry exceptional meaning since June 26 was his and Marisol's 41st wedding anniversary. It was also her and Matthew's 16th anniversary. She hugged her father, her heart filled with more love than it could contain.

§§§§§

Angilia and Eric greeted the band and Sam at the airport on Sunday afternoon, just in time to get them settled so they could catch up over dinner. Angilia hugged them excitedly, and she could feel how much weight Tim had lost since early March. She had also obviously noticed that he was bald, and she knew he was ill. She did not bring it up, though, at least not so soon. Tim looked very tired, and she prayed for him while everyone else chatted.

The next day, they all gathered in the basement recording studio, and soon they were learning the songs—except for the ones Eric and Angilia had written. Those would come later. Patrick's solo selection garnered some giggles, and since it was a late 1960s song, the band already knew that one. The songs selected for the trios were also covers, which they had all heard numerous times, so once they ran through the arrangements, the band was ready to record the songs.

Angilia convinced her father and her uncle that their vocals were consistently flawless, as did Sam. That meant they recorded most of the songs in one take each. By lunch on Tuesday, half of the trio songs were done. Twenty-four hours later, the remaining six trios were recorded. That left the three solo tracks, and they began with Patrick's song that afternoon.

Eric remembered his brother blaring the song in the early 1970s, from his 8-track player and later from his motorcycle radio. Neither Eric nor Patrick had ever watched the film which had made the song a hit, but that did not dampen Patrick's fondness for the song. In fact, he enjoyed singing "Born to Be Wild" so much, he insisted on six takes that afternoon. Finally, he laughingly called it quits and agreed to let everyone go upstairs and relax before dinner.

Angilia watched Tim all evening, and noticed how worn he appeared. He ate very little at dinner, and she became very concerned. She had planned to talk with him, but after dinner he excused himself and went to his suite. Sam put an arm around her shoulders and pulled her aside. "Tim's been sick lately. I don't think he's over it completely yet. He's tired a lot, but he insists he just needs rest. He doesn't like to talk about it too much, but I've kept an eye on him, too, darling."

"I hope he knows he can trust Matthew and Dr. Taylor if he needs anything. I just keep praying for him. I wish there was something I could do to make him feel better," Angilia sadly told Sam.

"Aw, sweetie, you're doing the best thing possible. We'll just keep praying for Tim. God will do what's best."

"I know, Sam. I just don't want Tim to suffer."

On Thursday, the band spent a few hours that morning learning and rehearsing Angilia's solo. She played the music on the guitar, and the musicians perfected it, adding their instruments to the mix until they achieved the right sound. When they had, Sam turned on the control panel, knowing her first take would more than likely be pitch perfect and flawless.

Angilia and the band played the music, and for the first time she sang the lyrics. Eric and Patrick were stunned. All of the men were, but none were more emotionally moved than Tim. When they finished, Angilia surprised them by saying, "I'm having second thoughts about recording this."

"Why, baby?" Eric asked her.

"I mean the words, and they are true for me. I just wonder if they don't come across as too condescending or holier-than-thou. Prayers are supposed to be private, between someone and God, not flaunted in public," she explained, a look of consternation on her face.

Patrick started to speak, but Tim put down his electric guitar and walked to her. "You have to record this. A lot of people need this. Believe me. Knowing you changed my life, Angilia. I'm far from perfect, but I tried to do the right thing. I didn't always, but I tried. I need to tell you something, and I know you know I'm sick. I'm dying. After the ceremony in March, I felt weird, so I went to the doctor. Many tests later, they told me I have inoperable bone cancer. This is the last music I will play with all of you, and I want you to record this prayer and send it out into the world where it belongs. Do it, for me and for everyone on this planet."

John, Greg, Joe, and Sam stood ramrod straight and still, as did Eric and Patrick. They had never expected this news from their friend. Angilia put her arms around Tim and kissed his now-hollow cheek. "I love you, Tim. I was just thinking the other day about that first day I met you and Tom. To me, you two looked like rock stars. You are a rock star, Tim."

"You mean, we looked like hippies," he smiled. "Long hair and crazy clothes. Tom and I could not believe it when this tiny kid came out when we asked who was singing. Neither of us thought it possible, but you knocked the ground from under us. You still do. Ready to do it again with this song?"

Angilia nodded, and Eric and Patrick joined Sam in the control booth. Angilia had annotated the lines on which she wanted Tim to harmonize with her, and they looked at one another as they recorded together for the last time. In one take, they recorded the most perfect performance they had ever done together. Tim's voice was weaker than usual, but his emotions resonated powerfully as his voice blended with Angilia's. Angilia and the band hugged when they finished, knowing the last song of the album, Eric's solo, would be the emotional high point of their careers. After tomorrow, they would never perform together again.

§§§§

The next day was poignant for everyone for multiple reasons. Not only was Tim preparing for his death, but the following day was the 41st anniversary of Eric's and Marisol's marriage. She had died in late 1995; she and Eric were together as wife and husband only four years. Patrick stood with his arm around Eric's shoulders while Angilia ran through the music with the band and they learned it.

Finally, Eric sang it once with the band so they could make sure they got everything right. Angilia smiled at him, knowing that her mother was listening to her father sing the words he had written about her, words that captured his true love-at-first-sight for Marisol. Eric did not want to prolong the session, so he promised himself to record the song in one take. Tim wanted to make this album with them, but Eric knew that doing so expended far too much of the little energy Tim possessed.

Angilia had spoken with her father the previous evening, after talking with Tim, and they agreed that Sam, Joe, John, Greg, and Tim should stay for a while. Tim had told Angilia that he would likely die within three weeks, although he felt it would be sooner. She did not want him traveling, or worse, alone at his home. He had agreed to stay, but he had made her promise to fulfill his last wishes. She had promised, and she would do whatever she could to surround him with love, comfort, and joy.

Eric sat on a stool, closed his eyes, and sung into the microphone to his beloved Marisol. Tears filled Angilia's eyes as she felt the emotions in her father's voice. He need not have worried about recording the song in one take, for his first and only take was absolutely magical. Angilia and Patrick hugged Eric when he finished, knowing how much he missed having Marisol with him and how much he anticipated their reunion in Heaven.

Love at First Sight

All of my life I have dared never dream

That love at first sight could happen to me,

But the truth is greater than any dream.

With one look I know we are meant to be;

At first glance I knew we will be a team,

A pair in love throughout eternity.

You alone allowed me to believe

The truth of happily-ever-after,

That love is real and will never leave.

I sent up my prayer and have the answer.

In my heart and soul you forever weave

The story that writes my greatest chapter,

The rest of my life lived in blissfulness.

We share love, we share joy, and we share life;

Now I truly understand happiness.

I am yours, you are mine, to be my wife

For a lifetime of only peacefulness,

Not just this life, but in the afterlife.

You made my heart believe in fairy tales.

§§§§

"Angilia, can I ask you a favor?" Tim asked her when Eric's session wrapped up. "I'd like you to record one song that's stuck with me for 21 years. I heard you sing it just that one time, at Tom's funeral, but I've heard it every day since then. Will you sing it again for me? Will you record it for me?"

Sam, Joe, John, and Greg had tears in their eyes. Eric felt for his daughter, who was making Tim's journey from this life to the next as calm, peaceful, and love-filled as possible. Patrick smiled, knowing that Tim would face his death with peace, not fear.

"Of course, I will. It's been a long time since we've done it. Do we want to run through it?"

"I'm sure I remember it," John said. "I'm not sure why, but it just stayed in my head, I think."

Angilia and the band played through the song, which all of them did remember. That song had been too special and meaningful for any of them to forget.

"Sounds good. Ready?" Sam asked. Eric and Patrick went into the control booth, unprepared for the emotional gut-punch they received. Sam and Eric did not even try to stop their tears. Patrick leaned on his brother, feeling the others' sadness and pain.

Sam played Angilia's interpretation of Sandy Denny's "Who Knows Where the Time Goes?" when they finished, and Tim smiled while he sat on the sofa between Angilia and Greg. Tim leaned his head on Angilia's shoulder, and she kissed his cheek. He was so much weaker, and she knew his death was quite near.

"That's a wrap. The album's 16 songs are complete," Sam declared. "Do we have an album title?"

Angilia looked at her father and smiled. She had shown him and Patrick. "We do. It's from Book 8 of Milton's Paradise Lost. *'Be strong, live happy and love,'*" she quoted.

"That's perfect," Tim weakly said.

The men helped Tim up the elevator to the sitting room chaise lounge. Angilia covered him with an afghan and placed soft pillows under and around him. Eric summoned Matthew and Mitchell, but Tim said he was ready and just wanted to die surrounded by those he loved most. They sat with him, holding his hands, while he slept.

Angilia sat beside him all that night, and when the darkness gave way to the light, he opened his eyes. "Happy anniversary, Angel."

"Yes, darling, happy anniversary," Matthew said and hugged her when he entered the sitting room at that moment.

Angilia hugged and kissed Matthew, and told him with her expressive eyes that Tim would die soon. She stayed beside Tim throughout Saturday and Sunday, and he rested against her while she held him. Everyone sat solemn, quiet, and prayerful. At Tim's request, Tom's solo albums played. Just after 1:00, Tim smiled when Tom's very first hit song filled the room. "It's been an amazing life," he softly said.

"You are amazing," Angilia said. "You are my Scarecrow." Tim smiled, understanding her <u>The Wizard of Oz</u> reference. She had met him first and had an extra-special bond with him.

"It's time for me to go over the rainbow now. I love you, all of you."

"I love you, Tim," Angilia said, kissed his cheek, and felt Tim die in her arms. Mitchell confirmed Tim's death and recorded the date and time: June 27, 2032 at 1:13 PM. Tim was 80, and even with cancer ravaging his body, one of the most dynamic, energetic, and revolutionary electric guitarists in rock and roll history.

§§§§

Monday morning, Angilia and Matthew drove to the hospital, where she would do as Tim had asked. She prayed over his body, and watched as it was placed into the crematory. That evening, she held the urn when they returned home. At sunset, she gathered everyone for the ceremony.

They all walked to a hill in the distance, where Tim and she had sat when she was a child. He had liked the peace, quiet, and solitude there. It was a long, quiet walk, but once they arrived, Angilia told them why there were there.

"Tim asked me a few nights ago to fulfill his final wishes. He did not want a funeral. He wanted to be cremated, and there was one place he wanted me to scatter his ashes. He called it the Mystical Hill, because it's so quiet and peaceful here. He said he could hear God when he was here."

Angilia led them in prayer, and they all spoke briefly and shared their feelings about Tim. Angilia stepped onto the hill and opened the urn. "God bless you, Tim. We love you," she said, and spread his ashes over the hill.

"Wow, this is rougher than I thought it'd be," John said. "I'm gonna miss him."

"We all are," Greg said, and put his arm around John's shoulders. Joe and Sam joined the hug, echoing John's sorrow.

"It will never be the same again. I know we're older, but until now I just never thought about us starting to die. First Tom and now Tim. That stings, you know," Joe said.

"That's the sad thing about getting old. You see the people you love die and leave you," John admitted.

"They don't leave us, they just leave earth. If I've learned anything over the past 30 years of knowing Angilia, it's that. Tom and Tim are together again, and when we die, we'll join them. This band is gonna be together forever," Sam stated.

§§§§

Sam rushed the release of the trio album, and it went live on Monday, July 12. The album was dedicated to Tim, and included Angilia's poignant written tribute to her friend and colleague. The debut single from <u>Be Strong, Live Happy and Love</u> was the prayer that Tim wanted released. There was never any consideration of another first song. That song touched Tim, and he knew it would touch other people.

Tim was proven right. The song sold more than one million copies in its first 24 hours, demonstrating the power in Angilia's lyrics. "I'm glad you released it, Little One. Tim said it before I could, but he's right. People need and want prayers and inspiration. They always have, and they always will. Heck, if *you* feel this way, then hundreds of others do, too. Your song lets people know it's okay to feel that way, too. Just like you told me about my poem, "My Purpose," lots of people feel this way and need reassurance. Plus, you help them find the words to ask for God's forgiveness, just like David's Psalms do, Angilia. It's a beautiful prayer of confession and repentance," Patrick told her that evening as they sat alone.

My Soul's Prayer

I honor your word and try to obey

All that you dictate, preach, expect, and say.

Though my imperfection leads me astray,

When I falter you never go away.

Despite the sins I never see, you stay,

Your love shepherding me along my way.

When you do peer into my soul you may

Weep in sorrow at my utter decay.

To you, my dear Lord, I ceaselessly pray

For the gift I do not deserve today.

My paltry life can but hope to convey

What in my heart I want to display,

My fervent love that shines like the sun's ray.

My solemn vow is to never betray

The debts I will never hope to repay.

I beg from you my faults to allay.

My soul purify so sins fall away.

Chastise me daily with my judgment day,

So I stay earnest and keep sin at bay

And not spend eternity in dismay.

Dear God, please save my soul, to you I pray.

CHAPTER 4

After the sadness of the successive deaths of Katherine, Roger, Midnight, and Tim, the Royal Family prepared for Eric's week-long 40th Jubilee. Unlike the 20th Jubilee in August 2012, this one had been planned by the current Jubilee Committee for the past five years. The six-member committee financed the entire week through donations that had been placed in a Jubilee fund that had been set up 20 years earlier at the Banque de Valdavia. The people wanted to honor their King—and their Queen. Unbeknownst to her, Angilia's 20th Jubilee in 2049 was already being discussed.

Angilia glowed with joy and love in the days leading up to her father's Jubilee week. The amount of respect and affection shown to her father never failed to touch her deeply. Even more heartwarming for her was sharing the experience with her son, and watching his wonder and excitement. To commemorate the event, Bonnie took portraits of the family, including King Eric and Prince Eric together.

The week began on August 22, 2032 with a Service of Thanksgiving at Christ Church Valmondois. The family received cheers when they stepped onto the courtyard that morning for the walk to church. They greeted people and posed for pictures during the relatively short walk, and accepted flowers, cards, and gifts from those there to pay respect to King Eric.

"Mommy, this is amazing. All of these people came to tell Grandfather how much they love him. People are telling me how much they love him. This is really cool," Prince Eric told Angilia as they entered the church to greet the congregation.

"I know, Eric. I know we're rather biased, but I do believe that your Grandfather is the most universally respected and loved leader in the world," Angilia added with a smile.

She, Prince Eric, and Matthew wrote their messages in the tribute book, which was on a table in the entryway. Soon, they joined King Eric in the Royal pew, and rejoiced more passionately than anyone else that he was their father, grandfather, and King. Angilia's silent prayer thanked God for keeping her father safe 20 years earlier and for not letting his destiny be altered. She did not want to contemplate how Valdavia and the rest of the world would have transformed had that happened.

§§§§§

On Monday morning, the Royal Family gathered outside the Counseil de Valdavia building located in the center of downtown Valmondois. Eric knew only that there would be a dedication, but none of the details. Only Billy knew, since he had been the contact person who had assisted the committee after Roger's death. The members of Eric's Advisory Board greeted him and the Royal party before the dedication began. Angilia had known the Board members all of her life, and had long ago vowed to continue the Advisory Board. Now that Prince Eric better understood the Board's purpose, he likewise wanted to have an Advisory Board when he someday became King Eric II.

Finally, the Chief Advisor, Benjamin Gibson, stood at the podium and called the hundreds of attendees to order. Press photographers took hundreds of pictures throughout the event, especially when Mr. Gibson surprised everyone. "Your Majesty Queen Angilia and Your Royal Highness Prince Eric, we would like you both to do the honor and reveal the building's new façade." Angilia and Prince Eric smiled and walked to the large black curtain that covered the front of the two-story building that Eric had leased in 1992. Together, they pulled the gold cord, and the curtain fell to the ground.

112

In large gleaming gold letters appeared the new name of the building: Le Eric Roi de Valdavia Centre Pour le Comité Consultatif. Under the sloping cornice, upon the tympanum of the pediment, was a bas-relief depicting King Eric in his diadem, uniform, and robe. Everyone suddenly erupted in applause and cheers of appreciation at the Grecian-style tribute to their beloved Eric.

Eric was encouraged to speak, and he went to the podium. Even after 77 years in the public spotlight and 40 years as King, Eric was never truly comfortable having so much attention and focus. He preferred that people focus on global and social issues rather than on him and his achievements. "Good morning," he greeted the huge crowd who strained for the best view of him. "Thank you all for remembering me this week. I am amazed. I am honestly surprised by this, and could have never expected this. Now I understand why the main entrance was shrouded for months. When I asked about the work being done, I was told the façade needed some reinforcements. I'm not sure how it feels to see myself at the top of the building, though. It's rather peculiar," he commented to some laughter.

"This Advisory Board is invaluable to me. These men and this lady consistently provide me advice, information, and a broader perspective so that I can do the absolute best job I can do for all of you. No one told me to solicit these experts from various fields. No one told me to establish an Advisory Board. When I became King in 1992, I knew I had been well taught and trained by my father, King Gerard. I had learned from the best. But I wanted to extend my knowledge base and my point of view, and forming the Advisory Board is one of the two best administrative decisions I have made. The other is proclaiming Angilia my co-monarch.

"I have said many times how much I cherish all of you and your support. You make my life and my work more enjoyable. My work often does not feel like work, because you remain my inspiration and guiding force. That does not necessarily mean the work is easier. In some ways, it is harder, because I strive to do what is always best for all of you. That is far from a complaint, though. That is a blessing. You encourage me to think deeply, seriously, and knowledgably about every decision, law, and proposal so that you truly do benefit. You keep me excited and passionate in everything I do. I have so treasured working for you these past 40 years, and I vow to continue to do so for the remainder of my life."

Everyone applauded Eric for more than 20 minutes, despite his thanks and attempts to end the applause. He looked at Angilia, smiling but uncomfortable—no one else probably noticed, but she always did. She stepped to his side and put her arm around him. "I know you don't want to be the center of attention, but this is wonderful, Daddy. This is everyone's chance to show you how much they love and respect you and appreciate everything you do for us. They know it never affects your ego, which makes them love you all the more. At least you know that you're doing a good job, right?"

"I suppose, Angel," Eric said close to her ear. "Hasn't this gone on long enough, though?"

Angilia giggled and stood at the podium microphone. Finally, the applause quieted, and she saw her father heave a sigh of relief. "Thank you all so much for honoring my father. None of us had any idea what was planned today, and we were all pleasantly surprised. This is the perfect honor for my father, because the Advisory Board was his brainchild and creation. I was born hearing and learning about this very republican institution of an Absolute Monarch—quite the contradiction in philosophies. Now that I am closely involved with the Advisory Board, I know beyond certainty that my childhood vow to continue the Advisory Board is concrete.

"Popular worldwide consensus says that my father is the most effective, empathetic leader of the past 100 years. He is. I have seen this my entire life, but working closely alongside him has shown me just how much he truly cares—about all of us, about Valdavia, about the world, and about our collective future. By now it is a cliché to say that we are blessed to have him as our King, but we are, more than we actually know. Your love for him fills my soul with joy. Thank you," Angilia told everyone. Her deep love for her father showed in her eyes and in the tender kiss that she gave his cheek.

§§§§

Eric's 40th Jubilee week was filled with events and programs that praised and honored him, including the popular Garden Party. Prince Eric, at nearly 11 years old, was a fan favorite as he mingled with the guests, posed for pictures, and signed autographs. Eric watched his grandson all day, his love and joy clearly evident. The country's future was safe and secure with the boy who would become its next King.

The 40th Jubilee culminated on Saturday, August 28, with a concert. The performers remained secret this time, although the Gateway Arena was filled to capacity. The Royal party sat in the Royal Box, waving to friends, neighbors, and well-wishers.

"I wonder why they kept the performers secret?" Mitchell asked.

"Probably to surprise Daddy," Angilia said. "I'm going backstage, though, and see if I know anyone. I'll be back," she promised them.

Wayne Chambliss, the President of the 40th Jubilee Committee, appeared on the stage moments before the concert began. "Welcome to the 40th Jubilee Tribute Concert. We knew this concert would draw a packed house, simply because we all want to show our love, appreciation, and support to King Eric. We planned a very special and exciting concert as the finale to the official 40th Jubilee Week, and I know you will be thrilled. Without further ado, let's begin the show," Wayne smiled and walked off the stage as the lights dimmed.

The curtains rose, although the stage was devoid of lights and the audience could not see who was on stage. One spotlight suddenly shone on the front center stage, and the band began playing a very familiar song. On cue, Angilia appeared at the microphone, guitar strap slung over her shoulder, singing. The audience erupted in cheers when Patrick's voice joined hers and he manifested beside her while they sang "Little Girl Lost," the first song they had recorded together 12 years earlier.

The concert was indeed the perfect capstone to the week's festivities. Angilia and Patrick performed their well-known recordings, as well as several new songs. Near the end of the show,

Angilia paused to turn the spotlight on her band and to introduce them. "These musicians really are the absolute best. I am so blessed and honored to call them my friends. Joe Arnold on the drums. John Herbert on the bass. Greg Smithson on the piano. As you know, this is our first performance without our beloved Tim Hanley, and we want to do this next song for Tim. He requested that we record this song, the last song he performed with us." Patrick stood in the shadows, his head bowed, while Angilia, John, Greg, and Joe performed "Who Knows Where the Time Goes?"

"Thank you," Angilia told the audience when they applauded. "My next song is for someone very special," she added. The band sat quietly, their heads also bowed, while Angilia played and sang "The Gift of You." Mitchell placed his hand on Eric's shoulder, both of them recalling the late night of March 7, 2012 when Eric had played his daughter's loving tribute while she fought to stay alive.

Matthew and Prince Eric listened to and watched Angilia while she sang only to her father. She looked at him as she sang, her eyes gleaming with that familiar look of love. Patrick stole a glance at his brother, and he smiled when he saw the love emitting from Eric's famous turquoise eyes. That is how Eric had looked at Angilia when she had come to escort Patrick to Heaven 55 years earlier.

By the time Angilia finished, many people were sobbing, affected by the sheer love that filled the arena. She blew a kiss to her father, thanked everyone, and turned to Patrick. "We have one more song. Actually, Patrick does," she said and smiled when he stepped front and center.

"I wrote a whole lot of poems when I lived here, a whole lot. Angilia put one to music in 2016, and it's kinda snowballed since then. It does prove the larger reason behind my poems, because even though I hid them away, they're out in the world now. When we were planning this concert in top secret, I pulled another old poem out, and Angilia helped me put it to music. This is for you, Eric," Patrick said, smiled up at his brother, and stood at the microphone with his hands clasped behind him.

Patrick's emotive, sweet voice sang his words with honesty, love, and conviction. Patrick had written the poem in May 1972, when he was 14 and Eric was 17, the day Eric graduated from high school. Patrick had watched as Eric was forced into the global spotlight more than ever, the world's most famous high school graduate, heir to the throne of Valdavia, and touted as the dreamiest eligible bachelor anywhere. Teen magazines plastered his image on their covers, which surprised no one except for Eric. If Patrick resembled Elvis with his curled-lip smile, Eric resembled a more handsome, clean-cut Jim Morrison. Eric never let any of the fame and attention affect him. Patrick had good-naturedly teased him, even though Eric was the most focused, level-headed person Patrick knew. Patrick admired Eric, and although they differed in many ways, Patrick aspired to emulate his big brother.

When Angilia had read Patrick's poem about Eric, she had cried. Patrick's love and respect for his brother were stated so beautifully and honestly. Angilia looked at her father while Patrick sang, and she saw that he felt Patrick's emotions. Tears glistened in Eric's eyes, and a tender smile formed on his mouth. When Patrick finished, he saluted Eric, and the audience rose for a rousing standing ovation.

My Brother, My Hero

O brother, my brother, you are so wise,

So kind, loving, and always in control.

To me you seem an angel in disguise,

Such depth and truth I see within your soul.

God rightly destined you to be the heir.

You are a king already, that I know.

Among all men on earth you are so rare.

I never told you that you are my hero.

I learn so much just by watching you live,

Longing and wishing I could be like you.

You never take from me, but always give,

Especially your love that is so true.

You are far more than words can ever say.

My love for you deepens more every day.

§§§§§

Before they left for church on September 19, Angilia double checked with Antoine and Anthony that everything was ready for Mitchell's 82nd birthday party. They wanted to begin the party as soon as they returned home, because their gift for Mitchell involved travel, and they wanted to get the trip underway as soon as possible. Eric, Angilia, Matthew, and Prince Eric were packed, and Matthew would help his father pack after the party. The pilot was on standby, and Eric's plane would be ready to depart before the day was half over.

Everyone headed to the sitting room at 9:20, as usual after church, although they maneuvered Mitchell to the front so he could open the door to the decorated room. When he did, they all shouted "Happy birthday!," which brought a huge smile to his face.

"Thank you all. I'm a bit old for surprise parties, but this is nice," Mitchell told them as they gathered around him.

"Nonsense, Mitchell. Birthdays are a great excuse to show people we love them. Besides, we enjoy birthday parties. You've been part of the family for 20 years. You know that," Eric said and put his arm around Mitchell's shoulders.

"Nobody's ever too old for a surprise party, Grandpa," Prince Eric smiled up at Mitchell, and pulled him to the table where the cake waited.

Mitchell laughed, a sound which filled them with joy, and blew out the lone heart-shaped candle. Susan cut the cake and served everyone, and they all sat comfortably as they talked, laughed, and enjoyed the special day.

One wrapped gift awaited Mitchell, a joint gift from everyone. Inside were tickets and passes to museums, and special tickets for private tours of archaeological sites in Cairo, Egypt. Mitchell flipped through the pile, looking rather confused. "I've always wanted to go to Egypt," he said.

"Good. Let's get you all packed and set," Matthew said. "We're leaving as soon as you're ready."

"We are? Now?"

"Of course. It's your birthday, and a week's trip to Egypt is your present," Eric said. "What better time to leave than now?"

"You'll love it, Mitchell. My trip to Kenya was truly my dream come true," Eduardo said. "In fact, Bonnie is going to help me put all of my pictures together for an extensive article I'm writing. You can do the same when you return."

"I don't know what to say except thank you," Mitchell said, and he hugged everyone before he and Matthew walked to Mitchell's house so they could pack. One hour later, Eduardo drove everyone to the airport, including Mike and Nathan for security, Eric, Angilia, Matthew, Prince Eric, and Mitchell. They all settled on the plane, the luggage was loaded, and soon they were on their way to Egypt. Angilia and Eric smiled at one another, so pleased that Mitchell seemed happy. He deserved happiness and fun.

§§§§

Eric's plane landed at Cairo International Airport at 6:00 that evening, much to everyone's excitement. Their rented cars were waiting, and once the luggage was stored in the cars, they drove to their hotel. After freshening, they decided to stroll the area before deciding on a restaurant for dinner.

Angilia took Matthew's and Mitchell's picture near a fountain, her father's picture near an ancient building, and her son's picture below one of the oldest street signs. Although they resembled typical tourists, the Royal Family was soon recognized. People stopped them for autographs and pictures throughout the evening, and even Mitchell was included—much to his surprise.

"Why would anyone want my picture or autograph?" he asked with bemusement in his voice.

"Because you're you, and you are a hero," Angilia replied and put her arms around him. Mitchell blushed and hugged his daughter-in-law.

They finally decided to eat at Abou el-Sid restaurant, and they entered with smiles and happiness. Angilia slipped away long enough to arrange for the waiter to bring a birthday desert to Mitchell at the end of the meal. Prince Eric enjoyed the Egyptian song that the waiter sung to his Grandpa.

"What a beautiful way to wind down my birthday," Mitchell said. "This really is a dream of a lifetime. Thank you all. I could have never predicted all of this 20 years ago. You all mean the world to me. What a wonderful family we have," he said as he looked around the table at the people he loved most.

The next day, Eric had scheduled a private tour of the Giza Pyramids and the Sphinx. Everyone was fascinated by the beauty and history surrounding them. Outside one of the pyramids, Mitchell was pleasantly stunned when their personal guide told him he could enter one of the pyramids. Mitchell took his journal and pen with him. He sketched what he saw and wrote what he felt while inside Cheops' pyramid.

Mitchell emerged after more than one hour, his eyes misty and his mouth smiling. Angilia felt such elation for her dear Dr. Taylor. "You look like a child on Christmas Day. Oh, I am so glad you got to do this, Dr. Taylor," she said, her own hands clasped before her in joy.

Mitchell pulled her to him in an embrace that spoke far more than any words could about his love for the girl who had brought their families together in the midst of tragedy.

"This exceeds every expectation I had of visiting Egypt. Thank you all so much for making my dream come true," Mitchell smiled as he hugged Angilia, Eric, Matthew, and his miracle grandson. "I love you."

§§§§§

February 4, 2033

> *I really like school, but I can't wait until it's over today. I'm already ready. I got ready yesterday after I finished my homework. I have what I need packed in one bag, and that means Grandpa and I can start our weekend together as soon as I get home and change clothes.*
>
> *We are going camping this weekend, just the two of us. Well, not exactly. Nathan is going, too, but he'll have a separate cabin. It will be just like it's only Grandpa and me. We're going fishing, hiking, and row boating. We'll cook our own food. Grandpa's even going to teach me how to make rope out of vines!*
>
> *I love spending time with Grandpa. He might be older, but he's a really neat guy. I love him a whole lot.*
>
> *Okay, I will pack this diary and my pen in my duffle bag, too, so I can write down all the cool stuff each day and have the memories in here for all time.*

§§§§§

Angilia heard Prince Eric run up the stairs after school that afternoon, and she smiled at her father. Prince Eric breathlessly rushed into their office and hugged his grandfather. He turned and looked at his mother, his eyes twinkling with excitement. He held her close and said, "I'm going to miss you, Mommy. But Grandpa and I are going to have so much fun. I've waited for today for two whole weeks."

"I know, Eric. I'll miss you so much, too, but this weekend will be so wonderful for you and Grandpa. I think he's more excited than you are," she giggled. "It's all he talked about at lunch. Why don't you go change clothes and get ready, so you, Grandpa, and Nathan can get started?"

Prince Eric kissed her cheek, nodded, and ran down to his suite. Soon, they heard him run downstairs and out the patio door. Eric and Angilia smiled. "We should head down soon to say goodbye," Eric said. Angilia agreed, and she went to get a sweater from her room. Her phone startled her with her son's ring tone just as she slipped on the sweater.

"Mommy, please come. I need you," Prince Eric told her in a voice that sent chills through her.

"I'm coming, darling." She disregarded the elevator and walked as quickly as she could to Mitchell's house. When she entered, her heart skipped several beats.

Prince Eric stood beside Mitchell's favorite chair, staring at his Grandpa. Angilia looked at Mitchell, who was unmoving, appearing asleep. She knew, though, that he was dead. She walked to her son, put her hands on his shoulders, and kissed his head. She put her fingers over Mitchell's carotid artery, and did not feel a pulse. His heart was not beating, he was not breathing, and his skin was cold.

She held her son close to her. "Oh, Eric, darling. I'm so sorry."

"Grandpa's dead."

Prince Eric stood rigid in her embrace, and Angilia realized that he was in shock. Finding his Grandpa dead on what was supposed to be a happy day was traumatic.

Matthew was across the country at an official engagement. She could not call him with this news while he was at a public event. Instead, she called her father and told him to come to Mitchell's house.

Eric entered through the open door, and he, too, felt an ache in his heart when he saw Mitchell and knew he was dead. Tea and cookies were on the table beside the chair, and an open book laid upon Mitchell's lap. A few hours earlier, Mitchell had smiled constantly as he talked excitedly about his weekend camping trip with his grandson. Eric looked at the boy whose face had radiated joy moments earlier but now reflected utter heartbreak.

"I'm going to call Billy," Eric softly said, and stepped into the next room. Billy had accompanied Matthew, and rather than upset his son-in-law, Eric explained what had happened to Billy, who assured Eric he would handle everything and drive Matthew home as soon as possible.

Angilia cradled Prince Eric in her arms as they sat on the sofa, and she looked in gratitude at her father when he joined them. Two hours later, Matthew's ring tone sounded, and Angilia answered her husband's call. Before she could say much, Prince Eric gently took the phone from her.

"Daddy, Grandpa is with Grandma in Heaven."

§§§§

Two days later, Eric, Matthew, Angilia, Prince Eric, and Eduardo held a private service with Reverend Hutchins in the Royal Vault. Prince Eric placed his Grandpa's urn in the niche next to his Grandma's niche. "I miss you, Grandpa. I'm sorry we didn't get to go on our camping trip. But I know you're having a much better time in Heaven with Grandma. I know how much you missed her. Now you don't have to miss her ever again. I love you, Grandpa."

Matthew knelt and hugged his son while he spoke to his father. "I love you, Dad. I'll always love and miss you and Mom. We'll be together again someday, though. All of us." He kissed Prince Eric's cheek. "Right, Eric?"

"Yes. It just feels like such a long time." Eric knelt beside his grandson and put his arm around the boy's shoulders.

"I know it does, Eric. It feels like a very long time. I miss everyone so much, especially Grandmother," Eric softly said about Marisol. "No matter how many years I have to wait to join her, those years are nothing compared to the forever we will have together. Forever. Isn't that amazing?"

"Yes, Grandfather. I know it is. I do. But right now it just hurts too much."

"I know it does, Eric. That's okay. It's normal to hurt when someone we love dies. Your Mommy told me something wise when Roger died. Our pain equals our love. That's why it hurts so much.

You love Grandpa so very much, Eric. He knows that. So does Grandma. Death doesn't end our love. It just separates us for a while."

Prince Eric nodded and hugged his Grandfather. Reverend Hutchins prayed for God's loving grace to heal their pain. Angilia recited Mitchell's favorite Bible verse, which had been engraved on his urn: 1 John 4:7. *"'Beloved, let us love one another: for love is of God; and every one that loveth is born of God, and knoweth God.'"*

"Grandpa loved everyone. That's why he was a doctor. He wanted to help people and take away their pain," Prince Eric said.

"Dr. Taylor showed his love to us every day. He restored my trust in doctors, which was a tough thing to do," Angilia added.

Matthew smiled up at her. "He taught me what it means to be a doctor, a man, and a father. I owe who I am to Dad."

"Mitchell was a wonderful, true friend from the first moment. He helped me survive that nightmare. His compassion kept me sane and grounded," Eric said.

"Mitchell was great fun, but more than that a great friend. I'll never forget how well he cared for Mamá and Papa. They loved and trusted him so," Eduardo said as tears choked him.

"Grandpa took care of us all. He made our family complete," Prince Eric said. "I am glad he is my Grandpa. I'm so happy I got to know him and learn from him."

§§§§

Prince Eric opened his eyes when his alarm sounded, and he saw Angilia sitting next to his bed watching him. "Good morning, Mommy."

"Good morning, Eric. Happy birthday," she said and leaned over to kiss his cheek. "I love you, Eric." Her miracle son was now 12 years old.

"I love you, Mommy." Angilia handed him a card and a gift, and smiled at his confusion when he opened the gift and saw a box filled with game modules.

"These look neat, Mommy, but I don't have the system they need," he said with a lopsided grin that reminded her of Uncle Patrick.

"Oh? That's odd. I could swear I saw one in your sitting room," she replied with a straight face.

Prince Eric's eyes grew large, and he leapt out of bed, ran to his sitting room, and shouted for joy. Angilia watched him with a huge smile, and soon was joined by Eric and Matthew.

"Thank you, Mommy!" Prince Eric nearly shouted as he grabbed her in an exuberant hug.

"Games, huh? Someone's going to be a bit distracted at school today thinking about all of the fun waiting at home, I suspect," Matthew teased. "Happy birthday," he said and slid a large box into the room.

Prince Eric ripped the paper off and instantly gave his father a high-five. "This is so cool, Daddy. Thank you."

"A chemistry set? That should be fun," Angilia smiled. "Looks like something for you and Daddy to do together." Matthew giggled and Prince Eric nodded.

"Well, since we're doling out early morning birthday gifts, here's another one," Eric said and handed his grandson a small box. "That was my signet ring. My father gave it to me when I was 15. I want you to have it, Eric."

"Wow! This is awesome! We do have the same initial. Thank you, Grandfather. I will give this to my son someday." Prince Eric hugged his grandfather, and Angilia put her hand on her father's back as tears filled her eyes.

Eric cleared his throat. "I think we need to get ready for breakfast soon, or our birthday boy will end up late for school."

"I won't. I've never been late for school. Today's going to be really neat anyway. I don't want to be late."

"What's so neat about today?" Matthew asked.

"We each get to teach the class about a poem we got to choose from our book. I have my lesson on my computer," Prince Eric said and picked up his handheld computer.

Matthew grimaced and feigned horror. "Poetry? Yuck."

Angilia playfully slapped his arm. "Which poem did you choose, Eric?"

"I selected "Ozymandias" by Percy Shelley. I like how it's about history and Ramses II. We saw his mummy when we were in Egypt. Grandpa and I really enjoyed the museum. He bought me a book about Ramses II, and I'm using that today, too."

"That's an excellent choice, Eric," Angilia told him and kissed him before she left so he could prepare for breakfast and school.

"Yeah, it is, Eric. Grandpa will be listening and watching today from Heaven," Matthew smiled.

CHAPTER 5

"Abuela, we love you and miss you. You filled my life with love from its very beginning. I do remember your brown eyes shining when you held me the day I was born. Your skin was so soft and warm. I always felt safe, happy, and loved with you. I felt your love that first day and every day thereafter. I still do. Your love is such a wondrous gift."

Eduardo held his niece close as emotions rushed through his body. "That is so poignant, my Angel. Mamá's love was grand. Her love made her more beautiful than her physical beauty. Her love is what I longed for most during those long years. I had resigned myself to never seeing my family again. I had longed to see them for so long. I had dreamed about them for so long, until I had to force myself to stop. The pain of seeing them in my mind was too intense. Then the miracle brought me back to them both. I know Mamá didn't want to leave us, but I also know how much she wanted to be with Papa and Marisol. I miss them all so very much. So much." Eduardo leaned atop his mother's tomb, crying.

Angilia knew his tears ranged across a lifetime of emotions far greater than grief. He had felt so grateful upon his freedom that he had never allowed himself to truly unleash his emotions. He did so now, on the 10th anniversary of his mother's death, while his family and friends surrounded him with love.

"I love you, Mamá," Eduardo finally said and stood tall. "I love you, Papa. I love you, Marisol. I love all of you," he said, and turned to face his family and friends. He spread his arms wide, and they all met in a group embrace.

"I love you, Eduardo," Eric said with a smile.

"I love you, too, Uncle Eduardo," Prince Eric echoed. "I love Abuela and Abuelo and Grandmother a whole lot. Someday I will get to meet them and tell them that in person."

Angilia kissed her son and placed one dozen white roses atop her grandmother's tomb. She softly read the plaque aloud.

Juanita Calicia Lapira Martinéz

3 July 1930

10 September 2024

Thou shalt also be a crown of glory in the hand of the Lord,

and a royal diadem in the hand of thy God.

Isaiah 62:3

†

§§§§§

"It's so beautiful here. I still can't get over how beautiful it is. I just love being here and walking to my heart's content. It's been 22 years since our release, Eduardo. That's how long we were captives together," Bonnie said as she and Eduardo spent the afternoon strolling the palace grounds.

"I know. I hardly remember what that felt like, what being a prisoner in that room felt like," Eduardo added.

"I don't, either. Everyone here made me feel so welcome and free that I stopped thinking about it. It just vanished one day, but I don't know when. There hasn't been any reason to remember or feel all of that," Bonnie said, and breathed in the fresh air.

"No, there hasn't. Bonnie, you became a great, true friend all those years ago. I do remember how we shared everything. Maybe I should have done this years ago. But they always say it's never too late," Eduardo said, took hold of Bonnie's left hand, and smiled. "Bonnie, will you marry me?"

"Yes. Yes, Eduardo." He slid a diamond ring onto her left ring finger and pulled her into a kiss. They held one another for several moments. "Shall we share our happy news?"

Bonnie nodded, and she and her fiancé walked back toward the palace hand-in-hand. Moments later, Bonnie's smile disappeared when Eduardo suddenly collapsed to the ground. Angilia had watched the scene from a fourth floor window, and her heart had leapt for joy when she witnessed her uncle's engagement. Now, she screamed for her father and Matthew, and began walking down the stairs as quickly as she physically could. Eric very rapidly caught up to her, as did Matthew, and she frantically told them, "Uncle Eduardo, on the lawn, hurry."

Matthew ran swiftly to Eduardo, and Eric soon arrived. Bonnie lay across Eduardo's body, crying, and Eric gently lifted her into his embrace. Matthew did not feel a pulse, but he performed CPR for several minutes, to no avail.

Angilia reached them just as Matthew stopped. She fell to her knees beside her uncle, took his hand, and said, "I love you, Uncle Eduardo." She bent, kissed his cheek, and prayed. She reached for Bonnie's left hand, and the two women cried as Eduardo's death cut them with the unexpected suddenness of a saber. "I'm so sorry, Bonnie. Uncle Eduardo loves you. I've known that for years. He always said you are his best friend."

"He's mine, too. I never knew anyone like him. We knew and loved each other for a long time. We never talked about it. We didn't have to. Today is the happiest and the saddest day of my life. We were saying how we were prisoners of war together for 22 years and lived here in peace for 22 years. 44 years. We knew and loved each other for 44 years. I don't know life without Eduardo. What am I supposed to do without him?" she asked as she cried tears of heartbreak against Eric.

Eric fully understood Bonnie's pain, and he gently rocked her as he held her close, letting her cry until she could cry no more. She needed to grieve. Bonnie kissed Eduardo's cheek when the funeral director arrived to transport his body to the funeral home for preparations, a last kiss that expressed more than four decades of emotions.

§§§§§

Two days later, the Royal Family and their closest friends, as well as many who had known Eduardo, gathered in Christ Church Valmondois for his funeral. Yvonne hugged Prince Eric when she and her parents arrived. She never knew just what to say to her best friend that day, because Prince Eric's family had suffered the deaths of so many of their loved ones in the past five years. That seemed so cruel to Yvonne. As if sensing her thoughts, Prince Eric smiled at her and patted her shoulder.

After the hymn and Reverend Hutchins' prayer, Angilia walked to the pulpit to deliver her eulogy. "I met my uncle 22 years ago, when he and nine other journalists were finally freed from 22 years of captivity. I had hoped and prayed to meet my mother's brother, and that prayer was answered. I am so thankful that we were blessed to have him with us for those 22 years.

"Uncle Eduardo was filled with the most inspiring child-like wonder, always looking at every little thing as a wonder and a gift. I remember five years ago when we sat in the gazebo, and he watched an army of ants carrying bits of food back to their colony. Uncle Eduardo smiled as he watched the ants, amazed and awed. He never took anything or anyone for granted, because he knew what it meant to lose everything and everyone.

"Uncle Eduardo taught me so much about gratitude, appreciation, and living. The world had drastically changed during his 22 years in captivity, and he never wanted to miss anything else. He saw beauty in so much, and he never lost his love of living.

"Uncle Eduardo is reunited with his parents and sister now, a reunion he anticipated with wonder. We know he is happy, loved, and blessed. So are we. Our love for Eduardo is eternal, and we will admittedly miss having him here with us. How could we not miss him and his joie de vivre? We know, though, that we will be reunited with him someday.

"Uncle Eduardo loved life, his family, and his friends. For many years, I saw very special love between Eduardo and Bonnie Glaser. They met 44 years ago as prisoners of war, and their friendship and love outlasted every challenge, change, and moment. We love Bonnie. We cherish her friendship with Eduardo. They kept each other alive and positive when that should have been impossible. Eduardo told me eight years ago that Bonnie was his shining star during those 22 years they lived in one bare concrete room. She was there with him when none of us could be. Bonnie," Angilia smiled and hugged Bonnie when she walked to the pulpit.

"All ten of us bonded during our 22 years in captivity. Eduardo became my best friend quickly, though. He kept me going whenever I became fearful or depressed. He talked about his family so much, and I felt as if I knew them. His parents, Alejandro and Juanita, felt like safety blankets to me. Their love and support for Eduardo spilled over to me. They seemed so real to me.

"When I first came to Valmondois and met them, they were so familiar to me. They were like old friends. They welcomed me into their lives to share their love with me. By the time we were released, my parents were dead. Alejandro and Juanita became my surrogate parents. I love them so much.

"Eduardo's eyes always sparkled whenever he talked about his big sister, Marisol. He told me so many stories about her, and she, too, became so real to me. He even told me about Marisol's true love, a prince named Eric, whom I remembered seeing in the magazines. Eduardo speculated about his sister's real-life fairytale and how many children she and Eric had.

"Eduardo called me late the night he first arrived at the palace. His mind was swirling, and his emotions were all over the place. He was home with his parents. He cried and laughed simultaneously as he described that first sight of them after so many years. Prince Eric was now King Eric, and just as Eduardo remembered. Eduardo mourned Marisol's death, about which he had just learned. He described his niece Angilia, the girl we'd been told about after our rescue. He told me she really was our angel. Her name means Angel, he said, and that was no coincidence.

"His family became my family, and I love them. Eduardo blessed my life for 44 glorious years. What a precious gift. He is my soul mate for all time. Adjusting to life without Eduardo will be the most difficult thing I have ever done. My solace lies in knowing that he still lives and that we will be together forever someday."

Bonnie hugged Eric when she returned to the pew, knowing how much he must have hurt in recent years with the deaths of so many loved ones. She knew that she would adapt to life without Eduardo with his family's help. Angilia squeezed Bonnie's hand as she stood and walked to the piano.

After Abuela's funeral, Eduardo had asked her to sing his favorite gospel song at his funeral. "This is for you, Uncle Eduardo," Angilia said, and then played and sung "In My Father's House."

When she finished, the pallbearers stood and carried Eduardo's coffin into the Royal Vault, where they carefully lowered it into his tomb. Bonnie, Angilia, Susan, Nicole, Yvonne, Shannon, and Darlene placed flowers atop his coffin. Prince Eric placed a sealed card among the roses, and Matthew placed a bouquet of daffodils, the March flower. Eric placed a letter to Eduardo there.

Finally, the heavy lid was lifted atop the tomb, the plaque already engraved and affixed. Reverend Hutchins said a closing prayer, and Angilia held her father's and Bonnie's hands.

Eduardo Alejandro Martinéz Calicia

16 March 1957

9 October 2034

The gift of God is eternal life through Jesus Christ our Lord.

Romans 6:23

†

§§§§§

The early morning news focused on the momentous milestone of the year, as Angilia heard while she stood at the door to her father's suite. "Valmondois is besieged by reporters, photographers, and well-wishers today as the world celebrates His Majesty's 80th birthday. King Eric has reigned over Valdavia for 42 years, more than half of his life. Judging by the number of people on the mall and streets today, I am confident in saying that our King Eric is the world's most loved monarch." Franklin Sydney spoke with several people on the mall, all of whom said they wanted to show their love and respect to Eric on his birthday. People of all ages were shown, including students who hoped to see him before they had to rush to school.

Eric emerged from his bedroom in a navy suit, looking as handsome as any movie star. His silver hair gave him a debonair look that reminded Angilia of Cary Grant. Eric's dimpled smile lit his face when he saw Angilia there smiling at him. He held his arms open, and she walked into his warm embrace.

"I love you, Daddy. Happy birthday."

"I love you, my beautiful daughter Angilia."

"I have something for you," she winked and went to the hall to retrieve his gift. Angilia struggled to carry the large rectangular package, and Daniel rushed to help her lean it against a sitting room wall.

"What is this?" Eric asked in amazement. Angilia told him to find out, and he removed the wrapping paper, only to feel tears fill his eyes. "Oh, Angel, this is amazing. I will keep this here, where I can see it at the start and end of each day." Eric pulled her into another hug and kissed the top of her head. She felt the pendant under his shirt, placed her hand over it, and smiled up at him.

"I wear the pendant near my heart constantly, Angel. I find myself looking at it many nights, and you were right that seeing Marisol, me, you, and Matthew together is a blessing."

Daniel had no idea what Eric meant, but he smiled, understanding how much Angilia's portrait of Eric, Patrick, and their parents meant to Eric. He had known Eric's family, and he knew how close they were. "This is beautiful."

"Thank you, Daniel. Excuse me. I hear our other birthday boy," Angilia said. "Happy birthday, Daddy." She kissed his cheek before she went to Prince Eric's room. Angilia helped her son get ready, and then they went to breakfast together, joined by Matthew, Eric, Susan, Billy, and Daniel.

When they finished, Angilia carried two large boxes of cupcakes to the car and drove her son to school. She helped in Prince Eric's classroom that day, much to the students' pleasant surprise. After school, Angilia reminded everyone to come to the palace the next day for Eric's 13th birthday party. Angilia smiled when his classmates surrounded Eric, wished him a happy birthday, and promised they would celebrate with him on Saturday.

§§§§

Six weeks later, the Royal Family led the annual Christmas Eve service, highlighted by King Eric's recitation of the Christmas story from Luke Chapter 2. Angilia looked at her father in utter admiration, realizing that she had heard him recite the Christmas story for 38 Christmases.

Eric smiled at her when he finished. "The birth of Jesus is one of the two greatest miracles we will ever know. His death and Resurrection is the ultimate greatest. There have been other miracles throughout the centuries. I know. I experienced one of God's miracles 40 years ago today. My beautiful daughter Angilia came to me 40 years ago. Words can never truly impart how grateful and blessed my life is because God chose me to be Angilia's father."

Angilia joined her father at the pulpit, where they hugged with tears shining in their eyes. "We have been together for 40 years. We have loved each other for 57 years, since the day my Uncle Patrick died and I was his Spirit Guide. What once was a day shrouded in sorrow became a day of love and joy. I loved my father instantly. Leaving him and returning to Heaven was so difficult for me. My Uncle Patrick knows that. My father taught me what love really is from the very beginning."

Patrick smiled as Angilia and Eric sang an a cappella version of "Ave Maria." The congregation sat in awed reverence. Everyone felt the love shared between father and daughter on the holiest of nights.

§§§§

3 January 2035

My Beautiful Daughter Angilia,

What an amazing experience to share our testimony and faith with our friends and neighbors in the early morning hours of Christmas Day! Today you celebrate your 39th birthday, but you—your precious soul—came to me 40 years ago! That Patrick shared the holy anniversary with us is incredibly emotional. I had never thought I would ever see my little brother again until I died and went to Heaven. Your bringing him back to me, in soul manifestation, is such a blessed miracle, my Angel.

You are my most beloved and cherished miracle, my beautiful daughter Angilia! You never fail to send surges of love, joy, and gratitude through my veins. You are such an amazing daughter, wife, mother, friend, and Queen. You are more than practically perfect. You are perfect.

I love you so incredibly much, Angel, for all eternity!

All my heart,

Daddy

§§§§

"I love spending time with you, Mommy. You are so cool."

Angilia giggled. "I'm not sure how cool I am, but thank you. I love spending time with you, Eric. I love you."

Angilia reined in Starlight and dismounted, and Eric did likewise with Rocket. They let Starlight and Rocket graze for a few moments while the two of them sat on a large rock.

"Rocket is the best horse ever," Eric said. "I really like riding him, and I think he likes it, too."

"I know he does. So does Starlight. There's a magic in our relationships with Starlight and Rocket. We four were meant to be together, Eric."

"Just like you and me, Mommy." Eric smiled, stood, and hugged Angilia.

"Just like you and me, Eric. God made us mother and son, and I am so grateful," Angilia said as she hugged her teenage son.

"So am I, Mommy."

§§§§

"Good morning, Daddy," Angilia said, and walked to the elevator with him. In the dining room, they greeted Susan, Billy, and Prince Eric. Soon, they were joined by Matthew. They waited for Daniel as long as they could before Anthony served everyone so that Prince Eric would not be late for school.

Eric excused himself, and said, "I'm going to check on Daniel."

Eric did not receive an answer to his knock on Daniel's suite door, so he opened the door and went in. Eric looked in the bedroom and saw his friend in bed. Eric knew before he stepped to Daniel's bedside, but his shoulders drooped when he touched Daniel and felt a cold, lifeless body.

"Oh, Daniel," Eric whispered, and sat beside his second-longest friend. "I'm going to miss you, you know. At least you and Roger are together now." Eric held his friend's hand and prayed before he pulled his phone from his pocket.

Angilia walked Prince Eric to the car with Nathan, kissed her son, and returned to the foyer just as Matthew began walking quickly upstairs. "It's Daniel, isn't it?" Angilia asked him.

"Yes, darling. Your dad called me. I'm going to Daniel's suite so I can take care of everything."

Angilia joined Matthew, held his hand, and they walked slowly to the third floor together. When they entered Daniel's suite, Angilia hugged her father and held him close while Matthew confirmed Daniel's death. After getting his medical bag, Matthew filled out Daniel's death certificate.

Matthew put an arm around Eric, and said, "Daniel died of natural causes in his sleep. Given the state of rigor mortis, I estimate that he died four or five hours ago, while he was asleep. I doubt he felt anything. I'll call the funeral director soon, Eric," Matthew softly said.

The following afternoon, Eric, Angilia, Matthew, Prince Eric, Susan, Mike, Tony, and Nathan gathered at the church for Daniel's funeral. After Reverend Hutchins' prayer, Eric gave the eulogy.

"I met Daniel on my first day at university, and we became instant friends. We were 19, and we were together for 61 years. Daniel is the second-longest friend of my life. Roger is the longest. Now they are together, in what I know is the most glorious place in existence.

"I know that death is not sad, and is a natural part of the life process. That does not mean I won't miss my friend. The saddest part of aging is outliving my friends."

Angilia hugged her father before Matthew, Prince Eric, Billy, Mike, Tony, and Nathan carried Daniel's casket to the plot next to Roger's. Daniel had mentioned wanting to be beside Roger in the cemetery. Daniel was just a few months older than Eric, and died at the age of 81 on September 7, 2035.

Their once bustling home was one person less. Eric, Angilia, Matthew, Prince Eric, Susan, Billy, Mike, Tony, and Nathan walked home in thoughtful silence as Daniel's death hit them in stark reality. Eric had never needed a valet, but the role had enabled him to have his friend nearby every day for 57 years.

The Royal Family and their friends entered the palace foyer, where Angilia pulled them into a group hug. "We are a small, love-filled family. I love you all so much."

CHAPTER 6

"Her Majesty Queen Angilia turns 40 today, and the world celebrates. No official events are scheduled to mark the milestone, although that has not discouraged hundreds of people from filling the mall outside the palace," Franklin Sydney commented during the early morning news broadcast. "The only official acknowledgement of Her Majesty's birthday thus far is the release of three new photographs taken by Bonnie Glaser." Franklin showed the three photographs, one of Angilia alone, one of her with her husband and her son, and one of her with her father.

Eric finished dressing, and smiled while he watched the broadcast. His baby was born 40 years ago, and he looked at the portraits as they were shown on the television. Her hair was slightly different, but she looked the same as she had for years. To Eric, Angilia was ageless. He picked up a wrapped gift and letter from his desk and stepped across the hall to the suite she shared with Matthew. Prince Eric ran from his suite quickly, but stopped long enough to hug his grandfather.

Matthew soon emerged, and greeted his father-in-law. "Angilia is ready," Matthew smiled before he went downstairs.

Eric entered just as she stepped into her sitting room. "Happy birthday, my beautiful daughter Angilia."

Angilia hugged her father. "I love you, Daddy."

"And I love you, Angel," Eric smiled and handed her the present.

Angilia carefully unwrapped the package to see an advanced release copy of the Retrospective of Tom Greenfield's complete recorded work. Angilia looked at it with a smile and a few tears, and hugged her father. "Thank you, Daddy. This is more amazing than I ever imagined it would be."

"I knew you would enjoy this, and I could think of nothing better to give you today. I know you're launching the foundation soon, and I know how much Tom means to you."

"He does. We often talked about that day we met. Serendipity it wasn't, we both agreed about that. We were meant to meet that day. Tom was part of God's plan for me. I know that. I also know that I was not supposed to be with him on the day of the accident. If I had been there, I would have gotten on the plane, and I would have died then. Eric would have never been born. The rest of God's plan for me would have been left undone. I'm grateful that God preserved me so that Eric could live."

Eric pulled her close to him and kissed the top of her head. "I'm eternally grateful, too, Angilia. I know you felt guilty about Tom's accident, that if you had been there you could have prevented it. That's not true, baby. Tom's death was tragic, but you couldn't have stopped him. As you said, it only would have caused your death, too. I thank God for you every day and every night."

§§§§

25 January 2036

Her Majesty Queen Angilia officially launches the Tom Greenfield Foundation today, and inaugurates the Foundation with appearances at the King Stefan Middle School and the King Gerard Hospital. The Tom Greenfield Foundation supports music education through musical instrument donation and instruction to schools, hospitals, and other organizations.

Eric's Press Secretary, Carol, released the press statement early that morning.

After breakfast, Angilia kissed Prince Eric and promised she would see him later that morning when she came to his school. Two hours later, Mike accompanied her to the school, where students, faculty, and staff filled the auditorium. Sam and the band greeted Angilia when she arrived, much to her surprise.

"Sam! John! Joe! Greg! It's wonderful to see all of you! Thank you so much for coming today. Your approval means a lot to me," she said while she hugged and kissed her friends.

"We wouldn't miss today for the world," Greg told her with a smile.

"Yeah, we had to come, for you and for Tom," Joe added, with which Sam enthusiastically agreed.

"This is too important for us to not come," John said. "We thought we could have some fun with the children today if that's okay."

"If it's okay? That's awesome! Thank you," Angilia smiled, and grabbed them into a group hug.

Finally, the principal, Mrs. Stimpson, greeted Angilia and her band and walked on stage to introduce the Queen.

"Welcome to our very special convocation. As you all know, Her Majesty Queen Angilia is here to launch her Tom Greenfield Foundation. I know how excited everyone is, so without further ado, it is my extreme honor to introduce Her Majesty Queen Angilia."

Angilia walked on stage to a standing ovation, her smile radiant as she waved at the audience. "Thank you, Mrs. Stimpson. I am very happy to be with you all today for the official launch of the Tom Greenfield Foundation. Tom Greenfield was my mentor, teacher, duet partner, friend, and champion. My life is so blessed by him, and I am so grateful for Tom.

"The Tom Greenfield Foundation honors his love of music and belief that music changes people. Today marks the 25th anniversary of Tom's death, which seemed the perfect day to launch the Foundation. In the 25 years since his death, Tom's legacy has grown stronger. His music continues to touch and entertain millions of people the world over. Every week, I receive letters and messages from people who tell me how much Tom affects their lives.

"That confirms the mission of the Tom Greenfield Foundation. Our goal is to bring the joy, critical thinking skills, and means of performing music to schools, hospitals, and various other organizations throughout Valdavia and in many other countries.

"I begin here, at King Stefan Middle School, which is where my husband and I came to know Miss Yost, after whom this auditorium is named. Today, the Foundation is thrilled to gift the school with 50 each of the following instruments: guitars, flutes, saxophones, drum kits, portable keyboards, and violins."

The stage curtain rose behind Angilia, revealing a stage full of musical instruments. Everyone in the room erupted in a standing ovation, which took several minutes to subside. When she finally persuaded everyone to sit rather quietly, she introduced Sam, John, Greg, and Joe. People pleaded with Angilia and her band to perform, so they finally relented and used some of the new instruments for a 30 minute impromptu concert.

"Thank you so much," Angilia said when they finished. "Greg, Joe, and John would like all of you to come up here and have fun with them for a while." Students truly enjoyed their lessons and the chance to play each of the instruments. Prince Eric stood next to his mother, joined by Yvonne, all of them smiling as they spoke with students and teachers.

Finally, it was time for first lunch period, so Angilia, Sam, Joe, Greg, and John thanked everyone and left for a quick lunch themselves before the next event. Angilia had invited her father and her husband to the hospital, for she knew the event there would truly surprise them. She had worked in secret for almost one year to bring her idea to reality, and today would lay the final proverbial stone in completely erasing the past.

Just before 1:00, Angilia kissed her father and Matthew, and took her place at a podium. "Thank you all for coming to our Tom Greenfield Foundation event at King Gerard Hospital. I am so very happy to be here for this unveiling today. Today not only honors Tom on the 25th anniversary of his death, but all of you who are here today, and all of those who will follow you in the years to come.

"Our goal is to continue Tom's love of music by donating musical instruments to schools, hospitals, and other institutions. Tom understood the value and pleasure of music in each person's life, and so do I. We have donated 200 musical instruments to the hospital, with the hope that music allows you to express yourself, to have fun, and to help alleviate some of the fear and boredom of being here."

Everyone enthusiastically cheered at that moment, and some people even cried. Angilia smiled at the doctors, nurses, technicians, parents, and many young patients. She finally waved them quiet, took a deep breath, and shared her real surprise.

"Those who cannot yet leave their hospital rooms will have instruments of their choice brought to their rooms. For those who are able to leave their rooms, we have a beautiful new place for you to come when you want to perform music, read, play, or anything else you desire." Angilia noticed the many puzzled expressions, including Eric's and Matthew's. There had not been any recent additions to the building and no announcements by the Board of Directors.

"To my left is a large room that stood empty and locked for far too long, since 2012 to be exact. That had once been the office of Gregor Jamieson, but after his suicide, the office was locked and never used.

"I persuaded the Hospital President to let me turn what had been a place of bad memories into a place of happiness, music, and sunshine. The office space was totally renovated by a private sponsor into a safe place, a haven and play room, for children who visit the hospital. Never again will this room stay locked."

Eric and Matthew stared in awed surprise at Angilia, knowing that the private sponsor was her. She had paid to transform the scene of her nightmare and horror into a scene of hope and beauty. Sam, Joe, John, and Greg hugged Eric and Matthew, knowing the truth, too.

At that moment, as everyone clapped, Angilia walked to what had been Jamieson's office, and pulled a huge black drape away from the façade. Where curtained windows and locked doors had been, now stood shining windows, no doors, and bright, cheerful decor. Instruments, bookshelves, comfortable furniture, bright new toys, and sunlight filled the area.

"I am so honored to dedicate the Tom Greenfield Playroom and Playground," Angilia announced. Everyone then saw that the outside beyond the room had become a new playground for the children. "I do hope you have fun, and that this area does help take away some of the darkness and fear that come with being ill. I never want any children to feel lost and alone when they are sick. Have fun," she said, and motioned for the children to enter the playroom.

Instead, they rushed or were led to Angilia, hugging her, kissing her, thanking her, and crying what she had long called happy tears. While she was surrounded by children, Angilia smiled at her father, her husband, and her band. What had once been a nightmare was now a pleasant dream come true.

§§§§§

"Oh, Angilia, I love you so very much, more than I ever thought I would love anyone." Matthew pulled her closer and kissed her soft pink lips.

"I love you so much, Matthew. I am so blessed by you and our precious Eric. My life is so full of love, my dear. You are my soul mate, and my love for you is larger than the universe."

Matthew and Angilia kissed and cuddled for as long as possible before they showered, dressed, and went to the dining room for breakfast. No one else was there. The table was set, but the buffet was bare of food. Where was everyone? Angilia walked to the kitchen, which was spotless and vacant of people.

"Where is everyone?" Angilia asked when she returned to Matthew. Before he could answer, she went to the foyer telephone and called her father's cell phone. His phone rang several times, with no answer. Angilia hung up and looked at Matthew fearfully. "Daddy didn't answer. Something's wrong."

"Nothing's wrong. Someone would have told us if there were, darling."

"You're right, I know. This is just so strange, Matthew," she said, her arm around her husband as they slowly walked back into the dining room.

"Happy anniversary!" Angilia had rarely been as startled, and she looked at her family and friends with happy tears in her eyes. After lots of joyous hugs and kisses, Prince Eric smiled and told his parents to blow out the candle. Angilia laughed and held Matthew's hand when they saw a large Belgian waffle with whipped cream, strawberries, and a lit heart-shaped candle. They blew out the candle, and Matthew fed his wife a bite of the waffle.

A few hours later, the Royal Family and friends arrived at the Musée for a portrait unveiling. Prince Eric was excused from school for the event, which Angilia and Matthew rarely allowed. The Royal party was greeted by the Director, Stephanie Purvis, and escorted into the crowded Royal Portrait Gallery.

"Good morning, and welcome to our very special portrait unveiling, Your Majesties, Your Royal Highnesses, and esteemed guests. I am so honored to introduce His Majesty King Eric," Ms. Purvis said and curtsied to Eric when he came to the podium.

Angilia beamed when her father received a lengthy standing ovation. She knew how much people adored and respected her father, yet the public demonstrations of affection always made her emotional. Eric was now 81 years old, although he looked younger than his age. Eric had worked out for more than one hour every day for longer than Angilia had been alive, and he was extremely fit and muscular. Matthew, who gave his father-in-law annual electrocardiograms and stress tests, was impressed by Eric's physical fitness—including enviable washboard abdominals—and excellent health. Eric maintained a healthy diet, had never smoked nor drank alcohol, and made faith the center point of his life.

As Eric smiled and thanked everyone for the warm welcome, photographers captured his movie-star looks. His grey hair, turquoise eyes, and gleaming smile were joined by lines at the corners of his eyes and mouth. He was as handsome as ever, still eliciting screams and swoons. As if on cue, a woman in the audience shouted, "I love you!" to Eric, which made the audience erupt in cheers again while Eric blushed.

Finally, Eric succeeded in motioning everyone silent. "Thank you for this amazing welcome. I truly believe that nowhere on earth is as warm and supportive as Valdavia. I say it so often that it's a cliché by now, but I am truly honored to serve you. I know how blessed I am by all of you and by my family.

"I am especially blessed to work alongside my precious daughter Angilia. She and Matthew celebrate their 20th wedding anniversary today, for which I am so very grateful. We are here today to honor this happy occasion with a new portrait. I am so incredibly honored to ask my grandson Eric to unveil his parents' portrait."

Prince Eric smiled as he walked to the gold cord, pulled it, and uncovered Matthew's and Angilia's first joint portrait. Matthew was attired in a cream evening suit with lavender vest and bow tie. Angilia wore a lavender handmade lace off-the-shoulder dress. They held one another, and they smiled at each other. Prince Eric's smile was huge as he stepped to the podium beside his grandfather. "My mother and my father. Happy anniversary, Mommy and Dad."

Everyone cheered the young Prince, while many sobbed when Angilia hugged Prince Eric. At 14, Prince Eric was as tall as his mother and as handsome as his grandfather. Matthew, Angilia, Prince Eric, and King Eric relented to popular requests for pictures and posed together. Everyone noticed that Matthew's arm tenderly encircled his wife's waist and that she held his hand, leaned against him, and put her other arm around her son. Eric placed his hand over hers on Prince Eric's shoulder. Their body language expressed their eternal love far louder than any words ever could.

§§§§

After the calm, enjoyable summer, the Royal Family prepared for the annual Independence Day Celebration in honor of Valdavia's September 16 founding. Eric drove them to Valmondois' Central Park, the long-traditional location of the Independence Day festivities. They were greeted by hundreds of cheering Valdavians.

Bonnie had taken family pictures that morning, and Carol released them with a statement explaining everyone's attire. King Eric wore one of his father King Gerard's suits; Angilia wore one of her mother's dresses; Matthew wore one of Mitchell's suits; Prince Eric wore one of Patrick's suits; and Patrick chose to wear one of his grandfather King Stefan's suits. Each of them chose to honor their ancestors on this special day, which was a charming tribute to their heritage.

Susan, Billy, Mike, Tony, and Nathan smiled and stayed close to the Royal Family during the picture and autograph requests. Throughout the afternoon, they mingled with everyone who crowded the park, while enjoying the high school band who entertained everyone. Bonnie took occasional pictures for the family, until Matthew realized that they had not eaten since breakfast.

Everyone settled at a picnic table, and Matthew, Prince Eric, Patrick, Billy, Tony, and Nathan went to get trays of food and drinks for everyone. While his family and friends enjoyed their lunch, Patrick kicked an errant soccer ball to a group of boys. Despite his suit and Oxford shoes, Patrick joined the informal game of soccer for several minutes, much to everyone's delight. Many people took pictures and videos of Prince Patrick in action, and within minutes, several pictures and videos were available worldwide via the Internet.

When his family finished lunch, Patrick high-fived the soccer players and rejoined his family. He straightened his jacket and tie, smiled, and giggled. "That was fun. What do we do now?"

"Looks like you have some visitors," Billy said, as a woman pushed a man in a wheelchair toward the Royal Family.

Angilia smiled at her Uncle Patrick's still-askew tie, and she was adjusting it when the woman and man approached them. "Excuse me, Your Majesty," the woman said. When Eric turned and smiled at her, she curtsied and clarified that she meant Queen Angilia.

Angilia turned, smiled, and greeted the woman and man. "Your Majesty, my name is Tammy, and this is my husband Jack." Angilia shook their hands, and Jack jerked when she touched him. He grasped her hand with both of his, and looked at her.

"Queen Angilia, I have lung cancer. I will be honored if you will pray for me," Jack said with tears in his eyes.

"Of course I will," Angilia said, and put her other hand over Jack's. She closed her eyes and prayed. "Dear God, please protect Jack and keep him safe from illness and suffering. If it is your will, we pray that you heal Jack. We know that our lives are in your hands, and that whatever you will for us we must accept. Please let Jack feel your love as you hold him in your protective embrace. We love you and thank you for your blessings and grace. Amen."

Jack's whole body trembled, and Tammy tried to stifle her tears of fear. After a couple of minutes, Jack kissed Angilia's hands. "Thank you," he finally said through a tear-filled voice.

Tammy wheeled Jack away quickly, fearful that his condition had worsened. Unbeknownst to the Royal Family, Tammy rushed her husband to the hospital. Meanwhile, those who had witnessed the prayer hugged Angilia, despite her futile protests.

Eric smiled at his daughter, knowing she had done God's bidding. Soon, they and their family and friends resumed walking through the park and mingling with people. Before they realized the time, it was early evening. The Royal party headed toward the main entrance to thank those who had come for the celebrations.

Before Eric and Angilia could make their public comments at the podium, Tammy and Jack approached them again. Angilia was stunned and confused to see Jack walking, almost running, toward them. He grabbed Angilia in a hug before she could say anything. Tammy began crying. Angilia looked at her father in perplexity.

"Forgive my presumptiveness, Your Majesty," Jack said when he stood straight from the hug. "I am at a loss for words. I don't know what to say except thank you."

Tammy smiled through her tears. "We are both so happy and shell-shocked. I took Jack to the hospital after your prayer. I didn't know what was happening to him and why he seemed to be convulsing. We spent the past five hours there, and Jack was x-rayed, given MRIs, even needle biopsies and lots of tests. I don't know how you did it, Your Majesty, but Jack is fine."

"I don't have lung cancer anymore. The tumors are gone. We saw them on the most recent images from just last week, and this afternoon no one saw them on the images. I am cured. I can breathe. I am healthy. I owe you my life," Jack said, much to everyone's amazement.

Those close enough to hear Jack spread the news to those who could not hear him. Hundreds of people erupted in cheers for their Queen, well aware that she had performed similar miracles in the past. "I am so grateful to God, Jack and Tammy. Please don't thank me. I didn't do anything. All I did was pray. God performed a miracle healing, and he deserves all of the praise."

"I do thank God, but you intervened on my behalf. You did this," Jack insisted while he bent and kissed her hands. "Thank you."

"What a blessed end to Independence Day!" someone in the crowd shouted, to be echoed by several dozen voices. Jack and Tammy smiled and hugged Angilia, knowing that she was indeed an angel.

"It certainly is, I agree. Thank you all for coming today to celebrate Valdavia's founding. We live in the most wonderful country with the most wonderful people," Eric said to officially close the Independence Day celebration.

"Thank you. We love you all, and we love Valdavia," Angilia said and waved at everyone as she and Eric were cheered.

§§§§

That night, while Angilia sat at her desk and wrote about September 16, 2036 in her diary, Patrick came into her sitting room. She stopped writing, and smiled up at her uncle. Patrick motioned her to the sofa and closed the door.

"What's wrong, Uncle Patrick?"

"Nothing's wrong, Angilia, not really. I just want you to understand what's going on when things like today happen. You are far more powerful than you realize."

Angilia looked surprised, and shook her head. "No, I'm not. I love you for thinking so…."

"I don't think so, I know so," Patrick interrupted her. "I figured it out after you got me out of trouble that time with God. When I went to hide grandfather's robe on God's throne, the Cherubim stopped me. They forbade me to enter. I shed my physical manifestation and got through that way. I later asked Michael why I was stopped. Was it because they knew what I planned to do? No. Michael told me that angels have to have a selfless purpose for visiting God, for needing to confer with God. The Cherubim didn't know about my prank, but they did know that I was there for myself.

"When you went, you weren't even stopped, because you were there for me. Your reason for wanting to talk to God was totally selfless. You weren't there for fun and games like I was. You were there on my behalf. That's the difference, Angilia. Your entire existence has been about other people.

"God knows that, of course he does. Your heart is pure. That's why your prayers for healing are often fulfilled. God hears our prayers, we know that. Your prayers are for other people, like Jack, or even your father all those years when you lived in fear of Jamieson's threats. God appreciates your selflessness, and that makes your prayers very powerful, Little One."

"God made me. It never occurred to me to not obey and honor him. I've only done what he commanded and expected of me, Uncle Patrick. Thank you," Angilia told him with a smile.

"You are amazing, Little One, you really are," Patrick said. He pulled her close to him, kissed the top of her head, and thanked God for his niece.

§§§§

Two weeks later, Angilia awoke early and was smiling at Matthew when he put his arm over her and opened his eyes. "Happy birthday, my dear," she said and leaned close to him for a kiss.

"It is now," he smiled, and kissed her again. "We've enjoyed 20 years of happiness and love, my darling. I could never imagine needing or wanting more than I already have. You are my love, my beautiful wife. Our son Eric is the bright shining star in our lives. Patrick is the brother I never had, and Eric is a second father and a friend. Our family is everything important to me."

"I know, Matthew. You, Eric, Patrick, and Daddy are my most precious blessings," she agreed, kissed him, and smiled. "Does that mean you don't want this?" she teased and held a wrapped birthday gift.

Matthew laughed and grabbed for the present. "Give that to me." She finally let him reach for the gift. He ripped it open and smiled when he saw a new watch. He had worn the same watch since she had met him in March 2012, and when the band had been repaired for the third time, she knew a new watch was the perfect birthday gift for her husband.

When Matthew lifted it from the box, he noticed that the back of the face was engraved. *"Eternally yours, A"* Matthew pulled Angilia close to him and did not even try to control his tears. At 50, Matthew felt love fill his every fiber, more than he had on his wedding day.

§§§§

March 9, 2037

> *Today I will miss school, but for a very special occasion. Mommy, Daddy, Grandfather, and I are in Oxford, England. 25 years ago Mommy and Daddy met, or rather met again, when he was her cardiac surgeon. Mommy told me how God had brought them together and fulfilled our destinies. That is such a cool story, and I am proof of God's greatness and blessings. God kept Mommy alive so that I could live. That is so awesome.*
>
> *Today is going to be awesome, too. Today is the 25th Eric DeBruce Martineau scholarship ceremony. Mommy and Grandfather have spoken and performed at every ceremony. I've been to a couple, but I really look forward to today, because it will be extra special.*

§§§§

"Welcome to the 25th annual Eric DeBruce Martineau Scholarship for Musical Excellence. I am Stephen Cole, Dean of Christ Church College at the University of Oxford. We are so very grateful to Their Majesties for their commitment to our students. Ladies and gentlemen, I am so honored to introduce His Majesty King Eric de Valdavia and Her Majesty Queen Angilia de Valdavia."

Eric and Angilia walked across the stage to a standing ovation. Prince Eric and Matthew smiled at the love shown to Eric and Angilia. Eventually, the audience stopped, and the traditional question-and-answer session began.

"Angilia, you've been writing and recording songs most of your life. What keeps it fresh and new for you?"

"The short, simple answer is life. My inspiration comes from my life. It always has. However, nothing is simple about life, which is very complex and exciting. There are some predictable elements, but much of life is an unknown. That provides the wonder, experiences, ideas, and joy that fuel my creativity. Besides, music has always been part of me, so there is no possible way I could live without music," Angilia replied, to several cheers of approval.

Eric smiled and nodded. "Angilia's music has been a blessing to me since she was one year old. The first time I heard her sing was a totally earth-shattering moment. The first time she played one of her songs on the piano electrified me. I actually brought a surprise for all of you, and this is the perfect time to share it."

In moments, everyone in the theatre watched a very young Angilia sing several of her songs, sometimes accompanying herself at the piano and often on her guitar—which was almost bigger than she was. Eric's eyes glistened as he watched his little girl on the home movies. Matthew looked besotted. Prince Eric smiled through his tears seeing his mother so young and talented. The home movies lasted almost 45 minutes, and received another rousing standing ovation.

Angilia spoke into her microphone, convincing everyone to stop. "Thank you. I had no idea my father brought this, but since he did, there is a real treasure on there that you have to see."

"There is?" Eric asked, confused.

"Of course. A couple of minutes later, in fact. Is it all right if we continue the video?"

The home movies began again, and just as Angilia had promised, everyone witnessed a treasure indeed. A much younger Eric and Angilia were shown seated on her sitting room floor. Angilia played her guitar, and they sang one of her songs. On the video she smiled when they finished, and asked, *"Will you sing it for me, Daddy?"* Eric smiled and said, *"Only if you sing it with me, Angel."* Everyone sat enraptured, watching Eric and Angilia duet on what was now his signature song, "Sunshine on My Shoulders."

After another standing ovation, it was time for their concert. Eric and Angilia took their places at center stage, and she put her guitar strap over her shoulder. She plugged in her guitar and Eric whispered in her ear. Angilia nodded, smiled, and began playing the guitar. They opened with a duet of "Sunshine on My Shoulders," 37 years after the home video of their duet.

§§§§

On a beautiful May Saturday, Angilia went for a ride with her beloved Starlight. Ben, the stable assistant, put on the saddle for

153

her, and Angilia enjoyed a long, leisurely saunter with her palomino. The clear sky and sunshine helped Angilia relax. She and Starlight stopped far from the palace under a grove of trees.

Angilia dismounted and let Starlight rest for a while. She put her arms around his neck and kissed him. "I love you, Starlight." He kissed her cheek, and they stood quietly content for several moments before they headed back to the stable for his cool down.

One hour later, Ben removed the saddle for Angilia. She removed Starlight's blanket and bridle, led him to his stall, kissed him, and gave him dinner. She fed Rocket and spent a few minutes with him before saying goodbye to the horses. Starlight neighed in response.

§§§§§

Angilia went to her father's suite after she dressed for church, to find him standing thoughtful on his balcony. Eric sensed her there, and turned to face her with a smile. She smiled in return and joined him.

"It's a gorgeous morning. I love you, Daddy," she said and leaned up to kiss his cheek.

"I love you, my beautiful daughter Angilia," Eric said and kissed her nose.

"Today is very special and blessed. Our lives changed forever 60 years ago today. Uncle Patrick, you, and I were connected that day. You filled my soul and really taught me love."

Eric breathed deeply. "Oh, Angilia, you really are my miracle. I have loved you for 60 years, long before I knew the angel I saw that day was you. You brought Patrick back to me. I never expected to see my daughter and my brother together on earth."

Eric pulled her close. He and Angilia felt another set of arms embrace them, and they beamed. "Hey, Eric. Hey, Little One. I love you both so very much. The day I died was the day my life really began. That day set God's plan for us in motion. We are an awesome team, aren't we?"

Patrick's charming, smiling, and gleaming steel-blue eyes had not changed since the day he died. Patrick did not live to become 79, but he lived eternally. The three of them embraced while Eric said a prayer of love and thanksgiving.

§§§§

That afternoon Eric and Angilia went for a walk on the mall. The summer afternoon was comfortably warm. They went to the coffee shop, sat at an outdoor table, and enjoyed some lemon tea. "Today is so nice. This date used to remain shrouded in sadness, but that all changed 25 years ago, Angel. Now this is a day of joy."

Angilia smiled at her father. "That's why I shared everything with you 25 years ago. Even when Patrick doesn't visit us, we know he's all right, Daddy."

"I know. Patrick came to us when the time was right. You once told me that Patrick remained in the Angels Choir because he had an important mission," Eric said with a cheerful smile. "I am so awed by Patrick and you over the past several years. God has an important mission for Patrick that is much larger than this physical world."

Angilia held her father's hands. "Patrick is a far grander angel than he realizes. He is so very special. Patrick draws people to God just by being himself. Most people are hooked by his charm, talent, and looks, and then become closer to God by assimilation. Uncle Patrick is so amazing."

Suddenly, they heard Patrick's music blaring close by, and they smiled. Eric and Angilia enjoyed second cups of lemon tea and were almost finished when they heard screams and saw people run toward the church. Eric left €20 on the table, and he looked at his daughter when they heard girls and women yelling Patrick's name and his music booming louder.

Angilia held her father's arm, and they walked to the church. Angilia laughed and hugged her father. Eric shook his head, smiled, and laughed. The cemetery was filled with people, many singing and dancing around Patrick. 25 years earlier, on June 24, 2012, Eric had sat at his brother's grave and mourned. Now, on July 19, 2037, Patrick motioned for Eric and Angilia to join him and the revelers.

Eric and Angilia entered through the cemetery gate, to be hugged and greeted by those who filled the cemetery. One young woman greeted them and said, "We're all so grateful to have you here for our celebration of Patrick."

Angilia, Eric, and Patrick mingled with those who had gathered at Patrick's grave. They all prayed and sang together. Someone passed around festive cupcakes she had brought, the ideal party touch. "This is perfect, because today really is Patrick's eternal birthday," Angilia said. Eric hugged his brother, Angilia smiled, and everyone else cheered.

§§§§

Bonnie took and Carol released a portrait on the morning of November 17, 2037. Angilia wrote the statement that accompanied the portrait. *"My beloved father and son celebrate their birthdays today. My father, King Eric, is 83 years old. After 45 remarkable years of service, my father remains more dedicated and energetic than the rest of us combined. His namesake grandson, Prince Eric, is 16 today. My father and my son, the current and future Kings de Valdavia, are the shining stars of our country and my life."*

Early that morning, Angilia greeted her father with a loving hug and prayer, and her traditional early-morning gift. "I love you more than ever, Daddy," she said and handed him a small jewel box.

Eric smiled when he opened the box and asked where she had gotten the cufflinks. "How did I not know about these?" Eric asked.

"I'd hoped you wouldn't see them advertised before today. I don't think Eric has seen them, either. They are made in England, actually. Eric is really popular there. These were too neat and special not to get you," Angilia said about the Prince Eric 16th birthday cufflinks.

"They are perfect, Angel. Thank you."

§§§§§

The joint birthday party was after school that afternoon. Most of Prince Eric's friends attended, and when he greeted the guests he was cheered by the people on the mall. The chants and cheers were audible during the party, to the extent that a couple of his friends teased him that he should greet his fans.

"Actually, there is something we can do," Prince Eric said. "Can I take my second birthday cake outside to everyone?"

Eric, Angilia, and Matthew smiled at each other. Angilia had taken one of her 17th birthday cakes out to the courtyard for those gathered on the mall. Twenty-five years later, her son did the same thing. Prince Eric was loudly cheered when he came outside with his family and friends. The guards opened the gates and allowed well-wishers to greet the Royal Family.

Anthony brought the cake, plates, and forks outside, and Prince Eric, Yvonne, and their friends served everyone until the cake was gone. Billy smiled at his darling Queen Angilia and said, "I remember you gave me a piece of your birthday cake that had a large icing flower. You knew how much I liked icing." Angilia smiled and hugged Billy when her son handed him a corner piece of cake, one with more icing.

The Royal Family posed for pictures for several minutes before Prince Eric thanked everyone. "Thank you all for thinking of me today. I am honored and humbled by your birthday greetings and gifts. Thank you for everything."

Everyone waved, returned to the sitting room, and finished the birthday party. Soon, Prince Eric's friends had to return to their homes. Even for a future King de Valdavia, homework had to be completed before dinner.

CHAPTER 7

During breakfast, Bonnie could not stop smiling as she looked at the happy faces while everyone casually talked. "I know you weren't planning to do anything special today, but I would really like to take some pictures of you all this morning. May I?" Bonnie asked. While everyone looked at one another, she added, "There's such a happy atmosphere this morning. I'd like to try to capture it."

"We're already dressed for it, and it is Angilia's birthday," Matthew smiled.

"Of course, Bonnie. Why don't we do this before we leave for church?" Eric added.

So it was that Bonnie took several semi-formal pictures, some of which included Susan and Billy, in the light-filled sitting room. As they all looked at the pictures on Bonnie's computer, Prince Eric smiled and said, "I think these are awesome. Why don't we release them for Mommy's birthday?" Bonnie was pleasantly surprised.

While everyone else freshened for church, Bonnie sent the pictures to Carol, who released them to the press syndicates and the public as Her Majesty Queen Angilia's 42nd birthday pictures. When the Royal family and friends arrived at church, those who had seen the pictures realized they had been taken that morning. The Royal party was wearing the same clothes. During the traditional post-service receiving line, people wished Angilia a very happy birthday.

Many people noticed how Prince Eric smiled as he watched his mother, a look of love emotionally similar to how Angilia always looked at King Eric.

One woman clasped Prince Eric's hand and said, "My dear, I remember seeing you in your mother's arms when you were born and a few weeks later at your first Christmas service. To see you now, with your arm around your mother, is such a beautiful sight, Eric."

"Thank you, Mrs. McKee. My mother is very special. I love her so much," Prince Eric said, which elicited smiles from Eric and Matthew, and parishioners who were close enough to hear.

Angilia smiled up at her son, tears filling her eyes. "You are my precious gift from God, Eric."

"As you are mine, Angel," Eric softly said and hugged his daughter.

§§§§§

"Angilia, is it all right if I go to the Royal Vault this afternoon?" Bonnie asked one spring afternoon.

"Of course it is, Bonnie. Let me get the key for you."

"Thank you. I want to visit Eduardo today," she said with a small smile.

Angilia placed the key in Bonnie's left hand and felt the engagement ring Bonnie still wore. "I know how much you miss him, Bonnie. Someday, when you and Eduardo are reunited, you will have your happily-ever-after."

"I know, my dear. I think I'm ready for that, to tell you the truth," Bonnie confessed and kissed Angilia's cheek.

Hours later, as everyone gathered for dinner, Angilia realized that Bonnie had not returned. "Start without us. I'll go walk home with Bonnie. We'll eat together soon," Angilia said and walked to the church.

The Royal Vault was closed but still unlocked. Poor Bonnie really did miss Eduardo. Angilia quietly stepped in and called for Bonnie. The light was off, and when the room remained silent, Angilia turned on the light. Her heart lurched.

Angilia knelt beside Bonnie, who was on the floor next to Eduardo's tomb. Bonnie did not respond, but Angilia felt a pulse and quickly called an ambulance. Angilia went to the hospital with Bonnie, to be left alone when the doctors rushed Bonnie into an examination room.

Angilia called Matthew, who calmly relayed the information to the others. Eric placed his napkin on the table and said he was going to the hospital with Matthew. Prince Eric quickly followed his grandfather and father. Not only was Bonnie ill, but his mother was alone.

When they arrived, Matthew kissed his wife and went to Bonnie immediately. Prince Eric put his arms protectively around his mother, and Eric put his arms around both of them. They were soon joined by Billy and Susan, who were anxious to hear anything. They refused to leave as evening stretched into night.

Matthew reappeared at nearly midnight, his hands in his pockets. "There was nothing anyone could do. Bonnie is dead." Susan openly sobbed, and Angilia reached for her. "She had a brain aneurysm sometime this afternoon, and quickly lapsed from unconsciousness to coma."

"This wouldn't have happened if I had gone to check on Bonnie much sooner," Angilia said.

"Actually, it most likely would have, darling. Bonnie suffered a massive aneurysm, which caused heavy cerebral bleeding and hypovolemic shock. That led to her death. The neurosurgeons did everything humanly possible, but honestly, there was irreparable brain damage. I'm so sorry," Matthew explained.

"Bonnie wouldn't have survived? She lived for a few hours, and had she been conscious, she would have suffered horrifically. Then the blessing is that God did not let her feel the pain," Angilia added. Matthew nodded and hugged her.

Two days later, Eric, Angilia, Matthew, Prince Eric, Susan, Billy, and Reverend Hutchins held Bonnie's funeral in the Royal Vault.   Reverend Hutchins prayed, and everyone shared their memories of Bonnie. When they finished, Angilia placed Bonnie's urn where she knew it belonged, atop Eduardo's tomb. Bonnie's name, dates, and favorite scripture were engraved on the urn.

Bonnie Darlene Glaser

6 October 1959

29 March 2038

I have fought the good fight,

I have finished my course,

I have kept the faith

--2 Timothy 4:7

†

"Uncle Eduardo and Bonnie are together again for their eternal fairy-tale," Angilia smiled.

§§§§

9 June 2038

I feel so wretchedly selfish today. My problems and worries are nothing compared to Charlie's. He is such a beautiful, happy little boy who is dying before he can grow up to be a doctor and help other children. Charlie has bone cancer. I spent several hours with him. He is so funny. He made me laugh. He broke my heart.

No one should suffer as Charlie does. No one. I hugged him before I left him, and it was so hard to let him go. How can I ever forget Charlie? His bright eyes, smile, and love of life are remarkable. I feel so ashamed compared to Charlie. Forgive me for my shortcomings, God. Keep Charlie safe and warm as only you can. Amen

§§§§

"Angilia, a family is here to see you," Billy told her one morning as she and Eric worked on a proposal. She was perplexed, but told Billy to escort them to the office. Angilia stood when she heard footsteps approach the office, only to almost collapse when Charlie appeared in the doorway.

Nearly one month earlier, Charlie could not stand, let alone walk. Billy and Eric looked concerned when Angilia placed her hands over her heart and cried. Eric held her, suddenly fearful, and asked, "Angilia, what's wrong, baby? Are you all right?"

Angilia nodded her head and forced herself to stop crying. "Charlie," she tearfully said. "I don't understand. How did you get here?"

Charlie stood there smiling, knowing his news would amaze the Queen. "My parents brought me. I wanted to come here and see you before we went home. I hope that's okay."

"Before you go home?" Angilia looked at Charlie standing feet away from her. "Does that mean what I think it does?"

Charlie nodded. "The doctors did lots of tests and didn't believe it right away. I just woke up well one day after your visit, and no one understood. I'm okay. I'm not sick. I don't have bone cancer anymore."

Angilia held her arms open for Charlie, and she hugged him close. "Oh, Charlie, this is a miracle. Thank God."

Charlie's parents stepped into the office with huge smiles. "Thank God and thank you, Your Majesty. Charlie started feeling better within a week of your visit. Doctors kept him in the hospital for tests and retests until they couldn't deny that his cancer was gone," Mrs. Britt said.

Angilia held Charlie and started to protest, when her Uncle Patrick appeared in the doorway, behind Mr. and Mrs. Britt, smiling. She smiled at him, recalling what he had told her. "I'm so very grateful and happy, Charlie. When you are ready to enter medical school, I bet Matthew will be happy to help you."

"That will be nice, Angilia. Thank you for talking to God for me," Charlie said and kissed her cheek.

§§§§§

Anthony put the finishing touches to the buffet, and smiled at Angilia before he left. Eric called Mike and told him to come to the sitting room for something urgent. When Mike rushed in a moment later, Eric, Angilia, Matthew, Prince Eric, Tony, Nathan, Susan, and Billy shouted, "Surprise!"

"Are you kidding? A surprise party?"

"Of course, Mike. Your retirement is too important not to celebrate," Eric said and hugged his longest-serving security officer.

Angilia stepped to him and hugged him. "You're too important to us, Mike. You were with Daddy the day he brought me home after my birth. You have always been here. Thank you."

Mike cleared his throat. He had kept a professional distance most of his career, beginning his first day under King Gerard. He did not want to become emotionally attached to his employers. That all changed the day Angilia and Eric were shot. "You are all very important to me. I will miss you and working here, but I'm 80 and it's time for me to step down."

Everyone enjoyed the afternoon, taking time to show and to tell Mike how much he meant to them. Tony hugged his colleague and said, "I can never replace you, but I can sure try to emulate you."

"You'll be a great Chief of Security, Tony." Mike said his goodbyes to everyone. He kissed Angilia's hand and saluted Eric, which made Angilia cry. "Call me if you need me for anything," he said.

"You know you can call or visit any time, for any reason," Eric said and handed Mike a gift.

Mike smiled, nodded, and waved goodbye. He got the last of his bags from his suite, turned off the light, and left the palace.

For the first time since he was 24, Mike did not work for the Royal Family. Mike's first day as a Royal security officer had been June 7, 1982 and his last was October 23, 2038.

§§§§

Sam, Greg, Joe, and John arrived in Valmondois on Monday morning. Angilia had called them more than one week earlier and said she would travel to the States. They insisted on traveling to Valmondois, though, and one of Eric's planes was sent for them. Angilia picked up her four friends and drove them to the palace. They enjoyed brunch with Eric, Angilia, Matthew, and Patrick.

Angilia had anticipated what the men eventually told everyone. "Angilia, I know we've talked about this before. All of us talked about it more on the plane, and, well, this isn't easy for me," Joe said.

"It's not easy. We've known you, been with you, for 37 years. You are the light in our lives, darling. You were an amazing little girl, and you are an awesome woman. We love you so much," Greg added, tears forcing him to stop.

"We do. But we're all in our 80s, and it's time for us to bow out before we do you a disservice," Sam said. John was too emotional to speak.

"You could never do me a disservice, none of you. I love you all. You've done this most of your lives, and it's time for you to enjoy the other parts of life. I will miss working with you, but I understand," Angilia said.

Angilia, Sam, Joe, Greg, and John shared a group hug. "We will see each other, I promise," she told them.

§§§§

5 April 2039

Today, Sam will produce his last session, and Greg, Joe, and John will play their last session with Patrick and me. I knew they would retire soon, and the news is not surprising. The news is bittersweet, though, because these men

165

have been with me most of my life. I can never replace them, not because there aren't other talented musicians, but because they are among my dearest friends.

Today is extra special. We are recording two more of Patrick's poems, both of which are thoughtful and beautiful. The proceeds of these two songs go to the Tom Greenfield Foundation, which is more appropriate than ever.

Tomorrow, the guys will have a wonderful surprise. Susan is helping me organize a surprise party for them, and I called some of our entertainment friends to invite them. One of Daddy's planes will pick them up and have them here in time for the party. Dorion Collins even said he will perform at the party. How sweet. We have a lot to do today, so that tomorrow can be all about fun and togetherness.

§§§§

The three musicians quickly learned the two songs. Patrick and Angilia recorded their duets rather quickly, as well, since Patrick was never too concerned about perfection. He was more into the emotions captured in the lyrics, so each song was recorded in one take each.

That left the afternoon free, so after lunch the men went to the hospital with Angilia. They wanted to visit the children and spend some time with them. Angilia, Sam, Joe, Greg, and John surprised everyone, and had fun making music, playing games, and enjoying the playground. A few hours with the children there nourished their souls and filled their hearts with gratitude.

The following day, after Prince Eric got home, the surprise party began. Angilia asked the four men to join her in the music room, and everyone greeted them exuberantly. The afternoon was filled with music, talk, food, and a whole lot of love. Dorion Collins did perform, much to everyone's delight, for he wanted to honor the band and producer behind the music that had influenced him as a teenager in Michigan years earlier.

Angilia kissed her friends at the airport the next morning. She vowed to visit them in December for Christmas. She watched the airplane depart, knowing she was sending them to days for all of the other important parts of life they rarely got to enjoy. It was time for them to savor the things that mattered aside from music.

Two weeks later, the songs were released, and Angilia smiled as she listened, cherishing the wondrous talents of Patrick, Joe, John, Greg, and Sam. What a perfect song for one of their two last songs together.

The Greatest Mystery of All

Life is the greatest mystery of all.

Along with all the joy and the sadness,

The laughter and the many tears that fall

Come lots of unexpected blessedness.

Especially when things are torn apart,

Someone greater than we is in command,

Turning a broken heart into a blessed heart

And part of all he has destined and planned.

Not a thing in our lives is due to luck.

All is caused by the keeper of the stars.

His loving grace leaves me so awestruck.

Beyond space and time he intertwines our hearts.

§§§§

9 July 2039

Fifty years ago tonight my favorite love story began. Mommy and Daddy met, and their love was instant. Neither of them knew it that day, but they were destined to meet and fall in love. Abuela told me years ago that Mommy considered not going, because she found charity dinners very boring. Mommy got ready and left just one hour before the dinner started. Moments after she arrived, she was escorted to her table, and Daddy was introduced. He gave the pre-dinner speech, and Mommy was stunned! Daddy saw her from the stage, and he had to force himself to look at others as he spoke. He was mesmerized!

Today is a very magical, emotional anniversary. I know how deeply Daddy feels this date always, especially today. I know Mommy is with us, and that she is aware of today's significance. If Daddy agrees, I'd like to spend the day with him and have lunch with him in the most special place.

§§§§§

Angilia heard her father across the hall, so she went to his door and greeted him with a smile. Eric returned her smile. "Happy anniversary, Daddy," she said, which touched him deeply. He was very aware of the date and its importance.

"Oh, baby, today is such a beautiful memory," Eric said and kissed his daughter's cheek. They went to the Chapel and prayed together before breakfast.

Later that morning, Eric and Angilia went to the music room together. "Twenty-seven years ago, Abuela told me that Mommy loved you at first sight. I know she did. She knew she would marry you. You are the only man she ever loved," Angilia said as they stood on the balcony, sunlight embracing them.

Eric smiled. "I want to share something with you. I'll be right back." He went to their office and returned moments later with a book. Eric opened it to a specific page, quickly scanned it, and handed it to his daughter.

Angilia smiled up at him when she saw what it was. "Your diary from that night." Angilia read it, her soul overflowing with love. She smiled while tears filled her eyes, and she felt her pulse pound. Her father's diary entry expressed his feelings exquisitely.

10 July 1989

I am in love. I know love. I always had faith that she and I would find one another when the time is right. I never worried or really wondered. I left it up to God. He brought us together.

I saw her as I gave the speech. I knew at that instant. Love at first sight. Plain, simple, wondrous, and miraculous. She is the love of my life, my one and only. She is my future wife, the mother of our children.

I had to force myself to look at other people during the speech. My eyes quickly returned to her. She stared at me. We both know. We are meant to be together. We are.

It is not just that she is beautiful. Oh, she is very beautiful. It is far deeper than that. After the speech, I asked Roger to bring her to my table. We talked the rest of the night. She is everything to me.

Leaving her early this morning was the most difficult thing. We will see each other today and tomorrow, before I must return to Valmondois. I have been to Spain several times, and never saw her before. Our time is now.

I feel—what? Elated? Ecstatic? Buoyant? All of that and so much more. I have only heard men talk of love in this way in Shakespearean plays. Not in real life. I feel like poor Romeo. He was a child. I am 35. That has no bearing.

I am in love! I love Marisol. Marisol loves me. God has begun writing my love story.

"Oh, Daddy, this is more beautiful than I ever imagined. True, eternal love. You and Mommy. I love you both," Angilia said, and smiled up at him with loving tears in her eyes as she clutched his 1989 diary to her chest.

Suddenly, Angilia handed him the diary and skipped to the piano, her skirt flitting around her legs. She sat on the bench and immediately began playing a piece Eric had never heard before. Its lilting, joyous melody reminded him of Marisol. She had swirled, danced, and skipped so lightly and elegantly during those first two days in Spain. She had filled his heart with beauty, joy, and love. Angilia's music evoked her mother and their love so perfectly.

When she finished, Angilia turned and smiled up at Eric, who was smiling. His joyous smile was contagious. She leapt, grabbed his arms, and said, "I want to have lunch with you and Mommy today, just the three of us. Anthony has a basket packed, and we can go as soon as we are ready."

"That will be wonderfully beautiful, Angel. Let's go," Eric said. They took the elevator to the third floor, freshened, and went to the Royal Vault with their picnic lunch.

There, Angilia and Eric prayed at Marisol's tomb. Their hearts were light and blissful that day. Angilia spread the blanket alongside Marisol's tomb, and she and her father laughed and talked throughout the afternoon. They toasted their love by tapping their juice glasses against Marisol's tomb.

Eric told Angilia about his and Marisol's courtship, their dates, and their happiness. He told her about his first meeting with Marisol's family, on his second day in Spain when he picked up Marisol at her parents' home. Alejandro and Juanita charmed him and made him feel at home immediately. He loved them. Marisol's younger brother Eduardo, who never approved of his sister's beaux, hugged Eric right away.

"We felt like family from the beginning. I loved them. We were family. Despite the sadness, I know how blessed and loved I am, Angilia." Eric pulled the pendant from under his shirt, and they both looked in awe at the scene from the future that Michael allowed them to see. "I love you, my beautiful daughter Angilia. I love you, my beautiful wife Marisol. I love you."

§§§§§

"Happy birthday, Daddy," Angilia greeted her father early that morning.

Eric held his arms open for a hug, and she walked to him with a smile. She leaned up on her left foot, kissed his cheek, and handed him a wrapped box. Eric removed the wrapping and the lid, to see a beautiful handmade and illustrated book. Eric smiled when he realized she had made a book of his poem-turned-song, "Love at First Sight."

"This is gorgeous, Angel. What a perfect gift this year. What a treasure trove of rarities I have," Eric said and motioned to the handmade books she had given him since 2012.

§§§§§

By popular demand that morning when Prince Eric prepared to leave for school with Nathan, he posed for pictures in the courtyard. People requested Eric and Angilia, too, so Prince Eric opened the front door and called for them. People screamed in delight. Their beloved, suave King Eric was 85, and their handsome Prince Eric was 18. Queen Angilia celebrated that day, as well—10 years earlier, she had become Queen de Valdavia.

People gave the Royal trio flowers, cards, and gifts to commemorate the three milestones. "Thank you for remembering me. This was such a nice surprise to start the day. I do have to leave now, or I'll be late for school. Thank you," Prince Eric said with a wave. He waved again when Nathan drove away. Angilia and Eric held hands and smiled as they waved and returned to work.

§§§§

When Matthew, Prince Eric, and King Eric awoke on December 6, 2039, they found gifts from Angilia. All three men smiled when they opened the gifts and saw newly-printed second editions of Angilia's best-selling memoir. Now that her son was 18, she felt the time was right for the two important additions.

Prince Eric knew what his mother added, and he knew he would face questions. He believed his mother, and had his entire life. She had told him years earlier about their meeting in the Unborn Children Sphere. Eric did not remember any of it, but he had seen her drawing of him. He did resemble a younger version of the man in the drawing. He felt the overpowering emotions in his mother's account. How could he not believe her?

Matthew and Eric realized that the other update was Abuelo's death 18 years to the day earlier. Prince Eric did not remember his great-grandfather, but the account touched his heart. That his grandmother appeared to his grandfather and mother when she came as Abuelo's Spirit Guide was incredibly beautiful and uplifting.

Angilia had requested the first copies for her father, husband, and son. She dedicated the second edition to them. They were the most important people in her life. In their own ways, they were blessings and gifts from God. While Angilia remembered Abuelo and looked to the past, she watched her son get ready for school and looked to the future. As she had written in her memoir,

171

the past, present, and future were eternally bound in a precious synergy.

CHAPTER 8

Prince Eric joined his parents, grandfather, and Susan after school. They walked to the church together, and Angilia glowed to see their son put his arm around Matthew. She smiled and took Susan's hand, recognizing the dress she wore as one that Katherine had bought on her last day exactly ten years earlier. Eric sensed Angilia's emotions, and put his arm around her.

Inside the church, Eric unlocked the Royal Vault, and he let Matthew and Prince Eric enter first. Susan followed Angilia and Eric. They lowered their heads while Matthew prayed. After they said Amen, they stood silent for a moment, until Prince Eric spoke.

"I love you, Grandma and Grandpa. I vividly remember coming here with Grandpa that day while Mommy was in surgery. Grandpa let me choose Grandma's place, and I chose this niche, because the mosaic reminded me of Grandma and me. Grandpa kept me from getting too sad that day, and we made it all about love and happy memories."

"That's beautiful, Eric," Angilia said and hugged him.

"Yes, it is. Mom and Dad were all about love. There's no sadness, because I know they wait for us in Heaven. When God decides to call us home, we will be together. Angilia showed me the joy in that," Matthew said with a smile.

§§§§

Two weeks later, Valmondois overflowed with photographers, reporters, and Royal fans. All of them were there to witness Prince Eric's high school graduation. School dismissed at noon on the Friday before graduation, and Prince Eric was cheered and heralded when Nathan drove them through the palace gates. Prince Eric walked from the garage to the courtyard, surprising everyone. He spent a while talking with them, thanking them, and accepting graduation cards and gifts. He smiled a dimpled smile so like his grandfather's. He resembled King Eric, and possessed a nature much like his mother's.

The next day, paparazzi were camped on the mall outside the palace and outside Prince Eric's high school. The family, Susan, and Billy enjoyed a relaxed breakfast. By midmorning, Prince Eric dressed in a suit and took his commencement regalia in a garment bag. Angilia kissed him with a happy smile before he left with Nathan for the high school. Hundreds of people waited to see him, and he asked Nathan to let the convertible top down on the car. Prince Eric waved to everyone, his smile charming. As soon as the car passed, many people followed, headed to his high school.

After they watched Prince Eric leave, Angilia, Matthew, and Eric shared a few moments of nostalgia. "Our baby is a man now, Matthew. These 18 years have been beautiful and amazing. Watching Eric grow into the godly young man he is has made everything else worthwhile," Angilia said as she looked at her husband and her father.

"Yes, he is a true miracle. I am so grateful that God preserved you both during your pregnancy. You are both miracles, Angel," Eric said and smiled at his daughter.

"Yes, you are, darling. I can't believe our son is graduating today," Matthew added.

§§§§

Two hours later, Eric, Angilia, Matthew, Susan, Billy, and Tony arrived at the high school for the ceremony. Nicole and William greeted them with hugs, and echoed Matthew in marveling at the passage of time. Yvonne and Prince Eric, born just seven months apart, were lifelong best friends who had shared nearly every milestone. Now they shared their graduation.

Eric, Angilia, and Matthew were escorted to front row seats in the Stadium, where the ceremony was held, and were joined by Nicole and William. Soon the ceremony began with the greeting and welcome by the high school principal, Debra Gates. Following her was the national anthem, during which everyone stood. Angilia smiled as she sang the words of loyalty to Valdavia. Her smile grew broader when she noticed her son in the front row of graduates and saw him discreetly nod to her.

After the keynote address by actor Vince Craig, an alumnus of King Phillipe High School, the awarding of the degrees began. Principal Gates returned to the podium. "Our first diploma is awarded to our Valedictorian, who has maintained a perfect 4.0 grade point average throughout his four years at King Phillipe High School. In addition to his studies, he was a member of the Latin Club and the Chess Team, as well as a working member of our Royal Family. I am honored to present Eric DeBruce Martineau Taylor."

Angilia, Matthew, and Eric were utterly surprised, and watched in astonishment as Prince Eric came on stage, accepted his diploma and award, and stood at the podium. Matthew took several pictures of his son, as Angilia beamed through her tears. Angilia noticed the gold-embroidered sash over Eric's shoulders, trailing in front to the floor, as well as the gold tassel on his cap.

Prince Eric smiled at his grandfather, parents, the Alexanders, Billy, Susan, and Tony before he began his Valedictorian Address. "Thank you, Principal Gates. This was never my goal. I enjoyed school and learning, though, which I inherited from my amazing parents. I never felt any pressure to do anything except my best, which is what I have always done.

"Today, our hard work in high school is celebrated with this ceremony and many graduation parties. Today, one chapter in our lives concludes and the next chapter begins. Regardless of where your life leads you, never let go of the passion and joie de vivre which make each day a challenge, a joy, and so very fulfilling. What you do does not define who you are as much as how you do that. Love whatever you do, so that it never feels like a burden.

"So many people lose or forget the wonder and miracle in each day. We have that. We must not lose it, for the moment we do, we lose the joy in what most people refer to as the little things in life. I learned how to see beauty and wonder in everything from my family and from a man whom I never met. I got to know Arthur Brennan when I read his memoir. He lived to be 100 years old, and he never lost his childlike delight in the most mundane things.

"If I can maintain that spark within me, I will never experience a boring or monotonous day. I hope none of us lose that. In fact, my challenge to all of you in the Class of 2040 is to make a commitment to yourselves, for yourselves, to never overlook the beauty in each day. If we do that, it will spread by contagion among all who come in contact with us. If we do that, we will never feel drudgery.

"As we celebrate our achievements today, we look forward with gratitude for each and every day. We will take this world through the remainder of the 21st century, and if we do so in the emulation of Mr. Brennan's childlike wonder, we can overcome every challenge we face."

Prince Eric received a standing ovation, much to his amazement, but not to anyone else's. He finally thanked everyone, bowed, and returned to his seat. Principal Gates returned to the podium to present the diploma and award to the salutatorian. "The student with the second-highest grade point average was a staff member of the high school newspaper during her four years, serving as editor during her junior and senior years. I am honored to introduce Yvonne Alexander."

When Yvonne stepped on stage to accept her diploma and award, she smiled broadly at her parents and Prince Eric's family. Angilia and Nicole hugged, neither of them knowing ahead of time about their children's honors. Prince Eric and Yvonne had wanted to surprise their families.

Two hours later, all of the diplomas had been given, and the ceremony concluded with the traditional recessional. Prince Eric led his classmates, while the parents, family members, and friends in the audience gave him and his classmates a rousing standing ovation. One hour later, after spending time talking, the graduates found their families, posed for pictures, and finally began leaving. Many were hosting graduation parties, including Prince Eric.

Prince Eric, like his grandfather decades earlier, was inundated with picture requests, which he gladly fulfilled. He invited all of his classmates to his party, even if they could only attend for a few moments, which they promised to do even if they were having their own parties. Finally, the Royal Family left the high school, only to face several photographers awaiting the first sight of 2040's most famous graduate.

Prince Eric, his parents, and his grandfather obligingly posed for pictures. Prince Eric even agreed to pose for pictures alone, although he refused to pose with his award, not wanting in any way to brag. Prince Eric smiled and thanked the photographers. "We have to get home now before my friends arrive. Bye," he said with a wave as he, his family, and his friends entered their cars.

Back at the palace, Anthony and his staff had a buffet set up on the patio, including a large sheet cake to celebrate the graduates. Streamers and lights were strung from the trees, balloons in the school colors of purple and yellow were tied to weights and scattered around the grounds, and tables and chairs were clustered.

When the family drove out of the high school parking lot, they were greeted by hundreds of well-wishers congratulating and cheering Prince Eric. The convertible top was lowered so that everyone could see him. Angilia smiled through her happy tears at the love shown to her son, and Matthew put an arm around her and kissed her, which many people saw. The screams and response to the Duc's affection for his wife made Prince Eric's huge smile even more radiant. He had long known how much people adored his mother.

Finally, the Royal Family arrived at the palace, where they were cheered by hundreds of more well-wishers. The family surprised everyone by stepping into the courtyard, where Prince Eric posed for more pictures and accepted peoples' congratulations, hugs, cards, and gifts. "Thank you so much for taking time to think of me today. I am so honored by your kindness. I have to get ready for my graduation party now," he said in a loud, clear voice so similar to his grandfather's.

Prince Eric, Angilia, Matthew, and Eric smiled, waved, and thanked everyone before they entered the foyer. They headed to their third-floor suites to freshen before the party, although Eric saw his daughter smile wistfully as she watched her husband, son, and father chatting as they slowly climbed the stairs. Angilia turned away and walked to the elevator, which she now took alone since the deaths of Mr. Brennan, Abuelo, and Abuela. As the elevator door opened, she felt her father's arm around her, and she smiled up at him.

"Today is such a gloriously happy day, Angilia. It's also one of those milestones that make me pause and reflect. I remember the day Eric was born 18 and a half years ago. I also remember how you nearly died, but how God saved you. You really are my miracle, my beautiful daughter Angilia."

Angilia hugged him close and looked up at him. "The miracle is our eternal connection. You are my first and greatest love, Daddy. I loved you instantly, I knew it, and Uncle Patrick knew it."

"Yes, he did," Patrick said as he manifested in the elevator and put his arms around them. "We've got a party starting soon, so you two better get ready," he grinned. The elevator flew to the third floor without warning, and Angilia giggled when it stopped.

"At least you'll have lots of people your age here this afternoon," Eric teased his brother, who would have turned 82 that year had Patrick not died in 1977.

"And music, right? Can I be in charge of the music? I've got lots of great music in my room."

"I doubt they want 70-year-old music at their graduation party, Patrick," Eric told his brother with a smile.

"They'll love it, believe me," Patrick said. "See ya soon," he promised before he disappeared. Eric shook his head, but smiled at Angilia and kissed her nose before they rushed to get ready.

§§§§

Yvonne, Nicole, and William were the first to arrive. None of Prince Eric's other friends' parents were coming, but Nicole and William had been close family friends for years. "Besides, we can help with anything at all," Nicole said as she greeted her best friend Angilia.

Yvonne and Prince Eric welcomed their high school friends, and it was not long before three-fourths of the graduating class gathered on the back lawn. While they excitedly talked, laughed, and nibbled on hors d'oeuvres, "Also Sprach Zarathustra" blared from hidden speakers, surprising everyone.

"Good grief! What is that?" Eric asked, as everyone looked around for the source.

"That is Uncle Patrick," Angilia said with a smile. "He warned us at least. Excuse me," she said and went behind nearby flowering vines, where Patrick had set up his equipment. "You are amazing, Uncle Patrick. You know I expected this, and was actually surprised when I didn't see you out here earlier."

"Yeah. I wanted to surprise them."

"You did, Uncle Patrick," Angilia giggled while he inserted the next 8-track tape into the player and selected the Bee Gees' "Jive Talkin'." Soon Angilia grabbed his arm in excitement and smiled at him. The teenagers were dancing. Angilia told him to move out from behind the vines, and he did so.

"Hi, Uncle Patrick," Prince Eric greeted his granduncle. "I can't believe this stuff still works," Prince Eric grinned, pointing to the 8-track player and tapes. "What have you got here?" Prince Eric asked and looked through the tapes. He handed one to Patrick and asked him to play it. Patrick smiled, and soon some of the greatest hits of 1972-1974 filled the air.

Eric, Yvonne, and their friends danced to songs such as "Precious and Few," "Long Cool Woman," "Sara Smile," "Top of the World," "That's Rock and Roll," "Burning Love," and "Mandy." They enjoyed a slow dance to "The Air That I Breathe," and then gigged through the kumbaya moment when "I'd Like to Teach the World to Sing" played.

Eric chatted with his brother as they watched the graduates. "This is a time warp, Patrick. I had my doubts, but they are enjoying this."

"Yeah. Good music is good music forever," Patrick smiled. "This one's for you," he smiled at his brother.

John Denver's "Sunshine on My Shoulders" drifted gently through the air, and Angilia smiled at her father. Eric walked to her and asked her to dance. As they had on her wedding day nearly 24 years earlier, they gracefully danced to "their song" while the teenagers stood aside and watched with tears and smiles. Nicole, Susan, Billy, and of course Matthew felt love and awe fill them as they watched. Everyone applauded when the song ended. Patrick changed the mood with "Me and You and a Dog Named Boo."

§§§§§

"Twenty-five years ago today the world celebrated the wedding of the century when Queen Angilia, then the Princess Consort, and Matthew Taylor married. Their wedding is remembered for its pomp and grandeur but more so for its emphasis on love. Angilia's and Matthew's love story has charmed and touched people since 2012, and will continue to do so.

"A very special programming note. Today at 1:00 we will present an exclusive live program, an interview with the Queen and the Duc de Valmondois. This program will air twice only, live at 1:00 and again at 8:00 this evening. On a personal note, I have to say how extremely honored I am to conduct this very special 25th anniversary interview with Her Majesty and His Royal Highness, especially since this will be my last assignment for Valdavian News Network. I officially retire at the end of today. Thank you all for a wonderful and exciting career. I love my work and shall miss it, but

I will still remain active in the community," Franklin Sydney announced during the sunrise news on Wednesday, June 26, 2041.

§§§§

"Good afternoon, and welcome to the Palais Royale de Valdavia for our very special interview with Her Majesty Queen Angilia and His Royal Highness Matthew, Duc de Valmondois," Franklin Sydney announced at precisely 1:00 that afternoon. "Thank you for welcoming us into your home on this extraordinary day, Your Majesty and Your Royal Highness."

"You are always welcome here, Franklin," Angilia said. Matthew echoed his wife's comment.

"Happy anniversary. Your wedding 25 years ago is still the most-watched wedding in history. Those of us who witnessed your romantic wedding will always remember every detail," Franklin added.

"Thank you, Franklin. Matthew and I remember that day, as well, especially the overwhelming love that surrounded us. That day was all about love," Angilia said and looked at her husband with a joyous smile.

"Yes, it was," Matthew agreed, with his now famous amber eyes glowing. "We, Angilia and I, were destined to wed, and that day was the beginning of our life together. Love surrounded us that day and has surrounded us every day since."

"Yes, and it will cocoon us for eternity," Angilia added, her smile for Matthew only.

§§§§

Later that afternoon, Angilia and Eric worked in their office when Billy tapped on the open door. "Angilia, a package for you needs your signature," he announced. At her request, Billy escorted the deliveryman to the office, and Angilia was handed a huge box after she signed the form. Billy escorted the deliveryman to the courtyard, while Eric helped Angilia with the package. They

181

removed the brown wrapping paper to see a pink box with a large embossed gold label:

Commemorative Royal Wedding Set

Her Royal Highness Princess Consort Angilia

and

His Royal Highness Matthew, Duc de Valmondois

Angilia called Matthew and Prince Eric to the office so the family could open the package together. They were as surprised by the box as Angilia and Eric. Matthew lifted the lid carefully, to find an envelope addressed to Angilia. After she read it, she passed it to Matthew.

"It's from Robert Geppetto, the doll sculptor who made the doll of Uncle Patrick a few years ago. He made wedding dolls of Matthew and me for this anniversary, and he is donating 75 percent of the proceeds to the Tom Greenfield Foundation," Angilia explained.

"Wow, that's cool," Prince Eric said. "Let's see them, Mommy."

Angilia smiled and pulled aside the white tissue paper. She lifted a white silk pillow from atop the dolls, to look at the detailed replicas of Matthew and Angilia as they had appeared exactly 25 years earlier. Susan joined them, and gasped at the dolls.

"Those are amazing," she said.

Angilia carefully removed the dolls, placed them on the custom stand, and was very impressed. "It's bizarre to see my own face. These are so lifelike. The gown is just like mine. Look at Mommy's tiara and Grandmother's earrings. This is incredible."

"I always knew you are a doll, and now you really are," Matthew said, hugged his wife, and kissed her.

Prince Eric and King Eric beamed in joy, both overflowing with love for Angilia and Matthew. Susan dabbed tears from her eyes. If ever a fairy-tale existed, this was it.

§§§§

"Daddy, please come with me to the chapel," Angilia requested one hour later. Eric smiled at her and wondered what she would share with him. He held her hand, and they took the elevator to the main level. They walked to the chapel together, where Angilia led him to the altar.

She stood holding both of his hands in hers, and looked up at him with that so-familiar love shining in her eyes. "Today is very special. You and Mommy married 50 years ago. Your love story is the real fairy-tale. God blessed me immensely by declaring both of you my parents. I love you and Mommy so incredibly much."

Eric looked down at his daughter, and tears blurred his vision. "Mommy and I love you more than I ever knew it was possible to love. You are our blessing, Angilia."

They embraced while Angilia said a heartfelt prayer. "Dear God, Thank you for making us a family filled with such incredibly beautiful love. We love one another so very much, and will do so forever. We know the glorious eternal life that awaits us in Heaven. When we die, we will reunite there forevermore. That is our greatest blessing of all. We love you, God, and we strive to honor you. Amen."

§§§§

On Tuesday, December 6, 2041, Prince Eric received a package from his mother. Now a freshman at Université de Poitiers in Paris, Prince Eric missed his family. He enjoyed his studies in political science and his new friends, though he relished the letters, phone calls, and video calls from his family and friends in Valmondois.

Prince Eric knew well that it was the 20th anniversary of his great-grandfather's death. He had met Alejandro when he was just a newborn and, although he did not remember that, he knew

Alejandro well. His family made sure of that. In fact, Prince Eric had called his mother that morning before breakfast to let her know that he remembered the date.

He tossed his book bag in a chair when he entered his apartment. Nathan went to his private room there. Nathan guarded Prince Eric, as he had always done, without intruding. Prince Eric was glad he was alone as he sat at his desk and opened the package. A card and a wrapped gift were inside. "So soon after my birthday?" he said under his breath with a smile.

He read Angilia's card and his smile seemed to fill his face. He held it to his heart and said, "Oh, Mommy, I love you." He wiped his eyes with the back of his hand and opened the gift. He cried again when he saw one of her handmade books, a biography of Alejandro just for her son. On the cover was Angilia's watercolor interpretation of the first picture of Alejandro and Prince Eric, taken by Katherine on November 17, 2021.

CHAPTER 9

"How does it feel to celebrate your 50th Jubilee, Grandfather?" Prince Eric asked with a huge smile and put his arm around his grandfather.

Eric smiled at his namesake grandson as they met in the hallway outside their suites. "It does not seem like 50 years at all. All this fuss for doing my job. I can think of so much that the money and energy invested in this could help accomplish."

Angilia stepped from her suite at that moment and smiled. "You said essentially the same thing 30 years ago and 10 years ago, Daddy. People love you and want to show their love and respect. They wouldn't do this if they didn't want to."

Eric kissed her cheek and sighed. "I would much rather they donate the money to a charity."

"You are perfect, Daddy. Your humility and generosity make people love you all the more," Angilia firmly said.

"Mommy is right, you know. People love you more because you are so humble and compassionate," Prince Eric added.

"It is just a lot of ado about nothing."

"Everything. You are everything to us and to Valdavia," Angilia said as they went to breakfast.

§§§§

That morning, Eric, Patrick, Angilia, Matthew, Prince Eric, Susan, Billy, Nathan, and Tony walked to the church for the Jubilee Service of Thanksgiving. People were drawn to Eric as they had always been, and congratulated and thanked him for his kingship. As usual, Angilia smiled up at her father, always thrilled when he was the center of attention.

The Royal party was greeted by Reverend Hutchins, who refused to retire even though his health had been suffering for a while. As he had told Eric, "This is my life's work and blood. God will call me home when he is ready for me. As long as I have breath, I will do God's work the best I can."

That day, Reverend Hutchins spoke about Eric in a similar vein. "His Majesty did not choose this life. God chose it for him. Eric could have disregarded God's will for him and used his inherited wealth for selfish means. He never considered that. In his 50 years, Eric has proven himself as the most selfless leader, and that is how history is already recording his life and reign. On this day, let us give abundant gratitude to God for creating Eric Richard Constantin DeBruce Martineau as the 19th King de Valdavia."

Angilia and Patrick stood and walked to the piano. Angilia played and Patrick sang "I Asked the Lord," a hymn which perfectly suited the truth in Reverend Hutchins' sermon. When they finished, Patrick stepped to the pulpit, much to Eric's surprise.

"I was born 84 and a half years ago. In those years, I have known and watched my brother. Most of that time, I have watched him from Heaven, and I know for a fact how much Eric has God's love and approval. My big brother was literally born to be the King of Valdavia.

"Even before my death, when I was a teenager, I knew that Eric was the oldest child for a reason. I knew, I saw, how great a king he would become, and he has exceeded my expectations. Our grandfather is similarly impressed by Eric, calling him the overall best King that Valdavia has ever known.

"Eric has not exceeded God's expectations, however. He has lived up to them. God always knew Eric and the man, husband, father, grandfather, and leader he would be and is. My brother is living the life God always destined for him. Eric chose long ago to make God the cornerstone of his life.

"Eric was my role model when I was the seemingly-free-spirited and carefree kid. He never really knew exactly how much I admired and respected him while I was alive here on earth. I hope he does now. Eric is still my role model. I see what it means to live a godly life by watching and learning from Eric. I really am so blessed to know Eric and to be his brother. The world is blessed that Eric is the King of Valdavia. God does bless my brother, the King."

Patrick's smile literally radiated as he looked at Eric and went to him in a loving embrace. Angilia's tear-filled eyes shone with love, and she praised God for her family. They might be a small family, but their love was larger than the universe.

§§§§

Angilia returned from a School Board meeting and greeted her father with a kiss. She giggled when he pulled her onto his lap. They were, of course, older, but not much had changed between them in Angilia's 46 years. They were co-monarchs, but they were father and daughter above all else, and Eric relished expressing his love for and joy in his daughter.

"The proposal for the Project-Based Learning initiative was officially approved by the School Board today," she gleefully informed him of her most recent project.

Before Eric could reply, his phone rang and he reached for it. His tone became serious, and Angilia knew something had happened when he said, "Thank you for letting me know. I will be there soon."

Angilia started to move, but Eric held her. "Darling, Reverend Hutchins died a short time ago. Larry found him slumped in his desk chair."

"I will miss him, Daddy. His wisdom and understanding were invaluable."

"Yes, they were, Angel. Well, I promised to meet with Larry and discuss the funeral and his taking over," Eric said and patted her back.

"I will go with you if you want," she offered, and Eric nodded. They told Billy and Susan where they were going, and walked to the church.

There they talked with Larry Olson, Reverend Hutchins' young assistant, whom Eric officially named the new Reverend of Christ Church Valmondois. A formal statement was issued later that day informing the public of Reverend Hutchins' death and Reverend Olson's new position. Angilia, Eric, and Reverend Olson signed the official church documents in the church office as well, where they were locked with all of the church documents in a safe.

Reverend Hutchins' funeral was scheduled for the following afternoon, October 15, 2042, where Eric gave the eulogy to honor the man he had known since childhood. The church was standing room only, as hundreds of people wanted to pay their respects to the only minister they had known.

Angilia sang Reverend Hutchins' favorite hymn, "Mansion Over the Hilltop," the lyrics of which helped keep any sorrow away. Reverend Olson concluded the service by echoing those lyrics. "Samuel Hutchins devoted his life to serving God, and during his 91 years, his obedience and devotion earned him a home in Heaven. That is his eternal home, where he dreamed of living when his life on earth ended. What a glorious reward for a life well lived."

§§§§

A few days later, Angilia's phone rang, and she instantly recognized Greg's telephone number. "Greg! How are you?"

"I am as well as can be expected, darling. I've got some news to tell you, though."

He paused, and Angilia knew that one of them had died. "Who is it, Greg?"

"Sam. He did not answer any calls or messages the past couple of days, so I called the police near him. They found him this morning. Another of our pillars is gone, Angel."

"Oh, Greg, I will leave as soon as I can get everything together," she told him, and stood from her desk, intending to go to her suite and pack a suitcase.

Eric watched her in concern, even more so when she stopped walking and turned to face him. He went to her and put his hand on her back. She listened to Greg, sadness in her eyes.

"Are you sure?" she asked Greg.

"Yes, darling. Sam didn't want a funeral. He donated his body to science, and he left a document with his wishes. He didn't want a big deal over his death. He wanted us to remember his life and friendship. I wanted to visit him last month, but it just didn't happen. Sam knows how much we love him, Angilia. He knows."

"I know he does. I love you, Greg. Call me anytime. Let me know if you need anything anytime. I promise I will visit all of you soon, Greg. I'll call Joe and John today, too. I love you."

Angilia hung up and hugged her father. "Sam is dead. He is with Tom and Tim now. I knew him for 40 years. It is hard to say goodbye to so many of our friends, Daddy. I know I will be with them again, but I miss them."

"I know, Angel. I know," Eric softly said and kissed his daughter's head.

§§§§

Angilia and her son left the palace in her famous pink car. The people who had gathered on the mall to celebrate King Eric's 88th birthday and Prince Eric's 21st screamed when they saw him behind the wheel. They knew that Eric was headed to the Bureau de Permis de Conduire to get his driving license.

More fans awaited them when Prince Eric parked in front of the building and helped his mother from the car. They briefly thanked everyone and went inside. Prince Eric and Angilia waited until his number was called, and then he completed the written test. He received a near-perfect score, getting only one answer incorrect. As did everyone, Prince Eric had his vision tested, which was found flawless.

Finally, the driving instructor introduced himself, and Prince Eric drove his mother's car for the 30 minute test through downtown Valmondois. Angilia beamed when the men finally returned and the instructor congratulated Prince Eric. While Prince Eric had his license picture taken, Angilia quickly and quietly called Matthew.

After the clerk prepared young Eric's license, everyone inside the building applauded. Many snapped pictures, and several moments later Prince Eric took his mother's arm and left the Bureau building. When they neared Angilia's car, Matthew and Eric got out of another car, a new black sports car.

"What are you both doing here?" Prince Eric asked, confused. "We are just heading home."

"You don't need to drive your mother's car," Matthew said. Prince Eric looked more confused. "Happy birthday, Eric," Matthew said for the second time that day. He handed a car key to his startled son.

"Happy birthday, Eric. I heard you tell Yvonne that this is the car you wanted. I hope the color is right," Eric said and hugged his grandson.

"Are you kidding? This is wonderful. I can't believe you did all this for me," Prince Eric said with tears in his eyes. He hugged his mother, then his father, and finally his grandfather.

"No one deserves this more than you, Eric," Angilia said as Matthew slipped his arm around her.

"Thank you all. Grandfather, would you like to join me for the drive home?"

"I'd love that," Eric replied, and the two men entered Prince Eric's new 2043 model car to applause and screams from those congregated on the sidewalk. The handsome Royals were cheered again when they drove through the palace gates. Angilia and Matthew smiled at each other as they watched the current and future Kings de Valdavia pose for pictures and accept birthday greetings.

"We are so blessed, Matthew. Every day is such a beautiful gift from God."

§§§§

"Happy birthday, my Angilia," Matthew said when he opened his eyes early on January 3, 2043. He leaned over and kissed her. "I love you," he breathed.

"Oh, Matthew, I love you," Angilia told him as she pulled him close and returned his kiss. They kissed and cuddled until they had to shower and dress for breakfast.

A few hours later, Prince Eric and Angilia walked to the stable, where they greeted and walked their handsome horses. "It's beautiful today, and a nice day for a walk. I love spending time with you, Mommy. You mean the world to me. Did I tell you that?"

Angilia stopped walking and hugged her son. She was crying so much that all she could manage to say was, "Ditto."

§§§§

Angilia had just finished putting on her earrings early before breakfast, when her phone rang. She smiled when she saw her son's number on the screen, and quickly answered, "I love you, Eric."

"I love you, Mommy. Is he still getting ready?"

"Yes, but he is almost done. Let me take the phone to him."

"No, wait. How is he today?" Prince Eric asked.

Angilia smiled, appreciating Prince Eric's thoughtfulness. "He's fine, Eric. What about you?"

Prince Eric sighed deeply. "I'm okay. Ten years ago was a very tough day. I'll never forget it. I miss Grandpa every day. But I know he's healthy, happy, and in a place of love. I just want to keep the happy memories of him first in my mind."

"Yes, Eric, happy memories. We have so many to keep the pain and sadness away," Angilia said as Matthew came to her and put his hands on her shoulders. "Dad is right here. He wants to say hello to you. I love you."

Angilia handed the phone to Matthew, who proved he was all right by talking and joking with his son as he always did. When he said goodbye to Prince Eric, he pulled Angilia into a kiss. "I love my family," he enthused as they went downstairs to breakfast with Eric.

§§§§

"Angilia, Eric, do you have some time to talk right now?" Susan asked them from their office door.

"Of course, Susan. What's wrong?" Angilia asked and stood.

"Nothing's wrong." Susan sat in a chair across from their desks and took a deep breath. "I love you. Eric, you and Marisol trusted me and welcomed me into your home, the only home I've known for almost 48 years. It didn't take me long to love your family."

Angilia and Eric saw the tears fill Susan's eyes. "Susan?" Angilia asked, wondering what was wrong.

"I'm almost 68." Tears fell from Susan's eyes, and she grabbed tissues from the box on Angilia's desk. "I knew this would be hard, just not this hard. I never thought it would be this painful to tell you this." She dried her eyes, blew her nose, and quickly said what she wanted. "I love you. I love my job. But it's time for me to retire. I don't want to die on the job. Oh, gosh, that sounds so awful." Susan was crying again, and Angilia walked to her.

Angilia sat next to her friend and hugged her. "No, it doesn't, Susan. Your life has been tied to mine since I was born. It's normal to want time for yourself and for everything else. I love you, Susan. I always will. Nothing can change that."

"I love you. It's not that there is anything urgent. But there are things I want to do and places I want to travel. That feels so ungrateful. I'm so sorry."

Eric moved to sit next to Susan, and he hugged her. "No, it doesn't, Susan. You should do the things you want to now. I honestly expected this a few years ago. Never feel guilty for wanting time for yourself. Never."

"Thank you," she sniffled and smiled at Eric. "Thank you for everything."

Eric smiled. "I remember my and Marisol's first interview with you. We had a long list of questions we asked everyone. The meetings with the first applicants were rather stiff and formal. Ours was quite relaxed and informal. It felt so natural. I'll always remember how Marisol asked you to stay for lunch, and how you talked with us as if we had long known one another. Your concern for Marisol and Angilia impressed us, Susan, especially when Marisol got sick during lunch. You stayed with her until she felt better, all afternoon. She trusted you. So did I. I always have, Susan."

"I'm crying again," she said in response, and grabbed more tissues. "I could never have asked for a better life. I came here after high school, looking for a new place and a new life. I used to think how lucky I was, but I know how very blessed I am. I do love you all," she said and hugged them again before she returned to her office.

§§§§

1 June 2043

Today, Susan told Daddy and me that she will retire in October. I love her, not because of the invaluable job she does, but for her lifelong and invaluable friendship. I pray that her life is full of peace and happiness. Susan deserves that and so much more.

Now I must consider who will take over the job. Nicole and Darlene are married with homes and families. Amy and Amanda are, too, but they live in other countries now anyway. Among my closest friends, Shannon is the obvious choice, but accepting this position means quitting her job. She will face the same decision Billy faced when Daddy contacted him to take Roger's job.

I will call Shannon soon and schedule a day for us to talk about this. I know that Shannon will pray about her decision and do what is best.

§§§§

Shannon came to the palace that Saturday morning. Angilia greeted her friend at the main entrance with a hug, and invited her to the back patio where they could enjoy the pleasant summer weather while they talked. "What would you like to drink, Shannon? We have tea, coffee, lemonade, orange juice, and spring water." Shannon asked for iced tea, and Angilia went to the kitchen for their drinks.

After they chatted and caught up, Angilia mentioned the reason for their meeting. "Susan is retiring in October. I need to find someone to take over."

"Yes," Shannon immediately said.

"Yes, what?"

"Yes, I'd be honored to be your assistant and Lady-in-Waiting. That is what you were going to ask me, isn't it?" Shannon asked, too excited to withhold her enthusiasm.

Angilia laughed and hugged her friend. "Of course. Are you sure, Shannon? This job doesn't come with regular hours. You have to be ready for anything at a moment's notice. That means you'll live here."

"I know. I've known you and Susan for a long time, and I've seen her at work enough to understand what I'll have to do. I have to manage your calendar, all inquiries and paperwork, correspondence, and I have to accompany you to meetings, events, and trips, and assist you. I know it's not as simple as it sounds. I know there are times when several things go on at once. It's like what I do every day at work, but on adrenaline," Shannon explained.

"Before you commit, have lunch with us. You can talk with Susan and Billy. If you're sure after that, I'd like to ask you to work with Susan and me, like on-the-job-training. Would next month be all right for you to begin, Shannon?"

"I am sure, but of course I'll join you for lunch and talk to Susan and Billy. Next month is perfect. I'll submit my resignation on Monday, and start packing my things so everything is ready. I'm so excited and honored, Angilia." Shannon smiled and hugged Angilia before they went to the dining room for lunch.

Everyone welcomed Shannon, and Billy helped her move her belongings into her suite in the palace over the next few weeks. Throughout July, August, and September, Shannon worked alongside Susan in her office, eventually taking over most of the duties. She accompanied Susan and Angilia to Angilia's meetings and on short trips. By early October, the transition was all but complete. All that was left was Susan's surprise party that Angilia had planned for Friday, October 9.

§§§§

"Susan and Shannon, it's time for my meeting. I thought we'd conduct this one in the sitting room," Angilia reminded them from their office door.

"I can't believe this is my last meeting with you, Angilia."

"I know, Susan. Tomorrow we get to set up your new home. Are you excited?" Angilia smiled as they exited the elevator on the second floor.

"I am, actually. We'll make a girl's day of it."

195

"I'll like that, Susan," Angilia assured her just as they reached the sitting room. "Okay, ladies, this is a very important meeting. Ready?" Both said they were, so they entered together.

"Surprise!" Eric, Matthew, Billy, Tony, and Nathan shouted, startling Shannon and Susan.

"I told you this is very important. This is just our way to tell you how much we love you and to wish you all the very best as you begin this new chapter in your life," Angilia said and hugged her friend again. Susan was typically crying, which showed no signs of stopping as everyone hugged her and told her they love her.

"This is too much. I can't believe you pulled this off without my knowing anything. Oh, pooh, I'm crying again," Susan giggled through her tears.

"What else is new?" Matthew teased.

"Nothing," she replied, which made everyone laugh.

The rest of the day was spent in relaxed love and stories. Susan and Angilia hugged in the third floor hallway that night before bed. "You are welcome here whenever you want to come, Susan. You know that."

"I do, darling. I love you all too much to stay away. This is my last night here. It is time to write my next chapter, you're right."

§§§§§

The next morning after breakfast, Susan's boxes were loaded in a moving van and taken to her new house 15 miles from the palace. Susan drove Angilia, and they followed the van. Once the boxes had been taken to the appropriate rooms, the ladies began unpacking. The house had been cleaned, and the furniture moved in, two weeks earlier.

Susan and Angilia started in the kitchen, having fun hanging the curtains and organizing everything. Next, they unpacked the bedroom boxes and put everything away. Angilia helped Susan hang, fold, and put away her clothes. When Angilia picked up one of Katherine's dresses that Dr. Taylor had given Susan, she held it up and smiled. Susan noticed and put her arm around Angilia. "I'll always keep that dress. In fact, I want to be buried in this dress."

"Susan, that is such a beautiful tribute."

"I also bought the cemetery plot next to Roger and Daniel after Daniel's death. I want my body to rest there. I have it all written out, and it's in my Bible. Okay?"

"Okay." Angilia smiled at Susan and placed the dress in the closet.

The two women hung up the drapes and plugged in the bedside lamps. Next they unpacked the bed clothes and made Susan's new queen size bed. They put away the last little things in the bedroom and its en suite bathroom. Susan glanced at her watch, surprised at the time. "It's after 1:00. Let's have lunch and relax for a while. I want to cook my first meal in my new house," she smiled, and they enjoyed the spaghetti and salad while they talked, laughed, and shared memories for a couple of hours.

After they washed and put away the cookware, dishes, flatware, and utensils, they unpacked the living room boxes and spent the afternoon arranging furniture, placing art, and putting books on shelves. By early evening, Susan plugged in her new television and turned it on. She ordered them a pizza, and christened her first night in her new house by giving the delivery man a huge tip.

Susan turned on the perfect movie, <u>Joan and Ralph: Victorious Love</u>. "I love this movie, Angilia. I really do. I remember the Hollywood premier and how you outshone every star there. That tour of America was wonderful, wasn't it?"

"Yes, it was, Susan. My life is filled with an overabundance of memories, and you are part of most of them, Susan. I love you, my friend."

CHAPTER 10

Eric's plane landed at Charles de Gaulle Airport in Paris, France, and when Angilia, Eric, and Matthew stepped out, they were quite surprised to be greeted by screams. They were amazed that anyone other than Prince Eric knew they were coming. They figured out how people knew when Prince Eric walked up the plane stairs and hugged them. He had been followed by well-wishers and classmates. He put his arm around his grandfather and walked down the airplane stairs with him. Matthew and Angilia followed, their huge smiles showing their happiness.

Tony and Nathan carried the four suitcases, stored them in Prince Eric's car trunk, and Nathan drove them to the Université. "I want to sit with you and catch up," Prince Eric said to his family. The four of them sat in the back seat, and Tony sat in the front passenger seat. They were cheered and saluted as they left the airport, and Angilia beamed when she saw a large sign wishing her father a happy birthday. He was 90 years old, and inarguably the most popular and adored leader in the world.

"Julianne is so excited to meet you. We want to take all of you to lunch at our favorite restaurant to celebrate," Prince Eric told them with a smile. "We love each other. I know she's the one, I do. We'll get married. We've already talked about it. We have prayed about it. We can't wait to start our lives in Valmondois. Julianne is moving there after we graduate."

"Oh, Eric, I'm so happy," Angilia gushed. "We look forward to knowing Julianne, too," Angilia said as the car turned into the Université and finally parked.

Prince Eric assisted his grandfather from the car, while Matthew helped Angilia. "Julianne's class ends in about an hour, and she'll meet us here before lunch. I thought you'd like to see where I spend most of my time," Prince Eric told them as they entered the Arts and Humanities building. The Royal Family was instantly recognized and noticed, and several students stopped to wish King Eric and Prince Eric a very happy birthday.

After a tour of the building, they stopped at a seating area to relax. Eric stood staring out of the window with a wistful expression. "It's been a long time since I've been here. Sixty years, almost 61." Eric took a deep breath as memories flooded his mind. "So much has changed in those 60 years, but so very much remains the same. That is how things should be—evolve and adapt while remaining true to their heritage. The Université de Poitiers has managed that perfectly. I'd like to think that Valdavia does that."

"Valdavia does that better than most countries and institutions," Prince Eric replied with a smile. "You visited the Université?"

Eric turned, his hands casually in his pants pockets, and smiled, the lines at the corners of his eyes deeper now. "Yes, in May 1984. I was asked to give a speech here."

"What about, Grandfather?"

"Oh, achievement, dreams, goals, and the future."

"This wasn't just a speech, Eric. Your grandfather gave the commencement address that year. That address was amazing," Angilia beamed.

"Wow. I'll look it up in the archives. I'd like to see that," Eric enthused.

"You will the next time you are home. I have a copy," Angilia smiled.

"Cool. What don't you have in the family archives, Mommy?"

"Apparently, not much," Eric answered with a wink.

Just then, a young woman approached Prince Eric, and his eyes lit up. Angilia and Matthew stood, thrilled to meet Julianne. Prince Eric introduced her to his grandfather, and she held his hand in both of hers. "I feel like I know you already. Eric talks about you a lot. He loves and admires you so much. Happy birthday," she told King Eric.

"Thank you. Eric has told us quite a lot about you, too. I'm so happy to meet you, Julianne."

Prince Eric introduced Julianne to his mother next, and Julianne practically oozed. "I am so thrilled to meet you. You are my favorite performer and writer, honestly. I have all of your music. And all of your books. You are my role model. I don't know what to say. I'm saying a lot, actually. I'm babbling on and on. I'm so sorry. It's so wonderful to meet you."

"Thank you, Julianne. No one has ever said anything so sweet to me," Angilia said and hugged her future daughter-in-law.

Finally, Prince Eric introduced Julianne to his father, and Matthew likewise hugged her. "Did Eric tell you that we are treating you to lunch?" Julianne linked arms with Angilia, and Prince Eric put his arm around his grandfather's shoulders, while they all walked to Prince Eric's car. Soon they were escorted to their table in the French restaurant, where they talked, told stories, and laughed for two hours.

Afterward, they went to Prince Eric's apartment, where he helped his grandfather settle and unpack in his room, despite protests to the contrary. "I'll be fine, don't worry. I have an early class tomorrow, so it's better for me to be on the pull-out bed anyway. Then I won't wake anyone else. I'm so happy you're here, Grandfather. I love you," Prince Eric said and hugged his grandfather.

"I love you, Eric."

Matthew and Angilia unpacked in the guest room, while Tony put his things in Nathan's room, which they would share for the weekend. Julianne went to her afternoon class, after which she stopped at a market and bought food for dinner, including a birthday cake for a surprise desert.

She and Angilia cooked and prepared dinner, giving them a chance to talk and get to know one another while the men sat comfortably and talked in the living room. Julianne felt so at ease with Eric's family.

"I knew who Eric was when I first saw him. How could I not? I've seen his pictures all of my life. He's a few years younger than I am, so I mean that literally. I liked him right away. A lot of people sought him out, you know, because of who he is, and wanted to be his friend or girlfriend. I didn't want to come across like that at all. We took a class together, and one day in the library working separately on a project for the class, we started talking and decided to work together. That was the start of our friendship. It blossomed from there. I love him, Angilia."

"I know, Julianne. Eric loves you. Daddy, Matthew, and I are so happy for you both. Eric told us you want to move to Valmondois when you graduate. I'll like that," Angilia smiled.

"So will I. You are so awesome, but you make it seem so easy to feel relaxed and comfortable around you. You are so down-to-earth despite all of your fame and accomplishments."

"Thank you. Any credit for who I am goes to God and to Daddy." Angilia glanced around the kitchen. "If you have the peas and potatoes under control, I'll set the table," Angilia said and gathered plates, flatware, and napkins. She next helped Julianne carry the dishes to the table, and then they called the men to dinner.

Everyone enjoyed the dinner, which Angilia blessed with grace, and finally it was time for Julianne to bring the birthday cake to the table. Both King Eric and Prince Eric were pleasantly surprised, and they blew out the twin star-shaped candles. After dinner, Angilia and Julianne cleaned the dining room and kitchen before Julianne said good night and promised them a fun Friday since neither she nor Eric had any classes scheduled after midmorning.

After a day of sightseeing, they enjoyed an opera in the heart of Paris, where King Eric was saluted with a standing ovation, much to his embarrassment. Angilia beamed as always, which charmed Julianne. After Sunday morning church, Prince Eric and Julianne drove his family to the airport and gave them tearful hugs.

"We'll come for Christmas break, we promise. That's not too long to wait. And we graduate in May, so we'll be home for good after that. I can't wait," Prince Eric said as he hugged his grandfather. "I love you."

§§§§

During the late summer and fall months, both Billy and Shannon received requests for Eric and Angilia to speak about one of the most intriguing events in Angilia's memoir—her soul entering her father's heart. With the 50th anniversary of that event occurring on Christmas Day 2044, people wanted to hear from them about this unique miracle.

Throughout late November and December, Eric and Angilia fulfilled 60 discussions across Valdavia in addition to their other meetings and engagements. At each one, they were treated with respect and honesty, sharing what that life-altering moment meant for both of them. Prince Eric and Julianne accompanied them after they came home for the Christmas break, and Matthew was able to join them for the last discussion, one week before Christmas.

At a large Catholic church in northeastern Valdavia, Eric and Angilia shared the experience. "Christmas of 1994 was quite a typical Christmas in most ways. Marisol and I were in the sitting room, where we always have the Christmas tree. She was looking through the Christmas CDs and loading the player. Her back was toward me. I was near the tree, looking at some of the heirloom ornaments, and I saw two people on the balcony. This is when the Christmas suddenly became very unusual. First of all, the sitting room is on the second floor, so it's next to impossible for someone to just appear on the balcony without attracting the guards' attention.

"I went onto the balcony and didn't see anyone in any direction. I thought I'd been mistaken, that I was imagining it perhaps. As I stood there, the day was calm and quiet. There was no wind. The weather was nice. But I felt a push against my chest and a gentle pressure on my heart. I felt my heart skip a few beats, even seem to move within me. It didn't hurt, but it felt unlike anything else. It caused me to step back, almost as if I was losing my balance. It's difficult to describe, because I've never before or since felt anything remotely like that.

"I turned and walked to Marisol, and she spun and smiled at me. Her smile faded, though, and she looked concerned. She asked me what was wrong and took hold of my arms. I looked at her and heard myself say, *We are going to have a beautiful daughter. Next Christmas you will be pregnant with her.*' Angilia was born nine days after Christmas 1995.

"What I felt that day was my daughter's soul enter my heart. God sent her to me, because he knew what would happen. God knew that Marisol would die before Angilia's birth, and he sent Angilia to me so that I would know her and feel her before her birth. God's love and wisdom brought Angilia and me together before she was born as a human, because he knew it would be just the two of us. The bond forged between Angilia and me is the foundation upon which our shared destinies were built. God blessed me far more than I deserve."

"When did you realize that Angilia is an angel, Sir?"

"I knew it since my brother Patrick's death, but I repressed the memories surrounding my brother's death for years. Angilia was Patrick's Spirit Guide, and I saw her that day in 1977. I thought at the time that she was an ancestor. It wasn't until her 11th birthday that I accepted that Angilia was Patrick's Spirit Guide. My daughter, who had not yet been born, was the angel who came for Patrick, not an ancestor.

"I knew long before her 11th birthday, but I didn't allow myself to dwell on it. She was never like other babies or children, she just wasn't. Her musical prodigy was formed in the Unborn Children Sphere. Her incredible memory for details, this hyperthymesia, was a gift from God, because Angilia really does remember every detail of everything that happened in her life. And she said the most bizarre things for a toddler. She would watch the clouds and say, *'I wonder what they are doing today?'* They who, I would think?" Eric smiled and looked down at her.

"Who did you mean, Angilia?"

"Patrick, my Great-grandfather Stefan, Michael, Gabriel, and the other angels in the Angels Choir. I thought about them every moment. I wondered what new masterpieces Gabriel had written or what trouble my Uncle Patrick had gotten into or who sought my Great-grandfather's counsel and why."

"Patrick's manifestations are well known. When Alejandro died, though, Marisol manifested as her father's Spirit Guide. You both saw her. What was that like for you both?"

Eric took a deep breath and put his hand over the pendant he wore constantly, hidden from view under his clothes. Matthew smiled, knowing what only he, Eric, and Angilia knew.

"There are no words for how I still feel about that miracle," Eric said softly as tears of happiness filled his eyes. "My wife, my love, my best friend. I saw her, I felt her. God confirmed the truth that she is alive and waiting for me, for us, when our earthly lives end. I always knew that, but God allowed me to see her and literally feel that truth. There are no words to describe the beauty and joy in that."

"No, there aren't," Angilia agreed as she stood next to her father. "I saw my mother's dead body in her tomb when she was buried, the day after my birth. I saw her, alive and animated, the day Abuelo died. I saw her. She kissed my cheek. I felt her. Knowing that she escorted Abuelo to Heaven made his death far more joyous than sad. I know I will see them, and the rest of my family and friends, when I die and return to Heaven. That is the greatest miracle of all," she said and smiled up at her father as a radiant glow surrounded her.

§§§§

Angilia reread her curriculum proposal prior to that day's School Board meeting and made sure the file was saved to her microcomputer. She and Shannon prepared to leave, and Angilia stepped to her father's desk. "The meeting shouldn't last more than a couple of hours. I'll be home in more than enough time for our meeting with the Advisory Board." She bent and hugged him, and breathed in the familiar scent of his cologne. "I love you more than life, Daddy."

Eric kissed her cheek and smiled. "I love you, Angel."

Within minutes, Angilia parked her very familiar pink car at the School Board office, and she, Shannon, and Tony went in. Tony sat in the lobby, alert but reading a book he had brought. Shannon, as usual, took notes during the meeting, while Angilia discussed the details of the curriculum with the other board members.

Suddenly and without warning, Angilia felt lightheaded and weak, and as much as she tried to pass it off, her face reflected her distress. "Angilia, dear, are you all right? What's wrong?" Cathy Shuman asked and put an arm around Angilia.

Angilia tried to stand, but collapsed back into her chair and finally admitted, "I don't know. My legs don't want to move." Shannon was next to her, and she looked panicked, as did everyone else. Vince Everton called an ambulance, despite Angilia's breathless protests. Vince rushed from the meeting room to direct the EMTs, and Tony was immediately rigid and fearful.

"I'm coming with you," Shannon said. Tony climbed aboard the ambulance, as well. Vince followed in his car.

In the ER, the technicians and nurses quickly undressed Angilia, put a hospital gown on her, and did an EKG. A nurse inserted an IV in her arm, although he was unable to draw any blood. A lab technician rushed in to draw the blood, which took even her four attempts.

Finally, the ER doctor came in and sat beside Angilia's bed. "Angilia, we are going to transport you to your private room soon so that we can start to assess you, treat you, and make you well."

"Admit me? No, I can't stay. I have another meeting today, and we didn't finish the School Board meeting."

"Reschedule. You're staying here for a few days. There are a few things going on, all of which are serious and need to be treated. Your heart rate is dangerously fast. Your blood pressure is dangerously high. Your potassium and magnesium are dangerously low, as is your blood glucose. The cardiac doctors have been apprised, and they will take care of you."

"I don't have time for this right now. Matthew can take care of me when he returns from Montville in two days," Angilia protested.

"You don't have time to ignore this right now. Do you understand that if you leave, you will probably suffer a heart attack or stroke?"

"Can I talk to Shannon first?"

The doctor relented, and brought Shannon into the exam room. "Shannon this is a disaster. The curriculum is supposed to be voted on today. If you don't mind, you know enough about it to pick up where I left off. Just take notes about any changes I need to make, will you? Also, please go to the Advisory Board meeting with Daddy and Billy. My notes are on my microcomputer."

"The School Board has postponed the curriculum vote. Do you really think your father will still go to the meeting?" Shannon asked, just as Eric ran into the exam room.

"Of course not," he answered. "Oh, baby, when Tony called me, I was so scared." Eric stood next to her, held her hand, and kissed her forehead.

"I'm so sorry. They want to admit me, Daddy. This is the worst timing for this. Tell them I don't need to stay," Angilia pleaded.

"Absolutely not, Angel. You are not leaving until the doctors say you are healthy enough to leave. End of discussion."

"But…" She started to argue.

"End of discussion. You are staying, and you will do everything the doctors say. Understood?" Tears slid down Angilia's cheeks, but she nodded. "Don't worry about anything else, darling. I want you to think of yourself for once in your life. We want and need you healthy, Angilia. What is wrong with you? Shannon, tell the doctor I want to talk to him please."

The doctor apprised Eric of Angilia's condition, and Eric pushed his fear away. "Just take care of her please. Help my daughter get well. That is all that matters."

Just then the nurse came to take Angilia to her private CICU room, and Eric held her hand as they went. The CICU nurses lifted her into the bed and closed the curtains around her bed. They attached electrodes from the heart monitor, placed the blood pressure cuff on her right arm and set it to take a reading every 30 minutes, and attached fluids to her IV to combat her dehydration.

When they finished, Eric was allowed to stay for a short while, although he was forced to leave when a technician arrived with an ultrasound machine and said she needed to do an ultrasound of Angilia's aorta. Angilia watched, and she noticed a dark red spot. "Is that where the bullet entered?"

"Yes, it is. That's scar tissue. This thin dark line is where Dr. Taylor opened your aorta during the surgery."

"That was just over 33 years ago," Angilia said softly. The technician patted her hand and finished the ultrasound, saying she would forward it to the doctors.

Eric returned to his daughter's side while the nurse gave her medications for her blood pressure, potassium, and magnesium. "We need to elevate your glucose. Would you prefer apple juice or orange juice?"

Angilia swallowed her protest and said, "Orange," which was also her father's favorite juice. When asked what she wanted for lunch, she said she wasn't hungry, but took a deep breath and asked for a veggie burger and French fries. "Please order the same thing for my father. He needs to eat, too."

Eric ate lunch with Angilia, although he noticed how she stopped eating before she was half done. "You have to eat, Angel."

"I'm not hungry," she stated just as one of the doctors entered her room.

He frowned and pulled a chair next to her bed. "You have to learn to eat three meals—not nibbles—each day. Your body needs the nutrients and the fuel. Bluntly, if you don't, your body will shut down——your kidneys, your liver, your heart. You won't live much longer unless you change your lifestyle now. Is that clear enough for you?"

"It's very clear," Eric said firmly. "Angilia, you are the one who was so scared about my destiny being altered. Three days ago was the 33rd anniversary of the shooting. You nearly died then, and you know that your death at 16 would have altered your destiny and Eric's. How can you now totally disregard God's plan for you, Angilia? How?"

"I hadn't thought of it that way. I was wrong. I know that. I Corinthians 16-17. I promise. I'll learn to take better care of my body. I owe that to God, to you, to Matthew and Eric, and to Valdavia," she said to her father, and ate more of her veggie burger and fries. Thirty minutes later, she felt nauseous, though, and Eric rang for the nurse. The doctor ordered an IV of ondansetron to relieve her nausea.

The ondansetron made Angilia drowsy, and soon she was sleeping as peacefully as she could. Nurses constantly came to check her heart rate and blood pressure, and two hours after she fell asleep, a nurse reluctantly woke her to check her blood sugar.

"It's still low, but eating did bring it up some. The doctor wants to see where it is two hours after your dinner tomorrow. That will help him see how three regular meals affect you," the nurse explained.

"How long do I have to stay here?"

"That doesn't matter, Angilia. You'll stay until you are healthy enough to be out of the danger zone," Eric stated, at which the nurse patted her hand and agreed. Angilia obediently nodded and soon fell asleep again.

While she slept, Eric went to her door and motioned for Billy and Shannon. "Billy, pack my overnight bag with changes of clothes and my toiletries. Shannon, pack a small bag for Angilia with a change of clothes, her toothbrush, and Little Bear. After you bring the bags to me, Billy, go home and get some rest. Matthew is on his way, and he'll take charge of her care as soon as he gets here." Eric saw Vince still sitting in the hallway and thanked him for getting Angilia to the hospital quickly. "I can never thank you enough. One of us will call you when Angilia is released."

Angilia awoke when Billy brought the overnight bags, and she smiled and patted the bed. Eric put the bags on a shelf and sat facing her, holding her hand. "Daddy, you need to go home where you can get some sleep. You don't need to stay here."

"I want to stay here. I wouldn't be able to sleep not knowing what's going on." Eric stayed in a chair beside her bed.

Two hours after dinner the next day, Angilia's blood sugar was still very low, and she was given another glass of orange juice to increase her glucose. She fell asleep, and Eric rested in the recliner, watching the heart monitor. Eric silently prayed, *Dear God, Angilia and I are not afraid of death. I do not want her to suffer and be sick. I don't want her to die yet. Please take care of her. Please. Amen*

Eric felt a hand on his shoulder and warm air around him. "Hey, Eric. Michael sent me with God's answer to your prayer." Eric sat up and looked at Patrick, his eyes expectant. "You already know the answer. God will do his part, but Angilia has to do her part. If she doesn't, there's not much anyone can do. She has to put herself first now so that she can live to do everything she's supposed to do."

Angilia quietly listened to her uncle, and when he finished, she opened her eyes. "I know that now, Uncle Patrick. I promise to do what I have to, but this will be very hard for me. I will do this, but I need your help."

"Of course we will help you, Angel," Eric assured her.

"Sure we will, Little One," Patrick promised, and kissed her cheek. "Now go back to sleep. I need my favorite niece healthy so she can keep me in line."

Angilia giggled and kissed him. "I promise. I love you, Uncle Patrick."

§§§§

A few hours later, Angilia tossed and murmured Matthew's name. Eric sat up, alarmed, and heard frantic footsteps in the hall. Matthew ran into the room and to his wife's bedside, breathless and worried. "Matthew. You are here," she said groggily, suddenly awake.

"I'm here, darling. I'm so sorry it took me so long. I love you," he said and kissed her. "I'm going to take care of you and help you get well." Matthew stood and looked at the monitor, breathing deeply when he saw her heart rate of 210 and her blood pressure of 200/120. "I'm going to review your chart and tests so we can treat this aggressively yet safely."

Forty minutes later, Matthew returned. "I've looked at everything, and I've talked with the other doctors. I'm giving you an injection of an anti-arrhythmic drug, cordarone. That will help regulate your heart rate. You're already hooked up to the heart monitor, and that will show me what affects the cordarone has over the next several hours." Matthew administered the drug. "I need you to go back to sleep so that your body relaxes. That will also help lower your heart rate and your blood pressure." He kissed her, pulled a chair next to her bed, held her hand, and sat alert and vigilant until she woke the next day.

Eric had barely slept, either, which Angilia could tell. Her anxiety for her father caused her heart rate and blood pressure to increase again. Eric saw Matthew's concern. "Angilia, I'm fine. You know I've never needed lots of sleep. Matthew, order us all some breakfast while I shower and change."

After breakfast, Matthew gave Angilia another dose of cordarone, and she soon fell asleep. Matthew convinced Eric to take a nap, as well, while he monitored Angilia. Matthew watched his wife sleeping, and lowered his head in prayer. He was suddenly roused from his prayer.

"Eric," Angilia urgently said as she woke. "Eric." She sat up and grabbed Matthew's arm. Eric sat up and looked alarmed. "I have to check on Eric. Hand me the phone, Matthew."

"I'll call him in a moment. I need you to relax, darling. You're hyperventilating. Breathe slowly and deeply, Angilia," Matthew insisted and forced her to lay back down. Her panic increased, though, when Matthew could not get through to their son.

"Call Julianne," Angilia said, breathing quickly. When Julianne did not answer her phone either, Angilia began crying. "We have to go to Paris, Matthew."

"You are not going anywhere. You need to relax."

"How can I relax?" she asked, panicked.

"Hey, Little One, it's okay. I'll check on Eric," Patrick suddenly manifested and answered her. "Just please try to relax. I'll be back soon, I promise."

Patrick walked down the hall, to see Prince Eric suddenly run out of the elevator toward him. Prince Eric stopped in front of Patrick, fear evident on his face. "Mommy?"

"Your father is taking care of her. He and Eric are with her." Patrick told his grandnephew what was wrong, and Julianne caught up to them just as Prince Eric began crying. "She'll be all right, Eric. She will. She is concerned about you, so once you calm down, I'll take you to her room."

Eric cried, releasing his pent-up fear, and then washed his face in the men's room. Julianne kissed him in the hall before he went into his mom's room with Patrick.

"Hey, look who I found," Patrick said as Prince Eric rushed to his mother.

"Eric," she said and reached for him. He hugged her, and explained that he felt something was wrong and took the first plane to Valmondois. Matthew breathed a sigh of relief as Angilia's heart rate and blood pressure stabilized.

Three days later, Matthew released her from the hospital, and she returned home with her husband, her son, and her father. Matthew prescribed a potassium supplement for her. He also made sure she ate three meals each day. Her meetings for the week were rescheduled, and she worked from her home office.

Prince Eric and Julianne stayed through the week, despite Angilia's concerns about their missing classes. "We'll be fine, I promise. We have midterms next week, and we're both ready. We won't get behind. Grandfather's letting us use one of his planes to return after church on Sunday. We want to stay. We love you," he told his mother and kissed her cheek. So did Julianne.

§§§§

Eric, Angilia, and Matthew returned to Paris to watch Prince Eric's and Julianne's graduation from the Université de Poitiers. That same day, Yvonne graduated from Harvard University in Cambridge, Massachusetts in the United States. Soon after, the graduates and their families returned to Valmondois, where Angilia and Nicole planned a celebratory party for their children.

Angilia and Matthew surprised Prince Eric and Julianne by inviting her to live in the guest house that had not been occupied since Mitchell's death. Matthew and Angilia had packed his parents' belongings, donated the clothes to charity, and placed the books and special items in the palace sitting room.

Yvonne and Prince Eric helped Julianne move her things into the house, and the three of them became wonderful friends. Julianne got a job at the museum, which she truly enjoyed. She joined the family for breakfast and dinner every day, which they all relished.

The summer passed uneventfully, until Carol asked to meet with Eric and Angilia in June. "I love you all and I have truly loved working here. This has been my dream job, it really has. I can never thank you for trusting me for the past 52 years. It's time for me to retire, though. I am nearly 75 years old, and the time is right for me to turn the job over to someone else."

"Carol, I understand. We can't tell you how very much you mean to us. You will be tough to replace, but I'd appreciate it if you'll be part of the interview process, Carol," Eric told her.

"Of course. There's actually someone I think you should strongly consider, Eric. Yvonne Alexander."

"Of course. She did major in public relations. Didn't she intern with you three or so years ago?" Eric asked.

"She did. She spent the summer between her first and second years interning in the Press Office. She did subsequent PR internships during college, both in Valmondois during the summers and in Massachusetts while in school."

"She did very well in her courses. She was in the top five percent of her graduating class. She is considering a couple of job offers right now, so we should talk with her soon," Angilia added.

"Fine. Why don't you set up the appointment, Angilia?" She did so, for the next morning, during which Yvonne, like Billy before her, did her best to cloak her excitement. She instantly accepted, and began her training the following day, much to Nicole's and William's pleasant amazement.

Carol's retirement party was on her last day, July 10, which was Yvonne's first official day as Press Secretary. Prince Eric and Julianne were thrilled, and they took Yvonne out for a celebratory dinner that night.

"It feels wonderful to have more people here again, bringing their friendship and laughter," Angilia said during dinner that night.

§§§§

In early October, Angilia, accompanied by Shannon and Tony, flew to the United States to visit Greg, John, and Joe. Something intuitive told Angilia that she would not see them again.

She spent most of the flight in prayer. The plane landed in Los Angeles, California, where Angilia spent two days visiting John and Joe. The men shared an apartment now, and both were rather feeble. A visiting nurse came every day to help with their care. Although Angilia left them knowing she would not see them in this life again, she left happy and grateful. Her two days with them were filled with love, laughter, and music. She prayed for Greg as the plane flew to Portland, Oregon, where he lived. As soon as the plane landed there, Tony rented a car and drove them to Greg's house.

"Are you looking for Mr. Smithson?" a neighbor asked Angilia as she waited for an answer to her knock on Greg's front door. She explained she was. "Well, he isn't here. He's at the hospice now."

Angilia got directions to the hospice, and Tony drove there immediately. Angilia entered Greg's room, and sat beside his bed until he awoke and smiled at her. He was frail and pale, and she knew before he told her that he was dying.

"I'm okay with it, Angilia. I've had a long, exciting life. I'm ready. I'm not afraid. I couldn't be after everything you taught me."

"I am so blessed to know you, Greg. If it's all right, I'd like to stay with you."

"I'd like that," he said, his breathing becoming labored. He soon fell asleep, and when the nurse came in to check on him, she told Angilia that Greg would probably die by the next morning.

Tony and Shannon stayed in the hall and brought Angilia lunch and dinner, making sure she ate well despite Greg's impending death. She dutifully ate, although her spirit was not in it and she barely tasted the food.

Greg woke long enough for one last brief conversation with Angilia. As he gasped for each breath, he told her he knew he would die very soon. "I want to ask you to take my ashes back home with you. Scatter them where you scattered Tim's ashes. Please."

"I promise, Greg," Angilia assured him.

Greg smiled and closed his eyes. Just over one hour later, Greg died as Angilia held his hand. She smiled at the sight of Tim, who had come to be his friend's Spirit Guide. She thanked God when she saw Greg manifest and both men blow her kisses before they disappeared and went to Heaven.

The next day, Angilia arranged for Greg's cremation, and two days later when she returned to Valmondois she explained his last request to Eric, Matthew, Prince Eric, Julianne, Yvonne, Shannon, and Billy. They walked with Angilia while she carried his urn to the same hilltop where she had scattered Tim's ashes.

Angilia led them in prayer, stepped atop the hill, and scattered Greg's ashes. "Greg told me he was ready and unafraid to die. Tim was his Spirit Guide. How beautifully perfect. Someday we will all be together again. I look forward to that."

CHAPTER 11

3 *January 2046*

My Beautiful Daughter Angilia,

How much I love you! You are the light and joy of my life. You have been for more than 51 glorious years, since that Christmas Day miracle. You are the miracle of my life, the reason for my life. When you portrayed the Christmas Angel in the church's live nativity when you were six, I didn't know how true and right that actually was. You are literally my Christmas Angel!

Angilia, every day with you is a true blessing. I have been granted 91 amazing years, and I am so grateful to share life with you. You constantly awe and amaze me, take my breath, and fill me with such love. That God deemed me to be your father still overwhelms my mind and my heart. I remain at a loss for words to express my love and gratitude to God for such an incredible distinction. Being your father is the greatest honor I will ever know.

The past five decades have been full of remarkable surprises and unexpected wonders. I could have never predicted what would unfold starting with your birth. From the first moment, you were unique and special. I knew that. I saw that. Where that ultimately led us, especially you and Patrick, is all part of God's plan for you. What else God has planned for you, I know not, but I do know that it will be just as extraordinary.

Oh, my darling daughter, how can I ever tell you just how much I love you and respect you? I hope you know. I am sure you do. How could you not see it and feel it emanate from every fiber of my being? My love for you consumes me. My love for you grows with each day.

All my eternal love,

Daddy

§§§§

"Happy anniversary, my love," Angilia softly said when Matthew opened his eyes.

Matthew smiled, pulled his wife into an embrace, and kissed her. "Happy anniversary, my Angilia, my beautiful bride."

A few hours later, the Royal party arrived at the Museé National de Valdavia. Stephanie Purvis welcomed them into the standing-room-only Royal Portrait Gallery. "Ladies and gentlemen, we are so honored to welcome you here today for a very special portrait unveiling. We commissioned the portrait to commemorate the romantic Royal wedding of Her Majesty Queen Angilia and His Royal Highness The Duc de Valmondois. That historic wedding 30 years ago touched people in a way no other wedding has, for that was a ceremony not just steeped in majestic pageantry but in true and abiding love.

"We know you will be as thrilled with Katarina Sabozky's portrait as we at the Museé are. I would like to invite His Royal Highness Prince Eric to officially unveil Ms. Sabozky's portrait," she curtsied to Prince Eric.

Prince Eric's dimpled smile radiated when he stepped to the red curtain, and people were once more struck at how much he resembled his handsome grandfather and namesake. Prince Eric pulled the gold cord, and there was a collective gasp when everyone saw the portrait of Angilia and Matthew. They wore matching white shirts and embraced, Angilia's cheek against her husband's chest. Matthew's head rested on his wife's head, and as always his amber eyes shone with his love for his Angilia.

Thirty years after their marriage, Matthew and Angilia were more in love than ever. That was evident to everyone who looked at them, in the flesh or on canvas. Their love story was one for the ages, one that had already been depicted in books, art, and song. Prince Eric's heart swelled as he watched his beautiful mother and handsome father share smiles—and hold hands. He prayed his and Julianne's love would be just as strong and lasting.

§§§§§

Prince Eric called his father to come to the sitting room on the afternoon of September 30. Matthew had just returned from a hospital board meeting, and ran from his car to the second floor, afraid something had happened to Angilia or his father-in-law. Instead, when Matthew opened the sitting room door, he was utterly shocked when his family and friends screamed, "Happy birthday!"

Matthew placed his hand over his chest and leaned against the wall, his emotions racing from fear to surprise in mere seconds. "You nearly gave me a heart attack," Matthew half-jokingly told them. "It's not fair to tease an old man like this."

Angilia walked to her husband and pulled him into an embrace. "You aren't old, my dear. You were so young when we married 30 years ago." Angilia leaned up and kissed her husband's lips, a kiss which lasted several minutes.

When the kiss finally ended, Matthew smiled at his wife and said with a giggle, "You mean you were very young. We have been married exactly half of my life, the happiest 30 years of my life."

Prince Eric and Julianne hugged, delighted by his parents' love and affection. Everyone wished Matthew a very happy birthday, and he opened their cards and gifts before Anthony uncovered the birthday cake on the table. Prince Eric lit the heart-shaped candle, and Matthew laughed when he was prompted to blow out the candle, saying he felt like a little boy again.

The afternoon was spent in joyous friendship and love with the people who mattered most to Matthew. He could not help but say a silent prayer of thanksgiving to God for his immense blessings. Thirty-four years earlier, when he raced to a dying Angilia, Matthew could not have known how very blessed his life would become.

"I'm going to steal a line from my father-in-law, with all due respect. Today proves that I am the most blessed man alive."

§§§§§

14 October 2046

After church, I walked to the stable to visit Starlight and possibly walk him. I no longer ride him. My boy is over 40 now, and has lived longer than most horses do. For that I am very grateful.

I am also sad. Starlight is weak, barely able to stand, and seeing him struggling to stand when I entered his stall hurt me so. I do not want him to suffer. I don't.

I stayed with him all afternoon, and Eric brought me lunch and stayed with me. I called the vet, who told me what I already knew. Starlight is dying of old age.

I do not want him to die alone. I cannot let him die alone and live with that. He and I have been together since I was 10 and he was six months old. Over 40 years. I have to stay with him. Shannon rescheduled all of my meetings for this week so I can be with my beloved boy.

§§§§§

Angilia packed a tote bag with her diary, pen, blanket, apples, and bottles of water, and returned to the stable. She petted Rocket and sat with Starlight in his stall. She stroked his neck and softly talked to him for hours. At dinnertime, Matthew came to get her. "I'm not leaving Starlight, Matthew. I can't. I don't want him to die alone. I could never forgive myself if that happens."

Matthew understood his wife's feelings. He squeezed her shoulder and returned to the palace. In the kitchen, he prepared two plates, and placed them on a tray with flatware and juice. He explained where he was going, and returned to Angilia. Matthew sat beside her, kissed her, and uncovered the dinner plates.

Angilia smiled at him with tears in her eyes. "This is so sweet, Matthew. Thank you," she said and kissed his cheek.

"I don't want you to stay alone either, Angilia. This is too emotional for you to experience alone. I don't have anything important scheduled for this week, so I'm staying with you. I love you too much not to stay with you. We share everything," Matthew told her.

After they ate dinner, Matthew returned the dinner tray to the kitchen. He then told his family that he was staying with Angilia in the stable. He quickly went up to their suite and changed out of his suit into casual clothes. He grabbed two pillows and another blanket, and went back to the stable and Angilia.

Matthew's heart melted when he saw Angilia leaning close to Starlight's ear. She softly sang to him as she continued to stroke his neck. Matthew saw Starlight's ear twitch at the sound of her voice. The bond between Angilia and Starlight remained strong, miraculous, and impenetrable. Even as Starlight neared his death, his soul responded to Angilia.

Throughout the week, Prince Eric and Julianne brought meals, changes of clothes, and toiletries to Angilia and Matthew. By Wednesday evening, Angilia knew Starlight's death was imminent. She quietly explained this to Matthew, and when he placed a pillow on top of the straw, she lay down beside Starlight. Angilia kept one arm around Starlight's neck, and talked softly to him throughout the night.

Thursday morning, Prince Eric and Julianne brought breakfast for Matthew and Angilia. She refused to eat. Matthew did not force the issue, knowing that Starlight was dying. Prince Eric put the tray aside, and he and Julianne sat with Matthew and Angilia. Prince Eric recalled how she had held Midnight the day Eric's horse had died. He put his hands on his mother's shoulders, giving her strength and love without words.

One hour later, Eric arrived and sat beside his daughter. Angilia smiled up at him and kissed his cheek. Angilia felt Starlight struggling to breathe, and she gently lifted his head onto her lap. At that moment, Starlight moaned deeply and stopped breathing. Moments later, Angilia felt Starlight's heart stop beating. Her beloved friend was dead.

Prince Eric stepped outside and called Joseph and Ben. He told them that Starlight was dead, and explained that Angilia wanted him buried on the property. Although Joseph was in his 70s and nearing his retirement, he had to prepare Starlight's grave for his adored Angilia. Joseph enlisted the help of several gardeners, and together the men dug a large grave for Starlight. The work took several hours, during which Angilia refused to leave Starlight's side.

By midafternoon, the grave was finished, and the men came to lift Starlight onto a wagon for his funeral cortège. Prince Eric walked Rocket to the front of the wagon to lead Starlight's last ride. Joseph drove the wagon slowly, and Angilia followed close behind. Ben and her family walked behind her, and soon they arrived at the most perfect spot.

Angilia could not stop her tears when she saw where Starlight's grave was. Prince Eric put his arm around his mother, and said, "This is where we always stopped to let Starlight and Rocket graze. This is the perfect spot for Starlight."

"Yes, it is, Eric. Thank you Joseph and Ben."

Joseph, Ben, the gardeners, and Prince Eric lifted Starlight into his grave. Her family stood around her as Angilia watched Starlight's burial. When Joseph and Ben finished, Angilia bowed her head. "Dear God, thank you for bringing Starlight into my life so many years ago. With love and gratitude, I release his soul to Heaven. We know that animals dwell in Heaven, for you tell us so in the Bible. I know that I will see and ride Starlight again someday. Until then, I know that Starlight and Midnight live eternally free in the splendors of Heaven. Amen."

The following week, Angilia and her father walked to Starlight's grave after his tombstone had been installed. "This is so beautiful, Daddy. Thank you so much for this."

"I know how very special the love between you and Starlight is, Angel. It's only fitting and right to honor that love," Eric softly said.

Angilia smiled when she read the scripture her father had selected for Starlight's tombstone:

STARLIGHT

6 June 2005

18 October 2046

A righteous man regardeth the life of his beast

--Proverbs 12:10

†

§§§§

Her Majesty Queen Angilia and His Royal Highness Matthew, Duc de Valmondois visit the United States 12 November, 2046-9 December, 2046. The official itinerary is as follows:

Los Angeles, California　　　　　*12-18 November, 2046*

Provo, Utah　　　　　*19-25 November, 2046*

Wamego, Kansas　　　　　*26 November-2 December, 2046*

Taveres, Florida　　　　　*3-9 December, 2046*

§§§§

The Royal plane landed at Los Angeles International Airport early on the morning of Monday, November 12, 2046. Shannon and Billy disembarked first, followed by four security officers. Angilia and Matthew, with Tony and three security officers behind them, were greeted with cheers and screams when they stepped outside the plane. They stood at the top of the steps for several moments, waving at the well-wishers before they walked down the steps. The Royal couple briefly greeted people during an informal walkabout, and then were driven to their hotel to eat breakfast and prepare for the day's engagements.

That morning, the Royal party went to UCLA, where Matthew donated one of his paintings to the University's collection. After lunch with the University President, the Royal couple was escorted to the library, where Angilia autographed copies of her books. After a photo opportunity, the Head Librarian, Mark

Landthorpe, invited Angilia and Matthew into the Rare Book Room, where he safely placed Angilia's books alongside some of the rarest, most exquisite books in the world.

"My books do not deserve to be kept in this room. These books span the world's history, and are so very important," Angilia said in amazement.

"Your books are very important, too. The first edition of your memoir, alone, is a very valuable modern book. We would never allow that book in general circulation. We have four copies of its second edition in general circulation, so that we can preserve this pristine first edition, Your Majesty."

Except for short visits, Angilia and Matthew had not been to the United States since 2018. Their two-month tour with Eric that year had generated then-unprecedented attention. Angilia's and Matthew's return to the United States made superstar headlines globally. That was never more evident than during Wednesday evening's main event.

The press and fans packed the sidewalks outside the theater, waiting for a glimpse of the beautiful Royal couple. Their patience was well rewarded when Matthew stepped out of their car and assisted his wife. Hundreds of people erupted in screams at the sight of Angilia in a long white dress and tiara. They were there for the world premiere of the film <u>Of a Good Courage</u>, for which Angilia had written the script. The film truthfully depicted the life of King Christophe de Valdavia, the man for whom the country and monarchy had been created.

Angilia graciously answered questions from reporters, including the significance of the film's title. "I wanted a title that reflected King Christophe's Christian faith, loyalty, and fearlessness. I chose the phrase *of a good courage* from Deuteronomy 31:6."

Matthew was asked for his thoughts about the film. "I think it's fabulous, just wonderful. Angilia's passion for history and for her genealogy never fails to amaze me. She never fails to amaze me. My wife is so talented in so many areas, that I am amazed by her at every moment. I could never be happier or prouder than I am at this minute."

Critics applauded the historical film for its accuracy and attention to detail. The next morning's trade publications and newspapers headlined the premiere and Queen Angilia's blockbuster film. When King Eric and Prince Eric read the glowing reviews, they called Angilia that morning to offer their congratulations. Angilia and Matthew spoke with them until it was time to leave for the day's engagements.

Thursday, Friday, and Saturday morning proved busy, and the Royal couple's week in Los Angeles culminated in a free concert Angilia performed solo at the Hollywood Bowl Saturday afternoon. After church on Sunday morning, the Royal party's plane flew to Provo, Utah, where they spent the second week of the United States tour.

§§§§

When Angilia and Matthew disembarked from the plane at Provo Airport, they were once more received by thousands of screaming, cheering, flag-waving fans. As Angilia always liked to do, they greeted people during a brief walkabout before driving to the hotel and preparing for the busy week's agenda. They reviewed the agenda during lunch with Shannon, Billy, and Tony.

The first official event on Monday morning was a ceremonial tree planting in Paul Ream Pioneer Park, after which Angilia and Matthew spent time with elementary school students who were there on a field trip. After lunch, the Royal party went to Provo High School, where Angilia and Matthew spent the afternoon visiting several classrooms and speaking with the students and teachers.

After spending Tuesday morning at an elementary school, the Royal couple went to Springville Museum of Art. There, Matthew donated one of his paintings and gave a talk about his style and approach to art. Angilia glowed while she watched her husband, and she took several pictures that she sent to their son and her father. What she did not realize is that people took pictures of her taking pictures of Matthew. King Eric and Prince Eric smiled when they saw the pictures in the next day's news. Angilia's and Matthew's love for one another charmed everyone.

Wednesday was spent at a ski resort with children with disabilities and their families. Although Angilia could not ski because of her knee, she accompanied several children on carriage rides over the beautiful snow. Matthew joined several other children during ski lessons, letting them see him fall and make mistakes, which helped alleviate their fears and embarrassment. In midafternoon, Angilia and Matthew joined the children for hot chocolate and cookies. Angilia cried herself to sleep in Matthew's arms that night, her sensitive soul once more unable to bear the suffering of others.

On Thursday, the Royal couple arrived at Provo City Library at Academy Square, where they signed copies of their books and articles throughout the day. The proceeds of the book sales were donated to the library, which helped fund the purchase of new books as well as programs for the community. To accommodate the crowd, Angilia and Matthew agreed to stay and sign books and articles until the library closed that day.

They were asked to celebrate Thanksgiving Day with the Mayor and his family. It was the first Thanksgiving for the Valdavians, one which they immensely enjoyed. Sharing the warmth, food, and togetherness with the Mayor's family touched them all deeply. Angilia smiled with tears in her eyes and melancholy illuminating her face, and Matthew knew that she was homesick. She missed her father, her son, and her home.

Angilia and Matthew spent Friday at Brigham Young University, where they spoke to several classes throughout the day. They ate lunch with a group of students in the cafeteria, during which both of them recalled their own unique university experiences. Their visit proved very popular, and they were asked to stay and visit some early evening classes.

Saturday morning, the Royal party ate breakfast at a local restaurant, after which they visited several local shops. They ate lunch at a nearby Italian restaurant, which drew a huge crowd of fans and photographers. When they finished lunch, they returned to their hotel suite so that Angilia could rest and prepare for that evening's free concert.

Angilia took the stage at Covey Center for the Arts to a packed house. She entertained the audience for more than two hours, during which she sang songs that spanned her impressive 44-year career. Matthew's eyes glowed as he watched his wife perform and receive several standing ovations. Some people watched Matthew watch his wife just as much as they watched Angilia perform. The look of love on his face and in his eyes after 30 years of marriage besotted everyone who noticed.

After Sunday breakfast at a local restaurant, the Royal party attended service at a nearby Church of Christ, after which Angilia answered several questions about her memoir. She, Matthew, and their friends stayed as long as possible before they had to go to the airport. They were greeted by hundreds of well-wishers as they arrived and boarded their plane. That afternoon, they were yet again cheered when they disembarked at Wamego Municipal Airport in Wamego, Kansas, where they would enjoy the week.

§§§§

Enjoy the week they did, beginning with Monday morning's ceremonial tree planting in Wamego City Park. Despite the snow, the parks department staff managed to thaw the earth, dig the holes for the trees, and make sure the plantings were smooth and easy for the Royal couple. Several school classes attended the tree plantings, not only because of the historic significance, but because the students were anxious to meet Queen Angilia and Duc Matthew.

Angilia and Matthew relished spending two hours with the students and teachers before it was time for the school buses to return those students to their schools. Matthew, Angilia, Shannon, Billy, Tony, and the rest of the security officers then went to a local restaurant where they ate a late lunch.

On Tuesday, the Royal party spent most of the day at the Oz Museum, much to Angilia's sheer delight. Ever since a very young Angilia had seen the 1939 film starring Judy Garland, <u>The Wizard of Oz</u> had remained her favorite film. Eric had given her a complete set of the books on her fourth birthday, and she treasured them.

She excitedly pointed out a duplicate set of those books in one of the display cases.

Matthew smiled, enjoying her childlike glee. He knew how significant the film was to his wife, and remembered her multiple references to that film when they returned to Valmondois from Oxford in 2012. Matthew also recalled how Angilia had called Tim her Scarecrow. Angilia clasped her hands in joy when she saw the first edition of L. Frank Baum's <u>The Wonderful Wizard of Oz</u> from May 1900.

Angilia literally cried tears of joy and surprise when the museum director presented her with a pristine first edition of the iconic book. When Angilia opened the front cover, she was stunned to see that it had been autographed by the author himself. "I can never thank you for such a gracious, wonderful gift. Dorothy's adventure in the Land of Oz is so inspiring and hopeful. I'm not surprised that the book is as popular as ever 146 years after its publication. This is more than what naysayers claim, a mere children's book. This book teaches faith, courage, love, friendship, and the importance of family and home. This book is timeless."

Angilia and Matthew spent Wednesday with the children in local hospitals. Tony and the other security officers helped her deliver some of the hundreds of musical instruments donated on behalf of the Tom Greenfield Foundation. At each hospital, Angilia and the children played the instruments and sang songs in the common play areas. Matthew joined them, despite his lack of musical talent, instantly reminded of the week he had spent in Miss Yost's music class in 2012.

Throughout the day, Tony took several pictures of Angilia and Matthew with the children and sent them to Eric. Eric decided to surprise her, Matthew, and the children with a video call that afternoon. Everyone noticed how Angilia radiated love and happiness as she saw her father across the miles. Her eyes shone. The children screamed when Prince Eric suddenly joined his grandfather. The attention the children received from the Valdavian Royal Family made the children feel extra special and helped them forget their illnesses for at least a little while.

The next day, Angilia and Matthew visited Mount Mitchell Heritage Prairie, a state park honoring the state's commitment to end slavery. The couple climbed to the top of Mount Mitchell, enjoying the view and quiet peacefulness. They spent most of the morning exploring the prairie before they were escorted to the Mitchell Farmstead.

There, the Royal party ate a quick lunch before local students arrived for a field trip. Angilia and Matthew talked with the students and teachers for nearly one hour, and joined the students and teachers in listening to a talk by members of the local Historical Society. Angilia enjoyed the discussion immensely, thrilled that the students were interested enough to ask several questions.

After the discussion, one of the security officers handed Angilia her guitar case. She had agreed to perform several songs from the Civil War era, including spirituals that had often been sung by those involved with the Underground Railroad. One in particular affected her so deeply that she had to fight her tears as she sang "All My Trials." Angilia even asked the students to join her in singing "Swing Down, Sweet Chariot," which thrilled them endlessly. When Angilia's performance ended, she was besieged with autograph and picture requests, which she happily obliged. Matthew smiled, enjoying his wife's popularity, and once more took pictures that he sent to Eric.

On Friday, Angilia and Matthew signed copies of their books at the Wamego Public Library. Copies of their books had been made available for sale, and the proceeds donated to the library. The books sold out, as people completed their personal collections and bought several copies as Christmas presents. Matthew insisted on a half hour break for lunch, which they ate at a diner across the street from the library. They ended the day happy that the book signing had raised money for the library, and looking forward to the next day's Season of Lights.

The Season of Lights proved to be a full, fun, and magical day for Matthew, Angilia, Shannon, and Billy. They returned to the Wamego Public Library that morning for the Gingerbread Creations display. Angilia and Shannon in particular oohed and ahhed over the gingerbread houses and other buildings, including a working train station.

Angilia and Matthew were especially impressed by a gingerbread recreation of the Palais Royale de Valdavia. Angilia took several pictures of the gingerbread palace, which, as she pointed out, was very detailed and exact. "Look at the windows, the front door, the watchtower, the gates, and the statue of King Christophe! This is amazing. I can't believe how detailed and accurate this is. I have never seen anything like this."

Angilia met the woman who had designed and built the gingerbread palace especially for Angilia and Matthew to enjoy. Mary Turner asked that the display case containing her palace be opened so that the Royal couple could see all of the details. "Open the front door," Mary told Angilia. Angilia did so, and gasped when she saw a sweet replica of her father standing in the foyer wearing his military uniform.

"This is beautiful! I feel like Heidi when she got the snow globe of her grandfather!" Mary explained to an excited Angilia that the gingerbread palace was Wamego's gift to Angilia and Matthew, and would be carefully packed and taken to their airplane when they left Sunday afternoon. Matthew smiled, while his wife cried and hugged Mary in gratitude. "I will keep this as long as humanly possible in a place of honor," Angilia assured Mary.

When they finally left the library, Matthew, Angilia, and their party were given a tour along the streets to see the Holiday Decorated Windows. Angilia marveled at the winter wonderland and nativity scenes depicted in paint and lights in the dozens of windows. They paused at each window, taking time to enjoy each one and to speak with those who had created the window decorations. After close to two hours, it was time for the Royal party to follow their tour guides to the next event.

Children followed Angilia as if she were the Pied Piper, drawn to her as if by magic. They held her hands, arms, and coat, their short legs scurrying to stay close to her. When everyone entered St. Luke's Episcopal for Cookies by the Pound, Angilia and Matthew delighted the children by purchasing several pounds of cookies for them. As they nibbled the cookies, some of the children asked Angilia if she would sing "Silent Night" for them. Angilia did so, and everyone noticed that she radiated a magical glow as she sang. No one doubted that Angilia was an angel of God.

Finally it was time for the Holiday Home Tour. As the Royal party followed their tour guides, Matthew kept his arm around his wife's waist. They enjoyed seeing the decorated homes, outside and inside, and meeting the families who lived in them. Angilia was always touched when she saw a nativity scene and realized how many people honored the birth of Jesus Christ, the real reason for the holiday.

Finally, it was time for the final event of the day, the Colombian Christmas Show. Matthew, Angilia, and the Royal party relaxed in the theater and thoroughly enjoyed the Christmas show. After the show, the Royal couple took the opportunity to speak with the performers and congratulate them. After posing for pictures with the performers and audience members, the Royal party returned to their hotel for dinner and sleep.

After breakfast, Angilia, Matthew, Billy, Shannon, and Tony attended Sunday morning church service at New Life Baptist Church. They enjoyed the sermon and fellowship, and thanked everyone for their kind welcome before they went to the airport to board their plane. By midday their plane landed at Orlando Sanford International Airport for the last week of the Royal Tour.

§§§§

After the Royal party landed, they were driven the 40 minutes to Tavares, Florida. They spent the afternoon going over the week's itinerary in their hotel room, where they ate lunch and dinner. Their main agenda for the week was to highlight local businesses, attractions, and events. The week would not be too taxing or rigorous for either Angilia or Matthew. Nonetheless, Matthew insisted that his wife dine and bathe relatively early that evening so that she could get a full night's sleep.

Throughout the week, Matthew and Angilia had reservations to eat their meals at various Tavares restaurants. Angilia, Matthew, and the Royal party, therefore, ate Monday breakfast at AL's

Landing. Despite the attention they generated, they enjoyed the food and fresh juice. After spending time speaking with the other patrons, Matthew and Angilia did some Christmas shopping in the downtown shops. They were followed constantly by members of the press, which only helped to generate publicity for the businesses they patronized.

Monday afternoon, Matthew and Angilia did the obligatory ceremonial tree plantings on Main Street. Local business leaders and dignitaries were on hand for the ceremony, as were hundreds of Royal fans. After a walkabout, which lasted over one hour, Angilia and Matthew thanked everyone and returned to their hotel room.

Given that Tavares is known as America's Seaplane City, the official event for Tuesday morning was quite appropriate. Angilia and Matthew dressed casually in jeans and shirts for their first ride in a seaplane. Press photographers and reporters were on hand to cover the event, and King Eric and Prince Eric enjoyed seeing the coverage on the news reports that day. Watching the seaplane take off and land on the water was exciting for the two men. After Angilia and Matthew disembarked, they spent several moments answering questions from reporters and talking with the hundreds of people who had come to watch them.

By that evening, Angilia and Matthew sparkled in evening attire and received cheers of delight when they arrived at Boleros Cigar and Wine Bar. Although neither smoked nor drank alcohol, they had agreed to host a meet-and-greet at the bar, which was a popular establishment. Those who attended the meet-and-greet had purchased $500 tickets, the total proceeds of which were donated to the local Toys for Tots. What no one knew was that Angilia and Matthew had donated €5000 each to Toys for Tots so that more children could enjoy a happy Christmas. The total amount raised from ticket sales that evening was $95,000.

Matthew and Angilia continued to support local businesses by having lunch on Wednesday at Ruby Street Grille. The Royal couple, Shannon, Billy, Tony, and the other security officers enjoyed their lunches and the chance to speak with and meet Tavares residents. Although it still felt uncomfortable to Matthew, Shannon, and Billy, having their pictures taken as they ate was an expected and necessary part of the job. They knew that the pictures would provide attention and publicity for the restaurant.

This continued during Thursday night's dinner at Lake Dora Sushi and Sake, another popular restaurant. Angilia's veganism presented a challenge since she did not eat seafood, but she managed to find several dishes from which she could choose on the menu. The Royal party enjoyed the atmosphere and food, and agreed to pose for photographs with the staff. Despite the constant presence of press photographers, Angilia and Matthew spent time talking with other diners and even signing autographs.

On Friday evening, the Royal couple thrilled the passengers when they boarded the Orange Blossom Cannonball Christmas Express. The children in particular delighted in sharing the train ride through Tavares with the beautiful Queen and handsome Duc. Their presence made the train ride even more magical, especially since Angilia emitted a mystical glow. Press photographs captured her radiant smile, gleaming eyes, and apparent halo. Prince Eric printed a copy of one picture and had it framed and kept in his suite. He truly savored seeing how much his parents spread joy and happiness wherever they went.

The last official events of the Royal Tour occurred Saturday with Light Up Tavares: The Spirit of Giving. That morning, the Royal party bought Christmas gifts at the Craft Fair, and mingled with others who came to the events. Angilia particularly enjoyed talking with the children who waited to tell Santa Claus what they wanted for Christmas. The Royal party also enjoyed watching some local entertainers throughout the afternoon before it was time for the Christmas parade that evening.

Angilia and Matthew had been asked to ride on a float which had been designed just for them. They had agreed, and were glad they had when they saw the children's happiness. Children had always held a special place in Angilia's heart, and she wanted every child to feel love, peace, and joy. If she could bring a bit of that to them by riding in the Christmas parade, she was honored to do so. Angilia smiled up at her husband, and leaned close to his ear. "Oh, Matthew, doesn't it fill your soul with warmth to see how happy the children are?" Matthew smiled and kissed her cheek, a moment captured forever in photographs which were seen around the world.

After the parade, Angilia, Matthew, and Santa Claus were surrounded by hundreds of screaming children, all extremely excited to see them. Angilia and Matthew stayed for several hours to talk with, pose for pictures with, and sign autographs for the children. They were more than happy to do so, understanding that the simple acts brought so much cheerfulness to the children, especially at Christmas time. Angilia and Matthew went to sleep that night with visions of smiling faces filling their dreams.

The Royal party ended their Royal Tour by attending Sunday morning church service at Liberty Baptist Church. The congregation welcomed them with kindness and gratitude. Angilia and Matthew enjoyed the sermon, hymns, and fellowship before thanking everyone for their kindness. By early afternoon, they were safely in the air on their way home to celebrate Christmas with their family and friends in Valmondois.

§§§§§

Eric, Angilia, Matthew, Prince Eric, and Julianne decorated the Christmas tree in the sitting room on December 12, soon after Matthew and Angilia returned to Valmondois. After they finished, Angilia asked Tony to carry the gingerbread palace to the sitting room. Eric, Prince Eric, and Julianne had not seen the sweet replica of the palace, and they were as amazed as Angilia had been at the attention to detail.

"Isn't it astounding? I had Stephanie Purvis and her staff at the museum preserve this so that we can have it and enjoy it as long as possible. The archivist even made a custom acid-free box in which to store the gingerbread palace between Christmases," Angilia explained.

"I have never seen anything like this before," Prince Eric said, a comment which Julianne and Eric echoed.

"Open the front door, Daddy," Angilia requested with a smile.

Eric happily obliged his daughter, only to be pleasantly surprised to see his tiny confectionery counterpart staring back at him. Nicole, William, Yvonne, and everyone else who visited the palace that Christmas—and many Christmases to follow—were equally impressed by the gingerbread palace. In fact, the confection was so well preserved that Angilia's great-grandchildren would likewise marvel at it for several Christmases.

§§§§

25 February 2047

I spent the past several weekends auditioning band members, something I put off for as long as possible. I could not ignore the need for a new band any longer, though, since we are recording an album early next month.

The musicians are excellent, with lots of talent and experience. They all live in Valmondois, too, which will make it much easier for them to be available for recording sessions and concerts. Neil, David, Larry, and Robbie are not just talented musicians but wonderful men, and I look forward to knowing and working with them.

I will always miss Tim, Greg, Joe, and John, and no one will ever replace them, especially in my heart. I should visit Joe and John soon, once the album and few concerts are completed. Hopefully I shall be able to visit them in April.

§§§§

Angilia's new band joined her in the basement recording studio during the last week of February so they could learn the new songs for her next album. There were 12 songs that she would record solo, plus 4 bonus songs. Angilia wanted to record three duets, one with her father, one with Uncle Patrick, and one with Matthew. Matthew had tried to resist his wife's request, but like Eric had in 2012, he found it impossible to refuse Angilia such a simple—albeit embarrassing and very public—request. The fourth bonus song was one that Patrick had suggested and that Eric really liked—a duet between the two brothers.

On Wednesday, March 6, 2047, Angilia and her new band recorded her 12 solos in one take each, as she had always done.

Angilia chose not to replace Sam, but rather served as the producer. She realized now why Sam had taught her production so many years earlier, before she was a teenager. He had prepared her to take the reins and helm her recording sessions when he no longer could.

The next morning after breakfast, Eric and Patrick joined Angilia and the band in the recording studio. Everyone was well aware of the date although no one dwelled on the anniversary. Instead, the seven of them formed a prayer circle before they began work, which further lightened their spirits.

Angilia and Eric recorded their duet fairly quickly, in just two takes. After a short break, Angilia and Patrick finished their duet in one take. Finally, it was time for Eric and Patrick to record their very special duet, which they flawlessly completed in one take. Angilia played acoustic guitar on the track, and had to fight her tears and emotions as her father and her uncle sang to one another. When they finished and hugged each other, Angilia did cry, unable to force herself not to.

After washing her face, Angilia joined her family and the band in the dining room for lunch. The mood was light-hearted, although everyone noticed Matthew's nervousness. Eric empathized, remembering what his first recording session felt like and how he had done it only for his daughter. Matthew had tried to argue that he sounded like a toad frog when he sang, only to somehow find himself agreeing to record the duet with his wife.

So it was that Matthew found himself sitting across from Angilia at the microphone in the recording studio that afternoon. Only the four band members were present, and the six of them rehearsed the song several times before Matthew summoned the courage to record the duet. When it was done, Angilia placed her guitar on its stand and hugged her husband. "Thank you so much, darling. You are perfect, Matthew, just perfect. The album is finished!"

§§§§

The next afternoon, Angilia invited her family and friends to the recording studio to listen to the new album. Julianne in particular was overjoyed to be among the first to hear Angilia's new album, and she enthusiastically responded to each song, claiming each in turn was her new favorite. "Oh, it's impossible to choose just one favorite," Julianne finally admitted after the seventh song.

The four duets took everyone's breath, especially Eric's and Patrick's impassioned rendition of a song made famous nearly 80 years earlier, "He Ain't Heavy, He's My Brother." The brothers' love and emotions were more than evident to everyone, and like his mother had the day before, Prince Eric cried. His grandfather was 92 years old, yet more spectacular than anyone else on earth. Prince Eric deeply loved and respected his grandfather and granduncle. Their song of brotherly love touched him deeply, as it did everyone who heard it around the world when the album was released the following month.

Yvonne was the first to ask Angilia which song would be released as the first single, to which Angilia responded she wanted it to be her duet with Matthew. Matthew, however, made another suggestion. "I actually feel another song is better, and not because I don't sing on it. I know I'm biased, but my vote goes to the song you wrote for us," Matthew stated and gestured toward his son, Patrick, and Eric.

"So does mine, Mommy. I really love that song so much," Prince Eric said as tears threatened him once more.

Julianne hugged Prince Eric and offered her agreement. "All of the songs are wonderful and beautiful, but that one is truly special, magical, and true. It's all about your incredible love for your father, your uncle, your husband, and your son. The song captures the mystical, timeless love you hold in your soul for them. It's just so very beautiful." Yvonne and Shannon also added their support for that song, as did Billy and the band.

"Looks like I'm outvoted," Angilia giggled. "If you really want that song to be the first single, it will be." Two weeks later, millions of people also voted for that song by pushing it to gold record status within its first 24 hours.

My Love for You

My love for you is the most precious prize

From God above, and grows stronger each day,

Outsoaring the birds that fly through the skies

And my heart, where it will forever stay.

My love for you remains so pure and true,

More vibrant and alive than any dream.

A dream come true is my love for you,

Constantly surging life through my bloodstream.

My love for you lives for eternity,

The foundation upon which life is made,

The blessed gift that keeps me safe and free,

The surest treasure from which I never strayed.

Every wish on a star that shone like dew

Or answer to my prayers is my love for you.

§§§§§

Later that month, Angilia and her new band performed a sellout concert at Gateway Arena, during which she performed the songs from her new album along with songs that spanned her 45 year career. She garnered several standing ovations throughout the evening, especially when she played the very familiar guitar chords that opened "Our Dreams," her best-selling duet with Patrick.

When Patrick joined his niece on stage, the audience cheered relentlessly. Angilia and Patrick followed "Our Dreams" with their current duet, which earned even more screams. When that song ended, Patrick stepped offstage for a while, so that Angilia could introduce her band and her next surprise. "Please join me in welcoming our new band. David Baxter on electric guitar. Neil Stine on bass. On drums, Larry Moore. Robbie Gilmour on piano. Aren't they fabulous?" After the applause, Angilia said, "Now please join me in welcoming my father, Eric DeBruce Martineau."

The audience collectively jumped to their feet in a thunderous standing ovation that, to Angilia's delight, lasted nearly 30 minutes. Finally Angilia and Eric were able to sing their new duet, a story song she had written just for them. Another enthusiastic standing ovation delayed their next surprise for nearly 15 minutes. When Angilia called Patrick back to the stage, she knew that his and Eric's duet would send the crowd into the stratosphere. That was an understatement, for their emotional interpretation of the old Hollies hit proved to be the crowd favorite thus far.

Angilia ended the concert with her final surprise of the evening. "Ladies and gentlemen, I have one more very special guest to introduce. I am so thrilled to welcome my husband Matthew to join us." Matthew took a huge breath before he walked on stage to stand beside Angilia and sing their duet, a romantic ballad first recorded 89 years earlier in 1958--the year Patrick had been born. Just as the love between Eric and Patrick was evident in their song, the love between Angilia and Matthew shone brighter than the stars as they looked at one another and sang the Everly Brothers hit, "All I Have to Do Is Dream."

The concert was a rousing success, raising a total of more than €205,000 that was divided evenly between Angilia's Tom Greenfield Foundation, Eric's Open Heart Foundation, and Matthew's patronage (Patrick's former patronage) The Athletic Association of Valdavia. The Royal Family returned home that night elated, thankful, and blessed.

§§§§

Angilia returned from a School Board meeting with Shannon, only to have Billy stop her in the hallway. "Angilia, a lawyer from California is here to see you. He says it's very important, and he's been in the waiting room for almost two hours now."

Angilia appeared as surprised as she felt, unsure why an American lawyer would need to meet with her. Nonetheless, she asked Billy to show him to the office, which she entered to greet her father with a kiss. When Billy announced the lawyer, Eric asked if she wanted him to leave so the meeting could be private, but Angilia said that was unnecessary.

"Your Majesties, my name is Alan Palmer, and I represent the estates of John Herbert and Joe Arnold."

"Estates?" Angilia barely whispered.

"That's correct, Your Majesty. Mr. Herbert died last November, and Mr. Arnold died earlier this month. They hired me a few years ago to make sure their final wishes are carried out. I am here today to do that. They asked me to deliver this letter from them to you," Mr. Palmer told Angilia as he handed her an envelope.

Angilia quietly read the letter, took a deep breath, and handed it to her father so he could read it, too. John and Joe were cremated upon their deaths, and they wanted Angilia to scatter their ashes upon the same hilltop where she had scattered Tim's and Greg's ashes. "I had planned to visit them soon," she sadly said. "Of course I will do this for John and Joe. This is the least I can do for them after everything they did for me for so very long."

"Mr. Herbert and Mr. Arnold knew you would, Your Majesty. It is with my sincere condolences that I give you the urn containing their combined ashes," Mr. Palmer said as he stood and handed Angilia a ceramic urn. "I also brought some other things that Mr. Herbert and Mr. Arnold wanted you to have."

Mr. Palmer opened a large duffel bag, from which he pulled several music notebooks that had belonged to Tom. Angilia tenderly ran her finger over them and felt tears sting her eyes when she touched them. Mr. Palmer also handed Angilia a box containing photographs of Tom, the band, and Angilia that dated back to the early 1970s. When she glimpsed them, she had to dry her eyes of the tears that blinded her.

"Mr. Herbert and Mr. Arnold were especially adamant that you have something that had belonged to Mr. Greenfield," Mr. Palmer said and cleared his throat. Angilia looked at her father and reached for his hand, not knowing what to expect.

Angilia stood, still holding her father's hand, when she saw Tom's guitar case in Mr. Palmer's hand. She began crying, and her other hand covered her face. Eric stood and held his daughter close to him, knowing how emotional this unexpected visit was for her. Mr. Palmer carefully placed the guitar case on Angilia's desk and said, "I am so sorry for your loss, Your Majesty."

That afternoon, Angilia, with her family and friends, carried John's and Joe's urn to the hilltop, as they wanted her to. Just as she had done with Tim's and Greg's ashes, Angilia climbed atop the hill, bowed her head in prayer, and scattered their ashes. "Now the band is reunited and complete for all eternity. I miss my friends so very much, but I know I will join them and make music with them again when my life on earth is over. Until then, I have a lifetime of precious, beautiful memories to carry me through."

CHAPTER 12

"Good morning, and welcome to the sunrise news on this Monday, September 13, 2049. I am Brian Coleman. Our top story today: the dates and itinerary of Her Majesty Queen Angilia's 20th Jubilee. The Jubilee Committee announced the dates and schedule for the week-long events in a press release this morning.

"Her Majesty's Jubilee takes place the week beginning Sunday, November 14 with a church Service of Thanksgiving. That Monday is a day-long program in Central Park, with entertainment and food. On Tuesday, students from across Valdavia will perform various skits, songs, and orations in tribute to Her Majesty. On Wednesday, a parade consisting of marching bands and floats will make is way through Valdavia. The Committee has organized a charity luncheon that will benefit Her Majesty's Tom Greenfield Foundation to take place on Thursday. The traditional Garden Party is scheduled for that Friday, and the official Jubilee Week concludes on Saturday, November 20 with a concert.

"In its press release, the Jubilee Committee members say that they wanted to model Her Majesty's 20th Jubilee after His Majesty King Eric's 20th Jubilee. For those who recall His Majesty's 2012 20th Jubilee, you can see how similar Her Majesty's 20th Jubilee itinerary is to His Majesty's 2012 20th Jubilee. We are already inundated with messages of excitement from Valdavians who look forward to this week-long celebration of Her Majesty."

§§§§

"I'm so excited about your Jubilee, Mommy. Now it's finally time for everyone to show you just how much they love you," Prince Eric stated with a huge smile during breakfast.

"Well, I know better than to protest, especially after saying the same thing to Daddy before and during each of his Jubilee weeks," Angilia giggled and smiled at her father. "I just can't believe that they canceled school around the country for the entire week. That's one detail the members of the School Board never told me, because they knew I would object."

"It does make sense, Angilia, because so many students are involved in the week's activities" Yvonne added. "That's not an issue with your father's Jubilee weeks, since they happen in August when school is not in session."

"I suppose," Angilia relented as everyone went to finish getting ready for the church service that morning.

Eric, Patrick, Angilia, Matthew, Prince Eric, Julianne, Shannon, Billy, and Yvonne walked the short distance to the church, accompanied by Tony and Nathan. Several parishioners greeted them on the route, including Nicole and William, who were asked to join them. The Royal party was greeted at the front entrance of the church by Reverend Olson, who preceded them down the aisle, where they took their seats in the Royal Family's front pews.

"Welcome to Christ Church Valmondois for the National Service of Thanksgiving, during which we will praise God for the compassionate reign of Her Majesty Queen Angilia de Valdavia."

Reverend Olson bowed, and Prince Eric stood and walked to the pulpit. "Psalms Chapter 8. *'(To the chief Musician upon Gittith, A Psalm of David.) O Lord our Lord, how excellent is thy name in all the earth! who hast set thy glory above the heavens. Out of the mouth of babes and sucklings hast thou ordained strength because of thine enemies, that thou mightest still the enemy and the avenger. When I consider thy heavens, the work of thy fingers, the moon and the stars, which thou hast ordained; What is man, that thou hast made him a little lower than the angels, and has crowned him with glory and honour. Thou madest him to have dominion over the works of thy hands; thou hast put all things under his feet: All sheep and oxen, yea, and the beasts of the field; The fowl of the air, and the fish of the sea, and whatsoever passeth through the paths of the seas. O Lord our Lord, how excellent is thy name in all the earth!"* Prince Eric bowed his head in prayer, thanking God for his astounding mother. As soon as Prince Eric returned to his seat in the pew, Patrick squeezed Angilia's hand, stood, and walked to the altar.

The church pianist simultaneously took his seat at the piano, and the choir stood. Patrick sang the most passionate version of the hymn "How Great Thou Art," a hymn he chose because it so closely echoed the Psalm of David which Prince Eric had read. Everyone knew Angilia's affinity for David, and Prince Eric had intentionally selected her favorite Psalm by David to read at the National Service of Thanksgiving.

Reverend Olson nodded in thanks to Patrick, and then spoke his sermon. "Twenty years ago, we rejoiced when Princess Consort Angilia was proclaimed Queen Angilia de Valdavia by her father, King Eric de Valdavia. His Majesty shared with us that day that the inspiration for proclaiming his daughter as his co-monarch came from King David himself. From the time of Her Majesty's 2012 Father's Day sermon, many people have recognized the similarities between King David and King Eric, as well as between King Solomon and Queen Angilia.

"David and Solomon are known for their wisdom, physical beauty, and obedience to God. So, too, are Eric and Angilia. Already, Their Majesties' benevolence, godliness, wisdom, and of course their physical beauty are legendary. Valdavia's King and Queen in many ways belong to the world.

"Her Majesty, in particular, is a woman at the forefront of God's Army, a woman whose every thought, deed, and decision are guided by prayer and faith. Her tireless charity work extends far beyond the borders of Valdavia, impacting people in nearly every country. Queen Angilia understands that a true leader helps not only the citizens of her own country, but the citizens of the world. I dare say she would be the first to tell us that she learned her benevolent style of leadership from her father.

"We also know that Her Majesty imparted that lesson to her son, Prince Eric de Valdavia, our next King. The legacy of the DeBruce Martineau dynasty is one of faith, courage, and love. We see those traits daily in the lives of Her Majesty Queen Angilia de Valdavia, her father King Eric de Valdavia, and her son Prince Eric de Valdavia. Our descendants will benefit from this legacy for generations to come."

Reverend Olson stepped aside while the choir sang another Psalm of David, "The Lord's Prayer." When they finished, Reverend Olson returned to the pulpit. "Let us pray," he instructed the congregation, who stood with bowed heads. "Dear God, Thank you for the life of Her Majesty Queen Angilia. We know how blessed we are by Her Majesty, by her compassion and devotion. We pray for Queen Angilia's health, safekeeping, and well-being, and that you grant us her queenship for many years to come. In your holy name, Amen"

The congregation echoed Reverend Olson's Amen, and then the traditional receiving line formed near the pulpit. Not only did everyone in attendance offer their thanks and love to Angilia, they wished King Eric an early happy birthday. Eric's 95th birthday was just three days away, and Angilia typically beamed with joy at the love and appreciation people showed to her beloved father. Quite a few members of the congregation recalled Eric's 75th birthday, when he had proclaimed his daughter Queen Angilia.

When the congregation departed, Reverend Olson presented Angilia with the tribute book. She smiled, and said, "I remember writing the first message in Daddy's tribute book." Reverend Olson winked and asked her who she thought had written the first message in her tribute book. Angilia smiled up at her father and kissed his cheek gently. "I know," she whispered.

Angilia hugged her father while she cried when she read what he had written: *My Beautiful Daughter Angilia, you are the most amazing, awe-inspiring Queen, as I always knew you would be. I am so honored and blessed to work with you and to see you in action. I am far more honored and blessed to be your father. I love you.*

$$\S\S\S\S$$

Nathan drove the Royal party to Central Park at 10:00 on Monday morning, where people from across Valdavia were gathered already. They wanted to thank Queen Angilia for her lifetime of service, especially her 20 years as co-monarch. As soon as the Royal Family began walking through the park, people stopped them to greet them and to thank Queen Angilia. Prince Eric noticed how she beamed when people praised King Eric, as she always did, and he knew how she felt. He felt the same way about his mother.

The Royal Family, with Julianne, Billy, Shannon, Yvonne, Nathan, and Tony, slowly walked through the park, stopped frequently by people who requested pictures, autographs, or prayer requests from Angilia. Every time she prayed for people, they kissed her hands in gratitude. One young boy approached Angilia and asked her to pray, and his request stabbed everyone's heart.

"Queen Angilia, I need you to pray for my dad. He has a brain tumor, and the doctors say there's not much they can do. They told us he will die, and we don't want him to die. He's scared to die, I know he is, even though he never says anything. He doesn't want us to be scared. But I am. I see his fear in his eyes. I never talk to my parents about it, because I don't want to upset them. Please pray for my dad."

"Of course I will. What's your father's name?"

"Randy Meadows. I have the same name. I'm named after him."

Angilia put a hand on Randy's cheek, and held his hand with the other. "Dear God, Please lift Randy Meadows in your embrace. Please erase his fear, and let him feel your loving warmth surround him. If it is in your will, please release Randy from cancer. Whatever your will, please help Randy and his family find comfort in your love and the truth of eternal life. In your name we pray. Amen."

Randy was crying, and he looked up at Angilia. "Will my dad die?"

"Oh, Randy, I don't know. Only God knows. I will pray for you and your father every day, I promise." Angilia hugged him, kissed his cheek, and wiped his tears.

"Thank you, Queen Angilia. I just don't want him to die yet. I know everyone dies, but I don't want him to yet. He's still too young."

"I know, Randy. Pray. God hears our prayers. Believe me."

Randy nodded and walked away in tears. Angilia looked at Matthew with tears in her eyes, and hugged him. "It doesn't seem fair, does it?"

"It never does, darling. It's never easy, even for people of faith," Matthew said.

"I know God does everything for a reason, but I admit that sometimes it's very hard to see a reason for something like this. A young husband and father should never suffer like this," Angilia said against Matthew's shoulder.

Angilia did not see her Uncle Patrick manifest nearby and smile. Her compassion for people was so powerful, and he knew that God had heard her prayer. He did not know how God would answer, but Patrick knew that whatever the outcome, young Randy and his father would be all right.

Suddenly, Angilia felt a hand on her arm and heard a woman say, "Mr. Meadows will be fine. You will heal him."

Angilia looked at the woman, ready to protest, when she recognized the woman. "Elizabeth?"

The young woman nodded her head and smiled. "Yes. I know that you cause miracles. Toto was one of them. You healed him. I am eternally grateful to you, Queen Angilia."

"God healed Toto, Elizabeth. I'm so grateful my prayer was answered."

"It was. Toto was healthy for the rest of his life. He died at 19 years old. He lived a happy, long life with me. Thank you,"

Elizabeth said, and hugged Angilia. Elizabeth smiled at her former classmate, Prince Eric, and said, "Your mother is a saint."

People nearby applauded, which embarrassed Angilia. Matthew stood with his arm around her shoulders and said, "Thank you. My wife is quite a woman, I agree." The Royal party managed to finally walk through the park again, stopping at a bandstand to listen to one of the high school bands.

After an hour, they moved on, circulating among the people and enjoying the sights and sounds. Finally, it was midday, so Matthew steered them to a picnic table for lunch. He, Prince Eric, Billy, Nathan, and Tony got lunch for everyone. As Billy placed the drinks before each person, Angilia smiled up at him. "You did this for us 37 years ago at Daddy's 20th Jubilee, Billy. You got our lunch for us."

"I remember. Now it's Princess darling's 20th Jubilee," Billy smiled at her. Everyone smiled, as well, knowing Billy's now-legendary fondness for Angilia. His loyalty to Eric and Angilia, and their family, was widely known, as was evidenced in his face. He looked at them with such love and respect.

After lunch, the Royal party continued strolling through the park. People constantly stopped them to congratulate Angilia and to thank her and Eric for their service. All of them were asked to pose for pictures and to sign autographs, which they happily did. After three hours of walking and mingling with people, they decided to stop at another bandstand and enjoy the performance. This time, a young man sang many of Angilia's songs, which delighted her family and friends.

Finally, it was late afternoon, and a member of the Jubilee Committee approached the Royal party with a request. "Excuse me, Your Majesties and Your Royal Highnesses. We would like you to join us for a special announcement and presentation." None of them had any idea what was planned, but they followed Mrs. Joyner, only to be surprised when she led them to a stage near King Eric's statue.

They were more stunned when Mr. Gibson, another Jubilee Committee member, stepped to the podium. "Thirty-seven years ago, on the second day of His Majesty's 20th Jubilee, the foundation stone and sketch of King Eric's statue were unveiled. For nearly four decades, King Eric's statue has stood as a tribute to our King. For all those years, it has stood here alone.

"How appropriate that this changes today, on the second day of his daughter Queen Angilia's 20th Jubilee. The Jubilee Committee long ago planned the statue of Queen Angilia which we are delighted and honored to reveal today. Her Majesty's statue was designed and sculpted by Charles Jackson Schama, who joins us today for the statue's unveiling. Mr. Schama," Mr. Gibson introduced the sculptor.

"Thank you for inviting me to Her Majesty's Jubilee. When the Committee contacted me to sculpt the statue of Queen Angilia, I was astonished to say the least. I immediately accepted, instantly knowing the inspiration that would guide my work. Over the past few years, I was a frequent visitor to the Museé National de Valdavia. There, I studied and stared at one painting of Her Majesty, the one painting which I feel captures the truth and beauty of Queen Angilia. My desire was to translate that image into a three-dimensional sculpture made from the purest white marble. I would like to think that the statue will stand alongside the statue of King Eric for centuries, a visual reminder of the grace, strength, and beauty that is Her Majesty Queen Angilia."

Without further ado, Mr. Schama joined the Jubilee Committee members to release a large black cloth that encircled both statues. The cloth fell to the ground, at which point there was a huge collective gasp, followed by screams, cheers, and applause. The statue depicted Angilia as Matthew had painted her years earlier, in her flowing white gown and with large angel wings. She looked upward, at her father's statue, her left hand outstretched toward him, her long hair billowing around her.

Matthew stared at the statue, amazed and delighted that his painting had inspired Mr. Schama's sculpture. Prince Eric smiled in wonder as Julianne clutched his arm. Billy, Shannon, and Yvonne smiled, too, knowing how true Mr. Schama's depiction of Angilia was. Patrick radiated joy and happiness, and put one arm around Eric's shoulders.

With tears trickling from his eyes, Eric smiled and said, "She looks just as you appeared that first day 72 years ago."

"Yes, she does," Patrick softly said.

§§§§

The Royal Family and friends ate an early lunch on Tuesday so that they could arrive at Gateway Arena in time for the afternoon Children's Tribute to Queen Angilia. When they entered the Royal Box, the family received a standing ovation. Angilia, Eric, Matthew, and Prince Eric waved at everyone in gratitude. The applause finally ended after Mrs. Joyner came on stage for the welcome and introduction.

"Your Majesties, Your Royal Highnesses, members of the Royal household, and guests, we are honored and delighted to welcome you today for a very special program. Students from across Valdavia have come to honor Queen Angilia on the occasion of her 20th Jubilee. Throughout the afternoon, the students will voice their appreciation and admiration in a variety of performances that are guaranteed to delight and charm you. Without further introductions, we began the afternoon's entertainment."

The stage curtain rose, revealing a group of students of various ages and grades. They opened the show by performing Angilia's version of Ecclesiastes 3, which she had put to music years earlier. The words reflected Angilia's overriding philosophy of life: that everything happens for a reason when it is supposed to happen. Angilia knew that even when God did not cause events, he still intervened so that his will was done. She, her father, and her son were proof of that.

When the group finished, a second-grade girl walked on stage holding a microphone. The orchestra played the familiar notes of a song from Angilia's very first album, written and recorded when she was six years old. Angilia smiled and dabbed tears from her eyes as she watched and listened to the little girl. When she finished, the little girl curtsied to Angilia, thoroughly charming the audience.

Other similar performances delighted everyone as students paid homage to Angilia the performer at different ages throughout her career. One duo in particular thrilled Angilia. A middle school girl and a high school boy portrayed Angilia and Tom Greenfield, and performed two of their duets. Eric smiled and gently squeezed his daughter's hand, understanding how appreciative she was that Tom was included in her 20th Jubilee.

The climax of the tribute was a reenactment of Angilia's coronation. A high school girl, dressed in a long white gown, robe, and crown, portrayed Angilia, while one of the high school boys wore a white uniform and portrayed Eric. Another high school student portrayed Reverend Hutchins, and the three of them replicated Angilia's oath. Angilia and Eric smiled at one another and held hands, recalling that day in vivid detail as they watched the performance. "I love you, Daddy," Angilia softly said while the audience applauded.

A choir of students from every Valdavian school took the stage next. Appropriately, they sang the Valdavian national anthem, which had been sung at Angilia's coronation 20 years earlier. While most people in the audience expected that to be the conclusion, they quickly realized it was not. One very special performance remained, chosen as the finale for a reason.

A high school girl quietly walked to the center of the stage, held a microphone, and looked up at Angilia and Eric. A lone guitar sounded the opening chords of the most emotional song Angilia had ever written and recorded. Everyone in the audience looked up at Angilia and Eric as the teenager sang "The Gift of You," the song Angilia had written and recorded for her father the day before she had risked her life for him in 2012. How fitting that the final performance reflected the love and respect Angilia felt for her father.

§§§§

16 November 2049

Dear God, Randy Meadows is heavy on my heart. I know that everyone dies, and that those who believe in you have the promise of eternal life. I believe that you always know best and that you do what is best for each of us. Mr. Matthews, though, is a young husband and father, and I know in my heart that you, God, did not cause his brain cancer. I also know that you can help him and his family. If it is not your will to heal Mr. Meadows, I accept that, no matter how heartbreaking the situation.

God, I do know that you are the only one who has the power to heal Mr. Meadows. My prayer, as you know, is that you will heal Mr. Meadows so that he can not only support and raise his family, but so that he can build his nonprofit organization that works to help families who have lost a loved one. Tomorrow morning I will contact Mr. Meadows and offer my support and patronage to his Star of Hope organization. I know now that you brought Randy Meadows into my life for this purpose, and I vow to do all I can for Star of Hope. With my love and hope, Amen.

§§§§

Wednesday morning, Angilia awoke early and went to her father's suite door when she heard him in his sitting room. Eric looked at her with a smile and held his arms open for a hug. Angilia walked to him and held him close for several moments, savoring the very familiar scent of his cologne and the soothing feel of his warmth. She stood on the toes of her left foot, kissed his cheek, and said, "Happy birthday, my magnificent father."

"Oh, my beautiful daughter Angilia, how I love you so."

"I love you heart and soul, more than life, Daddy. I have since that first moment I saw you."

"And I you," Eric softly replied, tears shining in his turquoise eyes.

Angilia dabbed the tears from her own turquoise eyes and smiled up at her father. She handed him a card and a wrapped gift, and tenderly said, "Happy birthday, Daddy."

Eric lifted the lid from the gift to find a unique photo album of family portraits. On each page, Angilia had made watercolor pencil portraits of DeBruce Martineau family members. Although the family tree was far too immense to include every member, Angilia did represent the family's heritage dating back to the first verifiable ancestor she had traced in her research. The portraits ranged from biblical times to the present, ending with Prince Eric's portrait.

"Angilia, darling, this is stunning and amazing. There must be 200 portraits in this album. How you found the time to complete this with your busy schedule, I will never know. This is too much for me. This represents history, and belongs in a museum. Thank you, Angilia. This is exquisite. I will treasure this forever."

"Thank you, Daddy, but nothing I could give you is too much for you."

§§§§§

A few hours later, Angilia went to her office and called the Meadows' home. She explained the reason for her call to a very surprised Mrs. Meadows. When Angilia asked if she could meet with Mr. Meadows about Star of Hope, Mrs. Meadows swallowed her stunned stutter and said that Her Majesty was more than welcome to come. Angilia thanked her, promised to be there within the hour, and told her family she would return before lunch.

Mrs. Meadows greeted Angilia with a curtsy, and explained that her husband was resting in his chair in the family room. "Randy told us that he met you in the park on Monday. He also told me privately that you prayed for his father. I can't tell you what that means to me, Your Majesty. Thank you."

"Prayer is the least I can do. I hope I can do something more tangible," Angilia said just as they entered the family room. Mrs. Meadows introduced her husband to Angilia, and offered her the chair next to Mr. Meadows'.

"I'm so pleased to meet you, Mr. Meadows," Angilia said as she sat and shook Mr. Meadows' hand. She felt him shiver, and she wondered if he felt ill. Angilia said a silent prayer before she continued. "Forgive me for intruding, but when I learned of your Star of Hope nonprofit organization, I knew I wanted to somehow become involved. That's why I'm here."

"You want to help?" Mr. Meadows asked in a halting, flabbergasted voice. He looked at Angilia, then at his wife, and back at Angilia.

"Yes, I do. I want to do whatever I humanly can. It doesn't have to be public or grand at all. I just want to help," Angilia stated.

The suddenness and unexpectedness of Angilia's offer left Mr. Meadows speechless. As he struggled to find words, Angilia continued. "I can do anything that could help at all, from contacting people to donating money. Just let me know what Star of Hope needs, and I will do everything in my power to help."

"Star of Hope is only in its first year, and we were just beginning to make strides when I was diagnosed with cancer. There are a few counselors who volunteer their time to help families who are grieving, but the fundraising and outreach programs pretty much came to a halt with my illness. Just as we started spreading the word about Star of Hope, this happened. Despite my intentions and desires, Star of Hope has taken a back seat to the cancer."

"Then we need to put Star of Hope back out there on the radar. We need to make people aware of the organization's mission and purpose. If we do that, people will donate their services and money to help others. We have to get the message out there and keep it out there, so that no one forgets. This is too important for people to ignore or to forget," Angilia confidently stated.

"Advertising like that costs money, lots of money," Mr. Meadows replied. "How do we sustain public interest without the funds to do so?"

"That's what a patronage can accomplish. Have you considered asking someone to become the patron?"

"I did ask some of the local business leaders when I first launched Star of Hope, but none of them were interested," Mr. Meadows explained. "I just sort of dropped the idea after that."

"If you don't mind, I would like to be your patron, that is if you don't have any objections," Angilia offered.

"Objections? How could I have any objections?" Mr. Meadows asked in utter stupefaction. "Are you sure, Your Majesty?"

"Of course I'm sure. I wouldn't have offered if I did not want to do this."

"Thank you, Your Majesty. I don't know what to say."

"You don't have to say anything, Mr. Meadows. Thank you for allowing me to help. In fact, we can have our first event tomorrow," Angilia said.

"Tomorrow? But it's your Jubilee week," Mrs. Meadows said.

"I know. Tomorrow's event is a charity luncheon to benefit the Tom Greenfield Foundation. There is no reason the proceeds cannot be split evenly between the Tom Greenfield Foundation and Star of Hope. The plan is for me to issue a statement today reminding people of the purpose and cause of the charity luncheon. This is the perfect opportunity to tell people about Star of Hope, and to raise necessary funds at the same time," Angilia stated matter-of-factly.

"You'd do this for Star of Hope? You just met me," Mr. Meadows said.

"That doesn't matter. I want to do this, and there is no better time than tomorrow. In fact, if you and your wife feel up to attending, I would like to invite you to the charity luncheon. It will enable people to meet the man behind Star of Hope and hear from you directly. However, if you cannot attend, send me a written statement that I can read on your behalf."

"I'm overwhelmed. I don't know what to say, except thank you. We will be there tomorrow, I promise, even if I can't stay the whole time," Mr. Meadows assured Angilia.

"Thank you so much, Mr. Meadows. I appreciate your help more than you know. In fact, we can pick you both up tomorrow on our way to the charity luncheon. You can attend as our guests."

Stunned at the rapid turn of events, Mr. and Mrs. Meadows tearfully and gratefully accepted Angilia's invitation. "Excellent. We will be here around 10: 30 tomorrow morning."

§§§§

I am deeply honored that tomorrow's Jubilee event honors two very special organizations, both of which mean a great deal to me. The Jubilee Committee thoughtfully scheduled the charity luncheon for the afternoon of Thursday, November 18, 2049. One hundred percent of the proceeds raised will be split evenly between the Tom Greenfield Foundation and Star of Hope.

The Tom Greenfield Foundation provides musical instruments and lessons at no cost to hospitals, schools, and other similar organizations. Created to honor the legendary Tom Greenfield, the Foundation allows children the joy, freedom, and creativity that come with musical expression.

Star of Hope is a relatively new nonprofit organization founded by Mr. Randy Meadows. The mission and purpose of Star of Hope stem from compassion and empathy, providing support and counseling free of charge to families who are struggling with the grieving process. Families are at their most vulnerable, emotionally and often financially, after the deaths of loved ones, and Star of Hope provides necessary assistance and understanding at this most difficult time.

I am so humbled and appreciative that these two worthy causes are the recipients of the kindness and generosity of my fellow Valdavians. Thank you for being part of the work the Tom Greenfield Foundation and Star of Hope do on a daily basis.

§§§§

At 3:00 that afternoon, the Royal party arrived on Main Street for the Jubilee Parade. Bleachers had been set up along Main Street so that people could watch the Parade in comfort. A front row bleacher had been reserved for the Royal party, and Angilia linked arms with her father as they made their way to their seats. Matthew, Prince Eric, and Julianne closely followed them, and in turn were followed by Shannon, Billy, Yvonne, Nathan, and Tony.

Queen Angilia and King Eric received a boisterous standing ovation. Angilia beamed up at her father, typically elated and delighted at the reception he always received. Eric, though, smiled down at his daughter, knowing that people were there to celebrate her 20th Jubilee. Her love for her father, coupled with her humility, blinded her to the immense love and admiration people felt for her. It always had.

Angilia, Eric, Matthew, and Prince Eric—accompanied by Nathan and Tony—decided to do an impromptu walkabout. Angilia and Matthew walked across the street, while King Eric and Prince Eric spoke with people on the their side. Angilia suddenly noticed young Randy Meadows sitting alone, and asked him to join her family. She held his hand as they continued the walkabout, and Billy smiled, remembering the special relationship Angilia had forged with him when he was a child.

Finally, cheers from several blocks away indicated that the Parade was near, so the Royal Family and Randy took their seats on the bleacher. Leading the Parade was a marching band which played the Valdavian National Anthem. Floats depicting Angilia's life followed, beginning with her birth. That float illustrated Eric holding newborn Angilia as he left the hospital the day after her birth.

The second float recreated Angilia's first concert when she was six years old. The life-size likeness of Angilia wore a replica of the white floral dress she had donated years earlier to the Country Music Hall of Fame and Museum. As usual, a guitar was strapped across her shoulders, and people were struck by how very young and small she was when they saw that the guitar was almost larger than she was. To further prove that point, a life-size likeness of Tom Greenfield stood next to Angilia.

Another float presented Angilia's graduation from the University of Oxford when she was 11 years old. Shown in her regalia and holding her DPhil, Angilia appeared so mature despite her young age. This theme continued for the next several floats, including one which portrayed her as a 13-year-old literature professor and one which represented her first concert at Carnegie Hall when she was 14.

One of the most beautiful floats recreated Angilia's and Matthew's wedding day portrait. Angilia's one-of-a-kind wedding gown was replicated, as was Matthew's black tuxedo. No one could help but notice that the likeness of Matthew regarded Angilia with his trademark look of love, just as the real Matthew looked at his real Angilia at that moment. Prince Eric and Julianne smiled and felt tears in their eyes at the sight.

"Oh, it's Uncle Patrick," Angilia enthused when she saw a float that depicted one of Angilia's and Patrick's concerts. "I'm so glad he's part of this. Uncle Patrick is such an important part of our lives." Angilia and Eric smiled as they felt Patrick manifest between them and put his arms around their shoulders. Angilia leaned over and kissed his cheek and hugged him as people cheered at the sight of him. Patrick kissed her and Eric, and then waved to everyone.

People screamed Prince Eric's name when a float showing him as a newborn in his mother's arms appeared. Matthew, Angilia, and newborn Eric were represented as they stood outside the hospital the day they took baby Eric home. Matthew hugged his son and wife, tears once more shining in his eyes. Julianne also hugged Prince Eric, her wide smile reflecting her happiness. Not only was today King Eric's 95th birthday, but Prince Eric's 28th birthday, and that fact was cheered by everyone gathered for the Parade.

Another milestone captured in a float that elicited cheers and applause was a depiction of Queen Angilia's coronation. She and her father were shown as they appeared in their regalia sitting on their thrones. Their official portrait was recreated to stunning effect in the float that provided the perfect finale to the Parade. After the floats disappeared from view, the Parade ended.

The audience, however, spontaneously erupted in shouts of "God bless Queen Angilia!" After several minutes, Patrick leaned close to her ear and said, "They want you to stand, Angilia." She finally relented, but reached for her father's hand so that he could share the accolades. The King and Queen waved at everyone for more than 15 minutes, before Angilia curtsied her thanks and indicated that the Parade was now officially over. The Royal party returned home after driving Randy Meadows to his home, where he kissed Angilia in gratitude.

§§§§

As Angilia had promised, the Royal party arrived at the Meadows home at 10:30 on Thursday morning. Angilia and Nathan assisted Randy into the Rolls Royce, and Nathan placed Randy's wheelchair in the trunk. When they arrived at the Embassy Ballroom moments later, the Royal party took the elevator to a fifth floor banquet room, where the charity luncheon was held. The Jubilee Committee members and Angilia's band greeted them upon their arrival, and were pleased to meet Mr. and Mrs. Meadows.

The attendees began arriving soon after, and the Royal Family greeted each of them before the charity lunch began. Mr. Reid, a member of the Jubilee Committee, went to the stage to welcome everyone. "I and the members of the Jubilee Committee are so pleased and grateful for your generosity in attending this charity luncheon during Her Majesty Queen Angilia's 20th Jubilee week. Your purchase of a luncheon ticket supports two of Her Majesty's charities, the Tom Greenfield Foundation and Star of Hope. Shortly, Her Majesty and her band will perform while you enjoy the main course and dessert. Afterward, Her Majesty will tell all of us more about the beneficiaries of today's charity luncheon. We know you will enjoy today."

Angilia and her band members had eaten earlier so that they could perform during the meal. For 90 minutes Angilia, David, Neil, Robbie, and Larry entertained everyone with several songs that spanned Angilia's 47-year career. Billy and Yvonne had known Angilia their entire lives, and they thoroughly understood one another's love, awe, and privilege. Knowing Angilia was a gift that that they never took for granted.

Neither did Eric, Matthew, or Prince Eric. They watched Angilia's 20th Jubilee performance with utter reverence and love evident in their eyes and on their faces. Julianne leaned her head on Prince Eric's shoulder and regarded Angilia with a similar love apparent on her face. Those who knew Angilia appreciated how blessed they were by the experience.

Few people present felt as blessed as did Randy Meadows, who applauded louder than most when the concert ended. Angilia smiled at him when she placed her guitar on its stand, and stood at the microphone to address the audience. "Thank you all so very much. These amazing musicians deserve our thanks as well. David Baxter, Neil Stine, Robbie Gilmour, and Larry Malone are not just my band members, but have become friends as well as supporters of one of today's beneficiaries of the charity luncheon.

"One hundred percent of today's ticket sales will be split evenly between two organizations extremely important to me. The first is the Tom Greenfield Foundation, which honors my mentor, the amazing singer and songwriter Tom Greenfield. Founded with the goal of continuing Tom's love of music and his belief that music heals the soul, the Tom Greenfield Foundation donates musical instruments and instruction to schools, hospitals, and other organizations which work with children of all ages.

"I have seen the beauty and truth of Tom's belief every time I visit schools or hospitals or halfway houses not only in Valdavia but around the world. The ability to express themselves musically, freely and without judgment, boosts young peoples' self-confidence, engages creativity, or gives voice to emotions that cannot otherwise be expressed. The power in that is priceless and empowering.

"The second organization benefiting from your generosity today is Star of Hope, my most recent patronage. Founded this year by Mr. Randy Meadows of Valmondois, Star of Hope is a relatively new yet very powerful nonprofit organization. I was instantly drawn to the scope and purpose behind Star of Hope, and I am sure you will be, too. We are so privileged to have Star of Hope's founder with us today," Angilia said as she walked to the Royal party's table and held Randy's arm as he stood next to her.

"I could easily tell you all about Star of Hope, but that would be a disservice. As passionate as I am about Star of Hope's mission, no one can match the passion and emotion of Randy Meadows himself. I am so grateful that Mr. Meadows is with us today so that he can tell you about Star of Hope," Angilia said and handed the microphone to Randy.

Randy cleared his throat of impending tears and grasped Angilia's arm before he dared speak. "I am the one who is privileged to be here. A meeting between my son and Her Majesty on Monday led Queen Angilia to my doorstep. She had learned about Star of Hope, and she came to me with an offer to help. That was on Tuesday. Two days later, I am here at Her Majesty's invitation. As grateful as I am, nothing I do or say will ever express that gratitude.

"Early this year, I sought a way to help families who are struggling with grief. Yes, everyone grieves differently, and so many people remain mired in grief's depths and darkness. I wanted to help them find their way back to the light, to find peace, and to rebuild their lives. While the death of a loved one changes everything forever, we can learn to adapt and to live, to truly live, without the physical presence of the loved one who died.

"My goal in founding Star of Hope is to provide support and counseling services for families who are trying to find their way out of the darkness. Death is not easy for many people to plan for, to deal with, or to accept. My family knows that all too well. Due to my own recent illness, Star of Hope was forced to take an unfortunate backseat. I bemoaned that every day, more than I have ever told anyone, including my wife Marla. I longed so desperately to continue Star of Hope's fundraising and networking, so that we could afford more counselors and outreach programs. I regretted not having the finances, time, or energy Star of Hope so desperately needs.

"By some unexpected miracle, that all changed on Tuesday with Her Majesty's visit. Queen Angilia kindly offered financial and networking support, and suggested I find a patron who could spread Star of Hope's work and message to the public. In fact, Queen Angilia offered to become Star of Hope's Patron, to my complete and utter shock. I could think of no better Patron than Her Majesty Queen Angilia. In two short days my despair was turned to hope, and a huge weight lifted from my shoulders. I know that with Her Majesty's patronage, Star of Hope will shine and thrive in its mission to help grieving families. I sincerely thank Her Majesty Queen Angilia and all of you for your generous donations which will help the work of the Tom Greenfield Foundation and Star of Hope."

§§§§§

By midmorning on Friday, the Jubilee Committee and their volunteers, along with palace staff members, had everything set up and ready for the Garden Party. Local restaurants and florists provided the tables, refreshments, and flower arrangements, leaving the Royal Family and their friends free to greet the visitors and to enjoy the day. Billy smiled as he shared his memories of attending Eric's 20th Jubilee Garden Party in 2012. Julianne and Yvonne smiled also, enjoying the recollections of the little boy who had worshiped Angilia and who now counted her among his closest friends. Julianne understood that feeling well, for she had long admired Angilia, the woman who was now her friend and future mother-in-law. Angilia may be a world-revered icon, but she was so easy to know and to love.

The first guests to arrive knew that very well. Marla Meadows pushed her husband Randy's wheelchair across the courtyard and onto the grounds. Young Randy held his father's hand, and bowed to Angilia when she greeted him. "Hello, Randy. I am so very happy that you are here today," she said as she bent to shake his hand. Angilia then leaned over and kissed his father on the cheek, and said, "Mr. Meadows, it's so wonderful to see you. Your speech at the charity luncheon yesterday was amazing. So many people were impressed and touched that they donated another €8000 to the two charities. That could not have happened without your dynamic presence. Thank you."

"It is I who must thank you, Your Majesty. This entire week has been a dream come true, and we're all reeling from the whirlwind. I don't remember much of what I said yesterday, but I meant it when I called what you have done for me and for Star of Hope a miracle. It is. Whatever happens to me, I know that my work will continue through Star of Hope. Knowing that has given me such peace," Randy said as he held Angilia's hands in his.

"You give me far too much credit. Star of Hope is your creation, and you deserve all the credit," Angilia told Mr. Meadows.

"Your Majesty, Randy's right. Without your help and patronage, Star of Hope would have remained stagnant. You are our family's star of hope, our angel," Mrs. Meadows said and hugged Angilia.

"I am honored to do whatever I can to help. Please enjoy yourselves, and I'll catch up with you soon," Angilia promised them.

The Royal Family continued greeting the guests for the next hour, until the palace grounds were filled with hundreds of people. Eric, Angilia, Matthew, and Prince Eric with Julianne mingled with people throughout the afternoon, spending several minutes with each attendee. Everyone, it seemed, wanted to meet with Angilia and tell her how much they loved her and appreciated her work. She was constantly surrounded by fans and well-wishers.

Angilia smiled when she noticed that her father was likewise engulfed in a sea of admirers. He always was. King Eric was, at 95, the world's most beloved and popular leader, as was evidenced by the almost incessant coverage he received. His reputation as a benevolent monarch was by now legendary, as was his status as a suave, dashing man. Age had done little to diminish Eric's famous handsome looks. In fact, his grey hair, turquoise eyes, and smile remained as engaging as ever.

As if on cue, Scott and Darlene appeared at that moment, joining Angilia while she watched her father. "How is it possible?" Darlene suddenly asked.

Angilia turned, hugged her friends, and asked, "How is what possible, Darlene?"

"Your father is still the most gorgeous man I have ever seen," Darlene sighed. Scott hung his head in quiet resolution, realizing that his wife was indeed smitten for life. Darlene noticed, and said, "Well, he is. I can't help it if my King makes my heart skip beats. But I really came to wish my friend a very happy 20th Jubilee." Scott echoed his wife, and both of them hugged Angilia and walked away at the moment she was encircled by another group of well-wishers.

Matthew corralled his wife long enough for them to eat lunch, to which he invited members of the hospital Board of Directors. Angilia squeezed his hand in gratitude when Matthew led them all to the table where the Meadows family sat. For the next two hours, Randy Meadows was able to garner financial and professional assistance for Star of Hope.

After lunch, hospital board member Winston March introduced Randy Meadows to various business leaders and doctors. By the end of the Garden Party, Star of Hope received thousands of euros in donations and several promises of volunteer services. Angilia smiled up at her husband and hugged him close. "I love you, Matthew."

§§§§§

At 2:00 on Saturday afternoon, the Royal party arrived at Gateway Arena for the 20th Jubilee tribute concert. The Jubilee Committee had refused to release the names of the performers, which had generated much speculation. In fact, when they took their seats in the Royal Box, Prince Eric, Julianne, Yvonne, and Billy wondered why the secrecy. "It's probably because Angilia knows the performers, which would spoil any surprise," Matthew offered.

"You're probably right, Dad," Prince Eric said.

"Regardless of who the performers are, I know I will enjoy the concert," Angilia replied.

Daphne Chase appeared center stage as the lights dimmed. "Good afternoon, and welcome to today's tribute concert in honor of Her Majesty Queen Angilia's 20th Jubilee. All of us on the Jubilee Committee have truly enjoyed putting together this week of activities and events to pay esteem to our much-loved Queen Angilia. Thank you all so very much for making Queen Angilia's 20th Jubilee such an amazing success. The 20th Jubilee week culminates with today's concert.

"So many of you have voiced your appreciation to those of us on the Jubilee Committee, for which we are very grateful. Many of you have also asked all of us one question which we refused to answer—the list of performers in today's concert. We have a very good reason for not saying, which everyone will soon understand. Without further comments, the tribute concert begins." Miss Chase left the stage without another word, leaving everyone more befuddled than ever.

The arena lights went dark before the curtain was lifted and the band took their places at their instruments. The lights came back on just as Angilia's band began playing the opening chords of the first song. Her band was the performers? she wondered in surprise. Suddenly the audience exploded in screams and cheers as Patrick manifested on center stage in the spotlight. Angilia was more than pleasantly surprised, and her hands covered her face as tears trickled from her eyes. Eric smiled, tears filling his own eyes, and placed an arm around his daughter.

For nearly three hours, Patrick kept the audience in a frenzied fever. He sang his well-known solo songs, as well as covers of many of his favorite songs from the 1960s and 1970s. The Royal Family thoroughly enjoyed Patrick's surprise, none more so than Angilia. Her radiant smile and beaming eyes exhibited her joy and love.

Patrick glanced at his niece several times, thrilled to see her happiness. "Thank you all so much for joining me today and paying tribute to my exceptional niece, Angilia. The story of how she and I met is well known by now, and I think it's safe to say that you know how much I love her. We have one more song, one written just for Angilia."

Saving Grace

Another day, just a Tuesday,

Ignoring the restlessness deep inside

The whole while I silently pray

To the guardian angel by my side,

Unseen but felt for oh so long

Until I died to truly live in peace

In a place where nothing is wrong,

Blessed by the saving grace of my Angel, my niece.

CHAPTER 13

3 January 2051

With immense happiness, Her Majesty Queen Angilia and His Royal Highness Matthew, Duc de Valmondois announce the betrothal of their beloved son, His Royal Highness Prince Eric, to Miss Julianne Renée LeRoy, daughter of the late Mr. and Mrs. Thaddeus LeRoy.

His Majesty King Eric, Her Majesty Queen Angilia, and His Royal Highness Matthew, Duc de Valmondois are delighted. Their love for His Royal Highness Prince Eric and Miss LeRoy remains unparalleled, and they welcome Miss LeRoy to their family with joy.

§§§§§

People had begun arriving on the mall outside the palace gates before sunrise, hoping to see Queen Angilia. It was her 55th birthday, and people of all ages wanted to wish her well. They never expected the engagement announcement which Billy posted on the palace gate at 9:00 sharp at morning. Billy read the announcement aloud, which elicited stunned screams and cheers from the hundreds of people gathered.

The screams grew earthshattering when Eric, Angilia, Matthew, Prince Eric, and Julianne stepped onto the courtyard at 9:30. The guards unlocked the gate, and the Royal Family walked onto the mall to greet everyone. For one hour, they happily posed for pictures, signed autographs, and accepted gifts. Julianne smiled incessantly at the love shown to Prince Eric's family. She understood the love and respect everyone had for them, because she, too, had once admired them from afar. Now she was on the verge of becoming a member of that family, and she delighted in the congratulations she and Eric received that day.

At 10:30, the Royal Family thanked everyone and returned to the palace. Prince Eric and Julianne freshened before they had to go to the sitting room for their first joint television interview. Angilia knocked on her son's door, and he opened the door to her with a huge smile. She smiled up at him and placed a hand upon his cheek. Eric was quite tall, and Angilia recalled meeting him in the Unborn Children Sphere before they were born. She had looked up at him there, this man who was then her unborn son.

She had been drawn to him instantly. She had loved him instantly. God had made them mother and son. Their lives fulfilled God's plans for them, that Angilia knew. "I love you, Eric. I've loved you for so very long. I love you for all eternity, my son."

"Oh, Mommy. I love you," Eric replied and held her close to him for several moments. "I love you."

§§§§

"Good morning, and welcome to a very special program. I am Brian Coleman, and I am honored to bring you this historic interview from the Palais Royale de Valdavia on this January 3, 2051. The engagement of His Royal Highness Prince Eric and Miss Julianne LeRoy was announced earlier this morning, and they join us for their first joint interview. Congratulations Your Royal Highness and Miss LeRoy."

"Thank you, Brian," Prince Eric said with a smile.

"Thank you," Julianne echoed.

"Today is a very special day for several reasons. Not only is today Her Majesty's birthday, but the anniversary of your parents' engagement."

"Yes, it is. My parents announced their engagement 35 years ago today on my mother's 20th birthday. Julianne and I wanted to honor that anniversary, and we chose today to announce our engagement for that reason," Prince Eric stated with a smile.

"Yes, we did. There really was no other date we wanted for our engagement announcement," Julianne added.

"Your Royal Highness and Miss LeRoy, are there any details of the engagement that you can share with us?"

"Yes, Brian. Julianne and I had known we would marry when the time was right. On Christmas Day, we both felt that it was indeed our time. Two years ago, I had a jeweler make Julianne's engagement ring, which I kept locked in my grandfather's safe. I removed the ring that day, and I proposed to Julianne in the sitting room, surrounded by family and friends. She didn't know when I would propose, but because we had talked about it so often, the proposal was not unexpected," Prince Eric explained.

"Instead of choosing an heirloom ring from the Royal collection, you had Miss LeRoy's engagement ring custom designed. May I ask the significance of the design?" Brian asked.

Prince Eric and Julianne looked at one another and smiled. "I didn't choose an heirloom ring, but I was inspired by one. When my father proposed to my mother on Christmas Day 2015, there was only one engagement ring he wanted to give her—her mother's engagement ring. My grandfather designed that ring especially for my grandmother, with her emerald birthstone as the central gem and his citrine birthstone encircling it.

"I wanted Julianne's engagement ring to reflect the eternal, true love of my grandparents and my parents. I requested a similar ring for Julianne. There is only one difference between my mother's engagement ring and Julianne's engagement ring, the central stone. Julianne's diamond birthstone is the central gem, and is surrounded by my citrine birthstone," Prince Eric described the ring.

Prince Eric held Julianne's left hand, and lifted it so that everyone could see her engagement ring. "I've always thought that Her Majesty and The Duc had the most romantic, inspirational love story. I've always adored how The Duc honored Her Majesty's parents by giving her her mother's engagement ring. I also love how Prince Eric and I are part of this incredible love story that began with his grandparents," Julianne said with tears in her eyes and an abundance of emotions in her voice.

"That is so romantic, Your Royal Highness and Miss LeRoy. Miss LeRoy's engagement ring is not only beautiful, but symbolizes that bridge between past, present, and future that Her Majesty wrote about in her memoir so eloquently," Brian stated.

"Thank you, Brian. My family are the most important people in the world to me," Prince Eric said.

"Your family is well known for its love and support, Your Royal Highness. Miss LeRoy, you moved to Valmondois after you and His Royal Highness graduated from the Université de Poitiers. What has that transition been like for you? The Duc de Valmondois was the last commoner to marry into the Royal Family. What is it like from your perspective as you prepare to become a member of the Royal Family?"

"I had met Eric's grandfather and parents before we graduated, and I loved them instantly. They made me feel so at ease and comfortable. Moving to Valmondois was an easy decision, because Eric and I knew we would marry. His family welcomed me with open arms, and his friends became my friends. I have truly enjoyed everything about living here. People have made me feel so welcome here, and I have enjoyed getting to know our neighbors.

"As in awe of Eric's family as I was before I first met them, they really have shown me such love and support, and made me feel a part of their family already. I feel only love, respect, and gratitude to share my life with them," Julianne revealed. People noticed that Prince Eric smiled at her and squeezed her hand at that moment.

"We all love Julianne, and we look forward to sharing life with her," Prince Eric smiled.

"Those are beautiful sentiments, Miss LeRoy and Your Royal Highness. May I ask you both if you have selected a wedding date?" Brian asked the question everyone wanted answered.

Once more, Prince Eric and Julianne smiled at one another. "Yes, we have, Brian. June 26, 2051," Prince Eric stated.

Brian had not known the date in advance. No one had. "You and Miss LeRoy chose the same date that your parents and your grandparents married, Your Royal Highness."

"We did, Brian. Julianne and I will begin our eternal partnership on my parents' 35th wedding anniversary and my grandparents' 60th wedding anniversary," Prince Eric said with tears shining in his turquoise eyes.

§§§§

21 May 2051

Happy Birthday Mommy! I love you!

You were born 100 years ago today. God predestined your marriage to Daddy. Your love story remains my favorite, my inspiration. That love gave life to me, which in turn gave life to Eric. We would not exist without you. We know that. We love you. Daddy loves you eternally. His devotion to you touches my soul and fills me with warmth.

When my life on earth ends, and God calls me to Heaven, I will finally get to hug you and tell you how much I love you. You, Daddy, and I will reunite in Heaven, to never part again. How glorious that will be, my beloved Mommy.

§§§§

Angilia had just finished writing her diary entry early that morning, when she heard her father across the hall. She stood from her desk and walked to his door, where he turned to see her standing there smiling at him. Eric smiled in return, and said, "Good morning, my beautiful daughter Angilia."

"Good morning, Daddy." Angilia went to him, and hugged him close to her. "What a glorious, beautiful day."

"Yes, it is, darling," Eric said and kissed the top of her head. "My precious Marisol was born 100 years ago today. I fell asleep watching us in Heaven," Eric said and pulled the pendant from under his shirt. "What an utterly beautiful, breathtaking gift it is to see us together as we will be for all eternity."

"Oh, Daddy, it truly is," Angilia said as she leaned her head against her father and looked into Michael's pendant with him. "I do love all of you in my life here so very much, but I also look forward to that moment when I can actually hug Mommy. So many times, I have wanted to do that. There were times, especially when I could not tell you everything, that I longed for Mommy. I wanted, I needed, her to hold me," Angilia said as she began to cry.

Eric felt his heart break as he held Angilia close to him. He walked to the sofa with her, and cradled her against his chest as she cried. "Oh, my baby, I am so sorry."

Angilia shook her head, and said, "No, Daddy. No. You don't have anything for which to apologize. I do. I should never have said all of that. I didn't mean to hurt you, and I'm sorry I did."

"Oh, Angel, you didn't hurt me. You couldn't. It's normal for a girl to want her mother. Don't ever be sorry for that."

"I won't, I promise. I love you, Daddy." Angilia kissed his cheek, just as she felt a very familiar warmth near her. "I love you, too, Uncle Patrick."

"I love you, Little One," Patrick said and kissed her cheek. "I love you, Eric. Hey, um, Michael sent me out of the Angels Choir to regular Heaven to get something for both of you. Here," Patrick said and handed an envelope to Eric.

Angilia felt her father tremble when he took the envelope, and she looked at him in concern. Eric stared at the envelope. His and Angilia's names were written in a very familiar script, and Eric looked at Patrick. "Is this really from her?" he very softly asked.

Patrick nodded and put his arm around Angilia's shoulders. "Yeah."

Angilia looked at the envelope and gasped. "It's from Mommy." She looked at her father with such love in her eyes. Eric gently removed a sheet of parchment from the envelope, and held it so that both he and Angilia could read it together. Patrick smiled as he watched them, and said a silent prayer of thanksgiving for this miraculous gift for his brother and his niece just when they most needed it.

My Dearest Eric and Angilia:

I love you! I always have, and I always will.

Eric, my love, I have watched you from Heaven since my death. You fill my soul with such glorious peace. You are such an amazing man, my Eric. The world is so blessed by you. Our family is so blessed by you. You are the most godly king, husband, father, and grandfather. You are the epitome of what it means to be a man according to God.

Eric, I see that you have never removed your wedding ring since I slipped it on your finger. You always told me that you love me, and only me, for eternity. You have shown that every day. You have lived that every day. When you join me in Heaven, whenever that will be, we will live that for eternity.

Angilia, our beautiful daughter, how I love you. You are a miracle. You are the reason I was born. You are my life. What a magnificent woman you are! I have watched you since your birth, and I have been so amazed and awed by you, my daughter. God has destined you for such a wondrous life as one of his Supreme Angels. Words cannot tell you how much you fill my soul with joy. Angilia, you are such an amazing daughter, wife, mother, and queen. Your son Eric is a testament to you and to your father.

Oh my beloved Eric and Angilia, know that I do not regret one second of my life. I could never regret anything, because of you both. I lived my life for both of you and because of both of you. I am with you and I watch you, every moment, with all of my eternal love surrounding you. I love you both. I will be here waiting for you both. Until then—

Eternal Love,

Marisol

§§§§

"Welcome to our very special live broadcast on this Monday, June 26, 2051. We are delighted to bring you exclusive coverage of the Royal Wedding. I am Brian Coleman, and I am thrilled to join

273

you on this historic day. His Royal Highness Prince Eric and Miss Julianne LeRoy become husband and wife today.

"It has been 35 years since the last Royal wedding. In fact, it was 35 years ago today that Prince Eric's parents Queen Angilia, then the Princess Consort Angilia, and Dr. Matthew Taylor married in the most-watched Royal wedding thus far. That could change today as Angilia's and Matthew's popular son weds his college sweetheart, Miss LeRoy.

"Eric and Julianne became friends while they were both students at the Université de Poitiers in Paris, France. Julianne was born and raised in Paris, the only child of Thaddeus and Juliet LeRoy. Unfortunately, Mr. LeRoy passed away in 2028, when his daughter was 12. Mrs. LeRoy passed away four years ago. Julianne, therefore, has chosen not to be escorted up the aisle or given away during the wedding ceremony today. She will ride to the church with her maid of honor, and return to the Palais Royale de Valdavia alongside her husband Prince Eric in a carriage.

"Prince Eric and Julianne have selected two of their best friends to serve as best man and maid of honor, Leigh Graham and Yvonne Alexander. They have chosen not to have a traditional wedding party, but to be supported only by their two closest friends. Leigh Graham met Prince Eric at the Université de Poitiers, as well, and they have remained friends. Yvonne Alexander is the daughter of Her Majesty's close friends, Nicole and William Alexander, and was born just seven months after Prince Eric was born. As you probably know, Yvonne is the Royal Family's Press Secretary.

"The wedding of Prince Eric and Julianne is steeped in tradition and regality, but at the same time, it is a wedding that by all accounts will connect the past, present, and future seamlessly. This is the perfect time to do so, as we are currently halfway through the 21st century. The nation of Valdavia is in its 702nd year, and today we witness the marriage ceremony of our 21st monarch, the future King Eric II de Valdavia."

§§§§

Angilia awoke early that morning, and she heard her son return to his suite. She gently tapped on his door, and heard him say to come in. Prince Eric stood on his balcony, sipping some water, and he turned and smiled at her when she entered. He held his arm out to her, and she joined him on the balcony. "Today is so beautiful and perfect," Angilia sighed.

Prince Eric smiled, kissed the top of his mother's head, and said, "Yes, it is, Mommy. Today is perfect, and my life is perfect. My prayer is that Julianne and I remain as blissful and content for many years to come, just like you and Dad. Happy anniversary, Mommy."

"Thank you, darling. That's my prayer, too, for yours and Julianne's lasting happiness," Angilia softly said.

"Grandfather and Grandmother married 60 years ago today, and I know they love each other so very much. They were together for only four years. That's so unfair. I don't know how Grandfather has lived with the pain and heartbreak for so long. He's been without her for 56 long years. They should have had all of those years together here on earth, not separated by time and space. It isn't fair," Prince Eric said with tears choking his voice.

Angilia turned Prince Eric to face her, and she looked up into his eyes. "I know it seems unfair, Eric. It felt that way to me when I was growing up. There were so many times I longed for my Mommy, for her gentle embrace. I know how much Daddy misses her here with him. But, Eric, there is no pain and heartbreak. There couldn't be, not when Daddy knows for a fact that his wife is waiting for him in Heaven. Yes, 56 years is a long time to live without her here, but they will live together in eternal happiness when Daddy is called to Heaven. That's not painful or sad, Eric. That's gloriously beautiful and happy, and it makes the years without her here bearable and hopeful," Angilia told her son with such intense emotions in her eyes and in her voice.

"I know that's all true, and I believe you, Mommy. Grandfather is such a strong man, far stronger than anyone I know about. I hope to be as strong if he is, but I seriously doubt that I could bear what he has endured for so long. I pray I never have to."

Prince Eric cleared his throat, swallowed his tears, and smiled at his mother. "Enough of that. Today is a day for happiness and love. It's my wedding day, and I want only happy tears today," Prince Eric said and hugged his mother.

§§§§

After lunch, the carriages were prepared and everyone got dressed and ready for the wedding. Yvonne and Shannon helped Julianne in the guest house, as Leigh assisted Prince Eric in his suite. Billy helped Eric, while Matthew and Angilia prepared in their suite. Everyone was remarkably calm, while outside on the mall and the streets of Valmondois thousands of people exhibited anxious nervousness.

The wedding began at 1:00 in Christ Church Valmondois. When Prince Eric had stated that the Royal Family would make the short drive from the palace to the church, he received thousands of requests to reconsider. He and Julianne finally relented, and agreed that the carriage procession would follow the same route through the streets of Valmondois that had been taken on his parents' wedding day and his mother's coronation day. They understood that people wanted to see his family and wish them well. Like his grandfather and his mother, Prince Eric considered the desires of the people they served.

So it was that Eric, Angilia, and Matthew entered the first carriage of the procession. Angilia kissed Joseph before she stepped into the carriage, thanking him for his devotion and kindness on what would be his last duty for the Royal Family; he had officially retired one month earlier, but wanted to drive them to Prince Eric's wedding. The carriage was pulled by a white horse Joseph had borrowed from Mr. Holt's horse ranch. At 12:10 sharp, the carriage left the palace grounds to thunderous screams and shouts.

Angilia was seated between her husband and her father, and she smiled at both of them in utter happiness. She wore a pretty lilac chiffon dress and one of her mother's pearl chokers, her iconic long blonde hair simply pulled back at the sides and secured with one of her grandmother's diamond barrettes. Eric wore his military uniform, the same one he had worn on Angilia's wedding day.

Matthew wore a traditional morning suit. At 64, Matthew's dark blonde hair was mostly grey, but people noticed how he still looked at Angilia with those famous love-struck amber eyes. No one forgot it was Angilia's and Matthew's 35th wedding anniversary, which was heralded on dozens of signs through the streets of Valmondois.

Their carriage stopped at the church, and Tony alighted from his footman post on the back of the carriage to open the door. Like Joseph, he had retired as a security officer earlier that year, but wanted to be with them for Prince Eric's wedding. Eric stepped down unassisted, and turned to take his daughter's hand and help her from the carriage. Lastly, Matthew alighted, and the carriage pulled away. The three of them turned to wave at everyone standing across the street before they climbed the stairs to the church door. Before they entered, they turned and waved again, their radiant eyes and smiles showing their true happiness.

Meanwhile, Prince Eric and Leigh entered their carriage, driven by Ben and led by Rocket, for their journey to the church. Nathan acted as footman on the back of the carriage. As soon as the carriage appeared in peoples' view, the screams grew deafening. Prince Eric smiled, waved, and pointed to signs wishing his parents a happy anniversary. He picked up a handful of rose petals that people had thrown into the carriage, and tossed them back. Leigh enjoyed his friend's happiness, and he joined in the brief burst of fun as the carriage neared the church.

Finally, Prince Eric and Leigh stepped out of the carriage at the church. Prince Eric waved to everyone across the street, which delighted them. In a loud, clear voice so like his grandfather's, Prince Eric said, "I can't wait to greet you with my bride." Leigh laughed when that sent the crowd into a paroxysm. Eric and Leigh walked quickly up the stairs, turned to wave briefly, and entered for their joyous walk up the aisle.

Prince Eric smiled continuously, and he stopped frequently to greet friends and heads of state. When he neared the front pews, he hugged Nicole, William, Scott, and Darlene. Darlene began weeping, and said, "I can't believe my best friend's baby is getting married. You make your Aunt Darlene so proud, little Eric."

"Thank you, Darlene," Prince Eric said while Leigh, like Roger had before him, bit back his laugh.

Prince Eric walked to his family's pew and hugged Billy and Shannon. "I love you, Dad," he said to Matthew, and the two men embraced. "Grandfather. You are my role model. I love you." Prince Eric and King Eric hugged for a few moments before Prince Eric turned to his mother, tears once more shining in his turquoise eyes. He pulled her close and they held one another for several minutes, a scene which had many people weeping and Darlene sobbing. "Oh, Mommy, what can I say? I love you so very much."

"I love you, my Eric," Angilia said against him. "These are happy tears," she smiled up at him.

"Yes, Mommy, only happy tears today." Prince Eric and Leigh finally stepped to the altar to await Julianne, who would arrive shortly.

In fact, Julianne's carriage had left the palace grounds 10 minutes after Prince Eric's and Leigh's carriage. She sat alongside Yvonne in the carriage, which was driven by Wesley, a security officer, and pulled by another of Mr. Holt's white horses. People enthusiastically cheered Julianne, for she was the woman who made their beloved Prince Eric so happy. Julianne and Yvonne smiled and waved as they traveled through the streets of Valmondois, both of them knowing that Julianne and Prince Eric were meant to marry.

Their carriage stopped at the church, and Troy, a security officer acting as a footman, alighted and opened the door. Yvonne stepped down, followed by Julianne, and the women turned to wave at well-wishers before they climbed the stairs and went into the church.

People clamored for a glimpse of Julianne's wedding gown. Her white silk satin gown was a perfect reflection of her taste and style. The gown was long and sleek, it's only adornment a rhinestone band encircling the waist. Julianne's gown had a sweep train which barely touched the ground. Her mid-length two-tier silk tulle veil was held in place by a diamond tiara that Prince Eric had selected for her from the Royal jewels. In her hands, Julianne carried a bouquet of Angilia roses.

She and Prince Eric had chosen one of Angilia's piano compositions for the bride's procession, and Julianne felt tears sting her eyes when the church pianist began playing the piece. So did Prince Eric. He looked at his mother with a huge smile, and he saw the look of surprise and love in her eyes. He also saw his father gently hold her hand and smile at her. Prince Eric next looked at Julianne as she approached him, and said a silent prayer that their marriage would be as long and happy as his parents'.

Prince Eric smiled at Julianne as she stepped to the altar to stand beside him. She smiled at him, too, and nodded when Reverend Olson said the traditional marriage ceremony opening. "Dearly beloved, we are gathered here in the sight of God and in the face of this congregation, to join together this man and this woman in Holy Matrimony."

Prince Eric's and Julianne's marriage ceremony occurred in the middle of the 21st century, but was the traditional Christian ceremony that dated back centuries. The only omission was the question of who gave the bride away, because Julianne did not want anyone else to stand in her father's place. King Eric, Matthew, and Angilia completely understood. In fact, Angilia had prayed with Julianne in the chapel, where she had cried and told Julianne, "I would feel the same way, Julianne. No one could ever take Daddy's place, especially for something this important." Angilia's empathy had made Julianne love her even more.

That love was evident during the signing of the Church Register and Marriage License. King Eric, Angilia, and Matthew followed Reverend Olson, Prince Eric, Julianne, Leigh, and Yvonne into the Register Room. Prince Eric hugged his mother first thing, next his father, and then his grandfather. "I am so happy. I have no words to tell you," he gushed.

"You don't have to, son. We see it all over you," Matthew smiled.

Prince Eric turned to Julianne and grabbed her into a hug. "We are married. Isn't life perfect?"

Julianne laughed and kissed Prince Eric. "Yes, it is."

Everyone dried their tears and signed the Church Register, and then Prince Eric, Julianne, and Reverend Olson signed the Marriage License. Before they returned to the altar for the last portion of the marriage ceremony, Prince Eric pulled the 2016 Church Register from the shelf. He turned to June 26, and looked at his parents' wedding register page. "Thirty-five years ago. Isn't it beautiful to know that we share this special date with Mommy, Dad, Grandfather, and Grandmother?" Prince Eric asked Julianne as they looked at the register.

"Yes, Eric. This is such a beautiful way to start our lives together," Julianne said and kissed his cheek.

The wedding party and the Royal Family followed Reverend Olson back to the altar, where Prince Eric, Julianne, Leigh, and Yvonne took their places, while King Eric, Angilia, and Matthew resumed their seats in the pew. Reverend Olson gave the final blessing and prayer before the marriage ceremony concluded. Yvonne handed Julianne her bouquet, and smiled at her friend. "Honored guests, I am pleased to present His Royal Highness Prince Eric de Valdavia and Her Royal Highness Julianne, Princess de Valdavia."

Prince Eric and Julianne turned to face the wedding guests at that moment. He bowed and she curtseyed to King Eric and Queen Angilia before they walked down the aisle together. Two security officers opened the doors as the Royal couple approached, and those inside the church could hear the excited screams of the thousands of people gathered outside. Finally, Prince Eric and Julianne stepped out and smiled at the welcome they received.

Their carriage was waiting, but they paused for a few moments to allow everyone to see them. They waved and then walked down the stairs and entered the carriage. Ben drove slowly through the streets of Valmondois to allow everyone the best possible opportunity to see the newlyweds. People loved Prince Eric, their future king, and were happy that he had found his true love. The pair was cheered relentlessly on their return to the palace.

Eric, Angilia, and Matthew were also loudly cheered when they exited the church. People shouted anniversary greetings to all three, not forgetting that it was also Eric's and Marisol's wedding anniversary. That made Angilia emotional, and while she held her father's arm, she leaned up and kissed his cheek. Matthew smiled in joy, and put an arm around his wife and father-in-law. Angilia saw her father touch his wedding band. So did several people watching, and that moment was captured in several pictures.

Eric, Angilia, and Matthew waved, walked down the stairs, and climbed aboard their carriage. They were so well loved and respected, as the screams and cheers that accompanied them on their journey back to the palace demonstrated. When the carriage made its way down Main Street, a woman in the crowd held out a bouquet of roses and screamed Angilia's name. Angilia asked Joseph to stop, and motioned for the woman, who stepped under the police barricade and approached the carriage. Angilia leaned across Matthew to take the roses and thank the woman. Once she was back behind the barricade and safe, they resumed their journey to deafening applause.

By the time their carriage neared the palace gates, Angilia held six bouquets of roses. Suddenly a woman standing on the mall approached the carriage and handed two white roses to Eric. "Happy anniversary, Your Majesty," she said. Eric smiled and thanked her, while Angilia kissed her father's cheek. She, Eric, and Matthew waved before the carriage entered the courtyard.

After freshening, the Royal Family, Leigh, Yvonne, and dignitaries who had attended the wedding gathered in the throne room for the official wedding pictures. The most charming picture of the day was one of Prince Eric and his mother taken between official photographs. Prince Eric and Angilia had smiled at one another between pictures, and he had leaned down and kissed her cheek. Matthew kept a copy of that picture on his bedside table for the rest of his life.

Two hours later everyone went to freshen again and prepare for the reception, which would take place in the ballroom. Wedding guests began arriving, and were escorted to the fifth floor ballroom, where Eric, Angilia, and Matthew greeted them. At 6:00 promptly,

Billy introduced Prince Eric and Julianne, who entered the ballroom to applause. Julianne had removed her veil for the reception, and she looked elegant in her gown and tiara. Prince Eric was dashing in his black tuxedo. They made an attractive couple.

Because Julianne's father was dead, she and Prince Eric had decided that there would be no substitute for the father-daughter dance. The first dance would be between him and Angilia. When he was searching for just the right song, Prince Eric had mentioned his frustration to his granduncle. When Prince Eric had said that no song he had heard captured how he felt about his mother, Patrick had taken Prince Eric to his room and played a song from Barry Manilow's eponymous debut album from 1973. Prince Eric was amazed that a 78-year-old song was the perfect one for his mother-son dance.

Prince Eric went to his mother, took her hand, and walked to the center of the floor with her just as the disc jockey began playing "I Am Your Child." The lyrics were indeed perfect, and as everyone listened and watched, they fully understood Prince Eric's loving tribute to his cherished mother. Julianne, Matthew, and Eric cried as they watched. So did many of the wedding guests, including Nicole and Darlene. That first dance was the undeniable emotional high point of the reception.

Prince Eric's and Julianne's first dance as husband and wife was a close contender, however. In tribute to his parents, Eric and Julianne selected the same song that Angilia and Matthew had chosen for their first dance. When Elvis Presley's "Can't Help Falling in Love With You" began playing, Matthew and Angilia were pleasantly surprised. With tears in their eyes, they smiled at one another and kissed, vividly remembering their own first dance.

The reception was filled with emotional highlights, including Angilia's dance with her father. Unbeknownst to Eric, she had selected the same song that Eric and Marisol had danced to 60 years earlier at their wedding reception in the ballroom. They both had tears in their eyes as they danced to The Association's 1967 hit, "Never My Love." They smiled at one another as they danced, both recalling Marisol's phenomenal letter to them in May. At that moment, they felt warm air encircle them, and they knew she was with them.

The joyful, emotional reception ended around midnight, and after the guests left, the Royal Family went to the third floor. As they stood in the hallway, Prince Eric and Julianne hugged and kissed Eric, Angilia, and Matthew. "We are so happy," Prince Eric said and smiled at Julianne, who nodded and agreed with him. "Our wedding day was so full of love and happiness. Our prayer is that every day is as full of love and happiness. All of my life, I have seen love and joy surround you every day," Prince Eric told his parents. "That's my and Julianne's prayer for us. Thank you, Mommy and Dad, for showing and teaching me love," he said and then hugged his parents again.

"Thank you for welcoming me into your lives and your home. I love you all. Yesterday was my dream come true," Julianne said before she, too, hugged and kissed Eric, Angilia, and Matthew. She and Prince Eric went into the suite they now shared. They would leave after breakfast for their month-long honeymoon in Spain, a location they had chosen intentionally. Marisol's family was from Spain, and Prince Eric and Julianne wanted to visit there.

Angilia smiled up at her husband and her father, her smile and eyes reflecting her happiness. She hugged her father close for several moments, on the verge of happy tears, and like so many times before, breathed in the soothing, familiar scent of his cologne. "I love you, Daddy. Our family is so blessed by God. I am blessed by all of you every moment," she softly said, and leaned up to kiss his cheek.

Eric kissed her cheek, and then pulled Matthew into the embrace. "I love you both. We are indeed blessed. Our lives are blissfully perfect." Matthew hugged his father-in-law and told Eric he loved him before he and Angilia entered their suite.

Angilia and Matthew changed into their pajamas and cuddled in bed. "Oh, Matthew, I am so very happy for our son and Julianne. My prayer, too, is that their lives together are as happy and blessed as ours."

"Mine, too. Eric and Julianne will be happy, because they love each other. Love is the most important thing in this life." Matthew smiled at her, and said, "I love you, my Angilia."

Eric had also changed into his pajamas and robe, but instead of getting in bed, he sat on the balcony rail and looked up at Heaven. "Dear God, Thank you for your many blessings that you have given to my family. We love you, and we love each other. My prayer is that you protect and walk beside them, and that you surround them with love and happiness. Amen."

Eric smiled and pulled the pendant from under his shirt to witness the miraculous scene once again. The sight of him and Marisol together in Heaven always sent a rush of awe and joy through his soul. Even more extraordinary was seeing their beautiful daughter Angilia run to them. "Oh, Marisol, I do love you so. Our amazing grandson married the woman he loves yesterday, on our 60th wedding anniversary. You know that. Angilia and I felt you near us during our dance. Did you feel the love in my soul when she chose our wedding song? I am so incredibly happy, Marisol. I love you. Happy anniversary, darling."

CHAPTER 14

Angilia turned over, stretched her arm across Matthew, and groggily opened her eyes when she felt him kiss her. "Good morning, Matthew. I love you, my darling."

Matthew smiled and kissed her again. "Oh, my Angilia, I do love you. I have loved you since the first time I saw you, well, on this earth anyway," he said and giggled. "I am sure I loved you the first time I saw you in the Unborn Children Sphere, even if I don't remember that. How could I not love you at first sight?" Matthew pulled her closer and kissed her yet again, his love for his wife bursting through his veins.

"I knew you instantly that day in 2012. I knew you were my best friend from the Unborn Children Sphere, Matthew. I trusted you completely. I knew you weren't there by happenstance, but by God's will. We were always meant to be together, to be husband and wife, Matthew," Angilia said and ran her hand through his grey hair.

Matthew traced the curve of her waist with a finger, and said, "I know, my love. I am so grateful. Can you believe that it's been 40 years today since we saw each other again? God planned everything perfectly. You and I reunited, married, and gave life to our precious Eric. Nothing can ever be more beautiful or blessed than that, my darling, my love, my Angilia."

§§§§§

9 June 2052

Today is the 40th annual Father's Day. I treasure each Father's Day for the chance to publicly honor fathers. I cannot imagine my life without Daddy, nor would I want to. Daddy was the first real love in my life from the first time I saw him nearly 75 years ago. I loved him instantly, and I have loved him every millisecond since that moment. I will love him for all eternity.

My magnificent father is 97 years old. I thank God that Daddy is in perfect health, physically, psychologically, and neurologically. Although I was not supposed to, I learned in the Angels Choir that Daddy is destined to live past the age of 100. What an amazing gift that is, I know that. I never take one single minute with him for granted, for he is my greatest treasure.

I know that Eric feels similarly about Matthew. Today Eric and I will pay tribute to our fathers during the church service. I do love them each— Daddy, Matthew, and Eric. I thank God for them.

§§§§§

"Welcome to our Father's Day sermon," Reverend Olson greeted the congregation that morning. "Fathers hold a special place in God's hierarchy. Fatherhood is far more than a biological act. A real father loves his child. A real father protects his child from harm and danger. A real father provides for his child the necessities of life—food and shelter, for example. A real father teaches his child how to live.

"The most important lesson a father can teach his child is to know, to love, and to obey our Heavenly Father, God. God instructs fathers to do so not out of pride—for pride is a deadly sin—but so that fathers and their children will dwell in Heaven with God for eternity. A father is blessed by his child, and a child is blessed by her or his father. They are a comfort to one another. A man may accumulate many riches and awards during his life, but a father has no greater treasure and reward than his child.

"King David writes as much in Psalm 127, which he wrote for his wise son Solomon, whose name means beloved of the Lord. In verses 3-5, David writes, *Lo, children are an heritage of the Lord: and the fruit of the womb is his reward. As arrows are in the hand of a mighty man; so are children of the youth. Happy is the man that hath his quiver full of them: they shall not be ashamed, but they shall speak with the enemies in the gate.'* The fathers in this congregation should be happy indeed for raising godly children. God blesses righteous fathers and righteous children."

Angilia stood and walked to the pulpit, from which she smiled at her father before she began her portion of the day's sermon. "Reverend Olson spoke so eloquently about God's expectations for fathers. He was also correct in saying a child is blessed by her father. I know that so very well. My father has blessed me for nearly 75 years, dating back to 19 years before my physical birth. I loved him instantly, at first sight, and my already-immense love for him grows each day.

"Yes, I learned about God and obedience to God when I lived in Heaven prior to my birth. That was before I was human. Angels are godly and righteous, of course. Humans are not necessarily godly and righteous. We have free will, and God allows us the freedom to choose whether we believe in him and are obedient to him. God never forces us to choose him, despite his desire that we do so.

"An infant's earliest lessons come from his or her parents. Long before we go to school, we learn how to walk, to talk, to socialize, and to love from our parents. If we are blessed with Christian parents, we learn about God. Most of us here today did learn about God from our parents.

"I did, from my father. Long before he knew about my past, my father taught me about God. We attended church every week, we read the Bible, and we prayed. More importantly, I learned what it means to be godly on this earth by his example. He never had to preach or to lecture. He only had to live his daily life.

"God is the cornerstone of my father's life. He lives according to God's laws and commandments. He prays for God's guidance on a daily basis. From the beginning of my human life, I saw him lead this country directed by prayer. He prays about every decision, law, and deed. My father truly is a modern King David, a king who rules a country with faith and righteousness.

"Moses was another righteous man, who led the Israelites out of captivity to the Promised Land. On that perilous journey, God chose Moses to receive the 10 Commandments, for God knew that Moses was the most righteous among those on the journey. Moses wrote the first five books of the Bible, the Pentateuch. The fifth book, Deuteronomy, tells the story of this journey to the Promised Land. God blessed Moses with a long life, because God needed Moses on earth to guide the Israelites to the Promised Land. Moses was 120 years old when they neared the Promised Land.

"In the facts of that journey endure the lesson of Deuteronomy. God does expect us to be obedient, we know that. Deuteronomy shows us that obedience brings blessing. I see that evidenced in my father's life, not only in his long life and wealth, but in intangible blessings. In Deuteronomy 6:6-9, Moses wrote the words that God spoke to him, but that could have easily been spoken to my father. *'And these words, which I command thee this day, shall be in thine heart: And thou shalt teach them diligently unto thy children, and shalt talk of them when thou sittest in thine house, and when thou walkest by the way, and when thou liest down, and when thou risest up. And thou shalt bind them for a sign upon thine hand, and they shall be as frontlets between thine eyes. And thou shalt write them upon the posts of thy house, and on thy gates.'* There truly is no greater gift than a righteous father who teaches you about God, so that the two of you may spend eternity in the splendors of Heaven."

Angilia returned to her seat in the pew, and held her father's hand. Eric gently squeezed her hand just as the congregation stood for the hymn. Matthew held her other hand while they sang a hymn which perfectly reflected the morning's sermon, "Lead Me, Guide Me."

When the hymn concluded and the congregation took their seats, Prince Eric stepped to the pulpit. "I, too, know what a blessing it is to have a righteous father. My father taught me by example to live a godly life. Who I am is due to my parents. When I was in college, several people asked me why I was there. They were surprised that I was preparing for my future role, for the life

God intended for me. I was told several times that I should live the life of a playboy and have fun until I inherited the throne of Valdavia. That was never an option for me.

"Both of my parents lived extraordinary childhoods. My mother's was lived in the public eye, but my father lived his in relative privacy. He was not widely scrutinized or judged, and he had nothing to prove to anyone except himself. He could have easily used his genius as a proverbial get out of jail free card and not worked as hard as he did. He could have parlayed his genius into fame and wealth. He chose not to do that. He chose to become the cardiologist that God destined him to be.

"A father best teaches by example, showing rather than telling his child how to live. I think of my father as the equivalent of a church leader, whose duty is to teach the congregation how to live godly lives. The Apostle Paul wrote the Epistle of Paul to Titus, which gives his final instructions on church leadership to church bishops. Verses 11-14 illustrate how my father has lived and how he has instructed me. *For the grace of God that bringeth salvation hath appeared to all men, Teaching us that, denying ungodliness and worldly lusts, we should live soberly, righteously, and godly, in this present world; Looking for that blessed hope, and the glorious appearing of the great God and our Saviour Jesus Christ; Who gave himself for us, that he might redeem us from all iniquity, and purify unto himself a peculiar people, zealous of good works. These things speak, and exhort, and rebuke with all authority. Let no man despise thee.*"

Prince Eric returned to the pew, and Matthew hugged his son. Reverend Olson went to the pulpit and commanded, "Let us pray." The congregation stood to pray. Angilia and Eric put their arms around each other, and Prince Eric and Matthew put their arms around one another. The four of them felt happy tears in their eyes as they bowed their heads and prayed. "O Heavenly Father, Thank you for the immense blessing of our fathers. Let them feel the joy, love, and gratitude we have for them. We ask that you bless them as they bless us, and that you keep them safe, strong, and unafraid for as long as their earthly lives remain. In your loving name, Amen."

§§§§

"Wow, Grandfather, it's already your Diamond Jubilee Week. It feels like we just celebrated your 50th Jubilee. The past decade has passed quickly," Prince Eric said as he and his grandfather entered the dining room for breakfast.

"For some reason, the committee keeps doing this every 10 years. I'm flattered that people think I'm worthy of all this, but at this point, what more can be said or done?" Eric asked with incredulous bewilderment.

"Everyone can show you how much they appreciate you and love you, Daddy," Angilia said with a smile as she joined them and put her arm around her father.

"I'm just doing my job. It's not worth all this fuss," Eric insisted.

"Nonsense," Angilia said as they took their seats at the table. "You balked at a year-long Jubilee, which is what everyone wanted to do for you. The Queen of England had a year-long Diamond Jubilee in 2012. Valdavia wanted to do the same thing for you, but as soon as you got word of the plans, you insisted we not do that. I know why you did, Daddy. Your humility makes people love you even more. Your refusal to have a year-long Jubilee has made the committee plan an extra special Jubilee week for you," Angilia told her father with a smile as Anthony served breakfast before that morning's Thanksgiving Service.

§§§§

"Welcome to the Diamond Jubilee Service of Thanksgiving for the life and reign of our beloved and benevolent King Eric," Reverend Olson introduced that morning's church service. "Let us pray." The congregation rose, including Patrick, who stood alongside his brother on this most auspicious occasion. "Dear God, We join together in praise and gratitude for the life of our much-loved King Eric. You have granted King Eric long life and health, and by doing so you have blessed Valdavia immensely. For 60 years, Eric has worked for the betterment of all Valdavians, the benefit of the nation of Valdavia, and for the overall enhancement of the world. Our prayer is for King Eric's sustained blessings as he continues to fulfill your destiny for him. In your hallowed name, this we ask. Amen.”

Reverend Olson stepped aside, and Patrick walked to the pulpit for the Scripture reading. “King Solomon, the wise and righteous monarch of Israel, wrote Proverbs 3:1-2, which are very fitting on my brother’s 60th Jubilee. *My son, forget not my law; but let thine heart keep my commandments: For length of days, and long life, and peace, shall they add to thee.*”

Patrick returned to his seat between Eric and Angilia. The musicians and choir of Christ Church Valmondois performed a hymn that Prince Eric had selected. “Now Thank We All Our God” was a 17th century German hymn that Prince Eric believed reflected his grandfather’s relationship with God.

When the hymn concluded, Angilia walked to the pulpit. “When Solomon became King of Israel, he began his reign by visiting an altar to God, as recounted in 2 Chronicles Chapter 1. There, he sent up an offering and a prayer. When God appeared before him that night and told him to ask what God might give him, Solomon’s request was for wisdom and knowledge. God’s reply? *Because this was in thine heart, and thou hast not asked riches, wealth, or honour, nor the life of thine enemies, neither yet hast asked long life; but hast asked wisdom and knowledge for thyself, that thou mayest judge my people, over whom I have made thee king: Wisdom and knowledge is granted unto thee; and I will give thee riches, and wealth, and honour, such as none of the kings have had that have been before thee, neither shall there any after thee have the like.*”

Angilia walked to the piano, and Patrick followed and joined her on the bench. She played and Patrick sang a song that perfectly reflected Eric’s belief and faith. Angilia and Patrick had chosen a song from the 1945 musical “Carousel.” Their emotive rendition of “You’ll Never Walk Alone” brought tears to many members of the congregation, including Eric, Matthew, Prince Eric, and Julianne.

Eric said a silent prayer of gratitude for his family. The love and devotion they gave to him and showed to him literally filled his soul. He had said many times that he was the most blessed man alive, and that day he knew he was. When Angilia and Patrick returned to the pew, Eric hugged them close. Through his tears, he told them, "I love you."

§§§§§

"I wonder why the committee members asked us to meet them at the courthouse today. What could they possibly need us there for?" Eric asked at breakfast the next morning.

Billy, Matthew, Prince Eric, and Julianne shrugged their shoulders. "I have no idea, Grandfather," Prince Eric said.

"Billy?" Eric asked his trusted assistant.

"I really don't know, Eric," Billy replied. Yvonne answered similarly when Eric asked her. So did Matthew.

Shannon placed a huge forkful of food in her mouth at that moment, afraid Eric would ask her the same question. When he did, Shannon pointed to her mouth and shrugged her shoulders. In exasperation, Eric said, "Someone has to know something. Angilia?"

"I'm sure you will find out soon, Daddy," Angilia truthfully answered.

The truth was that only Angilia, Shannon, and the Advisory Board members knew why they were asked to convene at the courthouse. When the Royal party arrived, they were greeted by thousands of people and the members of the Jubilee Committee and Eric's Advisory Board. They all greeted the Royal Family, Billy, Yvonne, and Shannon, before Chief Advisor Dr. Gordon Furth stepped to a podium at the foot of the courthouse steps.

"Your Majesties, Your Royal Highnesses, members of the Advisory Board and the Jubilee Committee, and distinguished guests, welcome to today's special event honoring His Majesty on the occasion of his Diamond Jubilee. As a retired judge of the Supreme Court de Valdavia, I am delighted by today's special event. I am even more elated to welcome Her Majesty Queen Angilia, the crafter of today's decree, to the podium for a special announcement."

292

Angilia and Dr. Furth kissed each other's cheeks before she turned to the microphone. "Like Dr. Furth, I am delighted to make today's announcement. My father has served us well as our King for 60 years. I knew instantly what I wanted to do to honor him during his Diamond Jubilee. As you know, and as Dr. Furth can testify, Valdavia has the world's lowest crime rate. Valdavia's laws are never challenged in the Supreme Court. That means our Supreme Court is very rarely used, which is actually a very good thing, despite the boredom which Dr. Furth experienced on the job. That is due in very large part to my father, who has worked hard for 60 years to make this country as comfortable and safe as possible for us.

"With that in mind, I wrote the Proclamation which renames our Supreme Court. This institution is no longer known as simply the Supreme Court de Valdavia. As of today, August 19, 2052, this institution is officially known as The King Eric de Valdavia Supreme Court."

At that precise moment, a fake façade was lifted from above the pillars, and the new name revealed. In large gold letters spanning the building's architrave, the new name gleamed in the summer sunshine. The crowd erupted in loud cheers, and the Royal party was utterly surprised—except Shannon, who had been sworn to strictest secrecy.

No one was more surprised than Eric, who looked at his daughter in amazement. Would she ever cease to amaze him? Angilia's love for him never failed to awe him, and Eric felt tears in his eyes. Angilia smiled at him, her own eyes filled with tears. Eric walked to her, pulled her into a hug, and kissed the top of her head. As the crowd wildly screamed, Eric said the familiar refrain that always made her soul soar to the heights of happiness. "I love you, my beautiful daughter Angilia."

§§§§

On Wednesday afternoon, the Royal party would attend the usual children's tribute to King Eric. Another event in downtown, much to Eric's surprise, had been scheduled for that morning. "What does the committee have planned today?" Eric asked at breakfast that morning.

"We're as uninformed and out of the loop as we were on Monday," Matthew answered with a giggle.

"Not all of you were uninformed on Monday, right Angilia?" Eric asked and winked at his daughter.

"Yes, but at least I answered you truthfully on Monday," Angilia responded with a smile of her own. Eric smiled in reply and kissed her hand.

By 9:55, the Royal party arrived at the intersection of Main and Poplar streets in downtown Valmondois near the King Eric de Valdavia Supreme Court. A huge crowd had been gathering for hours and continued to grow as that morning's event drew near. The Jubilee Committee greeted the Royal party and mentioned how excited they were about the morning's event. The president of the Banque de Valdavia, Peter Marshall, greeted the Royal party, and spent several moments talking with Eric.

Finally he turned on the microphone he held and welcomed everyone. "First of all, I am so honored to be part of the Diamond Jubilee Committee. Planning this year's Jubilee has been a labor of love for each of us. Monday's event was a wonderful tribute to His Majesty, one that we were thrilled about when Her Majesty approached us with her Proclamation.

"Her Majesty pleasantly surprised us with the idea of changing the Supreme Court's name to honor her father. It's safe to say that we, the members of the Jubilee Committee, pleasantly surprised Her Majesty when we approached her with the idea of changing the name of Main Street. In order to change the street's name, Her Majesty needed to make it legal by drafting a law declaring the name change. She immediately did so, and the new street signs were installed before sunrise today. Main Street is now King Eric Boulevard."

No one had seemed to notice the new street signs earlier. Before Mr. Marshall had finished speaking, people began clapping and cheering, elated that their revered King Eric was honored in this way. Prince Eric took several pictures of the street sign closest to them, as he and Julianne smiled with glee.

Eric, however, appeared completely stunned. He looked over his shoulder at the street sign, as if to confirm that it actually said King Eric Boulevard. He looked at Angilia, who smiled up at him in radiant happiness, and pulled her into a hug. "You're too much, Angilia," Eric softly said against her ear.

The crowd was chanting for Eric to speak, and Angilia motioned for Mr. Marshall to hand Eric the microphone. Eric put his arm around Angilia's shoulders, took a deep breath, and said, "I really don't know what to say. I never once thought anything like this would happen. First the Supreme Court and now Main Street. Thank you for thinking I deserve having these two landmarks renamed for me. I can't say that I am totally surprised to learn that my daughter was involved in both," Eric said to laughter from the crowd. "I have said this thousands of times before, but it remains truer than ever. Valdavia is indeed the best country in the world, and you are the best friends, neighbors, and citizens in the world. It truly has been a blessing and an honor to serve you, to work for you, for these 60 years. I love you."

§§§§

That evening after dinner, Eric went to Angilia's sitting room while Matthew was in the shower. She had just finished that day's diary entry at her desk when he appeared in the doorway and smiled down at her. She stood and kissed his cheek, and Eric patted her back while he walked to the sofa with her. Too overcome with emotion to speak at that moment, Eric pulled Angilia onto his lap and hugged her close.

"Is anything wrong, Daddy?" Angilia quietly asked him. Eric shook his head and began to cry against Angilia's shoulder. "Daddy?" Angilia moved to get up, but Eric continued to hold her.

Eric took a deep breath, cleared his throat, and assured her, "Nothing is wrong, Angel. Nothing at all. This week has just overwhelmed me, that's all. I can't believe you managed to pull this off. Main Street has been Main Street for over 500 years. That was its first and only name until now. The Supreme Court has existed as it is for over 400 years. It belongs to the country of Valdavia. Why did you ever want to name it after me, Angilia?"

"Why did I. . . ? You really have to ask me that, Daddy? It's not just because you are the best, most wonderful father and grandfather in the world, which you are, but that you are the most righteous, compassionate, thoughtful, hard-working monarch this world will ever know. I love you. Matthew loves you. Eric loves you. Julianne loves you. Billy, Shannon, and Yvonne love you. The citizens of Valdavia love you. Everyone in the world loves you. That is the undeniable truth, Daddy.

"Your reign, your legacy, is cemented. Historians long ago began recording you as the most effective leader of the 20th and 21st centuries. Some have already proclaimed you as the most effective leader in history, especially given that you are an absolute monarch. Most absolute monarchs throughout history have been tyrants and dictators. You, more than anyone else, have shown and taught the rest of us in the world how to lead and to live with compassion and faith. You are absolutely extraordinary, Daddy."

§§§§§

Two days later, on Friday, the traditional Garden Party took place. As always, the Royal Family greeted those who came to wish King Eric a happy Diamond Jubilee and to thank him for his years of service. Many thousands of people attended the Garden Party throughout the day, all of them desiring to personally tell King Eric how much they loved and respected him.

Despite the long day and summer heat, Eric remained a gracious host. He circulated the palace grounds, speaking with as many people as he could. By 12:30, Angilia walked to her father and linked her arm through his as he spoke with a group of admirers. When they walked away, she smiled at Eric and asked him to join her for lunch. He relented for her sake, and the two of them enjoyed sandwiches and lemonade at a shaded table for half an hour.

Matthew noticed, and he walked to their table with one of the guests. The two men joined them, and just as Matthew prepared to introduce his guest, Angilia's face revealed recognition. "Charlie?"

"Yes, Your Majesty. I earned my college degree in May, and now I'm ready to pursue my dream of becoming a doctor. This wouldn't have happened without you, Queen Angilia. I owe my life to you. I can never thank you."

"Oh, Charlie, I'm so happy for you," Angilia said and reached for Charlie's hands. "You don't have to thank me. I'm so grateful that God healed you, Charlie."

"He did, thanks to your prayers. I have never had a recurrence of the cancer. I'm 24 now, and ready to start applying to medical school," Charlie said.

"Where do you want to go?" Matthew asked Charlie.

"My top choice is Cambridge," Charlie answered.

Angilia smiled at Matthew, and squeezed his hand in gratitude when he told Charlie, "Come by next week, and I'll help you, Charlie. I'll even write your recommendation letter if you want."

Charlie remembered Queen Angilia saying that Matthew would help him, but he had never expected such a generous offer. "You'd do that for me? Thank you, Your Royal Highness."

"I'm happy to do it. By the way, call me Matthew. Come with me, Charlie. I want to introduce you to some people from the hospital." Matthew kissed Angilia's cheek, and said, "I'll catch up with you later, darling."

"This is so wonderful, Daddy. I have thought about and prayed for Charlie so often over the years, and wondered how he was doing. I can't tell you how my soul feels seeing him so happy and healthy."

Before Eric could reply, a very familiar warmth surrounded them. "Hey, Little One. Remember what I told you? Your prayers are very powerful, Angilia. God has helped many people because of your prayers. That's pretty awesome."

"I remember, Uncle Patrick. I know God has a reason for everything he does, and I understand that I don't have to know the reason. But why do some people suffer and die from diseases, when others are healed? Randy Meadows isn't here today, because his condition has gotten much worse. His cancer has metastasized. He will probably die soon. That doesn't seem fair, Uncle Patrick."

"I know it doesn't, Little One. I know Randy doesn't want to die and leave his family and his work. But what did he ask you to pray for most of all? His healing? Or his fear of death?" Patrick turned Angilia to look him in the eye, and reminded her, "Didn't Randy tell you that no matter what happens his legacy is secure and his work will continue through Star of Hope?"

Angilia nodded as a tear slid down her cheek. "I was once were Randy was, afraid of death, not knowing what would happen after death. You know that changed as soon as I met you, Angilia. That changed for Randy, too, when he met you. He's not afraid of death anymore, Angilia. He's not. That prayer was answered. His prayer that his work live on after him was answered. Okay?"

Angilia nodded, hugged her Uncle Patrick, and kissed his cheek. "Thank you, Uncle Patrick. I love you."

§§§§

16 September 2052

Today we all spent the day in Central Park for the annual Independence Day celebration. 721 years ago today, King Phillipe VI of France created Valdavia for his friend Christophe. This year's Independence Day was directly tied to Daddy's Diamond Jubilee, with exhibits, bands, performers, and a fireworks display honoring him. How glorious! I know he is so humble and feels very uncomfortable with this sort of attention, but the rest of us just want to SHOW Daddy how much he means to us—all of us.

Today, young Randy came to the park and sought me out. The first time he did so was to ask me to pray for his father. This time, he told me that his father is in the hospital. Mrs. Meadows called an ambulance last night when Randy fell and could not get up when he tried to get out of bed. He can no longer support his body. Young Randy broke my heart when he told me he was resigned to his father's death, even though he does not want his father to die. He tried to fight his tears when he said that at least his father will not suffer anymore. He does not want his father to be sick and in pain.

I promised that I will visit his father in the hospital tomorrow, and I will keep that promise. Randy is a brave, kind man. I have grown to admire and to love him tremendously. I want him to know that I will never forsake Star of Hope no matter what happens. The work is far too important. Star of Hope is the legacy, the soul print on the universe, that Randy Meadows leaves. No matter how much my own heart aches, I must be there—for Randy, for Marla, and for young Randy. I must. God, I pray that you give the Meadows family strength, peace, and love as they face this heartbreak. I ask for strength and wisdom, as well, so that I can do what needs to be done for Randy, Marla, and Randy. I do not want them to walk through this alone. Amen.

§§§§

As promised, Angilia visited Randy in the hospital Saturday morning. Marla was sitting in a chair beside his bed, and stood to hug Angilia while she fought tears. "Thank you so much for coming, Angilia. We know you've got the Jubilee concert today, and you're busy. Randy told us that he saw you at the park yesterday. He really likes you."

"I like him, too, Marla. I had planned to come by your home yesterday afternoon for a bit, but Randy told me you were here. Is there anything I can do?"

"Well, I hate to ask, but I would like to go home, shower, change, and check on Randy. He's got a sitter, but I don't want to be away from him so much," Marla said.

"Go, Marla. I'll be glad to stay a while and keep Randy company," Angilia assured Marla, who kissed her husband and promised to return in a couple of hours.

Angilia kissed Randy's cheek, and sat in the chair beside his bed. He reached for her hand and held it as tightly as he could. "When the doctors told me I had brain cancer, I knew it would kill me. It is. I'm dying, Angilia. The thought of that terrified me before. It utterly terrified me, I won't lie. The idea of life ending and not knowing what came next was terrifying. I never said that to anyone. I tried to hide it from them. But Marla and Randy knew. They saw it in my eyes, my face. They knew."

"Most people don't know with certainty what death is like, Randy. Death and eternity are the greatest mysteries that exist. Few of us have first-hand knowledge of what happens after death. Lots of people, even people of faith, have some fear of death and wonder what happens when they die. When he was a teenager on earth, my Uncle Patrick had similar thoughts and feelings, Randy. He wrote about them in his poems."

Randy nodded his head and smiled. "Yeah, I know. I heard the songs. I read your autobiography, about how you met people in Heaven who had died. Are they really the same as they were on earth? God says in the Bible that when we die, we get a new body. What does that mean?"

"That means our bodies are whole and healthy for all eternity, Randy. That doesn't mean we look different. When my Uncle Patrick died, for example, his body was thrown against rocks under the water and severely, fatally injured. His spine was broken, and there was internal damage to his organs. When he died, his soul manifested in his new body, which looks exactly the same as his earthly body, only healed and healthy for all eternity. Yes, Patrick is the same person that he always was."

"So you're saying that when I die, I will still be Randy. I will still look like Randy. My body will look the same, but I won't have cancer anymore. The cancer can never come back?"

"The cancer will never come back, Randy. It can't. When we die, we are no longer physical beings but spiritual beings. Our physical bodies do die. Our souls do not," Angilia expounded.

"That's an awful lot to take in," Randy admitted. "I'm not sure I really understand all of this."

"Hi, Randy. Maybe I can help," Patrick suddenly said as he manifested and sat on the arm of Angilia's chair. Patrick extended his hand toward Randy, who reluctantly shook Patrick's hand. Randy looked at Patrick's hand, turning it over to examine it.

"You feel human. How is that possible?"

"Oh, you mean because I don't have any blood that keeps me warm? When we die, our bodies don't need blood and organs anymore. Instead of blood and organs, this body is made of my soul. Our souls are part of God, they come from God. Souls are full of God's love and warmth. That's why I don't feel cold and lifeless to your touch, like a dead body or a reptile does," Patrick explained.

"Okay, as unreal as this seems, I think I understand. Can I ask you something else?" Patrick nodded. "Angilia said your spine was broken and your organs damaged in the boat accident that killed you. Do you still feel the pain from that?"

"The doctors told Eric that I died immediately, but I didn't. I felt what happened. I remember the boat throwing me against the rocks and the indescribable pain. I remember looking up and seeing the sky through the water. But I couldn't move. I couldn't swim to the surface. Just as Eric and another man reached me, everything went dark. The last thing I saw before I died was Eric looking at me. The next thing I remember is standing next to Angilia beside my dead body. I watched my brother and my niece and the doctors doing CPR on my dead body. And the pain was gone. Angilia and I walked up to Heaven together. I have lived there ever since. I have never felt pain again," Patrick told Randy with his characteristic honesty.

"So when I die, my body will never get sick or feel pain again. I'll still be Randy, I'll still be me. And I will live in Heaven. I don't want to leave Marla and Randy and my life here, but if that's the way it has to be, then I can accept that now," Randy told Angilia and Patrick. Randy reached for Patrick's hand again, and clasped it as tightly as he could.

§§§§

At 11:30 on Christmas Eve night, Eric, Patrick, Angilia, Matthew, Prince Eric, and Julianne greeted parishioners as they entered the church. Marla Meadows and her son arrived, and Marla hugged and kissed Patrick and Angilia. Young Randy also hugged Patrick, and thanked him for helping his father. Angilia invited Marla and Randy to sit with them during the service. Just before midnight, the Royal Family, with Marla and Randy Meadows, took their seats in the Royal pew near the front of the church. Randy and Marla sat between Patrick and Angilia, and Randy held Patrick's hand throughout most of the service.

Reverend Olson's sermon focused on the divine birth of Jesus, and how his birth fulfilled a centuries-old prophecy. Jesus was unique among all who ever lived, for he was half human and half divine. His holy birth, which is celebrated on Christmas, was for one reason only. The miracle of his birth led him to his Crucifixion and the miracle of his Resurrection. Because of that, all people have the promise of eternal life.

Marla squeezed Angilia's hand and smiled at her. Randy had told her and their son about Angilia's and Patrick's visit, and that he really wasn't afraid to die. Randy reassured them that when he died, his body would be reborn healed and healthy. Meeting Patrick face-to-face had made that real and true for him.

Randy smiled up at Patrick, who squeezed the boy's hand and smiled at him. Eric smiled, as well, and thanked God that Angilia and Patrick had been able to soothe Randy's fears, as well as those of his wife and son. With a full heart, Eric stood and walked to the pulpit, where he recited the Christmas story from Luke Chapter 2. Patrick had never seen or heard his brother recite the Christmas story while he was alive, for Eric had begun the annual tradition in 1979. For 73 years, Eric had maintained this custom begun at the request of his father, King Gerard.

When Eric finished and returned to his seat in the pew, Patrick hugged him. A moment later, Patrick stood and walked to the altar, where he sung the perfect song for Christmas 2052. "There's a New Kid in Town" was written and first recorded in the mid-1980s, and was a song Patrick had heard Angilia perform. Its lyrics paralleled Reverend Olson's sermon perfectly, for they connected Jesus's birth as the son of Mary with the prophecy of the newborn Messiah, the son of God.

When the service ended, Marla and Randy profusely thanked the Royal Family. "Thank you, Queen Angilia and Prince Patrick for helping my father. He really isn't afraid anymore. Neither am I.

I don't want him to die, and I'll be very sad, but I know when he does that God will take care of him," Randy said and hugged Angilia and Patrick.

Marla patted her son's head, and smiled. "Yes, thank you both. Thank you for everything. You really helped Randy, but you helped us, too. I don't want my husband to die, either, and I will miss him. But I know God has a reason for this, even if I don't understand. I may never understand. I also know that Randy's work with Star of Hope will continue, and that means everything to him and to us. God bless you."

Angilia hugged Marla, and said, "You know we love you. Call me anytime for any reason." Angilia smiled down at young Randy and asked him, "Are you and your mom going to spend Christmas Day with your dad?" Randy nodded. "I thought you would. You'll see me tomorrow, then. If it's all right, I want to visit Randy tomorrow and wish him a Merry Christmas."

Marla and Randy said they looked forward to Angilia's visit, kissed her goodbye, and went home for some much-needed sleep. The Royal Family began their relatively short walk home, and Eric put his arms around Angilia's and Patrick's shoulders. "I know you prayed that Randy would be healed of his cancer, Angilia. You know that God would have done so if it had been in his plan. You know that there is something much larger at work here, Angilia. It's like what happened to Patrick," Eric said and smiled at his brother. "God has used Patrick to do great things in his name."

"Yeah, and I had to die in order to do that. I had to leave all the baggage of this world behind first. The day I died really is the day I started living, you know that, Little One."

"You've caused a lot of miracles, Mommy. This is a miracle, too, you know. You and Uncle Patrick erased Randy's fears of death. That's a big deal. I know. When Grandma and Grandpa both died, I missed them tremendously. All I really knew was that they weren't here anymore. I just wanted to see them again. I did not fully understand the whole idea of eternity. I do now. I know that I will see them again when I die and my soul goes to Heaven. Randy talked to me at the Garden Party in August, and he told me that even though he doesn't want his father to die, he knows they will see each other again someday. That's a very big deal, Mommy."

Matthew smiled at his son, and hugged him. Julianne kissed her husband's cheek in gratitude. Angilia smiled at them with tears in her eyes, and said, "Thank you all so much for easing my soul. I know there's a bigger purpose for all of this than I can comprehend right now. I just have to trust God and do the best I can for him. I love you all."

§§§§§

Shortly after breakfast on Christmas morning, Angilia placed a small Christmas tree and a bag of gifts in her car. Before she left, she kissed her family and told them, "I'll be home this afternoon. Thank you all for understanding why I have to visit Randy and his family today. This will be Randy's last Christmas, and I want him and his family to feel its magic and warmth as much as possible. I know they can't or won't forget what they're dealing with when they're stuck in a hospice room on Christmas. But maybe the tree, decorations, and gifts will help them some."

When Angilia arrived, she entered Randy's room with a huge smile. To the Meadows' surprise, she set the tree on a table across from Randy's bed and plugged in the lights, which instantly began twinkling. She placed the wrapped presents around the tree, and then turned to face the Meadows family. "Merry Christmas!"

"Merry Christmas," Randy said with a huge smile.

"Merry Christmas, Angilia. What is all of this?" Marla asked in amazement.

"This is Christmas! Angilia brought Christmas to us!" young Randy answered with glee.

Randy ruffled his son's hair, and said, "She sure did." He held his hand out toward Angilia, and she came to him. She held his hand, placed her other hand on top of his head, and bent to kiss his cheek. Randy hugged her close, and softly said, "Thank you for making my last Christmas special, Angilia."

"It's you who make my Christmas special, Randy," Angilia replied. She patted his now-bald head tenderly while he held her other hand against his chest.

"Please say a Christmas prayer for us, Queen Angilia," young Randy requested. Marla and Randy echoed their son, and Angilia smiled.

Angilia stood, her hand still on Randy's head, and held Marla's hand with her other hand. Marla and young Randy held Randy's hands, and they all closed their eyes. "Dear God, On this most blessed and holy of days, we thank you for your blessings. We ask for your continued embrace and love. We ask for your shelter and safekeeping. Surround us with your warmth, wisdom, and grace. Stand with us every moment so that we can better face whatever comes our way. Protect and guide our loved ones as only you can. Keep us free from fear and doubt. All of this we ask so that we may do your will in our daily lives. With our love we thank you for the greatest gift of all, your son Jesus. Amen."

The Meadows family repeated her Amen, and Randy smiled through his tears and said, "That was beautiful, Angilia. Thank you."

Young Randy motioned for Angilia, and walked into the hallway with her. "I opened my eyes during the prayer. I saw my dad. Something happened to him while you were praying. I don't know what happened. Mom didn't see it. She had her eyes closed. I didn't want to say anything in front of her and make her scared. I don't know what to do, Queen Angilia."

Angilia motioned for a nurse, and asked her to check Mr. Meadows. Angilia and Randy followed the nurse into the room, and sat quietly while the nurse examined Randy. After several minutes, the nurse surprised them by saying, "You seem to be breathing easier this morning, Randy. You don't have the shortness of breath you've had for several weeks. Your lungs are clearer. We'll keep monitoring this, but it seems something has eased your dyspnea. Perhaps Her Majesty's visit brought a Christmas miracle." The nurse smiled and patted Randy's arm before she left the room.

"What does that mean?" young Randy asked.

"It means I can breathe normally. It means breathing isn't hard or painful," Randy answered with a smile. "It means I can talk without having to stop for breath after every word."

"Does that mean you're better?"

Randy held his son's hand and smiled at him. "Yeah, I am better, Randy. Being able to breathe does make me feel better, a whole lot better. It really does. I think Nurse Nancy is right. I think Angilia brought a Christmas miracle."

"I do, too," Marla said, crying. She stood and hugged Angilia and said, "God bless you."

§§§§§

14 February 2053

Since today is the international day of romance, I want to do something special for Matthew, Daddy, Eric, and Julianne. It's so appropriate for us to share St. Valentine's Day. We share June 26, the very special day on which we all married. Daddy and Mommy married on June 26, 1991, 61½ years ago. Matthew and I married on June 26, 2016, 36½ years ago. Eric and Julianne married on June 26, 2051, 1½ years ago. Love binds us and connects us in every way. This evening, I want to honor that. I have made reservations at our favorite Italian restaurant, where I will take the four of them for an evening of love and camaraderie.

§§§§§

February 14, 2053

My beautiful Angilia surprised us all with a wonderful Valentine's Day dinner at our favorite Italian restaurant. The five of us shared a table and much love. I can only pray that our son Eric and Julianne share as many happy, glorious years as Angilia and I have shared. There was one person not present, physically present, at the table tonight to complete the three couples. Marisol. I think of Eric and can't help but feel incredibly sad. He and Marisol would have celebrated their 62nd wedding anniversary this coming June. But he has spent 58 of those years without her beside him. He has never loved another. That I do understand. I have never loved and will never love anyone except my Angilia. I could never imagine life on earth without her. In spite of everything I

306

know about Heaven and life after death, I could never live 58 years without her beside me. That is unfathomable to me. Yes, I know that Marisol's soul lives, but, God forgive me, that is nowhere near the same as having your beloved wife with you here on earth. Eric is a far stronger man than I could ever hope to be. My prayer is that neither my son nor I experience the pain and heartbreak that Eric has endured for 58 long years. The promise of eternal love and life is truly a beautiful blessing, I know that. Would that be enough for me? I never want to find out.

§§§§

14 February 2053

What a splendid St. Valentine's Day our beautiful daughter Angilia treated us to, Marisol, my love. I felt your spirit near me in the restaurant, and I know you shared this day of love with me. I love you.

I love our daughter Angilia, and I love our grandson Eric. You love them, too, Marisol. I know that. They know that. Matthew and Julianne love them and fill their lives with such joy and happiness. How blessed they are. My prayer for them is that they share many more love-filled years together. My heart and soul overflow with happiness and peace at the thought. I want them to enjoy many years of love and joy long after my soul joins you in Heaven, my love.

§§§§

Matthew returned home from a meeting rather late on the evening of April 2, 2053. He put his briefcase in his office, and then went to the sitting room, where Eric, Prince Eric, Julianne, Billy, and Shannon were sitting quietly and somberly. Angilia was not there. "What's wrong? Did something happen to Angilia?" Matthew asked in panic.

Eric shook his head. "Not like that, no. Randy Meadows died today. Angilia was with him and his family when he died."

Matthew's shoulders fell. "Oh, no. He lived longer than the neurologists and the oncologists thought he would, though, and far more comfortably. I know this hit her hard. How is she?"

"She's very sad, Dad. She's been in the chapel praying for a few hours. She refused to eat dinner," Prince Eric said.

307

Matthew nodded his head and walked to the window. "Poor Angel. I know how much she prayed for his recovery. She understands that God is in control and that he has a reason for everything, but that still doesn't make the pain any less for her." Matthew turned and walked to the sitting room door. "I'm going to check on her."

Matthew took the elevator to the first floor and went to the palace chapel. He quietly opened the door, not wanting to disturb his wife, but wanting to see how she seemed to be. Matthew was pleasantly surprised to see Patrick beside Angilia, holding her and talking to her. Matthew quietly closed the door, returned to the sitting room, and told everyone that Patrick was comforting Angilia.

§§§§

"It's okay to grieve and to cry, Angilia. Grief is normal, you know that. Even Jesus mourned when Lazarus died, but not for Lazarus. He identified with the grief of Lazarus' sisters, Mary and Martha. Jesus wept, yes, but he wept for them, not for Lazarus." Angilia nodded as Patrick held her. "You know that Randy is fine, Angilia. You know that. I know that you're not sad for Randy. You couldn't be sad for Randy, because you know that he's in the most wonderful place that will ever exist."

"You're right, Uncle Patrick. I do know that Randy is fine, and that he will always be fine. Even though we all expected this, that does not negate the pain involved. Marla and Randy were so devastated when Randy finally died. In spite of everything, despite knowing that Randy will no longer suffer, their grief hit the depths of despair when he actually died and it became their reality. There is nothing I can do for them, Uncle Patrick. Nothing."

"Oh, yes there is, Angilia. You've already done it. You came here, to the chapel, to pray for Marla and Randy. They are the ones who need prayers now. Your pain is in response to their grief, Angilia, just like Jesus' pain was in response to Mary's and Martha's grief. If the Son of God can feel that empathy and compassion for those who grieve, then there is no reason why you can't. After all, what did Jesus tell us in his Sermon on the Mount?"

"Blessed are they that mourn: for they shall be comforted."

"Exactly. Jesus will take care of Marla and Randy. He will ease their grief. He will comfort them. He has heard your prayers, Little One, and he will comfort them, and he will also comfort you."

CHAPTER 15

"Happy birthday, my magnificent father."

Eric smiled at his daughter as she stood in his suite doorway with a mystical glow surrounding her. He opened his arms, and Angilia walked to him and hugged him very close to her. She breathed deeply, feeling his oh-so-familiar warmth encompass her.

"I love you so very much, my beautiful daughter Angilia."

"I love you, Daddy, far more than words can ever express, far more than you can ever know."

"I do know, my Angel. I feel your love. I see your love. It shines in your eyes. I felt it and saw it for the first time on July 19, 1977," Eric said and kissed the top of her head.

Angilia smiled up at him. "There's something I've never told anyone. When I was in the Angels Choir, you know that everyone except Uncle Patrick believed I wouldn't remember anything." Eric nodded, recalling her 2012 revelations. "Once, I came upon Michael and Great-grandfather while they were talking. I had my diary and a quill pen in my hand, and I didn't intend to eavesdrop on their conversation. But I heard something very exciting and intriguing. About you."

Eric looked at her, curiosity evident on his face. "I don't know what they had said just before that, but Michael said, *'God has a lot in store for Eric, and that means your grandson won't join us here for quite a long time. God has destined Eric to live well past the age of 100.'* I stopped and stood still, staring at Michael. Great-grandfather saw me, and he cleared his throat. They changed the subject then and walked away. But I have never forgotten that. My whole life, I knew this day would come to fruition."

Eric stood still himself, comprehending what Angilia had just told him. Michael—God's Archangel—knew that Eric's life was predestined to last more than 100 years. His daughter knew that. Eric looked down at Angilia. "No wonder you so fiercely protected me. You mentioned my destiny so many times in 2012, but I never once imagined you meant anything like this. You've known this longer than you've been alive. You came to me knowing this. That's why you made sure nothing happened that would alter what God predestined for me. None of us know how long God intends our lives to last. But you've known this for so very long. Does Patrick know?"

"Of course, he does. I told him. We told each other everything. When I compared you to Moses a couple of years ago, that was intentional. God had a reason for Moses' long life, and he has a reason for your long life," Angilia smiled and kissed her father's cheek. "Nothing or no one was going to jeopardize your life, Daddy. First of all, you are too important to me. I love you too much to let anything happen to you. I have something for you. I'll be right back."

Angilia picked up a wrapped gift from her desk across the hall. She walked back to Eric and handed it to him. "Happy birthday, Daddy."

Eric smiled, always treasuring their early-morning birthday time. Her gifts touched his heart and soul, but more than the gifts, he cherished her and her love. Eric removed the gold wrapping paper, then the lid from the box, and beamed in pleasure. "Oh, Angel, this is extraordinary."

"I'd hoped you'd like it," Angilia smiled.

"Like it? This is priceless, another family heirloom," Eric gushed as he looked at a painting she had done of all 19 Kings de Valdavia, Eric front and center—with Angilia, the first hereditary Queen de Valdavia, beside him. "I love you, my beautiful daughter and Queen."

§§§§

"His Majesty King Eric is 100 years old today. Welcome to the morning news on this historic Tuesday, November 17, 2054. I am Brian Coleman, and we at Valdavian News join the world in wishing a very happy birthday to King Eric. The entire world, it seems, is marking this milestone. Several countries have produced commemorative stamps and coins, and many others have manufactured a plethora of items from tea cups to dolls. King Eric fever is at its zenith with this very important and remarkable birthday. King Eric de Valdavia is the longest-living monarch in history, a fact noted and commemorated around the world.

"Eric Richard Constantin DeBruce Martineau was born on November 17, 1954 to King Gerard IV and Queen Consort Matilda, the first of their two sons. As such, he was born Prince Eric de Valdavia and heir to the throne. He succeeded his father as King de Valdavia on September 15, 1992.

"Prince Eric married Marisol Martínez Calicia on June 26, 1991. Tragically, Queen Consort Marisol died on October 23, 1995, just over four years later. Their daughter Angilia Erica Charity, now Queen Angilia de Valdavia, was born on January 3, 1996. King Eric's grandson, Prince Eric de Valdavia, was born on November 17, 2021, His Majesty's 67th birthday.

"For 62 years, King Eric has reigned over Valdavia. Although Valdavia is an Absolute Monarchy, per the decree written by King Phillipe VI de France when he created the country of Valdavia on September 16, 1331, King Eric has led this country with compassion and empathy for those 62 years. He has been known as the King of the People for many decades due to his benevolence.

"King Eric is a superstar for other reasons, as well. Since 2012, he has been a singing star, with multiple diamond, platinum, and gold record awards. His handsome, suave looks have been plastered on magazines, newspapers, books, and posters since he was a teenager. His Majesty King Eric is revered not just for his kingship, but for his talent and looks.

"King Eric de Valdavia has publicly said many times how very blessed he is. How true that is. So are we. No wonder the world celebrates the 100th birthday of this man who has given and continues to give so very much not just to Valdavia but to the world."

§§§§

That morning, the Royal Family joined the congregation of Christ Church Valmondois, which was more full than usual. In fact, more people filled the church than ever before, many of them having come from across Valdavia and from other countries to attend the service. Brian Coleman had been correct—the whole world celebrated King Eric's birthday. Valdavian businesses and schools were closed that day in honor of King Eric's 100th birthday. In all but legality, the day was a national holiday.

The Royal Family greeted people until Reverend Olson approached the pulpit. Everyone took their seats in the pews, at which time Reverend Olson addressed them. "Welcome to our very special Service of Thanksgiving on this most extraordinary day. His Majesty King Eric de Valdavia celebrates his 100th birthday today. We rejoice and praise God for the gifts of long life and health that he has granted to King Eric.

"Not only has God blessed King Eric and the Royal Family, but God has blessed us, the citizens of Valdavia. Today we gather to publicly acknowledge our blessings. Let us pray." Everyone stood. "Dear God, We thank you for the life of King Eric, a life remarkable not just for its length but for His Majesty's godliness and compassion. Eric is the epitome of a father, grandfather, friend, and leader. Eric is that rare monarch who defines himself as your servant and our servant. Eric has always worked hard on our behalf, while turning to you for guidance. We thank you for ordaining Eric our King. We pray that your blessings and love continue to surround him. In your loving name, this we pray. Amen."

The congregation remained standing after they repeated Reverend Olson's amen. They sang Eric's favorite hymn, "I Vow to Thee My Country," the lyrics of which applied to Eric's feelings for both Valdavia and Heaven. Patrick smiled at his brother, understanding this more than almost anyone. When the hymn concluded, everyone except Angilia sat down.

Angilia walked to the pulpit, and smiled at her family and friends. "In Psalm 91:16, Moses writes that, *'With long life will I satisfy him, and shew him my salvation.'* On Father's Day 2052, I compared my father's long life to Moses'. God blessed Moses with a long life, because Moses had the important task of leading the Israelites to the Promised Land. God needed Moses. God had a purpose for Moses. Moses' life is recorded in the Bible so that we may learn from his life.

"God needs my father, too. God has a purpose for my father. I have known that since long before I was born. I have not shared that knowledge with anyone until today, when I told my father early this morning. When I was in the Angels Choir, I overheard Archangel Michael, who does have special access to God, tell something very earthshattering to my Great-grandfather. I was not intended to hear this, and I was not expected to remember it. No one except my Uncle Patrick expected me to remember anything from before my birth," Angilia said and smiled at her uncle. Patrick smiled in return and winked at his niece.

"God, however, knew with certainty that I would remember everything. He gave me this memory so that I would remember. What I heard Michael tell my Great-grandfather changed everything. Throughout my childhood, no one truly understood why I insisted that my father always have the protection of his security officers nearby or why I was especially concerned about his safety.

"I have always deeply loved my father, and have always wanted him safe and healthy. But I learned something from Michael that made my protection fierce and intense. I already knew from Uncle Patrick and my Great-grandfather that my father was the future King de Valdavia, which is a very important responsibility and role. What Michael said indicated a purpose far deeper than that, though. What did Michael tell my Great-grandfather? Michael said this: *'God has a lot in store for Eric, and that means your grandson won't join us here for quite a long time. God has destined Eric to live well past the age of 100.'* That revelation stopped me in my tracks, and remained imprinted on my heart.

"Like Moses, my father has work to do on behalf of God. Like Moses, my father changes lives and the world. Like Moses, my father's life is public so that others learn by osmosis. Like Moses, my father achieves all of this just by being himself and living his life every day. God intended all along for my father to reach this milestone birthday. That is a blessing. However, if we look at what Michael really said, we realize that we will be blessed with my father's earthly presence for years to come. Michael did not say that my father is destined to live to the age of 100. Michael did say that my father is destined to live well past the age of 100.

"God has a lot more work for my father to do. God still needs my father here on earth. We can praise God for that, knowing that we and Valdavia remain under the care and leadership of this remarkable man. God truly predestined my father, our King, and by virtue of that blessed us immensely. Our lives are inarguably wealthier because of him. I know how much you love him. I have always known and seen that, and I completely understand. I loved my father at first sight, and after my birth when I came to know him, I loved him even more.

"So many people love my father. God loves my father. My father loves all of us. That love for us is why he works as tirelessly as he does on our behalf. He does not have to do everything he does. He does not have to work as much as he does. No one told him he has to. He does not report to a direct supervisor or answer to anyone—except to God. My father does not have to do anything. As Reverend Olson said, my father is an Absolute Monarch. However, he wants to do everything in his power and ability for us, though. He wants to work so much for us, because he loves us. We love him because of that. We love him because he loves us. One short but powerful Bible verse encapsulates our feelings perfectly. 1 John 4:19. *'We love him, because he first loved us.'*

§§§§§

3 January 2055

My Beautiful Daughter Angilia,

Oh, how I love you! What more than that can I say? Words can never do justice to or truly express how I feel. My feelings are truly indescribable. My feelings transcend this universe. Mere words can never tell you how I feel, but words are all I have. Words will have to suffice.

Just nine days ago, we celebrated Christmas Day. We also celebrated a very special anniversary. Christmas Day 1994. 60 years. What a glorious, miraculous moment. That moment when our souls merged was the defining moment of my 100 years. That moment changed everything. That moment changed me. You changed me.

You changed me, Angilia. You changed me long before Christmas Day 1994. You changed me irrevocably long before I knew it was you who had come for Patrick. You touched my soul as no one else ever has or ever could. Long before I thought of becoming a father, you claimed ownership of my heart. I loved you the moment I saw you when I was at the depth of despair. While I was filled with grief for my brother, I was filled with love for you. I had never seen you before. I did not know who you were. I just knew that I loved you, that I deeply loved you. I did not understand that then, and I could not attempt to explain it. Love needs no explanation. Love just happens. Love consumes the whole being. That is what happened to me on July 19, 1977. I loved you.

Angel, you were born 59 years ago today, but you have been my daughter for all eternity. I have loved you for 78 years, most of my life. That summer day in 1977, I may not have known who you were, but I knew that I loved you. I have always loved you, my beautiful daughter Angilia. I will always love you.

My life's meaning and purpose come from you. You are the reason God created me. You are my soul, Angilia. I love you. What more can I say?

Eternally yours,

Daddy

CHAPTER 16

"Oh, my darling Angilia, I love you so," Matthew said as he awoke to the sight of his wife smiling at him. They kissed for several minutes, before Matthew smiled and said, "Happy birthday, my beautiful Angel."

"It's a very happy day, my love, because I am here with all of you whom I treasure and love with every fiber of my being. I am so incredibly happy and blessed," Angilia softly replied and kissed her husband again.

"Hmmm, I'm so happy you are here with me, my Angilia," Matthew murmured as he and Angilia tenderly expressed their love.

§§§§

Before breakfast, Angilia received three birthday letters, which she read alone while enjoying the early morning sun as she sat on her window seat. Tears slid down her cheeks as she reread the priceless missives. When she finished, she held them to her heart and said a prayer of thanksgiving for the three men who meant everything to her—her son, her husband, and her father. She placed the three letters in her desk drawer, where she kept all of the special letters and cards she had received. She smiled as she went down to the dining room, knowing that lifetime of letters was part of the legacy of love she would leave for Prince Eric and his children.

January 3, 2056

Dearest Mommy,

Happy birthday! I love you! Today is splendidly happy, because you are here with us. I am admittedly very selfish, and I am sure God understands since he sees into my heart, mind, and soul. I do not want to live without you here with me. I am not ready for you to leave me—us—and return to Heaven. Truthfully, I'll never be ready for that.

I have loved you forever, I know that. Even though I don't personally remember the Unborn Children Sphere, I know how true and pure our encounter there was. Like Dad says about his time there with you—how could I not have loved you? You are my mother. You have always been my mother! You will forever be my mother!

I have to tell you how much I treasure you. Not only did you give me life—the most blessed miracle—but you give me love, joy, and peace. Whenever anything seems too much, or when I am scared or upset, you make everything right. You. You possess what no one else does, Mommy. You possess a mystical, powerful quality that I can't describe or even see. But I feel it. I have felt it since infancy. It's my earliest memory—you holding me and emitting this feeling to me. It's calming, soothing, peaceful. It takes away fear or doubt or uneasiness or stress. I believe that's what Uncle Patrick felt when he died and you escorted him to Heaven.

I am selfish—I want that feeling forever! I love you!

Happy Birthday, Mommy!!

All My Love Forever,

Eric

January 3, 2056

My Darling Angilia,

You have owned me completely for 44 years. I loved you with my heart and my soul from the first second I saw you in 2012. Technically and actually, you have owned me forever. You have been my one and only since the beginning of our souls. You are why I never dated, never loved, never even briefly thought of such things as relationships and marriage. You.

I may not remember being in the Unborn Children Sphere, but I know that we met there. I know I loved you there. I know we forged an eternal bond there. I know. I believe. How could I not?

Oh, my Angilia, of course I have loved you forever, since time immemorial. I knew that when I first saw you. I knew that for an indisputable fact. I knew it in my heart. I knew it in my soul. Oh, I loved you so from that first second!

What a resplendent blessing God gave to us on that day, a day that reunited us in tragedy. God reunited us, for he predestined us to marry! We were meant to meet again on earth! Oh, my Angilia, you were correct on our honeymoon. I became a cardiologist so that I would be in the right place at the right time. I was meant to be the one who helped to save your precious life! I had to. I had to so that we could marry. That was predestined for us, my love.

God blessed me by steering my life in a direction I would have never pursued had I remembered my time in the Unborn Children Sphere and my passion for art. I had wanted to be nothing except an artist. If I had been, I would not have come back into your life 44 years ago. What an absolute tragedy that would have been! I don't want to think about that, though, because even in the midst of real tragedy, God worked a miracle!

So did your beloved mother! I sensed your Guardian Angel in the operating room, my love, and I know that Marisol brought your soul back to your body. I thank God that she did. Your mother must have known your destiny, Angilia, and preserved your life so that you could fulfill that destiny.

Eric and I are your destiny! What a magnificent gift from God! I do love you!

Happy Birthday, my love, my heart, my Angilia!

Your Matthew

3 January 2056

My Beautiful Daughter Angilia,

My heart and soul have so much love for you! Today they also feel such incredible happiness and contentment. My baby was born 60 years ago! My baby's earthly life began that day, and I am the fortunate and blessed man whom God chose to be your father. I cannot tell you, truly tell you, how much you have brought and given to me in these 60 years, Angilia.

Every moment with you is a priceless gift. Every moment with you overflows with wonder, awe, and joy. You have amazed me since your birth, my little girl. Long before I knew the truth about you, about your heavenly past, I knew how very extraordinary you are. I knew.

From the moment you were born and I first held you, I saw the most amazing, heart-stopping sight imaginable. I saw your love for me in your eyes! Every time I look at you, I see that, and every time I do, my heart and soul soar. I have never experienced anything else remotely as soul-shattering. Your love for me overwhelms me, my Angel. I do not deserve your love, but I am so utterly grateful for your love.

In my 101 years, I have never known anyone the slightest bit similar to you. How could I? You are truly unique among all of humankind. And you are my daughter! Every time I think that, it overpowers my mind. You are my daughter! Why was I, over all men, chosen for this blessing? In all honesty, though, the reason does not matter. What does matter is that I am your father and that you are my daughter. You are my greatest gift, Angilia.

For 27 years, you have been the Queen de Valdavia. I have worked alongside you, watched you, and learned from you in that time. I have been amazed by you every day. You take my breath. You are the greatest blessing this country will ever know, my daughter, my Queen.

You are the greatest blessing Matthew, Eric, and I will ever know. You bring such love and joy and sunshine to our lives. We love you. I love you!

Happy Birthday, my beautiful daughter Angilia!

Eternally,

Daddy

§§§§

At midday, Julianne appeared at Eric's and Angilia's office. Eric and Angilia were discussing the agenda for their afternoon meeting with the Advisory Board. As they talked, Angilia made notes on her computer, while Julianne smiled as she watched them. Eric suddenly looked at his watch, and said, "It's time for lunch, Angilia. Let's head downstairs now."

They noticed Julianne when they stood from their desks. "Julianne, what a nice surprise. Is anything wrong?" Angilia asked.

"Not at all. I came because it is lunch time. I'd like to take you to lunch today for your birthday."

"That sounds lovely, Julianne," Eric said with a smile. "You ladies enjoy yourselves immensely."

Angilia and Julianne did enjoy their time together over lunch at Angilia's favorite Mexican restaurant. They were accompanied by security officer Troy, who sat diligently but unobtrusively at the table next to theirs. "This is very relaxing, Julianne. Thank you for this."

"I wanted to do something with you today, and since it's a workday, lunch seemed like the perfect choice. I figured you'd be busy, and I was right. You're always busy. I don't know how you and your father do it. The two of you have more energy than anyone else, it seems. You constantly amaze me, Angilia," Julianne said.

"Oh, thank you, but there's nothing amazing about what I do. I adore what I do, so it never feels like work. You seem happy in your life since you and Eric married," Angilia smiled.

"I am so happy, Angilia. I really did enjoy my work at the museum, so I'm really pleased they became my first patronage. I still get to do what I enjoy, and that really does make all the difference, you're right. The fundraising, the meetings, none of it feels like work, because it means so very much to me."

"I'm so glad, Julianne. I knew it would. You and Eric have been married almost five years. Are you ready to take on more duties? How would you feel about assuming the role that Katherine had at Light Within?"

"Me? You want me to work with you at Light Within? I'd love to, Angilia!" Julianne enthused.

Angilia smiled and clasped Julianne's hand. "Wonderful. That's the perfect birthday gift."

"I really am happy, Angilia. My life seems too perfect to be true. There's only one piece missing in our lives. Children. Eric and I desperately want children. We've tried to get pregnant since we got married, but it hasn't happened. I get so discouraged by that. I try not to, but I can't help it. Eric tells me it will happen when God intends it to happen. I know that, but at the same time, I have to be realistic. I'm almost 40, and my time for having children is short. I'm so scared at this point that it won't happen for us, Angilia. Eric and I pray about this every day, we really do, but I'm still scared."

Angilia held Julianne's hands, and assured her, "Believe me, I understand, but don't give into fear, Julianne. Trust God. My mother was 43 when she got pregnant with me. My parents had longed for a baby since they got married, and God finally sent me to them. Their prayer was answered, just like yours and Eric's will be answered."

Tears trickled from the corners of Julianne's eyes, and she dabbed at them with a napkin. "Will you pray with me for that, Angilia?"

"Of course I will, Julianne." Angilia moved to sit beside Julianne, and she held her daughter-in-law while she prayed. "Dear God, We ask that you grant Eric and Julianne the blessed gift of children. My father, Matthew, and I know what a true blessing and joy children are, and our prayer is that Eric and Julianne know this first-hand, as well. We ask that you ease Julianne's fears, and that you keep her and Eric in the shelter of your love so that this new journey is as joyous as possible for them. This we ask in your holy name. Amen." Angilia kissed Julianne's cheek, and smiled at her. "I have a very strong feeling that our prayer will be answered this year."

"Oh, Angilia, I truly hope so," Julianne smiled.

§§§§

"I can reschedule my engagement and go to the doctor with you," Prince Eric told Julianne as they got dressed for breakfast.

"That's not necessary, Eric. It's just a simple blood test, and it doesn't take that long. I'll send you a message as soon as the doctor tells me the results," Julianne promised him. "I'm 12 days late, though, so it can mean one of two things. Either I'm pregnant or I'm premenopausal."

"I seriously doubt it's the latter, Julianne. You're only 39. We won't worry about that for a very long time. Mommy did tell you two months ago that she feels you'll get pregnant this year. I have a strong suspicion that I'll get a very happy message from you today," Prince Eric said and kissed his wife.

Two hours later, they kissed again when Prince Eric and Nathan left for the public engagement, and Julianne smiled as she got ready for her appointment. Julianne drove alone to her doctor's office, and as she waited for the test results, she felt her pulse pounding. She bowed her head in prayer, asking God for the only test result that she and Eric wanted.

"Well, Julianne," Dr. Morgan said as he reentered the exam room. She looked up at him, her face expectant. "Congratulations! You and Prince Eric are pregnant."

Julianne hugged Dr. Morgan, and cried the happiest tears of her life. "I promised to send Eric a message letting him know. Do you mind?" Dr. Morgan shook his head, and Julianne sent her husband the life-altering message from the doctor's office. Five minutes later, he sent her a short message, and Julianne laughed. "He asked if it's true," she told Dr. Morgan.

"Well, then, let me assure him that it is," Dr. Morgan smiled, took Julianne's phone, and sent Prince Eric a message that said it was indeed true. "I think this is for you, my dear," Dr. Morgan said to Julianne when Prince Eric replied, *'I love you.'*

§§§§

Prince Eric saw his mother attired in jeans and walking toward the stable on the following sunny Saturday afternoon. He quickly changed into jeans and ran to join her. He caught up just as she put the bridle on Rocket and brought him into the paddock for a walk. "It's a nice day for a horse ride. I'm afraid I haven't paid poor Rocket much attention lately," Prince Eric said and petted his horse's muzzle.

"You've had a lot on your mind, Eric. Both you and Julianne have. Rocket understands. Besides, I miss walking a horse," Angilia admitted.

"Why don't you take Rocket for a ride? He'll like that."

"Maybe you should, Eric. The fresh air and sunshine will do you both well."

"Let's both ride him, Mommy," Prince Eric suggested, and went for the saddle blanket and saddle. Soon, mother and son sat atop the saddle and enjoyed their ride.

"You were right," Prince Eric suddenly and cryptically said.

"About what?"

"Julianne is pregnant. We're having a baby," Prince Eric exulted.

Angilia dropped the reigns and looked up at her son. "Oh, Eric, my darling. How wonderful! I am more than happy for you and Julianne."

"I wanted to tell you first. Julianne had the pregnancy test earlier this week at her doctor's office. We're having a baby!" Prince Eric and Angilia hugged, sharing their elation. They walked

Rocket back to the paddock for his cool-down, and gave him some sugar cubes to celebrate the happy news.

When they returned to the palace, Angilia hugged her daughter-in-law and congratulated her. "Oh, Angilia, we have never been happier. We don't want to tell anyone outside of the family until the second trimester, but we just had to tell you first. Your prayers helped, we know they did," Julianne told Angilia. "Shall we tell everyone else now?"

Prince Eric asked his father, grandfather, Billy, Shannon, and Yvonne to gather in the sitting room. When they did, Angilia sat between her father and her husband and put her arms around them. "Julianne and I have the most wonderful news to share with all of you. We are having a baby," Prince Eric told them with a huge smile.

Matthew jumped from his seat and grabbed his son in a hug. "How wonderful, Eric!" He next hugged Julianne. "I'm so happy for both of you. You will be fabulous parents, both of you." Suddenly Matthew laughed, pulled Angilia into a hug, and said, "We are grandparents, my love!"

"Yes, we are, darling," Angilia gleefully agreed.

Eric stood, and said, "And I am a great-grandfather." He hugged Matthew and Angilia, and then walked to Prince Eric and Julianne. "I love you both, and I know how you feel right now. I have no words for how incredibly happy I am," he said with tears shining in his vibrant turquoise eyes. He embraced his beloved grandson and his granddaughter-in-law as love and happiness surrounded them.

"Congratulations! That makes me a great-granduncle!" Patrick unexpectedly shouted and joined the hug.

§§§§

15 May 2056

With utter happiness, His Royal Highness Prince Eric de Valdavia and Her Royal Highness Julianne, Princess de Valdavia announce that Her Royal

Highness is expecting twins. The twins will be born in November. Her Royal Highness is in excellent health, and is under the care of Dr. Henry Morgan.

Her Majesty Queen Angilia and His Royal Highness Matthew, Duc de Valmondois are ecstatic. Both of them look forward to welcoming their grandchildren into the world.

His Majesty King Eric de Valdavia's happiness exceeds mere words. With the greatest joy, he anticipates the blessings of being great-grandfather to Their Royal Highness' two children.

§§§§§

Julianne and Prince Eric asked his parents and grandfather to attend her five month ultrasound. "We want you to see the boys," Prince Eric explained.

So it was that the entire Royal Family witnessed the two baby boys the week before their shared wedding anniversaries. "They are absolutely perfect and precious," Angilia said as tears trickled down her cheeks.

Prince Eric hugged his mother, kissed her cheek, and agreed. "This is just so amazing. Every time we see them, we are completely blown away. They are alive and real. Our babies are healthy and growing," he gushed.

"Yes, they are," the nurse confirmed. "Both boys are well developed and healthy."

"This is so miraculous. Two perfect little boys, brothers forever. There is no one like a brother, so I know how blessed these two little men are to have each other," Eric softly said.

Angilia smiled and hugged her father. "They are very blessed, Daddy. So are we to have them."

"We get to hold them in five months. I can hardly stand the wait. Every time I have an ultrasound and see them, it makes me want them here now. I love them so much," Julianne said as she put a finger over one of the tiny hands on the ultrasound monitor.

§§§§§

"Welcome to the early morning news for Monday, June 26, 2056. I am Stacy Carpenter, and I am so pleased to join you on this special day. Our top story today is the triple wedding anniversary of our beloved Royal Family. Five years ago, in 2051, Prince Eric married Julianne Renée LeRoy, and now they await the joyous births of their twin sons. What a glorious fifth anniversary for them. Forty years ago, in 2016, then-Princess Consort Angilia and Dr. Matthew Taylor wed in a glorious and romantic ceremony. The first Royal couple to marry on June 26 was then-Prince Eric and Marisol Martínez Calicia, whose wedding occurred in 1991, 65 years ago.

"The love story of Eric and Marisol led Princess Consort Angilia and Dr. Taylor to select June 26 as their wedding date. That was a very personal choice, and a loving tribute to the Princess Consort's parents. Prince Eric and Julianne chose June 26 as their wedding date for similar reasons. In doing so, the couple paid homage to the groom's grandparents and parents.

"On this very happy anniversary, we at Valdavian News Network send our sincere congratulations to the Royal Family. True, lasting love is no stranger to them. These three love stories continue to touch peoples' hearts around the world and to inspire our collective belief in happily-ever-after."

§§§§

"Happy anniversary, Matthew, my love," Angilia greeted her husband when he opened his eyes as the early morning sun began to fill their bedroom.

Matthew smiled and gently pulled Angilia atop him. They kissed before he held her close and cried against her shoulder. "I love you, my Angilia. I love you so very much. I am so completely happy, my darling. I don't deserve this much happiness, but I am so grateful for it—and for you. I said it years ago, and it's true. My life would be wretched and meaningless without you. Thank God for you."

Angilia smiled and kissed Matthew. "Oh, Matthew, I thank God for bringing you back to me. You truly are the only man meant for me, God made sure of that. We are meant to be together. How beautiful is that? Our love and our marriage were meant to be, my

329

dear. Our love brought life to Eric, and now he is married to his one and only love. They have given life to our grandsons, Matthew."

"I know. That is beautiful, Angilia. We'll see them and hold them in just five short months. That is so amazing. Everything in our lives really is absolutely perfect, my love," Matthew smiled, and then kissed his wife again.

§§§§§

During breakfast that morning, everyone smiled constantly. The love and happiness were palpable to Billy, Shannon, and Yvonne. Julianne giggled when she asked for a second serving, and said, "These boys sure are hungry!" Prince Eric giggled, too, and kissed his wife. Eric, Angilia, and Matthew smiled at the exchange.

As breakfast neared its completion, Eric asked Billy if anything important had come up since dinner. "Nothing in particular, Eric. We've gotten hundreds of anniversary messages from around the world, which I'll bring to you this morning."

"People are so thoughtful, aren't they? We'll answer them this week, Billy," Eric replied with a smile. Angilia leaned over and kissed his cheek.

"The Press Office has also gotten thousands of anniversary messages and even requests. People want something special to commemorate today, a picture or something," Yvonne shared.

"Really? To tell you the truth, I hadn't even thought of doing anything public," Eric said. "What about the rest of you?" he asked Angilia, Matthew, Prince Eric, and Julianne.

"I hadn't either, Daddy," Angilia answered. Matthew, Prince Eric, and Julianne answered similarly.

"May I make a suggestion?" Billy asked everyone. "There is a huge crowd gathered on the mall, hoping to see you today. What if you make a balcony appearance? They'd really love that."

Eric, Angilia, Matthew, Prince Eric, and Julianne looked at each other, but finally agreed. "Sure, we can do that. It will give the people what they want and not take too much time away from our work," Prince Eric stated.

They all went to their suites, freshened, and then went to the fifth floor. Billy opened the balcony doors, and the crowd below erupted in shouts. The five family members stepped onto the balcony, with Eric between his daughter and his grandson. Eric's gold wedding band gleamed in the sunlight as he waved, and people could not help but notice. Sixty-one years after Marisol's death, he still wore his wedding ring. His love for and loyalty to his wife really were touching and inspiring.

Angilia and Prince Eric noticed, too, and both of them hugged Eric. Matthew and Julianne smiled at one another with tears in their eyes. Both of them felt the love surrounding the Royal Family, and both of them thanked God for that love. Both of them hugged their spouses, creating the perfect visual image of love on this most special day.

§§§§

"Happy birthday, Matthew, my love," Angilia softly said on the very early morning of September 30.

Matthew sleepily opened his eyes as he woke up, realizing that he had lain across Angilia sometime during the night. Matthew felt her heart beating, and he breathed deeply, cherishing the feeling. He smiled at her. "It's a very happy birthday, because you are here, my Angilia."

She giggled in glee when he kissed her neck, and then she gently lifted his head and kissed his lips. Matthew rolled onto his back and pulled her onto his chest. "Oh, Angilia, our 40 years together have been so incredibly happy. I can only imagine how wonderful our remaining years will be. You are like a magic tonic for me. I'm 70 now, but I don't feel 70. I may look 70, but I certainly don't feel that old."

"Oh, Matthew, you are as handsome as ever, darling. You aren't old, and you don't look old. You look perfect, my love,"

Angilia assured him, and as if to prove it, she slid her hand under his shirt to caress him while she passionately kissed him.

Matthew moaned in ecstasy and held her closer to him. "I don't care what I look like as long as you love me, my Angilia. That's all that's ever mattered to me." Matthew and Angilia continued kissing and cuddling for a few more hours, savoring their love and one another.

§§§§

"Happy birthday, my wondrous father," Angilia said, as always, from the door of Eric's suite early on November 17. He was standing on his balcony, watching the sunrise, when he heard her. He turned around, smiling, and beckoned her to him.

Angilia seemed to glide across the floor to him, and she hugged him to her. The familiar scent of his cologne filled her senses with a lifetime of happy memories. She breathed deeply against him, and sighed in contentment. "I love you, Daddy. I love everything about you. Oh, how I love you."

"That feeling is very mutual, my beautiful daughter Angilia," Eric tenderly said against her soft, shining blonde hair. "I am so very happy, my Angel. I was standing here remembering so many birthdays from my past. There are so many, and all of them are happy memories. The first one after Patrick was born, when he crawled into the cake, is a favorite memory," Eric giggled. "The first one I celebrated with Marisol, in 1989, is another. She made me a special dinner and a cake that night. My life has been long, and despite everything, it's been full of love and happiness."

"You are remarkable, Daddy. Not many people have that kind of positive, happy attitude after enduring pain. You are my role model and hero."

"Oh, I'm not a hero, Angilia, and I'm not remarkable. I love and miss Marisol, you know that. But you were our reason for living, and after her death, you were the only person who mattered. You have brought me such love and happiness, Angel. You fill my life. You give me a reason to stay happy and grateful. Our family is everything to me.

332

"Besides, I learned so much from you and Patrick about the truths of eternal life that I can't bemoan my life really. Yes, my brother died when he was so very young, and I missed him so for many years. Marisol and I weren't given decades together on earth, but our love buoys me. Our love lives in you, my beautiful daughter, and in Eric, my miracle grandson. I could never be anything but happy with both of you in my life, Angilia."

"Oh, Daddy, that is so beautiful," Angilia said and cried against her father's chest.

§§§§

Julianne called her husband, who was working with Angilia and Eric in their office, early that afternoon. "Eric, it's time. My water broke," she told him.

Prince Eric stood quickly and replied, "Really? Okay, just stay there. I'm coming, and we'll get you to the hospital." He ran to the office door, but stopped suddenly and told his mother and his grandfather, "Julianne is in labor." He ran down to their third floor suite as Angilia called Matthew to tell him.

Relatively soon, Julianne was admitted to the hospital and met by Dr. Morgan. Once he examined her, he allowed her family into her private delivery room. "Julianne is nearing delivery, so her labor will not be prolonged for several hours. Eric, you will stay with Julianne, as we discussed, and see your sons brought into this world. The rest of you will see them and Julianne as soon as all three are taken care of after the delivery."

Eric, Angilia, and Matthew hugged and kissed Julianne before they left. "I love you, Julianne. This is the answer to your prayers," Angilia said and hugged her daughter-in-law and son again before she, Matthew, and Eric left the delivery room. "This is a miracle. These little babies will share your and Eric's birthday, Daddy. Isn't that incredible?" she asked her father in the hallway.

"Yes, Angel, it is. First your son Eric, and now his two sons share a birthdate with me. What are the odds of that?" Eric smiled.

333

"I don't know what the odds are, but this is such an amazing day. Our grandsons will be here soon, darling," Matthew said and hugged Angilia.

The three family members sat in a nearby waiting room for a short while before Billy, Shannon, and Yvonne joined them. "We just had to come," Billy said. "This is too exciting to miss." Shannon echoed Billy's sentiments.

"I have to be here. Eric is my best friend, and Julianne is giving birth to their babies today," Yvonne enthused.

One hour later, Angilia sat rigid and grasped Matthew's hand tightly. "What's wrong, darling?" he asked her.

"I don't know, but something is wrong. I feel it. Something is very wrong," Angilia said and walked to the waiting room door. Matthew felt his heart lurch, knowing her instincts about Eric were always correct. He went to Angilia and held her. Soon, she was crying softly against him, and he took her to sit beside her father. "I'll find out how Julianne and the twins are, Angilia. I'll be back as soon as I find out." He kissed her and left, praying for everything to be all right.

Eric held his daughter against him while she cried. He had always sensed when something was wrong with her, and she had always known when her son Eric was distressed. Eric felt his own heart pounding as they waited for Matthew to return.

After 30 minutes of no news, Angilia announced she was going to find out why. Eric followed her from the waiting room, only to see several nurses enter Julianne's delivery room. "It's Julianne. Something happened to her," Angilia whispered.

She walked closer to the delivery room, followed by Eric, when they suddenly heard Prince Eric scream Julianne's name. Angilia's hand covered her mouth, and Eric put his arms around her. Something dreadful had happened. Yvonne joined them at that moment, and she began crying. What had happened?

Several minutes later, two nurses left the delivery room carrying the twins to the nursery. They saw Angilia and Eric, and stopped long enough for them to see the babies. When Angilia asked about Julianne, a nurse simply said that Dr. Morgan would talk to them soon.

"Oh, Daddy, this is Eric's worst fear," Angilia cried against him again. Yvonne sat slumped in a nearby chair, unable to face the reality of what must have happened. What exactly had happened?

Finally, Dr. Morgan came to them, and his expression said everything. "I'm so very sorry. It happened so suddenly, and without any warning signs. We monitored Julianne's health constantly during her pregnancy, and there were no pre-existing conditions or irregularities. The first twin was delivered normally, without any problems. A nurse was cleaning him, and we were getting ready to begin delivery of the second twin. Just then, Julianne had a massive heart attack."

Tears fell down Yvonne's cheeks. "How is she?" she asked. Angilia knew the answer before Dr. Morgan told them.

"She died instantly. We had to act very quickly at that point so that we could deliver the second baby by emergency Caesarian section. Both babies are healthy and fully developed. Dr. Taylor is with Eric, but Eric asked for you both. When you're ready, I'll take you in to him."

Angilia took her father's hand and nodded. They had to go to Eric. He needed them more than ever. Angilia's heart crumbled when she saw her son sitting ramrod straight in a chair, staring ahead. His face was void of emotion, and Angilia knew that he was in shock. She glanced at Matthew, who sat in a chair beside their son. His eyes were full of tears, and he shook his head as if to tell her that Eric was not doing well.

Prince Eric looked up and saw his mother at that second, and he looked totally devastated. "Mommy." That was all he said.

Angilia rushed to his side and hugged him against her. Eric held her tightly and cried, wailed. Dr. Morgan pulled King Eric aside and told him that his grandson had not cried until then, but that he had seemed to shut down emotionally when Julianne had unexpectedly and suddenly died. He had not even held his sons yet.

"We need to let him grieve, Dr. Morgan. This was supposed to be the happiest day of his and Julianne's lives. I understand what Eric is feeling and going through. I've been where he's at. The main difference is that Marisol's death was not unexpected and sudden. We all knew she would die. She had leukemia. Julianne was healthy. Eric needs to grieve Julianne before he can do anything else. He loves his sons, and he will give them a lifetime of love and devotion. He needs to come to terms with and accept Julianne's death before he can move forward with his life."

Dr. Morgan nodded, and said, "Of course. He has a strong support system with you and his friends, and that will help tremendously, I know. I'll leave you alone for a while," he whispered, and quietly left the room.

Close to midnight, Prince Eric stopped crying. He had cried for several hours, until he had no more tears left. He had cried until he had released all of his grief. He breathed heavily against his mother for several minutes as he regained control. He suddenly realized that she had been standing and holding him for all of those hours, and he pulled her onto his lap. "I need Reverend Olson," Prince Eric said.

"I'll call him," Matthew said, and pulled out his phone. He asked their minister to please come to the hospital as soon as possible. "He'll be here soon, son." Prince Eric nodded, but remained silent until Reverend Olson entered the delivery room.

"Julianne is dead, Reverend Olson. I'd like you to pray for her before they have to take her."

"Of course, Eric. I'm so sorry, my boy," Reverend Olson softly said and touched Prince Eric's cheek. He walked to the bed where Julianne's body still lay. He bowed his head and prayed. "Dear God, We ask for you to receive Julianne's soul into your Heavenly Kingdom and your loving embrace. Let her know that the love we feel for her will never diminish. Assure her that her and Eric's sons will always be surrounded by love and that they will know her and love her. We also ask for your comfort in our sadness and grief. Please, God, encircle Prince Eric with your love and protection as he mourns his dear wife. Give him the strength and the courage he needs as he deals with her loss while caring for their newborn sons. We pray for your loving kindness and mercy in our time of despair. These things we ask in your holy name. Amen."

The Royal Family repeated "Amen," and opened their eyes. Prince Eric patted his mother's back, indicating that he wanted to stand. He walked to Julianne's body and said, "I know that your soul is already in Heaven, my dear. But for now, this is all I have of you." He bent and kissed her lips. "I love you, Julianne. I will always love you. Goodbye, until we meet again."

§§§§

After Julianne's body was taken for funeral preparations, Prince Eric turned to his family and said, "I want to see the boys now." He called for one of the nurses to bring them, and she escorted the Royal Family to a private hospital room.

"I thought you could stay here until the babies are discharged, Sir. They can sleep in here with you, in bassinets, and you can feed them. We'll bring them to you."

In moments, two bassinets were rolled into the room, and Prince Eric bent and kissed both of his sons. He looked at his sons, smiled, and picked up the first-born twin. Holding the tiny boy cradled in his arms, Prince Eric smiled at his parents and his grandfather. "Meet my son Eric Richard Constantin DeBruce Martineau Taylor."

Angilia's eyes filled with happy tears as she looked at the newborn dark-haired boy. "You named him after Daddy! How beautiful and special," she said and hugged her father.

Prince Eric handed his namesake great-grandson to Eric, who beamed with love and delight. "He's perfect, Eric. Thank you for naming him after me. I'm honored."

Prince Eric smiled and picked up his other son. "Meet my son Patrick Alain David DeBruce Martineau Taylor."

Angilia gasped, and her hands covered her face. "He's named after Uncle Patrick! Oh, Eric!"

Prince Eric's smile expressed his happiness as he handed little Patrick to his mother. Matthew hugged his son, knowing what an emotional day and night it had been for him. On his 35th birthday, Prince Eric's two sons had been born and his wife had died. Matthew was stunned by all that had happened and at how strong his son was.

"Julianne and I knew their names as soon as we learned we were having twin boys. We wanted to honor Grandfather and Uncle Patrick. Now there is another Prince Eric. . . ."

"And another Patrick!"

"Uncle Patrick, I should have known you'd show up," Prince Eric smiled.

Patrick hugged his grandnephew. "I'm so sorry, Eric. This was so sudden. But Julianne is fine now. You didn't see him, but her father was her Spirit Guide. He took her to her new home in Heaven. She wanted to stay here with you and your sons, and she loves you all. But she's all right. She's with her parents again, and she really is fine."

Prince Eric patted Patrick's back and said, "I know, Uncle Patrick. I know she is. I love her, and I'll miss her, I won't lie. I'll miss her every single day. This is what I feared and dreaded more than anything. I told Mommy that several times. I guess I somehow sensed this would happen. The boys and I will be okay, though, because we have all of you and God."

Matthew also hugged his son. "You are just as strong as your Grandfather, Eric. I admire you both so much."

"So do I, my darling son, more than either of you know," Angilia said through her tears. "Uncle Patrick, here, hold your great-grandnephew Patrick," Angilia smiled and placed the dark-haired boy in his arms.

"Gosh, he's handsome. I really like his name, Eric," Patrick said, which made them all laugh. Angilia said a silent prayer of thanksgiving to God for Patrick. Patrick brought them what they needed most—reassurance and laughter. Both soothed their hearts and their souls.

§§§§

By 2:00 that morning, Prince Eric realized that the stress of the day had greatly affected his family. "Grandfather, Mommy, Dad, you need to go home and get some rest. You've been here a long time, and we've all ridden an emotional roller coaster. Go home, and I'll call you when the boys are discharged. You can come back and be here for their first public appearance."

"Are you sure, son?" Matthew asked. Prince Eric reassured his dad. Matthew and Eric kissed him and the babies. They motioned for Angilia, but she shook her head.

"I want to stay. I can help feed and change the boys. I'll be fine. You two go home, get some sleep, and we'll see you later. Take Billy, Shannon, and Yvonne with you. They don't need to stay in the waiting room any longer." Matthew and Eric understood, and both of them hugged and kissed her before they left. Soon, Prince Eric and his mother were alone with baby Eric and baby Patrick.

"Eric and Patrick are sleeping. Now's the perfect time to write the official announcement, so that Yvonne can release it in a few hours."

"Eric, you don't have to do that now, darling."

"Yes, I do. There's no sense in postponing it. Everyone will know soon enough. Julianne won't be with us when we take the boys home. I don't want people to find out that way, Mommy."

Angilia hugged her son, feeling such respect for him. Just like his grandfather, he thought of the public, of others' feelings, before his own needs. As much as he had feared losing Julianne and wondered how he would cope, Eric was incredibly strong. Angilia stood at the window staring at the stars, saying a silent prayer, while her son wrote the most difficult announcement he had yet written. He sent it to Yvonne, who tearfully released it early that morning.

18 November 2056

With conflicting emotions, I share with you the happiest and the saddest news.

Yesterday afternoon, my twin sons were born. Prince Eric Richard Constantin DeBruce Martineau Taylor was born at 4:40. Prince Patrick Alain David DeBruce Martineau Taylor was born at 5:17. Both boys are in perfect health, and I and my family love them tremendously.

My dear wife Julianne, Princess de Valdavia, unexpectedly and instantly died at 4:43 yesterday afternoon. Julianne's love for our sons will shine forever, and will be known and felt by Eric and Patrick. I shall love and miss her for the rest of my life.

Prince Eric de Valdavia

§§§§§

As soon as visitors were allowed, Prince Eric's close friend Leigh Graham arrived. The two men hugged for several moments. "I got here as soon as I could, Eric. I called yesterday evening to wish you a happy birthday, and one of the staff members told me Julianne was in labor. I called again very early this morning, and Yvonne told me what happened. I don't know what to say. Nothing I say will do much good, but I'm so sorry. My heart is broken, and I have no idea what you're feeling." Leigh hugged his friend again.

"Thanks for coming, Leigh. I'm doing better than I ever thought I would. This was my greatest fear, Leigh. Julianne is gone. This is my cross to bear, and it's going to be tough, I know that. But I'll be okay, I know that, too."

"I know you will. You inherited a pillar of strength from your family, that's for sure." Leigh turned to Angilia and smiled at her. "It's wonderful to see you again, ma'am. You don't look like a grandmother, though."

"It's nice to see you again, Leigh. Thank you. You're too kind."

"So, my best friend is a father! When can I meet your sons?" Leigh asked Prince Eric.

"Right now. It's almost time for their next feeding. Do you want to help? The nurse is bringing the bottles in soon," Prince Eric smiled at his bachelor friend.

"Sure. That'd be cool." Leigh bent over one of the bassinets and smiled at the tiny boy. "Which one is he, Eric or Patrick?"

"Patrick. They aren't identical. Eric not only was the first born, but he has turquoise eyes, too, just like my Grandfather. Patrick ironically has Uncle Patrick's slate blue eyes. Patrick is a bit taller, too, by two inches. Both have dark hair. They're incredible, Leigh, they really are," Prince Eric told his friend while Angilia smiled.

A few minutes later, a nurse brought the bottles of formula. Prince Eric picked up Patrick, while Leigh picked up Eric. Both men sat in chairs and fed the babies. "They are incredible, Eric. You made them. Wow," Leigh marveled.

"Life really is a miracle, a precious miracle," Prince Eric softly said and smiled at his sons.

§§§§

Dr. Edwin Howard, the twins' pediatrician, discharged them from the hospital a few hours later. He declared them both in excellent health. Matthew and Eric had arrived one hour after Leigh had, and both were grateful that Prince Eric's friend was there. As they began preparing to take the babies home, Prince Eric surprised them all, especially Leigh.

"Leigh, I am glad you're here. I've wanted to ask you to be my assistant. Stay with us a few days and think about it."

"Are you serious, Eric? Me?"

"I wouldn't have asked if I weren't serious," Prince Eric replied.

341

"I don't have to think about it, Eric. I'd love to, man. I was thinking about moving here, anyway, so we could see each other more. We rarely see each other anymore. This is the perfect solution! You've got yourself an assistant," Leigh said and hugged Prince Eric.

Angilia, Matthew, and Eric were thrilled. Prince Eric needed an assistant. More importantly, he needed his best male friend more than ever. Leigh carried the bags when they left the hospital. Prince Eric carried Patrick, and King Eric carried Eric. Angilia walked next to her father, and Matthew walked alongside his son. When they stepped out of the hospital, the several hundred people gathered there burst into shouts and applause.

The Royal Family stood for ten minutes, allowing people to see Prince Eric and his one-day-old sons. The sight of the young widower with his family touched peoples' hearts. His wife had died during childbirth. How incredibly tragic, people thought. However, Prince Eric's radiant smile pushed aside their sadness. Two beautiful babies brought sunshine and hope with them.

§§§§

Soon, they were home, and Prince Eric introduced the palace staff to his sons. After their exclamations and congratulations, the Royal Family took the elevator to the third floor and entered Prince Eric's suite. He beamed when he saw two heirloom bassinets there: his mother's and his grandfather's. Matthew had them brought from storage earlier that morning.

Prince Eric showed his sons around the suite, much to Angilia's delight, and told them, "This is your first room, guys. You'll stay here with me for several months. Think you'll like that?" Baby Patrick gurgled, as if to say he did like that, and Prince Eric kissed him and then baby Eric. "I do love you both. We're going to be fine, Eric and Patrick. We've got each other, our family and friends, and God."

Angilia kissed her son and her grandsons. "I love you, Eric, Patrick, and Eric. I love you."

§§§§

19 November 2056

What I never wanted my son to face has happened. His wife is dead. I was with them when it happened, and I feared for my son. For several hours, Eric was in the depths of heartbreak, and he cried his tears dry as Angilia held him. He expended his grief. He kissed Julianne goodbye, and then he focused on his two baby boys. They are his focus and purpose.

I had wondered if either Eric or I would be able to cope if either Julianne or Angilia died and left us without them. I have no idea how I would cope, but I was wrong about our son. Eric is so strong, just like the grandfather for whom he is named. These two remarkable men do not just share a name and a birthdate, they share strength and faith. Now they share widowhood.

In a short while, we gather in the Royal Vault for Julianne's funeral and burial. My father-in-law buried his Marisol there the day after Angilia was born. Now my son buries his Julianne. God, please give me strength so that I can support my son. He, too, is a far stronger man than I fear I will ever be.

§§§§

At 7:00 on Sunday, November 19, 2056, Julianne's private funeral began in the Royal Vault at Christ Church Valmondois. Eric, Angilia, Matthew, Yvonne, Shannon, Billy and Leigh surrounded Prince Eric, who held his sons. Julianne's body lay in repose, attired in her favorite dress. "She is beautiful," Prince Eric softly said. "She looks so peaceful."

Yvonne could not help crying, more because Prince Eric's observation was so true and beautiful rather than sad. Angilia smiled. "She is at peace, Eric. Mommy looked beautiful and so peaceful at her funeral, too. That was the image that soothed my heart when I was a child. They are at peace in Heaven."

"I know, Mommy. Julianne knows how much I love her and how much I'll miss her here with me. But I know she's happy in Heaven," Prince Eric said with a smile.

"That is the prevailing promise in death, Eric," Reverend Olson said. "Eternal life is the greatest gift given to those who believe in God. Julianne lives in eternal happiness and peace. We will, too, some day. Let us pray as we say our final farewells to Julianne's earthly body. We need never say farewell to her soul.

"Dear God, Our dear Heavenly Father, embrace Prince Eric as he learns to live without his wife Julianne's earthly presence. Embrace the new-born princes, Eric and Patrick, so that they feel their mother's love throughout their lives. Surround us constantly with your love, grace, and blessings, so that we feel joy rather than sadness. In this your divine name we ask. Amen."

Everyone repeated the Amen. Prince Eric handed baby Patrick to Yvonne and baby Eric to Leigh. He stepped closer to Julianne's tomb and placed a white rose over her chest. He bent and kissed her lips, and Angilia heard her father inhale sharply. He had done the exact same thing when Marisol was buried. He had laid a white rose over her heart and had kissed her lips.

Angilia put an arm around her father and looked up at him. Eric smiled down at her with tears in his eyes and a smile on his lips. He kissed the top of her head and softly whispered, "I'm all right, Angilia." He patted her back in reassurance, and she smiled up at him. He was all right, and her son would be all right.

Julianne Renée DeBruce Martineau Taylor

11 April 2016

17 November 2056

My beloved is mine, and I am his

--Song of Solomon 2:16

✝

§§§§§

After Julianne's private funeral, the Royal party gathered in Reverend Olson's office. There, Prince Eric and Angilia fed the babies and changed their diapers before the church service began. By 8:30, the Royal Family joined Reverend Olson at the front entrance to greet the parishioners. Everyone was stunned to see Prince Eric there, holding his twin sons. No one had expected to see him. Everyone commented on the beautiful boys, though, and congratulated him. No one dared mention Julianne, however, for fear of hurting Prince Eric.

When the service began, Reverend Olson led the congregation in a prayer, which was followed by a hymn sung by the choir. When the hymn ended, Prince Eric handed baby Eric to his father and baby Patrick to his mother. He surprised everyone except Reverend Olson by walking to the pulpit. What would he say? people wondered.

"'*Blessed are they that mourn: for they shall be comforted.*' Matthew 5:4, from Jesus' Sermon on the Mount. My mother taught me that verse and what it means when my Grandma Taylor died. More than ever, I know how very true this is. I mourn the death of my true love, my one and only, my friend and wife, Julianne. On what was supposed to be the happiest day of our shared lives, she died.

"She never saw our first-born son, Eric. She gave Eric and his brother Patrick life, though. Julianne's final act is the one that meant the most to her, giving birth to our sons. She had so looked forward to holding them. She can't. But she, her soul, surrounds them with her love every second. They feel her, and they will know her, even if they never see her.

"My Grandfather and my Mommy know what I and my sons are experiencing. They endured something very similar. My Grandmother died before her daughter was born. Grandfather had to accept his beloved wife's death while awaiting the birth of their child. I often wondered how he ever had the strength and courage to face that. How could he live without his wife?

"I now understand. His daughter and his wife. Grandfather's strength and courage, his love, came from his daughter, and he could not remain sad with her in his life. Grandfather never stopped loving and missing his wife. He still wears his wedding band as a symbol of that undying love. Grandfather knows that he will reunite with her someday.

"I love and miss Julianne, and I always will. I have two sons, though, whom Julianne and I loved from the first moment. I love them. They need me. They love me, and they love Julianne. My heart rejoices over their priceless lives.

"My heart is broken over Julianne's death at the same time. The first several hours after her death, I was mired in sorrow. Mommy held me for hours while I cried until I literally had no more tears to cry. I needed to do that. Grief is normal, as Jesus well knows. That's why he told us that when we mourn, he comforts us.

"He does. I know that. I feel that. Jesus was holding me, too, when Mommy held me. He let me cry. He knew I had to cry. I had to let the grief and the sadness out so that I could be here, truly here, for my sons. Jesus also comforts me by reminding me that he gives us the gift of eternal life. Julianne's body died two days ago. Her soul lives for eternity in Heaven. I know that, and that knowledge is the solace I have to lean on as I live the rest of my life on earth without my wife Julianne. I know that I will reunite with her someday."

§§§§

Eric and Angilia worked in their office on an early December afternoon. Eric alternated between drafting a speech and answering correspondence. Angilia opened her mail and answered letters which required replies. She opened an envelope from the Office of the Chancellor at the University of Oxford, her alma mater. She presumed it dealt with the scholarship, since the 45th annual Eric DeBruce Martineau Scholarship for Musical Excellence was occurring in early March, just three months away.

She presumed wrong, and the letter took her by surprise. "Oh," she quietly gasped as she read the letter.

"What's wrong, Angel? Is it bad news?"

"No, Daddy. This is from The Right Honorable The Baron of Darcy PC, who is the Chancellor of the University of Oxford. I expected his letter to be about the scholarship. After all, the 45th ceremony is soon."

"What did he write to you about?" Eric asked her, curious to know.

"He asked me to deliver the keynote address at the graduation ceremony on March 3. I don't know what to say. This took me completely by surprise."

"Say you'll give the address, Angilia. You should. Did you forget that March 2057 marks 50 years since you earned your DPhil from Oxford? I didn't," Eric smiled. "You were so incredibly young, Angilia, so young. Eleven. That still takes my breath away, baby."

"Oh, Daddy. I did forget, actually. I'll of course give the address. It's just that the Chancellor's request took me by surprise. I haven't been to an Oxford graduation in a long time. It will be nice to return," she said and smiled at her father.

§§§§

"Welcome, esteemed cabinet, faculty, graduands, and guests to the degree ceremony at the University of Oxford. I am Baron Darcy, Chancellor of the University of Oxford, and I am pleased to welcome you today. Every degree ceremony is special, because our graduands have worked extremely hard to reach this point. The degrees which they receive today reflect the work, talent, and dedication with which they undertook their studies. This is the moment for which they have worked.

"Fifty years ago this month, one very young lady received her Doctor of Philosophy degree at a ceremony much like this one. She made history twice that day. First, she became the youngest person to ever receive a doctorate from the University of Oxford at the age of 11. Not only that, she did so with a double major in Literature and in History while maintaining a perfect grade point average. Second, she became a member of the University of Oxford faculty that day, a career she held for five years until her retirement at the age of 16.

"Simultaneously to earning her doctorate, this young lady sustained a songwriting and recording career. She also was the heir to the throne of Valdavia, and as such, undertook Royal engagements. If that were not enough, she also managed to write books and articles which were published during and after her tenure at the University of Oxford. Quite a remarkable life for someone still a pre-teenager and teenager.

"I am delighted to present her as our Keynote Speaker today. Ladies and Gentlemen, welcome Her Majesty Queen Angilia de Valdavia." Baron Darcy kissed Angilia's cheek when she stepped to the podium. The audience gave her a lengthy standing ovation, and she tried to no avail to motion them to be seated. She smiled at her father, uncle, husband son, and grandsons, who had come to watch her historic keynote address. She radiated such happiness to see the six men who filled her heart and her life with tremendous love and joy.

Finally, the audience sat, and Angilia began her speech. "Thank you for your kind introduction Baron Darcy, and for this wonderful welcome back to the University of Oxford. I truly enjoyed my studies here, as I am sure all of you graduands understand. Working with the knowledgeable and talented faculty was a treasure for me, first as a student and then as a colleague.

"Those of you who receive your degrees from the University of Oxford today join a group whose members are among the most renowned and respected thinkers, writers, politicians, artists, and leaders going back centuries. We are blessed to be in their shadows. Future graduands will say the same about you, for the world is yours to impact, to change, and to lead. You are the world's future.

"While none of us can ever know with certainty what our futures hold, we do know that life is a gift that we must live to its fullest. Today you look forward with hope, excitement, and perhaps a tinge of fear. That is normal. The important thing is to never let go of the reason you came to the University of Oxford in the first place.

"You came here for various specific and personal reasons, but you all share that desire to make a difference. Each of you will make a difference, no matter your career. One need not command troops on a battlefield or create laws to make a difference. No one person in human history has truly changed the entire world except for Jesus Christ. You need only affect one person in order to effect change.   Affecting one person causes a ripple influence that continues for generations, long after you leave this world.

"You have already begun that here at the University of Oxford by sharing your ideas, your work, and yourselves with your peers and your professors. You have affected people in multiple ways, from making them consider alternative points of view, to sharing a new technique, or by offering help. Taking that beyond the proverbial and literal walls of the University of Oxford will be the most natural and useful way for you to continue changing the world one person at a time.

"You are the superstars here today. You bring a plethora of divergent thoughts, ideas, and dreams into the future. The future is constantly before you, not some far-distant light on the horizon. Your lives and your futures are full of such unimaginable wonders. Celebrate your achievements today. Tomorrow, fulfill your destinies and inhabit your lives. Do that, and you will change this world."

§§§§

"Welcome to the 45th annual Eric DeBruce Martineau Scholarship for Musical Excellence. I am Dr. Richard Gordon, Dean of Exeter College at the University of Oxford, and I am so honored to be the host for today's ceremony. Today, we award a full scholarship to a music student at the University of Oxford. Before the awarding of the scholarship, however, we have a treat indeed. Please join me in welcoming Her Majesty Queen Angilia de Valdavia and His Majesty King Eric de Valdavia."

The audience stood in an enthusiastic ovation, which saluted Angilia and Eric for several moments. They waved at the audience and greeted Richard, finally taking their seats when the audience stopped applauding. "Thank you so much for this warm reception," Eric said with his dimpled smile.

Angilia smiled, too, and also thanked the audience. "We are so thrilled to be part of this scholarship, and to help students see their dreams to fruition. My father and I have felt such elation in doing so for 45 years. Thank you for allowing us to share this with you."

Shortly, the traditional question-and-answer session was well under way. Near the end, one student in the audience asked Eric an interesting question. "Sir, 45 years ago, your singing career began when you recorded a song at Her Majesty's request. You had never performed publicly until the first scholarship ceremony in 2012. What has your singing career been like for you, considering it was never anything for which you planned or prepared?"

Eric looked at Angilia and took a deep breath. "I certainly never planned or prepared for it, and I never expected it to go further than that one song. I thought this was a one-time thing which I did for my daughter. I couldn't have ever expected this. What has it been like? Wow. It's been a constant surprise. Like I said, Angilia asked me to sing and to record "Sunshine on My Shoulders," and I did so just for her. I never even thought anyone else would care."

"Angilia, what does your father's singing career mean to you? Did you anticipate his success, or did you think, as he did, that this was something just for you?" a woman in the audience asked next.

Angilia beamed, and instantly replied, "My father's success never surprised me. I knew people would fall in love with his voice instantly, as I had before I was born. He never hears how amazing he truly is, but he is consistently humble, so that is not too unusual. My father astounds me. He never has to try, if that makes sense. He just sings from his heart, and he is impeccable."

"Well, this is perfect timing, actually, because Their Majesties will perform a short concert for us before the awarding of the scholarship," Dr. Gordon announced to cheers and applause. Angilia's band came on stage and took their instruments while Angilia placed her guitar strap around her shoulder. Minutes later, Eric and Angilia launched into a duet of "I Love You Because," which they had recorded years earlier. When the song ended, Eric charmed everyone by saying, "We dedicate that song to my great-grandsons Eric and Patrick, who are here with our family today." Angilia and Eric smiled down at the three-month-old boys and waved at them.

The concert could not conclude without Eric's "Sunshine on My Shoulders," which was a request shouted by a student in the audience. When he finished, Angilia and Eric walked to the center of the stage. "Thank you all so very much. My father and I are so thrilled to award this year's Eric DeBruce Martineau Scholarship for Musical Excellence," Angilia told the audience.

"We indeed are. This year, the scholarship is awarded to a young violinist who came to Exeter with the dream of becoming a classical violinist. I sincerely hope that this scholarship makes that dream easier for him to fulfill. This year we honor Stanley Chaddock," Eric announced.

Everyone applauded Stanley, who shook Eric's hand and kissed Angilia's hand. "I am so honored to receive this scholarship. His Majesty is correct. This award will help me continue my studies at Exeter without the burden of worrying about tuition. I am determined to make my dream come true, and as Her Majesty said at Saturday's Keynote Address, affect people. Music really does affect people, and if I can do that with my music, I will create my legacy. Thank you, Your Majesties."

§§§§

"Your EKG looks excellent, Eric, as always. There aren't any issues with your heart. The results of your blood work came back. Your potassium, magnesium, CBC, A1C, and cholesterol are all excellent. Your stress test was superb. You walked the treadmill for one hour without any undue exertion on your heart. You are in perfect health, my father-in-law."

"Thank you, Matthew. I try to take care of my body and stay healthy," Eric told Matthew as he buttoned his shirt.

"You do more than try. You are healthier than most men half your age. Are you sure you're going to be 103 tomorrow?" Matthew smiled.

"I don't believe it, Matthew. 103. I never expected to live this long. I don't feel 103," Eric said in bewilderment.

"You shouldn't, considering how healthy your body is. Let's go tell Angilia the good news, shall we?"

The men returned home and stood in Eric's and Angilia's office doorway together. She looked up from her desk, her eyes asking how her father's annual physical exam went. "Matthew has some news for you," Eric said, not realizing until he saw her face that his simple comment would scare her. She looked as if she expected the worst news. "Tell her," Eric quickly commanded his son-in-law.

"Your father's health is absolutely perfect, Angilia. He was just saying that he doesn't feel 103 years old, but in his condition, he shouldn't."

Angilia felt her heart lurch for a moment, and then she walked to her father and grabbed him in a hug. He put his arms around her as she cried against his chest. "Happy tears," she managed to say, while Matthew and Eric smiled. Tomorrow would be a real cause for celebration and happiness.

§§§§

"Happy birthday, my precious Daddy," Angilia said the next morning when she greeted him in his sitting room while he sat at his desk writing in his diary on the morning of November 17, 2057.

Eric smiled and pulled her onto his lap, kissed her nose, and said, "I love you, my beautiful daughter Angilia."

"I love you. Today is a glorious day, Daddy, because it's your 103rd birthday, Eric's 36th birthday, and little Eric's and Patrick's first birthday. I love you all."

"I love them so much, Angilia. I saw Eric just a bit ago when he went for the boys' bottles. He's happy. His little boys' birthday is today, and he's excited about the party."

"I know, Daddy. I know how much he misses Julianne, but he doesn't dwell on that. He's too busy with and focused on Eric and Patrick, for one thing. Two sons is twice the work of one son," Angilia giggled. "Still, you and Eric amaze me with your strength,

352

Daddy. I always knew he was like you in more than looks and name. He inherited your strength, courage, and faith.”

“Well, you possess quite a lot of those three traits yourself, Angel. I see quite a lot of you in Eric. He will be a fantastic king when the time comes for him to ascend to the role,” Eric said with a smile.

“Yes, he will, indeed, Daddy. King Eric II de Valdavia.”

§§§§

That afternoon, the Royal Family and their friends gathered in the sitting room for the twins’ first birthday party. Brightly-wrapped presents were stacked on the floor, and a large cake awaited them on the table. Angilia and Prince Eric sat the boys in their highchairs and tied bibs around their necks. Little Eric and little Patrick looked around in curiosity, seeming to wonder what was happening.

Suddenly, everyone sang the “Happy Birthday” song to them, and they both laughed and pounded their highchair trays. Everyone laughed in joy at the sight, and Yvonne took lots of pictures for Prince Eric. Prince Eric picked up the cake knife and cut a small piece of cake for Little Eric. He put it on a paper plate, which he placed on little Eric’s highchair tray. Little Eric put one fingertip in the icing, licked it, and began eating his piece of cake as neatly as possible.

Prince Eric placed another small piece of birthday cake in front of little Patrick, who smiled. Little Patrick then grabbed the piece of cake with both hands and smeared it all over his face. He tried to shove as much as possible into his mouth, but most of it ended up on his face. He leaned forward and grabbed more cake from the table, which seemed to horrify little Eric, who watched his brother with huge eyes.

Eric laughed uproariously, leaned on Patrick’s shoulder, and said, “He’s just like you were at that age!”

Angilia laughed so much she cried, but she forced herself to stop. Her father was laughing too much, so she told everyone the story of her father's fourth birthday when 11-month-old Patrick had crawled across the table into the cake. By then, everyone was laughing so hard they were either holding their sides or crying.

Little Patrick grabbed more cake, which only made them laugh more. Little Eric laughed as well, even though he never knew exactly why, and finally, so too did little Patrick. Eric picked up little Patrick and kissed him, getting cake on his face and his suit in the process. Patrick picked up little Eric and kissed him. Yvonne captured the priceless moment in pictures that Prince Eric framed and kept alongside his wedding picture, on his bedside table, for the rest of his life.

CHAPTER 17

Angilia had scheduled a rare Wednesday off work on May 1, 2058, but she still joined her father in their office after breakfast that morning. "Are you sure this doesn't cause any problems?" she asked her father.

Eric looked at her, took ahold of her hand, and said, "Of course it doesn't, Angel. You've worked nonstop for six months, and you deserve one day away from work. It's only one day, darling, and nothing will happen that everyone else can't handle. You and Susan just have fun and enjoy yourselves today."

"We will," Susan suddenly said from the office doorway. Angilia and Eric smiled when they saw her, and she walked to them. Eric stood and hugged Susan, one of his family's best and most-trusted friends. "Oh, it's so wonderful to see you, Eric. You look as handsome as always."

"Well, I don't know about that, but it's great to see you, Susan. You look happy and relaxed. Life has been good to you, to both of us, hasn't it?"

"Yes, it has, Eric. I just returned from Argentina last week. I had planned to stay two, maybe three, weeks when I went, but I ended up staying for five months. It was so nice, but it feels heavenly to be home," she smiled.

"It's nice to have you home," Eric smiled in return. "What have you ladies got planned for today?"

"Nothing is planned. We don't need a plan or a schedule. We'll just do whatever strikes our fancy. We can shop for hours or sit over tea all day. What's really important is spending time together, just the two of us, with no agenda," Susan gleefully said. Angilia laughed and hugged Susan.

"Both of you deserve this. Just have fun. We'll see you both later. Remember, you're staying for dinner, Susan," Eric told them. The ladies hugged and kissed Eric, then took the elevator to the first floor. Soon, they left in Angilia's famous pink car for a relaxing girl's day.

They decided to begin their day by browsing—and perhaps shopping—in downtown Valmondois' 12-floor department store. Angilia and Susan walked slowly, picking up items, chatting, laughing, and just having fun. They were instantly recognized, and although Angilia received autograph and picture requests, the ladies enjoyed relative peace on their rare day together.

They joined other shoppers in the elevator, and went to the toy department on the sixth floor. Susan wanted to get Eric and Patrick presents. "You're going to spoil them, Susan. You bring them gifts every time you come," Angilia smiled.

"Oh, pooh, they won't get spoiled. Besides, what little boys don't like toys?" Susan asked as she and Angilia browsed through the offerings. Finally, Susan excitedly asked, "Oh, how about one of these and one of those?" She pointed to a miniature piano and a toy drum set.

"Instruments? Already?"

"Why not? You were 14 months old when you played an entire Chopin concerto on the piano by ear. Eric and Patrick are your grandsons, after all."

"Are you sure you want to get these, Susan? These are pretty extravagant, after all."

"Of course I am, darling. I can't wait to see what the boys do with these this evening," Susan enthused, and arranged for a clerk to assist in getting the huge boxes to the register. Susan requested that the packages be delivered to the palace at 4:30 that afternoon, expecting that she and Angilia would return before then.

Angilia laughed in delight, and hugged Susan as they rode the elevator to the 12th floor restaurant for lunch. The two women sat across from each other at a table that overlooked Valmondois. Both ordered salad, vegetable lasagna, and lemonade for lunch, and talked while they ate.

"It's been far too long since we've done this, Susan. I'm sorry," Angilia said.

"No, darling, don't be. Life has been busy and full the past couple of years. We can't often have a day like today, but we do see each other a lot, actually. We will remain friends no matter what happens or how often we get together, we know that," Susan said as tears filled her eyes.

"I know, Susan. Oh, don't cry. I didn't mean to upset you," Angilia said with concern in her voice.

"Oh, honey, no, you didn't upset me. It's nothing like that. You know I cry when I'm emotional," Susan said, giggling through her tears.

The two women freshened in the ladies room, where Susan washed her face and reapplied her makeup. Soon, they were on the 10th floor, furniture and home goods. Susan considered buying an angel statue. "It reminds me of you, Angilia," she commented as she ran her finger along a wing.

Angilia picked up the statue, and walked to a register. After she paid, she smiled at Susan and put her arm around her life-long friend. "It's yours, Susan, your own guardian angel."

Susan began sobbing again, and Angilia steered her to the elevator, where they got off on the stationery floor. Angilia bought crayons and sketch books for Eric and Patrick, and a new leather-bound sketch book for Matthew. Susan bought Angilia a bound blank book with a pretty floral cover. "You're always writing," Susan commented.

They continued browsing until they noticed the time was 3:30. "Why don't we go home, where we can relax for a while? It'll give me time to visit everyone before dinner, too. Oh, and the boys' instruments get delivered at 4:30, so we want to be there for that," Susan suggested.

Angilia agreed with a huge smile, and soon they arrived in the sitting room with their purchases. "I'm going to let Daddy know we're home, and check on the boys. I'll be back in a few minutes. You know where everything is, so just help yourself, Susan."

Eric beamed when she walked into their office and greeted him with a kiss on the cheek. He kissed her cheek, and said he would gather Billy, Shannon, Leigh, and Yvonne, and go to the sitting room. Angilia quickly went to her son's suite, and smiled when she saw him feeding little Eric.

"I already fed Patrick, and Eric is almost done. We're almost ready to go visit with Susan," he said with a smile and kissed his mother's cheek when she bent to kiss his. She carried Patrick, he carried Eric, and together they arrived at the sitting room just as Matthew returned from an engagement and joined them.

Prince Eric and Matthew hugged Susan, and Prince Eric placed little Eric in her lap. "Oh, he is so handsome, and getting so big," Susan said while she gently bounced little Eric on her knees. "Let me see Patrick, too."

Angilia sat beside Susan, handing little Patrick to her while Matthew took little Eric. "Gosh, he really does look like your Uncle Patrick more each time I see him. They were certainly given the right names," Susan giggled. Little Patrick giggled, too, and clapped his hands. "Oh, Patrick and Eric, you are just too perfect, yes, you are, you little men." Suddenly, Susan looked horrified. "I sound like Miss Yost. Please, you have my permission to muzzle me if I say such a phrase ever again."

Matthew laughed until he bent double and clutched his sides, regaining control several minutes later. "You're too much, Susan," he managed to say as he gasped for breath.

Just then, a guard knocked on the sitting room door and said some boxes from Tamley's Department Store were there to be delivered. "Oh, they're here!" Susan excitedly exclaimed. Eric told the guard to have the boxes brought up.

Susan looked at little Patrick and little Eric, and told them, "Aunt Susan got you some new toys. Yay!" Little Eric and little Patrick clapped their hands in reply, and soon the large boxes were placed in the middle of the room. Susan handed little Patrick to Prince Eric and ran to get her camera from her purse. "I have to take pictures!"

Prince Eric handed Patrick to Leigh, got on the floor, and looked at the boxes in astonishment. "You got them instruments," he said, never expecting such gifts.

"Yes, I had to. I'm sure they inherited some of Angilia's talent. Open them," Susan happily instructed.

Soon, the piano and drums filled the center of the room, and Patrick reached for the drums, straining against Leigh's arms. "Put him down. Let him go at it," Susan said, her huge smile delightful.

Little Patrick ignored the drum sticks, and pounded on the toy drums with his hands—loudly. He did so for several minutes, even accompanying himself by trying to sing. Susan took dozens of pictures, while Yvonne filmed a video. Everyone responded, either laughing or clapping, and Patrick knew he had a captive audience. He performed another original composition, before little Eric wanted to get in on the fun.

Grandfather Matthew put him down, as well, and little Eric loudly pounded the piano keys to try to outdo his brother. He sang louder, too, and soon the little princes treated their enamored audience to their first performance. When they finished, Susan hugged both boys. "I knew these were just right for you two. You did inherit your grandmother's talent," she said.

Angilia hugged Susan, her happiness boundless that day. Susan was now 85, but she had never changed. She was as emotional and kind-hearted as she had always been. Angilia asked Yvonne to take a picture of Susan with little Eric and little Patrick. She wanted a visual image of the night's beautiful memory that she could leave for her grandsons, along with her written version that she recorded in the family history book she maintained.

§§§§

Ten days later, the Royal Family attended the King Phillipe High School's 2058 graduation, along with their friend Marla Meadows. Her son Randy received his diploma that day, and they were all thrilled. Watching him grow from a nine-year-old boy into the young man who joined his classmates on stage that day filled their hearts with joy.

When Principle Sumner handed Randy his diploma, Angilia beamed with delight and applauded loudly. She hugged Marla as they watched Randy stand for a moment and smile at the crowd. "Oh, Angilia, I feel Randy's spirit near us today. I know he's watching our son, too, and I know how happy he is," Marla said as she dabbed her tears with a tissue.

"I know he is, too, Marla. He is always near you and Randy. He always will be," Angilia responded.

A short while later, the ceremony was over, and the Royal Family and Marla found Randy in the throng of people. Marla hugged her son, told him how proud she was, and took several pictures. Randy asked Angilia to pose for a picture with him, and then he hugged her.

"Thank you for everything, Angilia. My dad wasn't cured of cancer, but his prayers were answered. Star of Hope is flourishing, thanks to you, and that's what he wanted more than anything," Randy told Angilia.

"Star of Hope is your father's creation and legacy, Randy. He lives through you, and he lives through Star of Hope. I am so very happy for you, my dear."

"I know he does, Angilia. I wanted to tell you that I'm going to Oxford to study psychotherapy. I want to take over where my father left off and be involved more directly with Star of Hope. I want to help people, which is what he wanted to do but couldn't," Randy said with a broad smile.

Angilia smiled at Marla and hugged Randy. "Oh, Randy, you are just as awesome and inspiring as your father."

§§§§

Angilia was awakened by very loud music outside the palace, on the mall, and when she opened her eyes, she saw that the sun was not yet shining. Suddenly, little Patrick began crying, which awoke little Eric, who also began crying. Angilia quickly put on her robe and rushed to Prince Eric's suite, while Matthew groaned and covered his head with a pillow.

Prince Eric held both crying boys, trying to soothe them to no avail. Angilia took little Eric, held him close to her, and gently rocked him. She softly sang to him, and he soon stopped crying and fell asleep. She gently placed him in his crib, and took little Patrick from her son. Soon he, too, was asleep in his crib.

Prince Eric mouthed his thanks, afraid to talk out loud, and kissed his mother's cheek. Angilia kissed Prince Eric's cheek and quietly left his suite. She silently went into her dressing room and put on jeans and a t-shirt. She wanted to know why there was such loud music on the mall so early in the morning.

When she stepped onto the courtyard, the people gathered screamed loudly. Angilia motioned them quiet and explained, "The babies are sleeping. Is everything all right?"

"We're sorry, Your Majesty, really we are," a young woman outside the gates said. "We didn't mean to disturb Eric and Patrick."

"But we came because of Patrick. We're hoping to see him today," another young lady said.

"Yeah, but we don't mean your grandson, Your Majesty. We mean your uncle," a third woman clarified.

Suddenly Angilia understood. "Today is July 19. Uncle Patrick died 81 years ago. Is that it?"

"Yes!" several women screamed. "We want to see him. How cool is it to see someone 81 years after he died?" a teenaged girl asked.

"Besides, how cool is Patrick, really? I mean, he's so handsome, and talented, and dreamy," another girl sighed.

"He sure is. Plus he's 19. He's forever 19. How cool is that?" yet another girl enthused.

Angilia fought her laughter. She knew how much people—especially women—adored Uncle Patrick. She knew how handsome, talented, and charming he was. She enjoyed their gushing, their sighs, and their protestations of love. How could she not?

"I'll make a deal with you. Wait a couple of hours, and keep the music down, until Eric and Patrick are awake. Once they are, I'll arrange for Uncle Patrick to visit you," Angilia promised them. They began to scream, but she put a finger over her mouth, and they forced themselves to stop. "Why don't you get some coffee or breakfast while you wait?" she suggested, and several of them obliged and grabbed breakfast at the coffee shop nearby. Others sat quietly on the ground, refusing to leave. "I'll be back once the boys have breakfast, I promise."

Angilia went inside, and leaned against the front door. Her father came from the kitchen with a mug of coffee and looked at her in concern. "Are you all right, darling? What's going on out there this early?"

"I'm fine, Daddy. It's July 19, that's what's going on out there," Angilia answered.

"Are you serious?"

"Yes, I am very serious. Patrick's fans are gathered out there by the dozens, and they were blasting his music. Normally, I would never mind, but it woke the boys."

"It woke both of us, too, it seems," Eric giggled.

"I got them to turn down the music until after the boys have breakfast. I had to promise them Uncle Patrick in return, but at least Eric and Patrick can sleep a while longer," Angilia smiled.

"You promised them Patrick?"

"Yes. They want to see Patrick today. So I made a deal that if they are quiet, I will ask Uncle Patrick to visit them."

"Groupies. Patrick would have them. He's the David Cassidy of the 21st century." Eric and Angilia giggled as they took the elevator to the third floor. They wanted to shower, dress, and start the day since they were already awake.

By the time they were finished, Prince Eric was getting dressed, as well, and he went for a cup of coffee before his sons woke up. By 6:30 that morning, Prince Eric and Angilia were feeding little Eric and Patrick, who both wanted to play. After they were bathed and dressed, Prince Eric placed them in their large playpen in his sitting room, where he worked at his desk.

"Eric and Patrick are awake and playing. It's time to keep my promise," Angilia said as Matthew stumbled from their suite.

"What promise?" he asked his wife and kissed her as she stood in their son's doorway.

"I promised to summon Uncle Patrick for a group of his fans on the mall," she explained.

"Huh? Is that what all the noise was earlier?"

"Yes." While they took the elevator to the first floor, Angilia told Matthew what had happened. "You get your coffee, darling, and I'll get Uncle Patrick." Angilia kissed him as they parted in the foyer.

When she stepped onto the courtyard again, the women who were gathered on the mall grew excited. "Thank you. Eric and Patrick have had their breakfast and baths. It's time for me to keep my promise." The women began jumping excitedly. "Uncle Patrick, can you please come to the palace courtyard now?"

Within minutes, Patrick manifested beside his niece, and the women screamed. "Hey, Little One. What's up?" he asked Angilia.

"It's July 19, Uncle Patrick," she replied with a smile.

"Oh," he simply said. "Hey, I'm here," he said to his fans with his familiar giggle. They screamed in response. "Thanks for remembering me."

"How could we forget you?"

"Why would we want to?"

"I love you, Patrick!"

"I love all of you, too, I really do," Patrick told them, which made them scream again.

"Happy birthday, Patrick," one young woman shouted.

"Hey, thank you! This is my real birthday. This is the date my eternal life began," he said with his famous slanted smile. He hugged Angilia, the girl who had made that birthday so joyous 81 years earlier.

§§§§

Angilia cooked the meal, set the table, and called her family to dinner. Eric, Matthew, Prince Eric, little Eric, and little Patrick walked to the dining area, where Prince Eric and Matthew placed Eric and Patrick in their highchairs. "I want some bread, please," little Eric said.

"No. We have to pray first," little Patrick reminded his brother.

Angilia beamed, and said, "Yes, we do. Would you like to say the prayer tonight, Patrick?"

"Okay," he answered. Everyone joined hands and bowed their heads. "We love you God. Thank you. Amen."

"That was a perfect prayer, Patrick," Matthew smiled at his grandson, a comment which great-grandfather Eric echoed.

"This is nice," Prince Eric said. "Being here, just the six of us, feels so relaxing and peaceful."

"Yes, it does," Eric agreed. "It's the perfect place to get away. It's also perfect for a very special birthday party tomorrow," he smiled.

"Mine and Patrick's," little Eric stated with a huge smile.

"And Daddy's," little Patrick said.

"And Great-grandfather's," little Eric added.

"Yeah. We have a lot of birthdays tomorrow," little Patrick said, which made everyone laugh.

"Yes, we do. That makes tomorrow very special. I am so very happy that your Daddy and both of you share my birthdate," Eric told his great-grandsons.

"You are the oldest," little Eric said to Eric.

Eric smiled, and said, "Yes, I am, Eric."

"How old will you be, Great-grandfather?" little Eric asked.

"104," Eric answered.

Little Patrick lifted his hands and counted his fingers. "Is that more than this?" he asked, holding up his ten fingers.

Eric laughed, and said, "Yes, Patrick, it's a whole lot more."

"Eric and I are this old tomorrow," Patrick said, and held up two fingers.

Little Eric looked at his brother and confirmed, "Two years old."

"Yes, my boys, you are getting so big and so smart," Prince Eric said and patted their heads.

Two hours later, after playtime, Prince Eric told his sons it was bedtime. Both obediently began picking up their toys and putting them away. He helped them put their toys away in the playroom, and then he led them to their bedroom, which had been built the previous year. Eric had additional rooms added for his grandson and great-grandsons, knowing the family would continue staying at the country house a few times each year.

After the boys were in their pajamas, Patrick returned to the kitchen, where Angilia was cleaning. "Grandmother, will you sing us our song?" he asked her.

Matthew and Eric smiled from their seats in the living room. Angilia smiled down at Patrick, took off her apron, and held his hand. Her heart swelled with joy, and she felt such peace and love as she had never before experienced. "Of course, I will, Patrick." Angilia walked to the twins' room with him, where Prince Eric had just tucked little Eric in bed. Prince Eric smiled at his mother, and watched her tuck little Patrick in bed.

"Are you going to sing it, Grandmother?" little Eric asked.

"Yes, Eric. I'm going to sing it just for you and for Patrick." Angilia kissed Eric's cheek, and then Patrick's. "I love you more than you know, Eric and Patrick."

"More than life," Patrick said, repeating a comment he had heard his grandmother say often.

Angilia said, "Yes, more than life." She sat on the edge of Patrick's bed and sang a lullaby she had written for them when they were born. They often asked her to sing it for them, and she always enjoyed doing so. Prince Eric felt tears sting his eyes as he listened to his remarkable mother and looked at his two amazing sons.

Sleep, precious boy,

Who fills our lives with joy.

Your family loves you heart and soul.

You make our lives complete and whole.

Sleep, precious boy,

Who fills our lives with joy.

You are a gift from God above,

A living, priceless proof of love.

Sleep, precious boy,

Who fills our lives with joy.

CHAPTER 18

"Happy birthday, my wondrous Angilia!" Matthew leaned across Angilia and kissed her pink lips, feeling his love pounding in his veins.

Angilia kissed Matthew's ear and whispered, "I love you, my white knight, my hero. You bring me such love and happiness that I don't deserve," she said as she ran her hand through his hair.

"Oh, no, darling, you deserve whatever I can give you and so very much more. You are the most awesome woman who ever lived. To say I love you seems so insipid compared to what I do feel, Angilia. You are literally everything to me, my precious wife."

Angilia smiled and kissed Matthew, their love, like their souls, eternal and timeless. Their love had begun in the Unborn Children Sphere long before their physical births, and came to fruition when he raced to her side on March 7, 2012. The proof of their divine love lived in Prince Eric and his sons, Eric and Patrick.

"Can we come in?" Eric asked from outside his grandparents' bedroom door.

"Yeah, can we come in?" Patrick echoed.

Matthew and Angilia smiled, and she said, "Of course you may, Eric and Patrick."

The now-four-year-old boys ran in and climbed onto the bed. They both grabbed Angilia in hugs as she put her arms around them and kissed them. "Oh, I love you, Eric. I love you, Patrick."

"I love you, Grandmother," Patrick said.

"I love you, Grandmother," Eric said.

"Happy birthday, Grandmother," Eric and Patrick said in near-perfect harmony.

"Thank you, darling boys. What a perfect start to my birthday, to be greeted first by Grandfather, and then by both of you," Angilia told them. She kissed their cheeks again.

"We got you something," Eric said, and handed her a card. Patrick handed her a gift.

"We wrapped it ourselves," Patrick proudly announced.

"You did a wonderful job, so neat and pretty," Angilia praised them. Matthew smiled, so utterly in love with his wife and his grandsons. "This wrapping paper is very pretty, and I want to keep it as a memento," Angilia added, which made Eric and Patrick smile happily.

The boys watched her very carefully remove the tape and unfold the wrapping paper. Angilia placed it on her bedside table to keep it from getting wrinkled or torn. However, both boys looked worried when Angilia cried once she saw the gift.

"Don't you like it?" Eric sadly asked.

"This is beautiful!" Angilia exclaimed, and grabbed Eric and Patrick in a tearful hug. "You couldn't give me a more perfect gift, Eric and Patrick. I love it, and I love both of you." Angilia kissed them both. Her father smiled as he watched from the doorway.

Angilia noticed him and said, "Look what Eric and Patrick gave me, Daddy." She held up a 5"x7" frame that contained a picture of the twins together, smiling. Eric walked to the bed and sat on the edge. He put his hands on his great-grandsons' shoulders, and said, "This is the perfect gift for your Grandmother, boys. You are certainly very thoughtful. I love you both." He kissed the tops of their heads.

"We love you, Great-grandfather," little Eric and Patrick said, and both boys kissed him.

"We asked Yvonne to take our picture so we could surprise you, Grandmother. We were going to get you a bracelet, but we thought you'd like this better," Patrick explained.

"It didn't cost anything, but we thought you'd like it better than the bracelet," Eric said.

Angilia kissed them again, and said, "I do, Eric and Patrick, so much more than a bracelet. This is more valuable than any bracelet. I love it. I love you. You are the perfect grandsons."

§§§§

"Why are people screaming?" young Eric asked during breakfast.

"Yeah, why are they screaming? Are they scared?" young Patrick asked.

"They're not scared, Patrick and Eric. They're excited, because it's Grandfather's and Grandmother's wedding anniversary today. They have been married for 45 years," Prince Eric explained.

"Are we having a party? With cake?" Patrick asked with a smile.

Matthew, Yvonne, and Leigh laughed. "I don't see why we can't have a party this afternoon," Eric said with a smile.

Angilia smiled at her father, and placed her hand over his. "It's Great-grandfather's and Great-grandmother's wedding anniversary, too, today. They were married 70 years ago. How special is that?"

"That is a long time, isn't it, Great-grandfather?" young Patrick asked.

"Yes, it is, Patrick. I love Great-grandmother very much," Eric answered with a smile.

"And I love Mommy very much," Prince Eric said while he looked at his sons. "Mommy and I were married 10 years ago today, Eric and Patrick. That was a very happy day. The happiest day ever was the day both of you were born."

"Mommy and Great-grandmother live in Heaven. We will go there, too, won't we?" young Eric asked.

Prince Eric beamed and kissed his sons. "Yes, they do, boys. We will go there someday, yes, and we will be very happy forever. You will meet your family and have lots of fun. Mommy will finally get to hold you, just like she wants to do. Doesn't that sound just wonderful?"

"Yes, Daddy," young Eric said.

"Yes, Daddy. I can't wait," young Patrick said.

Prince Eric felt tears sting his eyes—happy tears—and he hugged his dear sons close to him while he silently prayed, thanking God for his blessings.

§§§§

Before the Royal party left for church that day, Billy asked Anthony and his staff to please make a cake for an anniversary party that afternoon. The summer sun greeted the Royal party when they left the courtyard and walked to the church. Others on the way to Christ Church Valmondois smiled as they watched the Royal Family, with the young princes looking smart in their suits. Nicole and William joined their friends and their daughter Yvonne.

"Eric and Patrick, you are so handsome today," Nicole said as she smiled down at them.

"Thank you, Mrs. Alexander," young Eric said politely.

"Thank you muchly, Mrs. Alexander," Patrick also said.

Angilia asked Nicole and William to sit with them, which thrilled Yvonne, and the Royal pew was full that morning. Soon, Reverend Olson welcomed the congregation and led them in the opening prayer. This was followed by a hymn, and everyone stood to sing "Farther Along." Young Eric and Patrick held their father's hands, as if understanding the deeper implication in the song's lyrics. Angilia noticed, and she felt tears fill her eyes. As she sang, she silently thanked God for her precious grandsons. They were the true blessings in Prince Eric's life.

When the congregation took their seats, Reverend Olson began his sermon. "What a beautiful June 26, 2061 God has given to us, the beauty of the day very fitting to the three marriages which were consecrated on this date. *'I will betroth thee unto me for ever,'* says Hosea 2:19. That verse exemplifies the abiding commitment to his wedding vows and to his wife that His Majesty King Eric has upheld for 70 years.

"Eric and Marisol married in this church on June 26, 1991. He has lived on earth without her for 66 of those years. The love and devotion which he has shown for nearly seven decades is extraordinary. His Majesty does not feel it is, however, because his love for Marisol is so strong and powerful that it continues to fill his heart and his soul. There was never any thought or need of another romantic relationship." Angilia smiled at her father through her tears and held his hand. Eric gently squeezed her hand and smiled at her.

"We see that mirrored in his grandson, Prince Eric, who wed Julianne in this same church 10 years ago in 2051. Their fifth anniversary was the last which Eric and Julianne celebrated together. His love for her has remained strong and vibrant, and Prince Eric stays true to his wedding vows. Both men know that they will reunite with their beloved wives when God calls them home to Heaven.

"We associate happily-ever-after endings with royalty, and in these two cases, aptly so. Both King Eric and Prince Eric will indeed have their happily-ever-after endings when they do enter

Heaven to spend eternity with Marisol and Julianne. That truth has, more than any other, carried them through the sadness and grief and given them joy and hope. God will never let us suffer forever. He always replaces the pain with exultation. Let us each remember that."

Angilia once more tenderly patted her father's hand, and walked to the pulpit. "My father's love for my mother is legendary, and their love story is undeniably my favorite. His devotion to my mother has always filled my heart and my soul with so much awe and wonder. My precious son is no less awe-inspiring. My love, my husband, Matthew, is my soul mate and rock. I love these three men tremendously. There is no more appropriate scripture for today than Song of Solomon Chapter 8." Angilia recited the chapter, in which Solomon expressed the love between a man and a woman within the sanctified relationship of marriage.

Eric, Matthew, and Prince Eric watched and listened to Angilia with their love for her glowing in their eyes. Nicole, Shannon, and Darlene, who had supported Angilia on her wedding day, cried tears of happiness, as did Yvonne. Love dominated the day, as it should, and the congregation wished the Royal Family a blessed shared anniversary during the traditional receiving line.

After lunch, everyone gathered in the sitting room for the anniversary party. Young Eric and Patrick were delighted to see the cake, and they clapped. They also hugged their father, and told Prince Eric, "Happy anniversary, Daddy."

The twins walked to Eric and hugged him. "Happy anniversary, Great-grandfather."

Next, they hugged Matthew and then Angilia, and told them, "Happy anniversary, Grandfather and Grandmother."

Eric and Patrick brought tears to everyone when they stood in the center of the room and looked at their family. "We love you, Daddy, Grandfather, Grandmother, and Great-grandfather. You make us happy." Prince Eric, Matthew, Angilia, and Eric surrounded the twins with a group hug and with many kisses. Love did dominate the day.

§§§§§

After lunch on Monday, July 25, 2061, Angilia's phone rang as she talked with her family in the sitting room before she and her father returned to their office. "Thank you for calling me. I'll be there soon," Angilia told the caller. She stood and kissed everyone. Matthew asked her where she was going. "Susan died earlier today. When she moved, she told me her final wishes and asked me to make sure they were fulfilled. I'm going to take care of that now. I'll be home later today, darling."

Angilia drove to Susan's house and got Katherine's dress and the matching pumps from the bedroom closet. Angilia looked around, recalling how happy Susan was in her home. "I'm going to miss you, Susan. I love you," Angilia said as she left and locked the door.

Angilia drove to the funeral home where Susan's body had been taken. The director escorted her to a room where Susan's body lay covered by a sheet. Angilia could not help but cry when she saw her friend. She dried her tears, though, and handed the dress and shoes to the director. "Susan wanted to be buried in this dress. It belonged to my mother-in-law Katherine, and was given to Susan. These are the shoes that Susan bought to match the dress."

"Thank you, Your Majesty. Reverend Olson told me that you were the one that Miss Pierce entrusted with her funeral plans. He also told me that Miss Pierce bought a plot at the Christ Church Valmondois Cemetery. That is where her casket is to be taken for the burial, correct?"

"Yes. We'd like to have her funeral at Christ Church Valmondois, as well. Would Wednesday be too soon for that?" Susan wanted to be buried as soon as possible," Angilia explained.

"Wednesday is fine. We will take care of Miss Pierce, Your Majesty."

Angilia thanked him, and returned home, where her family still waited for her in the sitting room. "Are you all right, Mommy?" Prince Eric asked in concern as he sat on the floor playing with the twins.

"I'm okay, Eric. I'm sad. I'm going to miss Susan. She is the longest friend in my life. Life will never be the same without her."

Matthew hugged her and said, "It won't. In many ways, she was Mom's twin. They were so much alike. That's why they bonded and got along so well."

"I know, Matthew. I thought about that on the way to get the dress in which Susan wants to be buried. It's one that Katherine bought. Susan rarely wore that one so it would last until her funeral."

"Really? Wow, that's sweet of her. That makes me want to cry, though," Matthew said.

"If you do that, you'll be just like Aunt Susan, Grandfather," young Eric said. Everyone laughed.

"Yes, I will, Eric. And Grandma. She and Susan cried over darn near everything."

"I bet they cried when Susan got to Heaven and saw Grandma again," young Patrick said.

"I bet they did, Patrick. I bet they did. I'm sure they'll both cry each time one of us arrives in Heaven," Matthew added.

Eric stood and put his arms around Angilia and Matthew. "I'm sure you're right. In fact, they're probably crying now as they watch us. I know angels don't cry, Angilia, but I really don't think that rule applies to Katherine and Susan," Eric smiled.

"Tears were their laughter sometimes. That's how Aunt Susan explained it to us once," young Patrick said.

"That's a lovely thought, Patrick, and very true. Grandma and Susan cried more when they were happy than when they were sad," Matthew smiled.

"That is how I remember both of them. Happy," Eric smiled in return.

"I do, too," Angilia added. Prince Eric and the twins joined Eric, Matthew, and Angilia for a family hug.

"We do, too," young Eric said.

§§§§

"Welcome, Your Majesties, Your Royal Highnesses, and esteemed guests. We at the Musée are excited to add this latest portrait to our Royal Portrait Gallery in honor of His Royal Highness Matthew, Duc de Valmondois on the occasion of his 75th birthday. To introduce this very special portrait, please welcome His Royal Highness Prince Eric de Valdavia." Stephanie Purvis curtsied to Prince Eric when he walked to the podium.

"Thank you, Ms. Purvis. This is such a great honor for me for several reasons. First, I love my father, and I'm thrilled that this portrait in particular commemorates his 75th birthday. What makes this portrait so extraordinary? It was painted by my mother. That means he got to stare at her quite a lot while it was painted, and that shows. By now, we have all seen his expression when he looks at her, especially his eyes. He looks positively love-struck," Prince Eric truthfully said, which brought much laughter from the audience. "It's true! My grandfather first noticed it in early 2012. My father had it bad from the very beginning. My mother captured that perfectly. To unveil my father's portrait are his grandsons, Eric and Patrick."

People wildly applauded when the young princes walked to the gold cord. "Happy birthday, Grandfather," they said in unison, which charmed everyone. Young Eric and Patrick pulled the gold cord together and revealed Matthew's portrait. Prince Eric had been right. Angilia had memorialized the now-famous Romeo-like look of love in her husband's amber eyes.

The audience stood and cheered the portrait. They also requested that the Royal Family pose for pictures near the portrait. Eric, Angilia, Matthew, Prince Eric, young Eric, and young Patrick obliged, and no one could deny the truth. Matthew smiled at his Angilia with that same expression, 45 years after their wedding. His first and only love was more alive than ever.

§§§§§

Angilia stood in her father's suite doorway, waiting for him when he stepped from his bedroom looking as dapper as ever in a navy blue suit. He beamed when he saw her there, that ever-present, pulse-pounding look of love in her eyes. Eric walked to her, hugged her close to him, and said, "Oh, how I love you, my beautiful daughter Angilia."

"I love you, Daddy," she managed to say through the tears that choked her. She forced herself to stop crying, and she looked up at him. "I love you. Happy birthday, my magnificent father."

"What makes this day even more special is that our Eric is 40 today. What a strong, godly man he is, Angilia. He is amazing. And our little men are five years old today. Time has seemed to speed by since their births. They are growing up so fast, but so wise and handsome. They are so special, all three of them, Angilia."

"I know, Daddy. My baby is such a wonderful, kind man, just like you. Eric and Patrick really are perfect. Life is perfect."

"Yes, it is, Angel. I never could have dreamed of such a marvelous life, never. I never thought I would live this long. Sometimes, it's hard for my brain to wrap itself around the number. Why me? What did I ever do that God decided that I should live to be 107, Angilia?" Eric asked her in a thoughtful tone.

"Oh, Daddy, you know that. God still has work for you to do here on earth. He needs you here. Don't question it; just know that he has a reason. I am very grateful for that, you know. I will miss you so very much when God takes you to Heaven, Daddy."

Eric placed his hand over his daughter's cheek. "I know, darling, but never feel sad when he does come for me. That will be quite a joyous moment, we both know that. I will miss you so very much, my Angel. But we will be together forever someday." Eric placed a hand over the pendant he wore every day. "We know that. When I do die, I will go to Mommy for our eternal happily-ever-after. You will join us someday, and so will Matthew. Eric and the boys will, too. How gloriously happy we will be, together in Heaven for all of eternity."

"I know, Daddy. I know what a blessing and a gift that is, believe me. That will still not mean I will miss you less. In many ways, that will make me miss you more, because I will have to wait until I die to join you," Angilia confessed. "I'm not as strong and brave as you are, Daddy. I'm not." Angilia hung her head, crying, and Eric wrapped his arms around her.

"No, Angilia, you're not. You are far stronger and braver. I know that. I've seen that," Eric firmly stated. "You waited 17 years in the Angels Choir to see me again, from the day Patrick died until Christmas Day 1994. That felt like a lot longer, I know. You told me that. But God brought us together again. He will do so again in Heaven, darling. Believe me, waiting for that can seem agonizing at times. I know, though, that my reward is reuniting with Mommy and the rest of my family. They are worth the wait, Angilia, because eternity never ends. We will live together forever. You taught me the real truth and beauty of that, my beautiful, angelic daughter."

§§§§

That afternoon, the Royal Family was joined by Leigh, Shannon, Yvonne, Nicole, William, Darlene, and Scott in the sitting room. The triple birthday party was full of love, laughter, memories, and stories throughout the afternoon. Also present was Darlene's notorious adoration of King Eric. When she arrived, she hugged and kissed the twins and Prince Eric. When she approached Eric, however, she froze with her eyes huge and her mouth open.

"Hey, Eric, I'm here for the party! Hi Darlene," Patrick said when he suddenly manifested beside his brother.

Darlene gasped and fainted to the floor. "Oh no, not again," Scott moaned. "Matthew?"

Matthew revived Darlene, whose face turned bright red from her heightened emotions. "I'll be okay. I just need to pull myself together. Shannon, would you mind going to the ladies room with me, please?" Shannon led Darlene away, much to Eric's relief.

"Good grief. I thought Darlene was over that," Eric said.

"I'm so sorry. She'll never get over that, I'm afraid," Scott apologized in exasperation.

"This reminds me of Angilia's 17ᵗʰ birthday party. Darlene fainted two or three times that day," Nicole giggled.

"What is wrong with Darlene?" young Eric asked.

Everyone looked at each other, unsure what to say. "Darlene just has a huge crush on your Great-grandfather. She has for a long time," William finally explained.

"Yeah, she really likes my brother," Patrick said with a smile.

"Oh. That's why she faints?" young Eric asked.

"Yes, Eric. Darlene really likes Great-grandfather a whole lot. It's just too much for her," Prince Eric added.

"Oh. She fainted when Uncle Patrick showed up. Does she really like him, too?" young Patrick asked. Nicole, William, and Billy could not help but giggle.

"Yes, she does, Patrick. Darlene just can't help it, I'm afraid. I guess we're stuck with her obsession by this point," Scott said. They heard Shannon and Darlene returning, so everyone stopped talking about Darlene's condition.

"I'm sorry. It just felt warm in here," Darlene explained.

"Oh, yeah, that's because Uncle Patrick is hot," young Eric matter-of-factly replied, referring to the warm air that surrounded his great-granduncle.

"Yes, he is," Darlene said, flustered, taking the comment literally. "I need some water," she told Scott, who was afraid to let go of her arm lest she faint again.

"Here Darlene," Angilia said and handed a glass of water to Darlene. "Why don't we sit for a while?"

Thankfully, Darlene relaxed, enjoying the twins' stories and performance of their Grandmother's songs. "That was wonderful, boys. Talent and good looks sure do run in this family," she commented, "especially in men named Eric and Patrick."

"Why don't we cut the birthday cake now?" Prince Eric quickly suggested. The last thing he wanted was for Darlene to suffer another episode.

Everyone gathered around the table, where the cake stood. Young Eric and Patrick stood front and center, with their father and great-grandfather on either side of them. The four men blew out the candles together, and then hugged. Darlene sobbed. "This is so beautiful. This family is just surrounded by love. It's almost tangible," she said through her tears.

Nicole put her arm around Darlene's shoulder. "Yes, it is, Darlene. Love is the most beautiful thing."

"*Love is a many splendored thing,*" Patrick suddenly sung.

"Oh, Uncle Patrick, I love you," Angilia said and hugged him.

"So do I," Darlene muttered, and then fainted to the floor.

"Darlene did it again, Grandfather," young Patrick said.

"Yeah, but Uncle Patrick doesn't feel hot this time," young Eric said. Everyone laughed while Matthew knelt by Darlene.

"He does to Darlene," Scott said.

§§§§

6 December 2061

40 years ago today, my adored Abuelo died. He had come to me, in my sitting room, while I held Eric. Abuelo came to me. He died while I held him against me. There is something so precious and spiritual in sharing death with a loved one. I miss Abuelo, everything about him—his eyes, his smile, his wit, his strength and compassion, and his intense love. He was one of the first people I met the day I was born. I love him so. I always will. I know I will be with him again, someday, whenever God decides that my life on earth is over.

Abuelo's death is not surrounded by sad memories. It never could be. A miracle occurred that day. Mommy was Abuelo's Spirit Guide! I saw my Mommy! She kissed my cheek. How I love her, words are powerless to say. I saw her, I felt her! Mommy is alive! She lives in Heaven, where she waits for us—for Daddy, her one true love.

The real miracle that day is that Daddy saw her and felt her!! Oh, God, thank you for that priceless gift to Daddy! His love for her is legendary. His love for her is eternal. Mommy kissed his lips that day! It has been 40 years since then, but that one moment confirmed the truth—that she waits for him in Heaven!

Daddy is now 107, and I love and treasure him so. I don't know how many years of earthly life God has planned for Daddy. I am utterly selfish. God, forgive me. I want to keep him here. That is wrong of me. Daddy will never die, I know that. His body will. Not his soul. When you decide that his work on earth is done, you will take him to Heaven, God. Daddy told me not to be sad when that happens. I will try not to be. I won't be. Not really.

At that moment, Daddy will reunite with Mommy! God, you allowed me to see that—how can I ever express my gratitude for that? 45½ years ago, you allowed Michael to give me the divine pendant. Oh, how beautiful! You know that I gave the pendant to Daddy on his 75th birthday. The fulfillment of that scene is what awaits us upon our deaths. That is not sad. I know that.

I want Daddy to live eternally happy, together with Mommy. I do. I know I will join them when I die. Is it wrong to admit that I will miss Daddy? How long, how many years, must I wait for my death so that I can live with Daddy and Mommy? That is the most difficult part, God. Leaving Daddy and returning to the Angels Choir the day Uncle Patrick died—that was the absolute hardest thing I have <u>ever</u> done. You know that, God. You understand. Please understand now.

I want Daddy and Mommy to live happily-ever-after together. I do. They deserve that. I would never deny them that. Help me to stay strong, God, so that I can live the life you intend for me while I await my reunion with Daddy and Mommy in Heaven. I lived in Heaven, waiting to come to Daddy on earth. When he goes to Heaven, I will live here on earth, waiting to go to him in Heaven. Give me the strength to endure that wait, God. Please.

CHAPTER 19

"Welcome to the 50th annual Eric DeBruce Martineau Scholarship for Musical Excellence. I am Don Cross, Warden of New College at the University of Oxford. I am truly honored to host this very special ceremony on this March 6, 2062. Please join me in welcoming His Majesty King Eric de Valdavia and Her Majesty Queen Angilia de Valdavia."

The audience rose for an energetic 30-minute standing ovation. Eric looked at Angilia, as always uncomfortable with the attention. He heaved a sigh of relief when Professor Cross motioned Eric and Angilia to their seats when the audience finally sat. "Thank you. What a kind welcome," Eric stated.

"Thank you so much. My father and I are delighted to be here for the 50th straight year to award another scholarship in his name. Doing so is a true blessing," Angilia smiled.

Soon, the traditional question-and-answer session was under way. After 50 years, Eric and Angilia had been asked the same questions numerous times. However, they understood that those asking had not heard the answers before; many of them had not been born 50 years earlier. The repetition never bothered Eric or Angilia. This year, they were asked some new questions, though.

"I'd like to ask His Majesty what one music-related memory stands out most for him," one young man in the audience requested.

Eric sat quietly for a moment. "One memory? Just one? There are so very many. The one moment that still sends shivers down my spine is one I have recalled and relived many times. Angilia was two years old, and I had just tucked her in bed. She asked me to sing what she calls our song, "Sunshine on My Shoulders," to her. I began singing, and she sat up and smiled at me. After the first few lines, she began singing with me. I was dazed. My tiny little girl took my breath. Angilia didn't sound like a typical two-year old at all. Her voice was so mature, so perfect. I had never heard her sing before. That moment exceeds all other memories."

"Her music career began just four years later. Sixty years ago, Her Majesty recorded her first album. She wrote 11 of the 12 songs. What was that like for you, Sir, as her father?"

"Then, in 2002, I was really kind of dumbstruck. Everything happened so quickly. One day she was singing and playing music around the house, and literally the next day, she was rehearsing with Tom Greenfield. It was a whirlwind. I attended the first recording sessions. I watched my young, small daughter while she played the guitar and sang the songs. Tom and his band and producer were floored by her. Perfect pitch. Expert phrasing. Angilia's takes were faultless, just perfect. She recorded the 12 songs in just two days. The thing that I remember most is how much emotion was in her voice. She didn't sound like a child. She didn't. She constantly stunned me."

"Do you feel that Angilia's music career was pure coincidence or that it was meant to be?" a young lady asked.

"Oh, everything in Angilia's life was meant to be," Eric stated. "There is no question or doubt. God predestined everything. If you are familiar with Angilia's memoir, you know that she lived in Heaven prior to her physical birth. Everything about her was formed there, and stayed within her when she was born. That's why she never sounded like the young child she was, for one thing. Angilia was what many people call an old soul. Who she was in Heaven remained part of her when she came to earth. None of it was coincidence."

"My father is right. God created me centuries ago. God made me. God did not strip any of that away when I was born. It all came to earth with me. I can't and I don't take any credit for anything I have done. The credit goes to God and to my father. My father didn't know about my past until 2012, but he nourished my love of music. He taught me, he supported me, and he helped me to develop what God had gifted to me," Angilia explained.

Moments later, Angilia and Eric, with her band, performed a one-hour concert. They performed a mix of their solos and duets. One request for Angilia's first gold single was shouted, and she smiled when she played and sang Tom Greenfield's "So Many Rivers," the song that had caught his attention that day in 2002.

"Thank you. The past 60 years have been such a blessing. I have met many wonderful people and had so many amazing experiences due to the music. Music is one of the most divine gifts we can give to ourselves and to each other," Angilia said. "I learned that from Gabriel in the Angels Choir and from Tom Greenfield here on earth. Make your music for yourselves and for all of humankind."

§§§§§

"That concludes our meeting for April 19, 2062. Our next meeting is scheduled for 11:00 A.M. on Wednesday, May 11. Meeting adjourned," School Board Secretary Karen Wittier stated. The School Board members began leaving the building, and several walked out with Angilia, Shannon, and Troy. As they were talking, they heard a small voice say, "I need your help, Queen Angilia."

Angilia looked down at a little girl who appeared like she had been crying. Angilia handed her briefcase to Shannon and knelt down. "What can I do for you, darling?"

"Save Tiger. We were playing, and a car hit him. He's hurt."

"Oh, darling, of course. Let me stay with you and Tiger and call a vet. We'll get Tiger to an animal hospital," Angilia said. "Where is Tiger?"

"I live over there," the girl pointed to the corner nearby. "I want you to pray for Tiger, Queen Angilia."

"Of course, I will." Angilia took the girl's hand and walked toward her house. Shannon and Troy quickly followed, as did the School Board members, all of whom were frankly horrified by the girl's request.

The girl's cat was lying by the side of the road, not moving. Angilia bent and gently felt for a heartbeat. She did not feel one. Neither did Troy. The cat was not breathing. What could Angilia do? "Shannon, call a vet, and tell him what happened. Tell him to come here right away. Tell him it's my request, and I'll take care of everything. Hurry," Angilia instructed. Angilia never used her title to take advantage of situations, but in this case, with time critical, she had to get a vet there as quickly as possible.

The little girl was crying uncontrollably. "I don't want Tiger to die. I love him. Pray for him, please pray for him, Queen Angilia."

"Of course, darling. The vet will be here soon, and he will let us know what he can do. I'll pray for Tiger and for you while we wait," Angilia said, not sure if anyone could save Tiger—except for God. Angilia placed her hands on Tiger and began praying. "Dear God, I know that you alone have the power to help Tiger. You can do what none of us can do. If it is your will, please heal Tiger. Please do not take Tiger from his loving friend yet. We know and believe that you alone cause miracles. We ask you for a miracle today for Tiger. Please, God, heal Tiger if that is your will. This we ask in your holy name, God. Amen."

Everyone standing around Angilia, watching, echoed the Amen. Tiger, though, did not move. Angilia looked at the little girl in sadness. The little girl began crying loudly, and threw herself against Angilia. Angilia tried to soothe her, to no avail. Finally, the little girl sadly asked, "Does this mean that Tiger is dead? He's gone forever?"

"I'm so sorry," Angilia said, tears in her eyes.

The little girl nodded. She bent and picked up Tiger, intending to carry him to her back porch so that her father could bury him later. Suddenly, the little girl stopped walking and ran back to Angilia. The vet arrived at that moment. "Tiger moved, Queen Angilia. He moved."

Everyone was stunned. "Let me see him," the vet demanded. The vet gingerly felt Tiger's legs and abdomen. Tiger meowed, not liking the stranger's touch. "Put him down, please, so I can examine him better." The little girl put Tiger on the ground. The vet reached over and gently squeezed the cat's abdomen again, checking for obvious signs of injury, when Tiger hissed and scratched his hand.

"That's not nice, Tiger. The vet just wants to make sure you are all right. Be good," the girl scolded her cat. "Tiger doesn't like strangers. I'm sorry."

"May I hold him?" Angilia asked. The little girl nodded and placed Tiger in Angilia's arms. "Can you examine him now?" she asked the vet, who listened to Tiger's heart and other organs with a stethoscope.

"Well, there's no sign of internal damage and no obvious broken bones. Why don't we take Tiger to my office for x-rays, just to make sure?"

Angilia, the little girl—who finally told them her name was Nancy—and the vet went in his car, while Troy and Shannon followed. Two hours later, the vet told Nancy that Tiger was in perfect health. "I don't know how severely he was injured, but he's fine now."

"He was dead. He wasn't breathing, and his heart wasn't beating. Tiger was dead," Nancy said.

"It sure felt that way," Angilia added.

"Well, follow up with Tiger's regular vet in a few days, Nancy, just to make sure, but Tiger seems fine," the vet smiled.

Shannon and Troy were stunned when they heard the vet's verdict and saw Tiger. The School Board members had followed them to the vet's office, too, wanting to know the outcome. They were just as amazed when they saw Tiger in Nancy's arms.

"Queen Angilia saved Tiger. She brought him back to life. Thank you, Queen Angilia," Nancy said and kissed Angilia's cheek. No one present could deny that Angilia had caused a miracle that day.

§§§§

"Yvonne, can you come to the sitting room for something important?" Angilia asked Yvonne over the telephone on a sunny summer afternoon.

"Of course. I'll be there in a couple of minutes."

"She's on her way. Everyone stay out of sight until she's in the room," Angilia told her family and friends. Only she and Eric were sitting on the sofa when Yvonne entered and asked what they needed. At that moment, Eric said, "We want to tell you something."

That was the signal for everyone to jump out and yell, "Happy birthday!"

Yvonne was startled, not expecting a surprise party. Her hands covered her face, and tears filled her eyes. "I can't believe this. How did you manage to pull this off?"

"Easy. We invited everyone, and we all hid until Mommy and Grandfather got you in here. I knew you'd never suspect anything," Prince Eric told his best and life-long friend.

"I didn't. Thank you all for coming on a workday. Oh, Mom and Dad," Yvonne said and hugged Nicole and William. "Darlene and Scott. Shannon. I've known you all my life," she said to the COC friends and hugged them, too. "Leigh, I'm so glad you're here," Yvonne told Prince Eric's close friend and hugged him. "This is wonderful. You are the people who mean the most to me."

"Happy birthday, Yvonne," young Eric said.

"Happy birthday, Yvonne," young Patrick repeated.

"Thank you, Eric and Patrick. Gosh, you are both so handsome and big now," she replied and bent to kiss their cheeks. "I can't believe you're five years old already. Where has the time gone?"

"That's what I've been asking myself today, Yvonne," Nicole said as she wiped a tear from her eye. "My baby is such a lovely woman. It doesn't feel like 40 years," she added as she hugged her daughter.

"I don't feel 40," Yvonne said. "I really don't. Do you, Eric?"

Prince Eric smiled and shook his head. "No, I don't. Age is just a number, really. It doesn't define us. I learned that from my Grandfather. He's incredible, and if I can be half the man he is, I'll be doing well."

"You are quite an amazing man, Eric," Eric said to his grandson. "Age is a number, yes. We control how we feel and our mental attitude. You two are doing right, taking care of yourselves and surrounding yourselves with those you love. You've got many decades ahead of you," Eric smiled and hugged Yvonne and Eric.

"Has this family discovered the elixir of life or some magic potion? Everyone is so beautiful and healthy," Darlene marveled.

Yvonne giggled. "I'm not a member of the family, so don't count me among the young and the beautiful."

"Well, but you live here and work here. It's spread to you, too. What's the secret, really?" Darlene asked.

"There's no secret, Darlene. Faith, healthy living, and love. Those are the three all-important components of the formula,"

Matthew said with a smile. "I learned that when I came here in 2012. It's not magic or fairy dust or potions," he giggled, referring to press speculation. "It really is as simple as living a godly life. Look at my father-in-law for proof of that," Matthew said, realizing his mistake too late.

"Oh, I do, Matthew. I do, believe me," Darlene admitted, her face red due to her heightened emotions.

"Well, let's indulge in a little birthday cake now. Yvonne is the birthday girl today, and she gets to blow out the candle. What's a birthday party without cake?" Prince Eric quickly diverted the focus.

"Thank you," Nicole whispered to him as everyone walked to the table.

Yvonne blew out the candle, and cut pieces of cake for everyone. They all sat comfortably on the sofas and chairs while they ate the cake, talking and laughing and sharing memories. "The first birthday party I attended here was Angilia's 17th. Darlene, Scott, and Shannon were there also. That's the day that Matthew gave Angilia a pre-engagement promise ring. That was so romantic," Nicole shared.

"Yes, it was. I'd never known anyone who'd received a pre-engagement ring. And it was a very special ring. I remember what it looked like. It had a small diamond heart, and it said, *True Love*. That ring was beautiful," Darlene added, and wiped a tear from her cheek.

"It was," Nicole agreed. "Of course, it had another meaning to us because of COC, but most of the guys we knew from high school would have never given a girl a ring like that. Of course, Matthew was more mature than the high school boys, but still. That was, to me, his way of accepting who Angilia was and what she believed."

"Thank you, Nicole. It was my way of showing Angilia and Eric, her protective father, that I respected her beliefs. She and Eric are the ones who brought God back into my life after all the years of science. They didn't force their beliefs on me ever. They just lived their lives, and it sort of rubbed off on me," Matthew smiled. He looked at his wife and his father-in-law, feeling such immense love for them both.

"Well, once I learned about Angilia's past with Matthew in the Unborn Children Sphere, I knew that they were meant to be together. Their marriage was meant to happen. I knew God was in control. That's how our lives have been in the 50 years since then. All of us are meant to be family and friends. We entered one another's lives for a reason," Eric said definitely but with a smile.

"That's beautiful, Eric. I believe that. Angilia and my mother became friends 50 years ago. Eric and I were born just seven months apart and have been best friends all of our lives. It's like a cycle of love that spreads from one generation to the next. That is such a beautiful thought and a beautiful feeling. I'm so glad God brought us all together. I love you all," Yvonne said with what Angilia perpetually called happy tears.

§§§§

"His Majesty King Eric's Platinum Jubilee begins this morning with the National Service of Thanksgiving in Christ Church Valmondois. Welcome to our very special coverage on this glorious August 20, 2062. I am Chad Glover, and I am so honored to host our live broadcast of the National Service of Thanksgiving.

"Valdavia and the whole world celebrate King Eric's 70th Jubilee. What an amazing milestone. King Eric is the most revered and respected leader in the world, and the nation of Valdavia is so blessed by this man. In moments, the Royal Family is expected to arrive at the church, at which time we will begin our coverage of the National Service of Thanksgiving.

"In fact, the Royal Family's car has just arrived, and His Majesty and Her Majesty step out first and link arms. His Majesty is dressed in a classic navy suit, accented with a red-and-white striped tie, the colors of the Valdavian flag. Her Majesty wears a red and white dress, also paying tribute to the national colors. What a beautiful sight on this magical morning."

§§§§

"Welcome to the National Service of Thanksgiving as we pay honor to King Eric de Valdavia on his Platinum Jubilee. What a magnificent blessing God has given to us in the life and the reign of this righteous man. King Eric is truly a godly king, one who leads with prayer and compassion. Eric's love for God and for people is his guiding force. No other modern leader has based his or her administrative decisions, laws, and deeds solely upon prayer and faith. Eric does. He has done so since he assumed the throne on September 15, 1992. By placing God at the center of his life, Eric has made Valdavia the most peaceful, serene country in the world. We live in peace, without war and poverty and strife, and we owe this to His Majesty King Eric.

"Let us pray. Dear God, We thank you for the life and reign of King Eric. His life has been about serving you and serving us. Long before he became King Eric, he began working for our best interests. He prepared for his future role. He followed your commandments and laws, turning to you for guidance. That only strengthened when he became King Eric. We constantly reap the benefits of that, and for our many blessings we are grateful. Continue to embrace King Eric with your love and your grace. In your name, this we ask. Amen."

The congregation repeated "Amen," and most of them took their seats in the pews. Angilia and Patrick, however, walked to the piano. Patrick stood behind his niece while she played the hymn. They sang a hymn from 1834, one which meshed with the message of the National Service of Thanksgiving, "My Hope is Built." Eric watched and listened to them with such love. What an absolute miracle to have his brother and his daughter together.

When the hymn concluded, Angilia hugged her Uncle Patrick and returned to the pew, where she held her father's hand. Patrick stepped to the pulpit for a scripture reading. "1 John 2:10. *'He that loveth his brother abideth in the light, and there is none occasion of stumbling in him.'* I love you, Eric," Patrick smiled at his brother before returning to sit alongside him.

Angilia stood and walked to the pulpit for her scripture reading. "Psalm Chapter 112. *'Praise ye the LORD. Blessed is the man that feareth the LORD, that delighteth greatly in his commandments. His seed shall be mighty upon earth: the generation of the upright shall be blessed. Wealth and riches shall be in his house: and his righteousness endureth for ever. Unto the upright there ariseth light in the darkness: he is gracious, and full of compassion, and righteous. A good man sheweth favour, and lendeth: he will guide his affairs with discretion. Surely he shall not be moved for ever: the righteous shall be in everlasting remembrance. He shall not be afraid of evil tidings: his heart is fixed, trusting in the LORD. His heart is established, he shall not be afraid, until he see his desire upon his enemies. He hath dispersed, he hath given to the poor; his righteousness endureth for ever; his horn shall be exalted with honour. The wicked shall see it, and be grieved; he shall gnash with his teeth, and melt away: the desire of the wicked shall perish.*" Angilia smiled at her father, tears shining in her turquoise eyes. She returned to her seat between Patrick and Matthew, and both men gently squeezed her hands.

Matthew went to the pulpit for his scripture reading, and he smiled at his father-in-law. "Psalm 5:12. *For thou, Lord, wilt bless the righteous; with favour wilt thou compass him as with a shield.*" Matthew hugged Eric before he resumed his seat.

Prince Eric walked to the pulpit. "Proverbs 20:26. *'A wise king scattereth the wicked, and bringeth the wheel over them.'*" He smiled at his grandfather before placing a step-stool at the podium. When he returned to the pew, he patted his son Eric on the back.

Young Prince Eric walked to the pulpit, climbed upon the step-stool, and smiled at his great-grandfather. He held a card in his hand, from which he read his scripture. "Psalm 106:3. *Blessed are they that keep judgment, and he that doeth righteousness at all times.'* That's what my Great-grandfather does. I love you, Great-grandfather."

Eric held his arms open, and young Eric went to him in a hug. "I love you, Eric."

When his brother was seated, young Prince Patrick went to the pulpit and climbed atop the step-stool, a card in his hand, too. "Genesis 15:6. *'And he believed in the Lord; and he counted it to him for righteousness.'* I love you, Great-grandfather."

Patrick ran to his great-grandfather for a hug, as well. Eric fought his tears as he said, "I love you, Patrick."

§§§§§

Troy drove the Royal party to Central Park for Monday's traditional day of mingling, tributes, and programs. Angilia and Prince Eric walked on either side of Eric, and she linked an arm with her father's. As usual, Eric was constantly surrounded by well-wishers and fans throughout the day.

The Royal party had lunch at mid-day, at which point they found themselves once more besieged by people from across Valdavia and around the globe. They all wanted to tell Eric how much they loved and admired him. A Platinum Jubilee was quite rare, and people wanted to take advantage of the opportunity to wish Eric congratulations.

At 3:00 that afternoon, Tamara Courtney, a member of the Platinum Jubilee Committee, approached the Royal party. "Your Majesties, Your Royal Highnesses, we would like to ask you to join us for a very special program at the park's main entrance."

"Of course, Ms. Courtney," Eric graciously said, although he wondered what the program involved. When they arrived, Byron Lee announced the ceremony on the loud speakers, and within 20 minutes, most of those in the park were gathered. The six committee members excitedly stood near a podium, anxious to begin. "We are so happy that you could join us today. What a great honor it is for Valdavia to host His Majesty's Platinum Jubilee, the first in the nation's history. We could not let this auspicious occasion pass without somehow commemorating this milestone," Norma Vance said.

"No, we couldn't," Denise Turner added. "We are so thrilled by today's announcement, which we promise we will make very soon.

"Indeed, we will," the Committee President, Raymond Thacker said. "We desired to keep this as much a secret and a surprise as possible. We had to tell one person, however, to make this official. Her Majesty Queen Angilia quickly signed the decree making this legal."

Eric looked down at her in surprise, wondering what on earth she had done this time. She smiled up at him. He soon learned, along with everyone else, what the Jubilee Committee had enlisted Angilia's help with to honor Eric.

"Central Park is now officially known as King Eric Celebratory Park," Mr. Thacker announced just as the new sign was uncovered. The crowd loudly cheered, noticing a plaque which commemorated the date and occasion of the new name.

"The park, Angilia? Really?" Eric asked her, incredulous.

"Of course, Daddy. Isn't this fantastic?" she exclaimed.

"This is cool, Great-grandfather," young Eric said.

"Yeah, this is really neat, Great-grandfather. People love you an awful lot," young Patrick said.

"Yes, they do. They always have, and they always will, Patrick and Eric," Angilia happily said.

§§§§

On Wednesday, August 23, 2062, the Royal party joined thousands of people for a program at Gateway Arena. Clark Wynter welcomed everyone. "Good afternoon. We are so delighted about today's event for Platinum Jubilee Week. The Committee members and I were thrilled when we received word of this. We were contacted over one year ago and asked if this could be part of the week-long events honoring King Eric. Of course, we replied. Please join us in welcoming His Excellency Marcell Poirier, President of the French Republic."

Eric and Angilia were the first to stand, which the rest of the Royal party and the audience likewise did. President Poirier received a warm standing ovation. He looked up at the Royal box and saluted Eric, which elicited screams of delight and approval. "Thank you so much," President Poirier finally said.

"I am thrilled to be here during His Majesty's Platinum Jubilee. What an amazing and distinct milestone for this extraordinary man. I have known Eric since before I was elected

President, and I have always been impressed with his benevolent style of leadership. There is no mystery why Eric is the undisputed most-loved leader in the world. I say that in all sincerity and with no envy. Eric is the leader most of us wish we could be. There is no one better to emulate, that is the truth." The audience applauded their enthusiastic agreement.

"France and Valdavia have maintained a close connection since 1331 when Valdavia was created a sovereign state. What once was part of France became the nation of Valdavia. Since 1331, Valdavia has had 19 Kings and one Queen. Eric is, of course, your 19th King. You could not have a better, more effective King than Eric. Everything he does is for you, the citizens of Valdavia. God comes first in his life, followed by his family, and then by you. You rank quite high on Eric's hierarchy, and that means he works tirelessly on your behalf. You know that.

"Valdavia is quite an oddity in the latter half of the 21st century. Valdavia has never had a war or a revolution. There has never been poverty. There is no unrest. You have a stable, thriving financial institution. Your crime rate is all but nonexistent. No other modern country experiences the peace, contentment, and livelihood that Valdavia does. The rest of us constantly marvel at Valdavia, I must tell you.

"France wanted to do something public to honor Eric during his Platinum Jubilee. The best way to share this with you all is by live feed," President Poirier said while a large screen showed a view of the Arc de Triomphe. "Near the Arc de Triomphe stands France's tribute to King Eric de Valdavia." At that moment, the camera panned into an area near the famous Arc. Everyone in the audience gasped and then stood for a roaring standing ovation.

"That's you, Great-grandfather!" young Patrick exclaimed.

"Oh, Daddy, this is gorgeous!" Angilia enthused and grabbed his arm.

President Poirier looked up at the Royal Box and motioned for Eric to stand. "Ladies and gentlemen, this statue of King Eric de Valdavia stands in the heart of Paris, near where the first King de

Valdavia lived and worked." Angilia held her father's arm and stood with him. "Eric, France is proud to count you among her descendants," President Poirier smiled while the audience cheered.

§§§§

The next morning, the Royal party attended another portrait unveiling at the museum. Director Stephanie Purvis opened the ticketed event in the Royal Portrait Gallery. "Good morning, and welcome to the Platinum Jubilee commemorative portrait unveiling. Thank you for attending. Your ticket purchase is donated to His Majesty's Open Heart Foundation, which we are thrilled to support. We at the museum are absolutely delighted to add this portrait of His Majesty King Eric to our already-impressive collection. This portrait will serve as yet another tangible reminder of His Majesty's 70th Jubilee for many generations to come.

"This portrait was painted by His Majesty's son-in-law, His Royal Highness Matthew, Duc de Valmondois. As you know well, His Royal Highness is a very talented and accomplished artist, and the museum is proud to house a collection of the Duc's paintings. We, the staff at the museum, adore this portrait of His Majesty. We know you will, too. I would like to ask Her Majesty Queen Angilia to unveil the portrait of her father."

Angilia kissed her father's cheek, and walked to the portrait. She pulled a gold cord to open a red curtain and reveal Matthew's portrait of Eric. The audience responded with a rousing standing ovation that lasted half an hour. The Royal Family posed for pictures near the portrait, which depicted Eric at the amazing age of 107. His grey hair shone, and his famous turquoise eyes sparkled. His dimpled smile captivated as always. The lines and wrinkles did little to diminish Eric's charm.

Young Eric and Patrick smiled, pointed to their great-grandfather's portrait, and hugged him. Eric bent and kissed both boys, never embarrassed by public displays of affection. The fact that the Royal Family was never afraid to show their love was one of the traits that perpetually enchanted people. That trait had been passed from Eric to Angilia, to Prince Eric, and to young Eric and Patrick. People watched four generations of the DeBruce Martineau

397

dynasty, knowing that love would continue to lead and to dominate the ruling family for generations to come.

§§§§

On Friday, the traditional Garden Party was held on the palace grounds. The Royal Family greeted guests, who seemed to arrive steadily throughout the day as people wished to offer congratulations to Eric. He was constantly surrounded, as he had been at the park on Monday. Angilia beamed to watch the respect shown to her father. She always had.

Two hours into the Garden Party, Angilia asked two staff members to bring her surprise onto the back patio. She delightedly turned it on, which pleasantly surprised her family, friends, and the guests. Shannon and Billy smiled, remembering the giant jukebox from Eric's 20th Jubilee pageant in 2012. So did Matthew, who walked to his wife.

"What a nice thing to bring out today, darling. I remember how much you liked this when you first saw it. I was so afraid you'd find it before Christmas that year," Matthew giggled. "I'm so glad I was able to get it for you."

Angilia put her arms around Matthew's shoulders and smiled. "So am I. This is so special, Matthew. Eric and Patrick will have this for many more years. Their children will get to enjoy the magic of Daddy's song. What a treasure to leave to our grandchildren and their children."

"So this is your family heirloom, Angilia? I can't believe this thing still works," Eric said as he joined them. "I can't believe you brought this out here and turned it on."

"Oh, Daddy. This jukebox is so awesome!"

"Wow! What is that?" young Eric suddenly asked.

"Yeah, what is that? That's Great-grandfather's song, but what is that machine?" young Patrick asked.

"That is the coolest jukebox ever created, Eric and Patrick. It's more than awesome. It's breathtaking," Darlene said as she stared at the giant jukebox with equally giant eyes.

"Are you going to get sick again, Darlene?" Patrick asked.

"She won't. Uncle Patrick isn't here to make her hot," young Eric explained to his brother in a very serious tone.

"I'm okay," Darlene murmured. "This is just too much for me. I think I need some ice water," she said and asked Scott to help her to a table.

"Darlene is nice, but she acts funny," young Patrick said.

"That's just how Darlene is, Patrick. That's how she's been since we met her. She can't help it, but she is sweet and kind," Matthew said with a smile. "I wouldn't expect Darlene to change now, not after all these years."

"Some things haven't changed in 50 years," Billy smiled.

"No, they haven't, Billy. That's a very comforting thought, actually. Time constantly moves forward, but so much remains consistent. I'd like to think that's how it will always be," Eric said. Angilia agreed and kissed her father's cheek.

§§§§

On Saturday afternoon, the Royal party returned to Gateway Arena for the Tribute Concert. Eric was cheered when he arrived in the Royal Box, and he made Angilia stand to share the applause with him. Minutes later, Angilia kissed her father and Matthew, and told them, "I'm going backstage to talk with the performers. Don't worry if I'm not back before the concert starts."

"All right, darling. Have fun," Matthew smiled.

Angilia leaned down to her grandsons, and whispered, "I'll send Troy for you when it's time. Okay?"

Eric and Patrick nodded and kissed her cheeks. They were very excited about the special surprise they had planned with Grandmother. They knew Great-grandfather would like it.

Moments later, Raymond Thacker came to center stage. "Welcome to today's Platinum Jubilee Tribute Concert. I and the other Jubilee Committee members have truly enjoyed planning this Jubilee Week and seeing it come to fruition. What a majestic milestone for our treasured King Eric. Today's concert provides the perfect official finale for our week-long Platinum Jubilee. We know His Majesty will enjoy this concert, and you will, too. So, without prolonging the start, let the Tribute Concert begin."

The arena went dark for a few moments. Everyone recognized the opening chords to "Our Dreams," however, and erupted in cheers just as the lights came on. Angilia's band was on stage, with Angilia and Patrick front and center. She curtsied and he bowed to Eric, and they sang their first hit duet.

"Wow, I had no idea. This is so cool," Prince Eric smiled.

"Yes, Eric, it is. This is a miracle," Eric said with tears in his eyes. Matthew reached over and put his hand on Eric's shoulder. The two men smiled at one another as they watched and listened to Angilia and Patrick. The concert lasted two hours before Angilia paused to introduce her band. That was Troy's cue to bring the twins down.

"Where are you going?" Prince Eric quietly asked them when they stood up.

"We have to go to the bathroom, Daddy. Troy will take us," young Eric whispered.

Prince Eric saw security officer Troy hold the boys' hands and lead them from the Royal Box. He knew that Troy would guard them with his life, and he was not worried. He smiled when his mother said, "We have one song left to do for my father. I wrote this just for him, and Patrick and I decided to make this our final song of the Tribute Concert. This is not a duet, however. This is a quartet. Patrick and I have two very special guests joining us for this song. Eric and Patrick," Angilia smiled.

Everyone screamed when Angilia's grandsons walked onstage. The boys wore navy blue suits and carried microphones. They stood between their mother and great-granduncle. Prince Eric stared with his mouth open, never suspecting this. Matthew smiled, elated to see his handsome grandsons on the stage. Eric clasped his hands in front of him, prayer-like, overcome with emotions. The sight of his brother, his daughter, and his two great-grandsons was something he had never expected to see this side of Heaven.

"Thank you so much. Eric and Patrick make their professional debuts today just for their adored Great-grandfather."

"We love you, Great-grandfather," the twins said simultaneously. Eric blew them a kiss as tears trickled from his eyes. The tears nearly blinded him as he listened to the song that Angilia had written for his Platinum Jubilee.

I can never tell you just what I feel,

How very much you have filled my being.

I can't explain it, but it is more real.

It owns me, chains me, but is so freeing.

How can I tell you what I can't explain?

Words will never say what I feel inside,

For they remain trite and too mundane

To express what can never be denied.

But how else can I ever let you know

All this emotion oh so powerful,

That spark you lit with your vibrant heart-glow

That brought life to devotion immortal.

I cannot tell you, but I can show you.

Shining in my eyes, my pure love so true.

CHAPTER 20

"Happy birthday, my magnificent father," Angilia greeted him as always on his birthday. Eric turned from his desk and smiled to see her framed by the early-morning light that shone through the windows. He held his arms open, and she walked to him for a hug. She breathed deeply, always comforted by the familiar scent of his cologne. "I love you, Daddy."

"I love you, my beautiful daughter Angilia. I love you."

"Oh, Daddy, I am so happy," Angilia smiled up at him. "Please forgive my selfishness, but I feel so blessed and grateful that you are here with us."

Eric smiled. "That's not selfish, Angel. That's love. Never apologize for loving someone so much that you don't want to be separated from her." Angilia looked confused by his pronoun. Did he mean her mother? "You. I don't want to leave you, Angilia, when I do die. You know how I long to be with Mommy again, but that does not mean that I want to leave you. The only comfort is knowing that someday, many years from now, you will come to us."

"I know, Daddy. Even if we didn't already believe that, Michael showed us. I know what a gift and a miracle our eternity in Heaven is, and that is the reward God grants us for our lives here on earth. I know that. But every day that we are together here is a beautiful gift from God, too," Angilia smiled.

"Yes, it is, Angel. It truly is."

"I have something for you. Happy birthday," she smiled, and pulled a box from her pocket.

Eric smiled when he took it, knowing her gift to him would touch his heart. It did. When he opened the box, he saw another of her one-of-a-kind handmade books, this one of her song from his Platinum Jubilee, "What I Feel." As always, she had illustrated it, and Eric felt tears in his eyes when he saw the last illustration: his great-grandsons, Eric and Patrick, as they appeared at the Tribute Concert, singing the song.

"Oh, Angel, this is exquisite. What a treasure this is. I will never forget that performance, darling. What an astounding miracle that was, seeing and hearing my brother, my daughter, and my great-grandsons together. What a miracle you have brought to my life, Angilia," Eric said through his tears and pulled her close. "I love you."

§§§§§

"What a historic day. Good morning, and welcome to the sunrise news on this amazing Monday, November 17, 2064. I am Jason Fuller, and I am delighted to start this day with you. This really is a historic day. King Eric is the longest-living head of state and head of government in history. Today marks His Majesty's 110th birthday.

"What a remarkable life King Eric has lived, most of it in service to the nation of Valdavia. His accomplishments and deeds are far too numerous to cover, but suffice it to say that King Eric is known as the most effectual leader of the modern world. The entire world does indeed seem to celebrate His Majesty's birthday.

"As we can see from this footage, there are parties and celebrations occurring around the world. In Zimbabwe, there was a feast in King Eric's honor. In France, today is declared a national holiday. In the United States, there are street parties, birthday parties, and teas planned to celebrate this milestone. In Great Britain, the House of Lords will mark the day by debating King Eric's contributions to the world. In Japan, the day will be noted by an official toast by the Prime Minister. The President of the Government of Spain, Queen Consort Marisol's birth country, issued a decree declaring today King Eric Day in Spain.

"Souvenirs to commemorate this historic event have been issued by numerous countries. Stamps, coins, dollars, china, and a variety of other items are readily available as King Eric fever once again rages across the world. Valdavia is host this week to visitors from around the world, all here to see His Majesty on the occasion of his 110th birthday. All of us at Valdavian News Network sincerely wish King Eric a very happy birthday. We also want to take a moment to publicly thank King Eric for his dedication and compassion, which have made Valdavia the best place to live."

§§§§

Before breakfast, Yvonne released the official birthday pictures. One showed Eric and Angilia smiling at each other, their love plainly evident. Another showed Eric with his grandson and two great-grandsons, the current and future Kings de Valdavia. The third was Eric alone, wearing his military uniform, looking quite commanding. The fourth and final picture showed the DeBruce Martineau family together: Eric, Patrick, Angilia, Matthew, Prince Eric—who turned 43 that day—and the twins, Eric and Patrick—who were eight years old now.

During breakfast, the loud shouts, screams, and cheers from the huge crowd on the mall could not be ignored. "Valmondois is packed with people. The hotels are booked here and in the surrounding towns. We've never had this kind of public reaction to anything before. Your 110th birthday is the big event of the 21st century, Eric. This is unbelievable," Billy said.

405

"It sure is. The Press Office staff is working overtime just to handle the messages, requests, and birthday greetings. It's been like this for a week, and it's on overdrive today. In fact, I need to head back up there very soon," Yvonne added.

"Yes, it's quite busy around here lately. Even our office is getting a ton of messages and calls. It's incredible to see how much love and respect people have for you, Sir," Leigh commented.

"Thank you, Leigh. This is just a birthday. People have them every day. This isn't such a big deal, but people are kind and thoughtful," Eric replied.

"Daddy, this is a very big deal. Not many people celebrate their 110th birthdays. This birthday proves how surrounded by God's grace and blessings you are. Your life parallels that of the patriarchs of the Old Testament. Those men were granted long lives so that they could do God's work and will on earth. That's exactly why God predestined your long life. Michael said so. You are amazing, Daddy. So, yes, this is a very big deal," Angilia stated.

"Yeah, this is a big deal. All the other kids in school kept giving Eric and me birthday wishes and cards for you last week, Great-grandfather. We have a whole stack in our room to give you," young Patrick said.

"There was a whole unit about you last week, Great-grandfather. The government teacher, Mr. Kinter, taught us about your work, the laws and programs you've done. There's never been another monarch like you anywhere, anytime," young Eric added.

"No, there hasn't. Your great-grandfather is unique in all of history, Eric and Patrick. You are so blessed to know him and to learn from him," Angilia beamed.

"We know, Grandmother," both Eric and Patrick said, smiles illuminating their faces.

§§§§

The Royal Family decided to make a balcony appearance in mid-morning. The twins' birthday party was that afternoon, and despite the zeal surrounding his birthday, Eric wanted to finish a report before the party. "This is exactly why you are already recorded in the history books as the best leader of the modern era, Grandfather. You work endlessly for this country. You are mind-blowing," Prince Eric said as they got off the elevator on the fifth floor.

Billy opened the curtains and the double doors to the balcony, and the thousands of people filling the mall cheered their approval. Angilia smiled up at her father and linked her arm through his. They walked out with Matthew, Prince Eric, and the young princes. As soon as they saw Eric, the people began screaming, saluting, and jumping. Their excitement was intense and unprecedented. Eric was stunned. He was the only one who was.

"Wow, Great-grandfather, this is more than anything I've seen before. They really love you a lot," young Patrick said.

"They really do. I bet we won't see anything like this ever again," young Eric said.

"I think you're right, Eric. People do love your great-grandfather tremendously, Patrick. This proves it, Daddy. You are the most loved and respected leader of the modern era," Angilia smiled and kissed his cheek.

"I thought the crowds were huge when we came home from Oxford in 2012, but this is spectacular. I'm not surprised, though. I've known you too long to be surprised, Eric. Everyone sees the love people have for you. Well, everyone except you. You're far too modest and humble for that," Matthew said as they waved to and watched the crowd below.

"I'm honored people appreciate what I do. It's my duty. I couldn't respect myself if I didn't do the best I can do. These people are my fellow citizens, my friends and neighbors, and if I sold them short, I'd be committing the worst crime," Eric replied.

"Hey, Eric! That's why God loves you so much, you know," Patrick said as he suddenly manifested and put his arm around his brother's shoulders. The people on the mall screamed even louder to see the two iconoclasts together on this historic day.

Angilia smiled, kissed her Uncle Patrick and her father, and said, "God loves both of you. You are both revolutionaries and soldiers of God. I love you, Daddy and Uncle Patrick."

§§§§§

Since the country had declared the day a national holiday, much to Eric's chagrin, the twins' classmates were free to come over after lunch for the birthday party. Prince Eric and his sons greeted their guests at the main entrance, and Eric and Patrick were cheered by the crowd still on the mall. Soon, everyone gathered in the sitting room for the party, where the young princes played with their friends.

"Look how grown up they seem," Prince Eric said as he and his parents sat on a sofa watching the children. "My little boys will be men before I know it. I want to enjoy every second with them. They are my treasures."

Angilia leaned against her son as she hugged him to her. "Oh, Eric, you are an amazing man and father. I knew you would be. Of course Eric and Patrick will be wise, godly men, just like you, Dad, and Grandfather. They have the best role models in the three of you."

"Well, I certainly learned so much from Dad and Grandfather. I pray that I teach what I learned to Eric and Patrick," Prince Eric smiled at her.

"You do. You are a wonderful father. You will be a fantastic King one day, too," Eric said as he sat beside his grandson and patted him on the back.

"I hope so. I've learned so much from you and Mommy. I want to do you both justice."

"You will, Eric, of course you will," Angilia told him and kissed his cheek.

After more than two hours of games, it was time for young Eric and Patrick to blow out the candles on their birthday cake. Their friends sang an enthusiastic version of the birthday song before the princes blew out the candles together. Their friends cheered, and Angilia smiled as she cut and served the cake. Prince Eric scooped ice cream for everyone, and the children enjoyed talking and joking as they sat around the table.

Eric, Angilia, Matthew, and Prince Eric enjoyed the sounds of the young voices and the laughter, realizing how blessed their family really was. Angilia's smile enlarged when she felt a very familiar warmth. "Uncle Patrick, you're back!"

Patrick kissed her, Eric, Matthew and Prince Eric before sitting on the arm of the sofa. "Yeah, sure. I couldn't miss this! It's my great-grandnephews' birthday party. Gosh, they're handsome and so smart."

"They are, Uncle Patrick. They constantly take my breath. I mean, I helped to create them, and that's pretty heady stuff," Prince Eric said.

'Yeah, I bet it is," Patrick wistfully said. Angilia placed her hand on his arm just as the twins and their friends finished the cake and ice cream.

Young Eric and Patrick ran to their great-granduncle and greeted him with a hug. Their friends smiled and greeted Patrick, as well. Suddenly, young Eric asked, "Uncle Patrick, will you still visit us when we're grown? You won't forget us, will you?"

"Hey, no, I can never forget you guys! You bet I'll visit you, Eric and Patrick. When you're King," he said to Eric, "and you're a Duc," he said to Patrick, "I'll come by all the time and keep you company. I'll take your children for flights around the room, just like I did your dad and both of you. We'll always have tons of fun, you guys. I promise."

Patrick did their secret handshake with young Eric and Patrick, who both smiled and hugged him. "We can't wait, Uncle Patrick," young Patrick said.

"Dad, is it all right if we take our friends to our room for a while?" young Eric asked.

"Of course. Have fun." He smiled as he watched his sons go upstairs with their friends. "Life sure is wonderful. You were right, Grandfather. The happy moments overshadow the sadness by a long shot. I love you all." He collected his family in a group hug that expressed his love far more than mere words ever could.

§§§§

Five weeks later, the Royal Family welcomed their fellow parishioners to the midnight Christmas Service. Patrick stood beside his brother, and kept an arm around Eric. He glowed when people still wished Eric a happy birthday and thanked him for his decades of service. When Darlene and Scott arrived, she hugged Angilia, and said, "Gosh, look at you two snappy young men. Why, I remember when you were just tiny babies in your daddy's arms at your first Christmas service. Merry Christmas, Eric and Patrick."

"Thank you. Merry Christmas, Darlene," young Eric said.

"Yeah, thank you, Darlene. Have a super Merry Christmas," young Patrick told her.

"I swear, they're just like the other Eric and Patrick," she marveled to no one in particular. Scott wished his friends a blessed Christmas, and led Darlene to their seats.

Moments later, the Royal Family took their seats in their pew, and Reverend Olson opened the service with a prayer as always. When the congregation repeated the "Amen" and took their seats, Reverend Olson offered his sermon on how the Angel of God had told Mary of her divine baby's birth.

Eric walked to the pulpit, where he recited the Christmas Story from Luke Chapter 2. He had done so every Christmas since 1979. 2064 marked the 85th straight year he had recited Luke 2. Angilia's eyes filled with tears. Patrick noticed, and he put his arm around her. He could feel her love for Eric coursing through her body. He had since she had first seen her father, the day Patrick had died. He would never forget the look in her eyes that day.

Angilia had stared at Eric with the purest love shining from the depths of her soul through her eyes. She had loved her father at first sight, Patrick had known that. The intensity of her love had made her cry that day. She had not wanted to leave Eric and return to Heaven. Patrick and she had looked back at Eric, and Eric had stared at Angilia. Eric had not seen Patrick. Eric had seen his unborn daughter, even though he had not known who she was. He had loved her just as intensely nonetheless. That moment had seared both Angilia's and Eric's hearts and changed them forever.

Patrick had never seen or known of a truer, purer love than Eric's and Angilia's. He felt such awe to have been the one who had brought them together. He knew that his death served several purposes. God used him for his will, yes, but more importantly to Patrick, he was the catalyst for Angilia's and Eric's epic bond. Patrick smiled as he held his niece and listened to his brother. "Thank you, God," he silently said.

As if sensing Patrick's thoughts and feelings, Angilia kissed his cheek and smiled at him. Eric smiled as he watched them from the pulpit, and when he returned to the pew, he kissed them both. Angilia gently squeezed Patrick's hand and walked to the altar. There, she sang an a cappella rendition of "Silent Night," while a mystical glow surrounded her. Eric and Patrick smiled at one another. To them, she looked just like the angel who had appeared to them 87½ years ago on the day that Patrick had died.

Prince Eric was mesmerized by his mother's appearance and performance. She was an angel, of that there was no doubt. Young Eric and young Patrick stared at her, equally entranced. They knew of her heavenly background, and they believed her. Of course they did. But she literally looked like an angel, with a halo, a mystical glow, and the boys were hypnotized. So was Matthew, as always. He looked at his Angilia with his love illuminating his amber eyes as if they were lanterns. Angilia had the entire congregation spellbound.

When the Royal Family arrived home at 2:00 on Christmas morning, they went to their third floor suites. Patrick hugged and kissed them. "Hey, this was magical. I'll see you later. Merry Christmas." They all hugged and kissed Patrick and smiled as he disappeared and returned to Heaven.

Soon, the others went to their suites and got ready for a few hours' sleep. Angilia and Eric stood in the hallway together. "Oh, Angel, I love you. Patrick's right. Tonight was truly magical," Eric softly said.

"I love you more than life, Daddy. I love you," Angilia said through her tears and hugged him.

"Oh, darling, I know. I've always known. I saw it from the first second. Your love is the greatest gift I will ever know." Eric kissed her cheek and smiled at her. "We best get some sleep before the Christmas excitement begins in a few hours. Have a blessed night." Angilia kissed her father's cheek and went into her suite, where she changed into her nightgown, got in bed, and snuggled close to Matthew.

Eric went into his dressing room and changed into his pajamas and robe. When he stepped to his bed, he noticed an envelope addressed to him. He picked it up, recognized Angilia's handwriting, and smiled. He sat in his chair and read her letter.

25 December 2064

My Magnificent, Beloved Daddy,

What a blessed day Christmas is for us! It always is. This one is a little extra special, you know. 70 years ago, my soul entered your heart. Michael brought me to you, and I saw you again after 17 very long years. Oh, how I had longed to return to you! I can never truly tell you what that moment was like for me. I saw you again! Oh, Daddy, I had longed for nothing but that moment. I lived in the Angels Choir waiting for that moment. When Michael told me that my soul would enter your heart, I knew such joy as I have never known. When I entered your heart, my soul felt whole, complete.

I loved you at first sight. I never wanted to leave you. But I had to. I could not remain on earth until it was time for me to be born. Had I stayed, I would have jeopardized everything. Those 17 years between Uncle Patrick's death and Christmas Day 1994 were not that long in the scheme of time. I've told you how they felt longer than eternity. They did. My heart and my soul longed to be with you. That made the waiting feel torturously long.

My love for you is boundless and eternal. My love for you is larger than the universe. Oh, Daddy, my love for you is the first and most powerful love I will ever know. I loved you before I saw you. But once I did see you, I could never live without you. You are my everything. You. I love you, Daddy.

Eternally Your Loving Daughter,

Angilia

Eric walked onto his balcony and looked upward. "Dear God, Thank you for gifting me Angilia as my daughter. She is my greatest blessing, and I am so grateful for her. I love her, and I love you. Thank you. Amen." Eric stood staring at the Christmas stars, tears sliding down his cheeks.

After several minutes, he looked down at his wedding band. "My darling Marisol, Merry Christmas. I love you. How I love you. Our little girl is such a blessing to me, my love. You know that. I love her. I long to be with you again, but leaving our Angilia will be the one pain in that. Still, I know she will join us when God calls her to her eternal home. He showed us what a miracle awaits us," Eric said to his wife as he placed his hand over the pendant. "How happy we will be together forever, my love. I love you, Marisol."

§§§§§

When Matthew left his suite, he saw his father-in-law at his desk in his sitting room across the hall. He smiled and stopped long enough to say, "Angilia is ready, Eric."

"Thank you, Matthew." Eric stood, picked up a letter and a gift, and walked to his daughter's sitting room. Angilia stepped from her bedroom at that moment, and smiled at him. She went to him, and hugged him near. "Happy birthday, my beautiful daughter Angilia. I love you."

"Oh, Daddy, I love you."

Eric motioned them to her sofa, where they sat next to one another. He handed her the letter and gift, and she smiled up at him. "I treasure your letters so, Daddy. I've kept them all, you know," Angilia said and placed the letter and gift beside her on the sofa. "I will read this later, when I'm alone. Your letters mean so much to me. You mean everything to me."

"You mean the universe to me, Angel," Eric said and put his hand over her cheek. "I am going to miss you, my darling."

"Daddy?"

"I'm dying, Angilia." Tears filled her eyes, and she shook her head. "My life here is almost over. I've done what God wanted me to, and now he's calling me home." The tears fell from Angilia's eyes. "Don't be sad, Angel. Don't be sad."

"How can I not be sad? I want to stay with you, Daddy."

"You will, in here," Eric said and placed his hand over his heart. "You will come to me when God calls you home to Heaven. We will always be together, Angilia."

Angilia nodded her head and looked into her father's eyes, the eyes that had branded her soul so long ago. "Part of me is happy for you, even though my heart is breaking. You will be with Mommy. After being separated from her for 70 years, you will be with her. I know how much you have waited for this, Daddy." She smiled. "I feel selfish, because I know I won't have to wait anywhere near as long to come to you."

Eric smiled and pulled the pendant from around his neck. "When you gave this to me on my 75th birthday, I told you that you would wear this again when I die. This is yours once more, Angilia." Eric placed the pendant around her neck and kissed her cheek. "You will give this to Eric, and this will remain a beacon of hope for our family for all time."

Angilia nodded her head. "I promise." She held her father close to her for a long while as they sat in silence. They felt each other's love as if it were tangible. Eric grew more tired, and he rested his head on her shoulder. She kissed the top of his head, and he gently squeezed her hand.

At that moment, they felt a very familiar warmth when Patrick manifested beside his brother. Patrick saw the sadness in his niece's eyes, and he nodded to her. "I'm here, Eric."

"You are my Spirit Guide, Patrick," Eric said with a smile.

"Yeah. You are my important mission, big brother. I've known about this since before Little One left the Angels Choir. I never knew until just now when I would come to escort you to Heaven. We get to go together, Eric."

"I'm glad it's you, Patrick," Eric said.

"So am I," Patrick smiled. "Let's pray together one last time, okay?" Angilia and Eric nodded and closed their eyes. "Dear God, Thank you for loving us. Thank you for giving me the honor of being my brother's Spirit Guide. We know you will welcome Eric into Heaven with joy and love. Our family knows this, too. Wrap them in your love, God, as they adjust to life without Eric here with them. Let them feel the peace in knowing that Eric will be with his true love Marisol and the rest of our family forever. Let them feel the joy in that, not sadness. We love each other, and we love you. Hold us in your embrace always, God. Amen." Angilia repeated the Amen, and Eric whispered Amen.

"I have to leave you now, Angilia. This is not goodbye. We will never say goodbye. Instead, I will see you soon."

"Never goodbye, Daddy. Never goodbye. I love you."

"I love you, my beautiful daughter Angilia," Eric said for the last time on earth, kissed her cheek, and died in her arms.

Tears fell down her cheeks when she saw her father's soul manifest. He bent and kissed her cheek again. "I love you, Daddy." Eric nodded, smiled, and went to Heaven with Patrick.

§§§§

"Angilia, Eric, are you two coming to breakfast?" Matthew asked as he neared his and Angilia's sitting room. The sight he saw when he entered stopped him in his footsteps. Angilia sat on the sofa, holding Eric's body to her, her head against his. "Angilia?" Matthew softly asked.

"Uncle Patrick was Daddy's Spirit Guide. That was the important mission he had."

Matthew walked to the sofa and sat beside his wife. He put his hands on her shoulders and kissed her cheek. "Oh, darling." Matthew could say nothing more as tears overcame him.

"He is with Mommy again. That is what he longed for, and now they are together forever. That is so beautiful, Matthew. I miss Daddy, and I will until I die and return to him. Living without him and waiting to go to him are the hardest parts, I won't lie."

"I know, darling. I know. What can I do?"

"We will have his funeral service on Tuesday. That's the perfect day. It's the anniversary of Uncle Patrick's birth. Daddy will wear his military uniform," Angilia said as tears trickled from her eyes.

"I'll take care of everything, Angilia. I'll call Reverend Olson and handle everything," Matthew said, meaning the death certificate and funeral home.

"It happened at 6:26. Years ago, Daddy picked out a white coffin just like Mommy's. I want him here, in the chapel, until we have to take him to the church, Matthew."

"Of course, darling. When do you want me to call people?"

"You can do that soon, Matthew. I'm going to stay with Daddy until they come. Then I'll write the official announcement. Matthew, ask Eric and the boys to come here, please."

Matthew nodded, kissed her, and went to the dining room, where everyone was waiting to start breakfast. "Eric, Patrick, and Eric, I need you to come with me. The rest of you can go ahead and eat."

Prince Eric and his sons were concerned and confused. What was wrong? What had happened? They were silent as they took the elevator to the third floor and went to Angilia's and Matthew's suite. They froze, stunned. Prince Eric ran to his mother, though, fell to his knees, and hugged her. The twins began crying, and Matthew put his arms around them.

"Great-grandfather is in Heaven now, boys. He is with Great-grandmother again, and we know how very happy they are, right?" Angilia said.

"Yes, Grandmother, but we love Great-grandfather," young Eric said while he cried.

"I know, darlings. I know. He didn't want us to be sad, though. He wanted us to be happy, because he is with Great-grandmother and his parents. He's alive and happy. We love him, and we will miss him a whole lot. I will always miss him," Angilia said.

Prince Eric held his arm out for his sons, who went to him. They hugged him, and then they hugged and kissed their grandmother. "Why does it hurt so much when someone dies?" young Patrick asked.

"The more you love someone, the more pain you feel when that person dies. The pain equals the love. My heart is shattered, Patrick. I have never hurt this much. That's how it should be, because I love Daddy so much, and I miss him," Angilia explained.

"God doesn't think it's wrong to hurt?" Patrick asked.

"Of course not. He understands that our deep love makes our pain deep. He knows and he understands. God will get us through this. We will help each other through this," Angilia said and kissed her grandsons.

"It's gonna be tough, but we can do it. Great-grandfather did it when Great-grandmother died. We can, too," young Eric said. Young Patrick put his arm around his brother, living proof that they would help one another through their grief.

Matthew smiled, and then stepped into an empty suite to call the funeral director and Reverend Olson. Matthew placed Eric's military uniform in a garment bag and gave it and Angilia's request regarding the coffin and lying in state in the chapel to the funeral director when he arrived. Angilia followed her father's body until the hearse left the palace. She then went to the office she had shared with her father and closed the door. She wrote the official announcement of his death and sent it to Yvonne for immediate release.

3 January 2065

At 6:26 this morning, my magnificent, beloved father King Eric de Valdavia died. He was with me, and I want to assure you that he did not suffer. My heart is utterly shattered. I love and I miss my father more than words can say. I know, though, that he lives eternally in Heaven. He resides in the most beautiful, most perfect place ever to exist.

My father did not want anyone to be sad upon his death. One of the last things he said to me this morning is to not be sad, because he will live forever. He is now reunited with my mother, his only love. That is such a comforting, happy truth. I pray that you find consolation in that, too.

My father's state funeral will be Tuesday, 6 January 2065 at Christ Church Valmondois. The service will be open to the public. His entombment in the Royal Vault will be attended by invited guests. Both will be broadcast live so that all may pay their respects to this remarkable man whom I am so blessed to call my father.

§§§§

That afternoon, the funeral director and his assistants arrived with Eric's casket, which they carried into the palace from the back patio entrance. Angilia led them to the chapel, where one man positioned the bier. Eric's coffin was carefully placed atop the bier. "Thank you for taking such good care of my father. I really appreciate your kindness," Angilia told them and shook their hands.

"It is our honor, Your Majesty. Please let us know if we can do anything else," the funeral director said before the men bowed and left.

When the chapel door closed, Angilia opened the casket and smiled down at her father. His gold wedding band had been removed when he had been taken for embalming. Angilia slid it on his left ring finger, where it would remain for all time. "Oh, Daddy, I love you. I love you and Mommy both. Now you are together again. I have to let that truth carry me through this. I can't lie. I'm in so much pain right now. I miss you so much. I pray that I do not have to wait too many years to see you again."

Angilia had not heard Matthew come in, but she felt him put his hands on her shoulders. "Oh, my darling Angilia. What can I do?"

Angilia shook her head. "I love you, Matthew. But there's nothing anyone can do. I know Daddy is fine and happier than ever now. I know that. My pain is so deep, though. I wonder if it will go away, or if it will last until I die."

"I pray it doesn't last, Angilia. I don't want you to hurt. Eric never wanted you to hurt. God doesn't want you to hurt, either. He will take care of you, darling. Lean on God and us. We will help you, and you will help us. We all love and miss Eric, although no one's pain is as great as yours. The whole world is hurting. Thousands of people are calling, and thousands more are gathered on the mall. They all love Eric, and they are all grieving. You don't have to go through this alone, darling."

Angilia smiled at Matthew and kissed him. "I know, dear. I love you all so much." She walked from the chapel into the foyer and toward the front door.

"Where are you going?" Matthew asked.

"I want to talk with the people on the mall," she answered, and opened the door. Matthew heard loud screams and wails from outside, and he quickly followed his wife. The guards at the gates were surprised to see her and by her request to open the gate. "It's all right," she told them as she stepped into the midst of a huge throng of people.

People hugged her, cried, gave her flowers, and told her how sorry they were. They all said how much they loved Eric. "Thank you all so much. I know how much you love and respect my father.

Your kindness and thoughtfulness mean a lot to me," Angilia told them as they continued to gather around her.

Prince Eric noticed from a second floor sitting room window. "I have to go down there," he said. The twins and Leigh joined him at the window and said they would go, too. When Prince Eric, young Eric, and young Patrick came onto the courtyard, the people cried and grieved louder.

Prince Eric and the young princes joined Angilia and Matthew. Prince Eric also spoke to everyone in a strong voice so very like his grandfather's that people cried at the sound. "Thank you all for coming today. Your love and support mean quite a lot to me and my family. We love and miss my grandfather, and we know that you love and miss him, too. We will never forget him."

Young Eric and Patrick shook peoples' hands, accepted flowers, and consoled those who grieved. "Don't be sad. My great-grandfather didn't want anyone to be sad. He wanted us to be happy when we think of him," young Patrick said.

"We'll always love and miss him, but we don't have to stay sad. Think of the happy memories. Great-grandfather made us all happy, and he loved us. Think happy thoughts," young Eric said.

"We see so much of King Eric in you, Angilia and Prince Eric. He also lives in you two wise young men," a woman in the crowd said as she hugged Angilia, Prince Eric, and the twins. "King Eric will never die. He lives in each of you and those who have yet to be born."

§§§§

That night, Angilia sat alone in the chapel, where she read the birthday letter from her father. The poignancy of the letter, coupled with the emotions of the day, made her cry. She reread the letter as tears choked and nearly blinded her. She prayed to God, thanking him for her father and asking him to give her strength. "I want to honor you and Daddy, God, and I need you to help me stay strong. Help me put the sadness aside, so that I can do as Daddy asked. I need and want to be strong for Eric, Patrick, and Eric, for Matthew, and for all of the people who mourn. I ask you to help me to stay strong so that I can do everything I must do. Help me live without Daddy until you decide that my life is over. Amen."

3 January 2065

My Beautiful Daughter Angilia,

I love you. You are my life. You own my heart. You are my soul.

I have watched you for 69 years now. What an astounding woman you are, my little girl. Everything you do takes my breath—you stun me at every turn. I am so overwhelmed to know that I had a part in your creation. You were created for me, to be my daughter! Is there a more staggering realization than that?

Angilia, I write this early on your birthday. You will read this after I die. I am dying, my darling, I know that. Please do not be sad. I will miss you, and I know you will miss me. That is part of love. Know that I am not afraid. I have never been afraid. As much as I will miss you, I will of course be happy in Heaven. Mommy and I will be together again, and we will never part. I have longed to see her for so long, Angilia. You know that.

Michael showed us that we will all be together in Heaven. You know the indescribable miracle in that. As much as we will miss one another, know that our separation is temporary. You will run to me and Mommy someday, and we will finally be together, the three of us! Hold onto that until we are together. Knowing God's promise of eternal life and that Marisol and I would reunite forever is the one thing above all else that kept me strong all of these years. It will keep you strong, too, my dear.

I love you, and I am so proud of you! Carry me in your heart, as I will carry you in mine.

Eternally Yours,

Daddy

§§§§

On Tuesday morning, Angilia awoke early, showered, and put on her black dress and a pair of her mother's pearl earrings. She placed the heart pendant that her father had given her on her 16th birthday around her neck. She quietly went to the chapel, where she prayed for several hours. Finally, it was time for Eric's funeral to begin, and Prince Eric escorted the military pallbearers into the chapel. He kissed her, and said, "We're all outside, Mommy. We'll be with you and Grandfather."

"Thank you, Eric. I know you will. I'll be all right, I know that now. I love you, Eric." She leaned up and kissed his cheek.

Prince Eric went onto the courtyard, where Matthew, Eric, and Patrick stood facing the gun carriage onto which Eric's casket would be placed. Seven soldiers carried the casket slowly and reverently onto the courtyard, followed by Angilia. The casket was draped with the Valdavian flag, and a wreath of white flowers— Angilia's carnation, Eric's chrysanthemum, and Marisol's lily—laid on top. Angilia had placed the wreath there earlier that morning.

The soldiers carefully placed the casket on the gun carriage, and thousands of people gathered on the mall and the streets began crying loudly. As soon as the casket was on the gun carriage, the seven pallbearers saluted, and three soldiers gave King Eric a 21-gun salute. At that moment, the church bells began ringing the slow, somber funeral toll. The gun carriage began its measured march to the church.

The five members of the Royal Family walked behind the gun carriage to form the cortege: Prince Eric, young Patrick, Angilia, young Eric, and Matthew. As soon as the cortege left the palace courtyard, thousands of crying people began following. Thousands more people crammed the streets around the church, and when the gun carriage arrived, most of them began crying and wailing. They threw white roses at the casket, blanketing the street with the fragrant flowers. Many saluted Eric when the seven pallbearers carried his casket into the church.

The church was packed with people, many of whom stood in every available space. The entire congregation rose as Eric's casket passed, and remained standing while the pallbearers placed the casket on the bier. They still stood when they realized that Queen Angilia had not taken her seat, but that she greeted many of those present. When Reverend Olson approached her and held her hands, they were struck by how small she looked. She appeared far younger than her 69 years, and the sight broke many hearts.

Reverend Olson spoke with the Royal Family for a few moments before he walked to the pulpit. "In gratitude, we gather to pay respects to King Eric, our much-loved and righteous leader. Eric was greatly blessed by God, and so were we. Eric's 110 years were devoted to us, the people of Valdavia. Most of us never knew another King. We know how unique and benevolent our King Eric was. Our nation, our lives, and the lives of all future generations remain better because of Eric. He loved us. We love him. We will remember him with fondness and respect all the days of our lives."

Reverend Olson bowed to Angilia, and she stepped to the pulpit. She would deliver her father's eulogy. "Thank you all for your immense kindness over the past three days. Your concern for me and my family has overwhelmed us, but your love for my father has not. He was so easy to love and to respect. I know that so well, for I loved him at first sight. My father was the first love of my life. I do love him so. I understand your love for him.

"As I explained to my precious grandsons, Eric and Patrick, the pain we feel when someone dies equals the love we have for him. Grief and pain are normal, and God expects us to hurt when we are separated from those whom we love. Believe me; I know that all too well. My pain is immeasurable.

"However, my father did not want tears and sadness upon his death. He died on the morning of my 69th birthday. It was our tradition to give one another cards and gifts early on our birthdays. He always wrote me a birthday letter. He came to my sitting room Saturday morning, and gave me a gift and a letter. He told me he was dying, and as much as my heart broke, he told me not to be sad. He told me to hold onto the beautiful truth that he, his incredible soul, lives for eternity in Heaven. He is once again with my mother, and that is a blessed miracle.

"I understand the pain you feel. But do not feel sadness when you think of my father. You can shed tears, or you can instead smile because he lived among us. He was our gift from God. My father lived among us here on earth. Now he lives with

God and his family in Heaven. We will see him again. Let that knowledge keep the sadness away.

"Remember my father's love for all of us. Remember his smile. Remember his remarkable turquoise eyes that shone with his emotions and his love of living. Remember his compassion. Remember him, but not in sadness. One of my father's favorite Bible verses was Hebrews 13:1. My father lived his life according to this verse, and I know we saw that in action every day. *Let brotherly love continue.*"

Angilia walked to the piano, where she played and sang one of her father's favorite gospel songs, "Reach Out to Jesus." When she finished, she returned to the pew, where the seat to her left was now vacant. Matthew put his arm around her, amazed at her strength and faith. He knew how much she missed her father and how much she hurt, but she had somehow found the strength to put her sadness and pain aside and do as Eric wanted. Angilia would not dwell in sorrow. She would live in hope.

Reverend Olson returned to the pulpit for the closing remarks and the prayer. "King Eric did not want a prolonged funeral service, and those who knew him at all understand why. He never relished being the center of attention. He much preferred that any credit or honor be bestowed upon God. He considered himself foremost a servant of God. That is how I will remember him.

"Join me in prayer," he said, and everyone stood and bowed their heads. "Dear God, Thank you for the life and service of King Eric de Valdavia. You blessed Eric with a long life, which was spent in your service and fulfilling your will. We know that you have rewarded Eric with eternal life. We remain grateful that we were the ones fortunate to know him, even if from a distance. Eric's life touched us, taught us, and will influence this world as long as people exist. Now that you have taken Eric to his eternal reward, please comfort us who mourn his absence. Ease our pain, so that we may fulfill his wishes and smile when we remember him. In your holy name, this we ask. Amen"

Those in the church repeated the Amen, after which the seven military pallbearers carried Eric's casket into the Royal Vault for the entombment.   Angilia and her family followed, with Reverend Olson behind. Next, those friends who had been invited entered: Billy, Shannon, Yvonne, Leigh, Nicole, William, Darlene, and Scott. The vault door was closed, although, as Angilia had promised, the entombment was broadcast worldwide.

The pallbearers lifted the casket into the tomb, with the flag and wreath still covering it. Matthew, Prince Eric, and the twins placed white roses atop the casket. The others in attendance placed yellow roses. Darlene burst into tears when she placed her rose on Eric's casket, and Angilia held her friend.

"I'm sorry. I am so sad right now," Darlene cried.

"It's all right, Darlene. The sadness will go away, it will. We have a lifetime of happy memories," Angilia comforted her friend.

"Sure we do.   Great-grandfather was all about making people feel better and making them happy," young Eric said. Those watching cried, seeing so much of King Eric in his great-grandson.

"King Eric's life centered on his love of God and his love of all people. Let us mimic that in his honor," Reverend Olson said.

Scott held his crying wife, and Angilia stepped closer to her father's tomb. She placed an envelope addressed to "Daddy" on the casket, a sight which generated more tears. The seven pallbearers then lifted the heavy lid onto Eric's tomb. "I love you, Daddy," Angilia said as the camera zoomed in on the plaque.

Eric Richard Constatin DeBruce Martineau

17 November 1954

3 January 2065

The grace of our Lord Jesus Christ be with you all.

--Revelation 22:21

✝

CHAPTER 21

atthew opened his eyes and saw Angilia standing on their bedroom balcony. He got out of bed and walked to her, putting his hands on her shoulders. He kissed her neck, and said, "Happy birthday, darling. I love you, my Angilia."

"I love you, Matthew." Angilia turned to face him, put her arms around him, and leaned her head against his chest.

"How are you today? Are you all right, darling?"

Angilia took a deep breath and looked into his eyes. "I'm all right. I miss Daddy, Matthew, you know that. This is about the time he usually came in with his letter for me. I love him, Matthew. I love him."

"Oh, Angilia, I know. Do you want me to stay with you?"

Angilia smiled at him, touched by his concern. "No, you don't have to, darling. You go have your coffee. I'll be fine. I just want to stay here a while with my memories and my prayers."

"Okay. I'll come back in about an hour to take my shower and get ready for church. I love you," Matthew said, kissed her, and went to the first floor.

Angilia pulled the pendant from under her dress and watched her parents together in Heaven. "I love you, Daddy and Mommy."

"Hey, Little One," Patrick softly said and put his arm around her.

"Uncle Patrick, I love you. I was just watching Mommy and Daddy," she told him, fingering the pendant.

"Yeah. They're so happy, Little One. They are."

"I miss them. I just want to be with them, Uncle Patrick."

"You will be, you know that. Eric and Marisol want that, too, Angilia. They love you so much, and they watch you with such joy."

"They do? Really?"

"Yeah, sure. Hey, um, I have something for you. Here." Patrick handed Angilia an envelope, and her heart suddenly skipped several beats. She shivered, unsteady on her feet, and Patrick put his arms around her.

Angilia began crying, and she hugged him. "This is from Daddy."

"Yeah. It's your birthday. This is tradition."

"I never thought I'd read another letter from Daddy. Oh, Uncle Patrick, thank you. Can you. . .is it possible for you to take a letter to Daddy? Could you?"

"From you I can, sure," Patrick smiled.

Angilia rushed to her desk and picked up a sealed envelope. "I wrote this letter early this morning. I was going to leave it in the Vault today, but. . . ."

"Sure thing, Little One, no problem. I'll leave you alone now so you can read his letter. I'll give this to him as soon as I get back. I love you, Little One. Happy birthday." Patrick hugged her, kissed her cheek, and held her letter to Eric as he disappeared and returned to Heaven.

Angilia held the precious letter from her father, and went to her window seat—where she had often read his birthday letters. She bowed her head. "Dear God, Thank you for this gift. You know what this means to me, and I thank you. I love you, and I am so grateful for your blessings and love. Amen." Angilia smiled and watched the birds in the trees outside her window. The beauty and grace in nature were yet more gifts from God.

Angilia took a deep breath and traced her name on the front of the envelope. Her name, written in her father's familiar script. She carefully opened the envelope and slowly removed the piece of parchment. Tears of love and joy flowed from her eyes when she read her father's birthday letter to her.

3 January 2066

My Beautiful Daughter Angilia,

Oh, my darling daughter! I love you so. Mommy loves you. We love you, Angilia, and we wait for the time you join us here. Heaven is more incredible than I ever imagined! You were right—the beauty, the peace, the love are beyond earthly comprehension. Oh, Angilia, how wondrous it is to live here!

As you know, time does not exist here, but Patrick is my link to the human world. I know what date it is today, because he told me when January 3 began at midnight. One year. I have been here one year. I remember you and Patrick commenting on the concept of time on your engagement day. Now I understand. Eternity is timeless, truly timeless.

I am so proud of you, Angilia. You are truly remarkable. You have put your sadness aside for the sake of our family and our fellow Valdavians. Your grandfather even remarked on your strength and faith over this past year, Angilia. We are always with you. I am always with you. Know that. We live in one another's souls. We share souls. I love you.

With my eternal love,

Daddy

§§§§

Angilia and Shannon walked to a meeting at an office near the coffee shop. After the meeting, they decided to have lunch at the coffee shop. "It's such a lovely spring day, Shannon. Why don't we sit at an outdoor table?" Angilia asked her friend.

The ladies sat eating their salads, sipping their tea, and chatting. "You seem happy, Angilia. Are you?"

"Yes, Shannon. I am happy," Angilia smiled.

"I'm glad, I really am. It's been 15 months. I know how much you miss him."

"I do, Shannon. I always will. I'm okay, though. I know for a fact that Daddy is so happy. He and Mommy are, both of them. That really does make me happy. Their love is so epic, Shannon. Daddy lived without her for 70 years. 70 years. I can't fathom that. He was so faithful all of those years, and he lived so that he would be with her again. Now he is. As much as I truly miss him, I can never be sad for long," Angilia said with a smile and gleaming eyes.

"I can't wrap my head around that either, how long he waited for her. Not very many people could or would do that. Your father was really one of a kind," Shannon replied.

"Yes, he was, Your Majesty. I am so honored that he was my King."

Angilia looked up at a man who stood staring at her with tears in his eyes. "Thank you, Sir. That's very sweet."

"Your father became my King, yes, but before he was my King, he was my teacher. May I join you?" he asked, and when Angilia nodded, he pulled another chair to their table. "Your uncle, Patrick, was supposed to teach a class at the high school in the summer of 1977, a four-week class that started in late July. It was a literature class, just something for anyone who was interested. I enrolled. I was seven, and it seemed fascinating, especially with Patrick at the helm. He seemed so cool to me, and I was excited."

The man's eyes grew sad. "Patrick never got to teach the class. The school was going to cancel the class, and of course we all understood why. I remember getting a telephone call from a secretary at the school a few days before the class was supposed to begin. She said the class had not been canceled, and to make sure I bought the textbook before the first class. She never said who would be teaching the class.

"Imagine my surprise—everyone's surprise—when Prince Eric walked into the classroom when the first class began. Your father took over the class for his brother. Prince Eric led so many absorbing conversations about the poems, plays, and stories we read. There was such sadness in his eyes, and we all knew that the pain of his brother's death was deep and raw. We all knew what had happened to Patrick, and that Eric had been there.

"We saw, we felt, his pain. But what struck me most is how he put that aside and taught the class in his brother's place. I'm an old man now, but I remember that well. I tell you this because you are your father's daughter. I see the pain in your eyes, but I see how you push that away and do what you have to do. You are just as strong and compassionate as your father, Your Majesty. I am honored that you are my Queen."

The man stood, bowed, and walked away before Angilia had a chance to say more than a stunned, "Thank you." She truly was stunned. "How did I never know this, Shannon? Neither Uncle Patrick nor Daddy ever told me this. How could they not?"

"Because they, like you, never flaunted what they did. You really are your father's daughter, Angilia. I love you."

§§§§

Angilia opened her eyes to Matthew's kiss and the loud cheers of people on the mall. "Happy anniversary, my love, my Angilia."

Angilia snuggled closer to him and kissed his shoulder. "Happy anniversary, darling. I love you, Matthew."

"I love you. I have always loved you. Literally," Matthew giggled.

Angilia smiled up at him. "Yes, you have. Our friendship and love were born centuries ago, long before we were."

Matthew gently pulled her atop him and kissed her pink lips. "For that I am so grateful," he said between kisses.

"So am I, my love. Our lives together have been dreamy."

"Better than any dream. My dreams could never be this fabulous, my Angilia. Our reality is far more wonderful than any dream."

Matthew and Angilia cuddled and kissed until they absolutely had to shower and dress for breakfast. When they entered the dining room, everyone else screamed, "Happy anniversary!" Matthew and Angilia laughed joyously, a sound which thrilled their friends and family.

"Thank you," Angilia said as Matthew held her chair for her. "We're happy, aren't we, darling?"

"Absolutely!" Matthew answered.

"It's your 50th anniversary. We need to take a picture to mark this date," Prince Eric said.

"Yes, that will be nice. People actually expect something like that," Yvonne mentioned.

"Really? Okay, well, why don't we take one after breakfast?" Matthew asked his wife.

"All right," she answered.

After breakfast, Matthew, Angilia, and Prince Eric went onto the back lawn. Matthew led Angilia to the red rose bushes, which were the perfect romantic backdrop for their anniversary picture. Matthew stood behind Angilia, wrapped his arms around her, and rested his head against hers. Prince Eric took the picture, and Yvonne released it moments later.

After they freshened in their suite, Matthew and Angilia went out to the mall, along with their son and grandsons, to meet with the well-wishers. Many of them requested autographs and pictures, and many others offered the Royal Family flowers and cards. "Happy anniversary, Angilia and Matthew. What a romantic day!" one woman told them and kissed their cheeks.

"Thank you," Angilia smiled and looked up at her husband. "Today is very special. My parents were married 75 years ago, and this is their sixth anniversary together," Angilia said, reminding people that Eric and Marisol had celebrated just four anniversaries together before her death and two together since his death.

"That is beautiful, Queen Angilia, just beautiful. We all love you and your family. We love King Eric, and we do think of how happy he is with his Marisol."

"Yes, we do, Your Majesty. We wish you and the Duc many more years of happiness together. We love you."

§§§§

A couple of hours later, Angilia picked up a small book and two dozen white roses from her desk, got the key to the Royal Vault, and left the palace. People still gathered on the mall greeted her. "Where are you off to on this special day, Your Majesty?" a woman asked her.

Angilia smiled and answered, "I'm going to visit my parents."

"Wish them a happy anniversary from us," someone else shouted.

"I will. Thank you."

Inside the Royal Vault, Angilia stood between her parents' tombs. She placed 12 white roses above the plaque on her mother's tomb, and bowed her head. "Dear God, Thank you for my beautiful mother. Even though I have yet to meet her, she has been my comfort and protection. I know that. I feel that. Her love gave life to me, even though her own life ended. Her love kept me alive 54 years ago so that Matthew and I could marry and give life to Eric.

Thank you for my strong, brave mother whom I love so very much. Thank you. Amen."

Angilia opened her eyes and smiled at her mother's tomb. "Happy 75th anniversary, Mommy. Oh, how I love you and Daddy. You are the person I long to meet most when I die and return to Heaven. You. I long to see your sparkling brown eyes and your lovely smile. I long to feel your embrace. I long to know you, really know you. I love you, Mommy."

Angilia turned and placed the other dozen white roses on her father's tomb. Tears filled her eyes as she traced his name with a finger. She bowed her head and prayed through her tears. "Dear God, Thank you for my magnificent Daddy. I love him so. I long to return to him, to stay with him for all time. I miss him so much, but I know I am still here because you have more for me to do on earth. I will do as you command me to do, as I have always tried to do. Daddy taught me how to do that while turning my pain and sadness over to you. With your help and his, I will continue to do so until you decide that my life on earth is through. Until then, I thank you for the lifetime of loving, happy memories that make the pain and sadness easier to bear. Thank you, God. Amen."

Angilia smiled and said, "Happy anniversary, Daddy. I love you. I love you so very much. I always have, and I always will. You are my first and greatest love. I know how very happy you and Mommy are in Heaven, and I hope you know how happy that really does make me. I can't lie, though. I do miss you terribly. I live for the day I can return to you, to you and Mommy. What a glorious day that will be, Daddy. We know that," Angilia said and placed her hand over the pendant. "Your birthday letter to me was the most wonderful miracle, Daddy. Thank you.

"You and Mommy married 75 years ago today, in this church. Yours is my favorite love story, I've told you that many times. Yours and Mommy's love story truly is epic. People remember that today is also your anniversary, and they have asked me to give you and Mommy their wishes. People love you. They always have.

"I brought you something for your diamond anniversary. I don't know if you can read it from where you are, but I will leave it here for you. Oh, Daddy, I love you," Angilia said as she kissed his name on the plaque. She placed one of her handmade books on his tomb. On the cover was a painting of her parents, as they looked in the pendant from Michael, under the title <u>Eternal Love</u>.

§§§§

"Happy birthday!"

"Are you kidding me?" Matthew asked with a smile when he entered the dining room for lunch. "I'm way too old for surprises. But thank you." Matthew hugged his son and grandsons, kissed his wife, and took his seat.

"You don't seem old, Grandfather," young Patrick said.

"Thank you, Patrick, but, believe me, I'm old," Matthew giggled.

"How old are you today, Grandfather?" young Eric asked.

"I don't suppose there's any sense in lying, since my birthdate is public knowledge," Matthew joked. "I'm 80 today, boys."

"Oh," young Patrick said with a shrug of his shoulders, and took a bite of his salad.

"Oh? That's it?"

"Well, yeah, Grandfather. I thought you were going to say 100 or something," young Patrick replied.

"Well, I suppose compared to your amazing Great-grandfather, I'm not as old as a person could be. I sure feel old, though," Matthew grimaced and rubbed his shoulder. "I think your Great-grandfather was super-human, boys, I really do." Angilia smiled at her husband and kissed his cheek.

"Nah. Great-grandfather was touched by God more than most people are," young Patrick matter-of-factly said.

"He sure was. I bet he's got a place of honor in Heaven," young Eric said. Tears filled Angilia's eyes and slid down her cheeks. "I'm sorry, Grandmother. I didn't mean to make you sad. Please don't cry."

Angilia shook her head and walked to her grandsons. She hugged and kissed them, and reassured them, "I'm not sad, Eric and Patrick. What you both said is so beautiful. You've touched my heart deeply. These are happy tears, darlings. Only happy tears."

§§§§§

The sitting room overflowed with people there to celebrate the double birthday—Prince Eric's 45th and the twins' 10th. The party began after school, and four dozen of the young princes' school friends filled the palace with laughter and happiness. Angilia pleasantly surprised the children by revealing their special treat.

"There is pizza, popcorn, and drinks waiting for you in the media room. There are plenty of movies to watch and games to play. Go have fun. Anthony and his staff are there, and we'll check on you later."

"Wow! Really, Grandmother?" young Eric asked.

"Of course, Eric. The media room is all yours."

"Thank you, Grandmother," young Patrick said, kissed her, and ran to catch up with his friends.

"Thanks for arranging that, Mommy. They'll have a blast. They deserve to have fun this year," Prince Eric said.

Darlene suddenly began crying. "Oh, it doesn't feel right without your father here, Angilia."

"I know, Darlene. I miss him every moment. I understand. Just remember how very happy he is now. He and Mommy are together, and that's the one happiness that keeps me going," Angilia told her friend.

"I know. I just expect to see him like I always did, so handsome and dashing. I loved him. I still love him," Darlene cried louder. Scott held her, trying to comfort her to no avail. Prince Eric brought her a glass of ice water, but she nearly choked when she tried to take a drink while she was crying.

"Hey, why all the tears?" Patrick asked as he unexpectedly manifested.

"Darlene's sad that King Eric isn't here," Scott explained.

"Oh. Hey, Eric's fine, Darlene. He's happy. You'll see for yourself someday," Patrick said, trying to cheer the perpetually love-struck Darlene.

"I want to see him now," Darlene sobbed. "Why can't I?"

"Because you're not dead yet," Patrick answered.

"But I can see you, and I'm not dead," she moaned.

"Yeah, but it's different with me. I'm an envoy angel. Not all angels are envoys. God sends me to earth to do work on his behalf," Patrick explained.

"Why isn't King Eric an envoy angel? Why doesn't he visit us?" Darlene asked, trying to dry her tears.

"Eric had a very long life on earth, and he worked very hard. God's letting Eric enjoy his life in Heaven after 110 years of work."

"So, King Eric is retired? But you're not, because you only lived 19 years?" Darlene asked, trying to understand in her unique way. Scott and William rolled their eyes, and Nicole sighed.

"Yeah, I guess you could say that. If God wanted Eric to still work, he would have let him live forever."

"I wish he would have," Darlene said and sobbed again.

"I don't, Darlene," Angilia said.

"What? But he's your father! You miss him," Darlene said in horror.

"I do miss him. I love Daddy. But it wouldn't have been fair to him to prolong his life just for our own selfish desires to keep him here with us. I had to realize that, Darlene. I wanted Daddy with me for the rest of my life. That was for me. That wasn't for him. I didn't put him first until I realized that. He isn't dead and he isn't lost. He lives in Heaven, with God, Mommy and the rest of his family. That's what he deserves after 110 years of work. He deserves his eternal life. That is his well-deserved reward."

Darlene sat, her head bowed, for several moments. Finally, she looked at Angilia. "You're right, Angilia and Patrick. I know that. I am selfish, and I'm sorry. Heck, I'm almost 73, so my life will probably be over in a few years. Then I can see King Eric all I want," she smiled. "Isn't that wonderful, Scott?" she asked and hugged her husband.

"Oh sure, Darlene. I bet Heaven won't know what hit it when you see Eric for the first time there and faint. That will be a new one for the angels, I'm sure," Scott drolly said. Darlene playfully swatted his arm and giggled.

"You can count on that," Patrick agreed with a smile.

§§§§

"Hello, and welcome to the 55th Eric DeBruce Martineau Scholarship for Musical Excellence. I am Travis Fortner, the Provost of The Queen's College at the University of Oxford, and I am delighted to host today's ceremony. This scholarship began when Angilia DeBruce Martineau was a 16-year-old doctorate graduate of and a Literature professor at the University of Oxford. Every year since 2012, she has attended the award ceremony, and we are honored to welcome back Her Majesty Queen Angilia de Valdavia."

Angilia walked across the stage to a standing ovation, and after she greeted Travis, she waved to the audience. She motioned them to sit, and they did so. "Thank you so much for your support of the Eric DeBruce Martineau Scholarship for Musical Excellence. From the very beginning, I wanted this scholarship named in honor of my father. That was before he had recorded, but I had been blessed to hear him sing since before my birth. For 55 years, the world has heard the beauty and splendor in my father's voice. I am more proud than ever that this scholarship honors his musical legacy."

The audience gave Angilia a standing ovation once more, showing their love and respect for her father. "We are honored to have the scholarship in King Eric's name," a man in the audience shouted, which garnered screams of approval from the audience.

"Thank you so much. I know how much my father's music touches people around the world. He truly never knew just how incredible he is, but the rest of us do," Angilia smiled.

"Your Majesty, do you plan to record again?" a young woman in the audience asked.

"I don't know. I may. I have some piano pieces that my father enjoyed, and I just may record those for him."

"You should, if I may be so bold," a young man stated. "Your Majesty, you and your father recorded your massive hit album <u>Heart-Glow</u> 55 years ago yesterday. Today is March 7, the 55th anniversary of the assassination attempt that nearly ended your life. What are your thoughts on this anniversary?"

"I hadn't realized it was the anniversary of that, to tell you the truth. That day caused many components of my family's destiny to come together, and for that I am grateful. My husband Matthew was my cardiologist that day. We were meant to marry and give life to our amazing son Eric. Eric was meant to have his handsome sons, Eric and Patrick. If I think of this particular event at all, it is as a blessing. God turned what could have been—but wasn't—a tragedy into a blessing." Angilia smiled at Matthew, Prince Eric, Patrick, and Eric as they smiled at her from the front row.

"That is such a positive attitude, Your Majesty. Your deep love for your father led you to save his life and to risk your life. Has the assassination attempt in any way influenced your music?"

"My first instinct is to say no. The threat that loomed over my father is the basis for the song "Victory" from <u>Heart-Glow</u>, but that was written before the shooting. That day specifically hasn't influenced my music. My fierce love for my father has, of course it has. His soul print is embedded in almost everything I have written. My father is the strongest influence on my work. Gregor Jamieson had next to no impact on my work."

The audience stood and applauded again. When they finally sat, one young woman said, "You are such an inspiration, Your Majesty. Your strength, courage, faith, and love color your work like one of God's rainbows colors the earth. Rainbows come after the storm to bring beauty and hope. Your music is just like a rainbow, spreading beauty and hope over the whole world. Thank you."

Angilia bowed her head, overcome by tears and unable to speak. Her grandsons ran on stage and hugged her, an impromptu act of love that brought tears to many people. Eric took the microphone from her hand. "Our grandmother is the most incredible woman we have ever known. She is so strong and wise, and she cares about all people so much that she puts all of us above herself. I love her so much." Eric kissed her cheek, and Patrick took the microphone.

"Yeah, Grandmother is pretty amazing. I love her." Patrick kissed her cheek, and the audience stood yet again in grateful applause.

What no one could see is that Patrick, Eric, and Marisol watched the ceremony from Heaven, with smiles and, yes, tears. Their love for Angilia, Matthew, Prince Eric, and the young princes was so overpowering as it came together in a massive force, that those in the auditorium heard a loud clap of thunder at that moment. Angilia hugged her grandsons, smiled, and said a silent prayer of thanksgiving to God for her precious family.

§§§§

Angilia worked in her office for a few hours one summer morning, and then went across the hall to Shannon's office. "Shannon, is there anything important on my calendar for today?"

"Mr. Trainer called and asked if he could meet with you about Light Within. He has an idea for a new advertising campaign he'd like to go over with you," Shannon explained.

"Isn't he the co-owner of TRW Advertising?"

"Yes. He's interested in sponsoring Light Within, Angilia."

"How kind. Schedule a meeting for this week, here at my office," Angilia requested.

"Of course. I'll call him soon. There aren't any meetings today, although you asked me to remind you about the School Board curriculum revisions. You planned to work on them today," Shannon said as she looked at Angilia's calendar for July 19, 2067.

"Thank you, Shannon. I want some fresh air and sunshine for a while. I'm going to take a short walk. I've got my phone if anything urgent happens, so please call me immediately if it does. I'll be back soon, I think."

"Do you need someone to go with you?"

"No. I want to be alone for a while, Shannon," Angilia smiled.

Angilia slowly walked to the church cemetery, and entered through the gate. A woman was kneeling at Patrick's grave praying. When she finished, she placed a bouquet of flowers on the grave. She stood and told Angilia, "Your uncle is amazing. God bless you." Angilia thanked her, and the woman left the cemetery.

When Angilia was alone, she sat on the bench near her Uncle Patrick's grave and bowed her head in silent prayer. After several minutes, she opened her eyes and stared at Patrick's tombstone. She softly spoke to her uncle. "You really were so young, Uncle Patrick. I'm so sorry. You had to die because of me, and I'm sorry."

Tears spilled from her eyes as Angilia felt the guilt of that wash over her. She was the reason her cherished Uncle Patrick had died. "You sensed it would happen. You knew. Your life should have been long and happy, with a family of your own. Your life was cut short because of my life. That's not fair. It's wrong, and I am so sorry, Uncle Patrick. How can you ever forgive me?"

"Hey, Little One, there is nothing to forgive," Patrick said and pulled her into a hug. "My life wasn't cut short. My life was the way it had to be. My death was part of God's plan, you know that. You've never gotten mopey about me before. Why now?"

Angilia shook her head. "Oh, Uncle Patrick. It's a combination of things. It's the 90th anniversary of your death today. And these past three Julys have been harder without Daddy. I can't explain why, but they are."

"It's been 90 years? Really? Wow. Hey, but I do know why you're sad now. It is because Eric isn't here. This is the day you and he saw each other for the first time. Heck, I knew it. I watched you both that day, and I saw the love between you. Why do you think I wasn't sad, Little One? I wasn't sad," Patrick gently said and smiled at her.

"I know. I saw you, too, you know. But still. . . ."

Patrick interrupted her. "There's no *but still.* There's only what God ordained and predestined. You and Eric were meant to see each other that day. Your love was supposed to be formed that day. That day was beautiful, Little One." Angilia nodded and leaned her head against his chest. "Eric, Marisol, and I were talking about that day a while back with Michael and Grandfather. See, Michael knew everything from the beginning, 'cause he has an inside track with God. Michael knew how and when I would die. He knew that you and Eric would love each other from that moment you came down from Heaven. He knew. God knew. God planned it that way.

"You would know that Eric is your father, but he wouldn't know yet that you're his daughter. But he would love you instantly. And he did. You loved him, and you knew he's your father. That's why you didn't want to leave him and return to Heaven. That's what Grandfather feared. He knew you would love your father and that once you did, you would have a very hard time returning to Heaven. He tried to arrange another Spirit Guide for me, but God was adamant. It had to be you. Only you. Grandfather watched from Heaven, and he saw the love between you and Eric right away, too.

"That love is so strong and impenetrable, a force of its own. When the five of us were talking a while back, Eric said it always felt as if your soul and his soul were parts of one soul, like one soul had spilt. You know what? He's right, Angilia. Michael said so. Your soul and Eric's soul belong together. When Michael told us that, Marisol smiled and said, *That explains everything.*"

Angilia looked up into Patrick's eyes, her own eyes glowing. "That's what it does always feel like, Uncle Patrick," she whispered.

Patrick nodded and softly said, "There's a third part of that soul, Little One."

Angilia gasped and barely said, "Eric's."

Patrick nodded and smiled. "Yeah. Your father, you, and your son are one soul split in thirds. Michael told us that, and it all finally fell into place. You three really are meant to belong to one another, Little One. The three of you literally share a soul. Without your father here, there really is a part of your soul missing."

CHAPTER 22

On Christmas Eve 2068, the Royal Family welcomed the Christ Church Valmondois parishioners as they arrived for the midnight service. When the family took their seats in the Royal pew, everyone noticed that King Eric's seat was, as always since his death, empty. The sight of his empty seat was somehow comforting, as if he were not really gone.

Reverend Olson went to the pulpit for the sermon. "Christmas is one of the two most holy days. Easter is the other. One could never exist without the other. Christmas is the commemoration of Jesus Christ's birth, a birth which fulfilled ancient prophecies of the Messiah's birth. Easter commemorates the fulfillment of another prophecy, that of the Messiah's Crucifixion and Resurrection.

"Jesus was born in the most humble of circumstances. He was raised with love by Mary and Joseph, a man who chose to be the earthly father of God's son. From Joseph, Jesus learned the skill of carpentry, a fitting trade for the man destined to mold and to shape peoples' souls. Jesus visited the temples when he was young. He listened to and he learned from the scholars there. His early life was spent in hard work and preparation for his public ministry.

"That public ministry spread the truths of faith, obedience, and the promise of eternal life. That public ministry was the foundation for the Christian church. That public ministry was a threat to the godless men whose positions were jeopardized as more people learned that God is the one most powerful entity. That public ministry was done out of love. Jesus loves us enough that he risked everything for us. He paid the ultimate price for us. He was viciously murdered for us. He died for us.

"Jesus' death had to happen, and he lived his life knowing that. He lived so that he could die. He died so that he could be resurrected and live again. That is our Christmas gift. Eternal life. When we die, we are reborn in Heaven. What a miracle.

"Join me in prayer." The congregation stood and bowed their heads. "Dear God, Thank you for the gift of your Son, Jesus Christ. Through him, we have everlasting life. We pray that you continue your watch over us, that you lead us down the path you destined for each of us, and that you know how much we love you. In your blessed name we pray. Amen."

Reverend Olson bowed, and Angilia walked to the pulpit. This marked the fourth Christmas that she recited the Christmas story from Luke Chapter 2. The tradition that began in 1979 at the request of her grandfather, King Gerard, did not end with Eric's death. Angilia would recite Luke Chapter 2 at every midnight Christmas service for the rest of her life. It would continue after her death, as well. Prince Eric had told his mother after the 2065 service that he would carry on the tradition. His son Eric had said he would do so, as well.

Angilia smiled as she recited the story, and people noticed that her turquoise eyes sparkled more than usual. She felt warmth encompass her, a stronger warmth than Uncle Patrick's. She knew that her father was with her. His soul stood with hers during the Christmas story, a custom they now truly shared. When she finished, she smiled and barely whispered, "I love you, Daddy."

ՏՏՏՏՏ

Angilia gently kissed Matthew, and he opened his eyes and smiled. "Mmmm. Happy birthday, my darling Angilia. I love you," he murmured and kissed her again.

"Oh, Matthew, I love you, my dear. Thank you for being you and for making my life so wonderfully happy."

"Making you happy is my most important task. I want you to be happy, darling. Your happiness and health are the most important things in the universe to me," Matthew said and held her close to him. "I admit it. I am very selfish. I want you here with me for as long as possible," he said with tears choking his voice.

Angilia looked up at him and smiled. "That's very sweet, Matthew. Thank you."

"You are very sweet," he smiled and kissed her pink lips. "Very sweet."

Angilia giggled and ran her hand through his hair. They held one another and kissed for a long while, until she tickled his stomach and went to the shower. He sighed and decided to shower and dress, too. Despite it being his wife's 73rd birthday, he had an engagement in a nearby town that morning. Besides, he needed his morning coffee.

He finished and dressed in a suit. Matthew walked to her vanity in her dressing room while she brushed her hair, and he bent to kiss her neck. "I'll see you downstairs soon. I love you."

"All right, dear. I love you."

Moments later, Angilia walked to her desk in their sitting room, intending to write a diary entry that morning before breakfast. She felt so many emotions that she wanted to capture in her diary. What she saw on her desk made her pulse pound. "Daddy." She picked up an envelope with his very familiar handwriting on the front. A birthday letter! She held the letter to her heart and closed her eyes. "Thank you, God."

She went to the widow seat to read his letter, like she had so many times before.   "I love you, Daddy," she said before she carefully opened the envelope and removed the parchment sheet. She could not stop her tears as she read his letter, especially after what Uncle Patrick had told her last July.

3 January 2069

My Beautiful Daughter Angilia,

I love you, my darling daughter. I love you. Happy birthday, my precious little girl. It has been four years since I left you and came to Heaven, Patrick reminded me. In many ways it feels far longer than just four years. Now I truly understand what you meant about time—the wait does feel so much longer than it actually is. It feels so very much longer, Angel.

I know why. We know why. Patrick shared Michael's revelation with you. Patrick told me about that day in the cemetery. Oh, Angilia, I wish you didn't feel pain, but I know now that, regardless of your strong faith and knowledge of Heaven, you can do nothing to stop the ache. What Michael told us explained everything between you and me. Nothing in our lives has been a coincidence. Nothing. God planned everything, Angilia. Everything.

We knew that you were created my daughter, and I was created your father. We have always known that. What we didn't know is that we really do share a soul. Eric is part of the same soul, literally part of us. Oh, Angilia, this is how I knew when Mommy became pregnant and the baby was you. Mommy knew there was something unique and almost magical between you and me. What Michael told us clarified everything. Mommy said that explained why you responded to me so intensely from the beginning. You are our child, Mommy's and my, but you and I are part of one soul. God planned it that way.

Angel, as hard as the wait is, remember one thing. No matter how many years your life lasts, we will be together again. We will be together forever. We will regain a missing piece of our souls when you come to me. Many years from now, when Eric joins us, we will be complete. Just hold onto that, and know that the pain will then subside. It will.

Oh, Angilia, I do love you, my beautiful daughter.

Forever and Always,

Daddy

§§§§

March 16, 2069

    Rocket died this morning, sometime after Ben checked on him and fed him. I went to the stable to visit with Rocket, just to spend time with him. He was dead. He was a wonderful horse, and I will miss him. I felt such sadness seeing Rocket on the floor of his stall. I will never see him again this side of Heaven. He's been with me most of my life. I was 9, almost 10, when I got him. I am 47 now. Rocket was with me for 38 years.

    Gosh, I remember that Friday when Mommy picked me up from school and took me to Mr. Holt's ranch to pick out a horse. I knew it was Rocket right away. I knew his name. I loved him. I enjoyed riding him. Mommy and I used to ride Starlight and Rocket together, and I cherish those memories. I really do. Those were such special moments between Mommy and me. What beautiful memories I have, I really do. I am so blessed, and I thank you for that, God.

    I asked that Rocket be buried next to Starlight, because that just seems right and perfect. I requested that his tombstone have a Bible verse that Mommy said when we buried Rocket: "All flesh shall see the salvation of God. Luke 3:6" She told us when Midnight died that animals live in Heaven. I believe that, and I look forward to riding Rocket there someday. I like to think that Grandfather rides Midnight there. Somehow that thought is very soothing to me. I love and miss Grandfather so much.

    I wish I could talk to Grandfather. He is so wise, and he had a way of making things better. So does Mommy. They are so alike, it is quite eerie. It's almost like they are two halves of the same person. God forgive me, but I dread the day I have to let Mommy go to Heaven. I don't know how I will be able to live without her. She is such a part of my heart and soul. I don't know how else to explain it, but you must understand, God.

    I know Mommy will be in Heaven and that she will live forever. She will never truly die. I do know that. But I just feel as if I will lose part of myself without her. That doesn't make complete sense to me, but that is what it feels like when I think of life without her. I have felt that since I was a child. I remember writing that on her birthday in 2029, the year she was coronated. 40 years. My remarkable Mommy has been Queen de Valdavia for almost 40 years. Thank you for that, God. I love her.

§§§§§

Huge crowds turned out on July 10, 2069 for Angilia's official engagement in the Valdavian town of Toulouse, where she opened the King Eric Hospital. After the two-hour opening ceremony, Shannon and Troy accompanied her on a walkabout to greet those who had waited several hours—days in some cases—to see her. Angilia spoke to hundreds of people, making each one feel special.

Shannon's arms were quickly filled with flowers and gifts, which she hurriedly placed in their car trunk. Angilia was given so many flowers and gifts that Shannon made multiple trips to the car to unload her arms. After three hours, Shannon mentioned that Angilia should end the walkabout. She remembered Angilia's past health scares, and she wanted to err on the side of precaution. Troy agreed and said that Angilia should leave soon.

"Are you sure? There are so many people I haven't met yet," Angilia said to Shannon and Troy.

"I know, Angilia, but you know what Matthew always says about your long walkabouts," Shannon reminded her. "I really do think you need to stop now."

"Please Queen Angilia, don't go yet. I really need to speak to you," a girl in the crowd said.

Angilia turned just as a young woman pushed a teenager in a wheelchair through the crowd. Angilia told the police officers to let the young ladies across the barricade, and they approached her. "Hello. Were you waiting long?" Angilia asked them.

"Yes, Your Majesty, but we still didn't get to the front of the crowd. I really hoped—prayed, really—to speak to you," the girl in the wheelchair said.

"What can I do for you, dear?"

"Make me walk. Please make me walk. I believe in you."

Angilia knelt and took the girl's hands in her hands. "Oh, darling, I wish I could."

"You can, Queen Angilia. You can. I know you can. I know about the miracles you have done. I believe. Please make me walk," the girl pleaded and cried.

"I'm Bess. Please help my sister. Please. You're the only hope she has. Eleanor was born unable to walk, and she wants nothing more than to walk. The doctors can't help her. Please."

To prove that Eleanor could not walk, Bess held her arms and helped her stand. Bess let go of Eleanor's arms, but the girl wobbled and then began to fall. Those watching gasped in fear, and Bess grabbed her sister. "She can't even stand. Please help her."

"I can't cure anyone, as much as I wish I could. Only God can. I will pray for you and ask God to heal you, Eleanor," Angilia said. Eleanor cried and nodded her head. Angilia knelt and held Eleanor's hands again. "Dear God, Please hold Eleanor in your strong arms. Let her feel your love and strength. We pray that, if it is your will, you enable Eleanor to walk. Regardless of your destiny for Eleanor, let her and Bess feel your love and find the peace that only you can give to them. In your loving mercy, this we pray. Amen." Angilia hugged Eleanor for several moments as the girl cried.

"I love you, Eleanor. God loves you," Angilia said, and kissed her cheek. "Please let me know if there is anything I can do for you." Eleanor and Bess thanked Angilia.

Angilia slowly and reluctantly walked away, heading toward the car, when she heard people gasp and Eleanor shout, "Your Majesty!" Angilia turned, stunned to see Eleanor walking to her. "It worked, Queen Angilia! It worked! I can walk!" Angilia—and everyone else—stood frozen, watching Eleanor take her first faltering steps. When Eleanor reached Angilia, she looked at Angilia with tears and a smile. Eleanor hugged her Queen. "Thank you, Queen Angilia. I knew you could make me walk. I believed you could, and you did. Thank you!"

Bess stood crying, her hands over her face. Someone in the crowd shouted, "God bless you, Queen Angilia!" Everyone erupted in shouts of praise, applause, and tears. Bess ran to her sister and Angilia, and grabbed them both in a hug. "God bless you, Queen Angilia. You made Eleanor walk. Thank you."

Angilia began to protest, and said, "I didn't. . ." just as her Uncle Patrick manifested beside her and put his arm around her. Angilia looked at him, and Patrick winked at her. Angilia smiled and nodded. "I'm grateful my prayer helped, Eleanor and Bess. God is truly awesome. I am so grateful that he helped you to walk, Eleanor. I'm so grateful." Angilia kissed the girls and then her Uncle Patrick. "Thank you, Uncle Patrick," she whispered.

§§§§§

"Happy birthday, dearest Matthew," Angilia smiled down at him when he stirred. She had sat up in bed, and during his sleep, he had lain his head in her lap. Matthew groggily moaned and snuggled against her. Angilia smiled and placed her hand on his back. "Sleep awhile, darling. I love you," she whispered.

Two hours later, Matthew awoke and opened his eyes. "You're awake," he said, surprised, when he realized that Angilia was sitting up in bed.

She smiled. "I've been awake. You looked so peaceful and comfortable. I just enjoyed watching you."

"What time is it?"

"6:40."

Matthew moaned. "I guess we better shower and dress. Breakfast is soon. It's also Monday, the start of another work week."

"It's also your birthday."

"Don't remind me," he moaned again. "You make me feel like a pervert again. How can you still look nearly the same, while I look ancient?"

Angilia giggled in that familiar way that charmed him. "Don't be ridiculous. You do not look ancient, Matthew, and I most definitely do not look the same."

"Oh, yes, you do. Everyone comments on it. Everyone sees it. You've barely changed since we met again. You really are otherworldly. If I didn't know about you, I'd swear you were a witch. Only God and magic potions can make someone look like this for decades. Matthew pulled her down to him. "I'm not complaining at all, Angilia. You are perfect. I love you." She giggled again, and they kissed—"made out," as Matthew said—until they had to hurry their showers in time for breakfast.

§§§§

Angilia enlisted the harpist and a violinist from the local orchestra to record with her the instrumental album she had mentioned at the 55th scholarship ceremony. After a series of evening rehearsals, the three musicians convened in Angilia's basement recording studio. They recorded the 12 pieces over two Saturdays: November 2 and November 9.

Angilia dedicated the album to her father and titled it <u>Piece of My Soul</u>. Most people presumed the title referred to the fact that her music came from her soul. Only her Uncle Patrick knew the truth behind the title. "Hey, Little One! So you finally recorded those instrumentals. I'm glad you did. So is your dad. He really likes the title, Angilia." Patrick manifested as she finished her work in her office on the following Friday evening.

She smiled up at him. "He does?"

"Yeah, sure. He said it's the perfect title. Hey, tomorrow's Saturday. You want to record a song together?"

"Tomorrow? That's short notice for the band, but I can call them now," Angilia said, and reached for the telephone.

"We don't need them for this one. Just your guitar."

"Oh, okay. What did you want to record?"

"The last poem I ever wrote," Patrick said. Angilia stared into his eyes, not speaking. "Wrap it up here, and let's go to my room."

Angilia nodded, and told Shannon that unless anything urgent happened, she was finished in her office for the day. Shannon smiled, happy that Angilia ended her work day relatively early for her—it was 6:30.

Angilia and Patrick took the elevator to the third floor. They went into the twins' rooms first, and visited with Eric and Patrick for a few minutes. Finally they went into Patrick's suite, and he closed the door. She smiled as she watched him retrieve a notebook from another secret hiding place. This notebook was in a large envelope stapled to the back of Patrick's desk.

He removed the notebook and turned to the last page on which he had written. He handed the notebook to Angilia. She noticed the date in the upper right hand corner: July 19, 1977. She looked at him, her eyes filled with pain. "I wrote that before breakfast that morning. It's the last thing I wrote," he said matter-of-factly. "Read it."

Angilia read his poem and immediately walked to the patio door, tears in her eyes. "Well? What do you think?" Patrick asked.

"This is the saddest, most poignant poem I have ever read, Uncle Patrick." She went to him and hugged him tight.

"I did meet my destiny that day, and it did set me free. So this isn't sad anymore. See, that's the thing, Little One. I felt these things and let them put fear and dread in me, and I was afraid of, yet resigned to, dying young. But as soon as I did die young, bam, everything was okie-dokie."

Angilia could not help but laugh. "You are incredible, Uncle Patrick. Of course this will make a great song. Just your voice. There doesn't need to be anyone else. This is 100 percent you," she insisted.

"Well, okay, I guess. But you have to write the music and play guitar for me," Patrick said, with a hint of trepidation in his voice.

"I will." Angilia picked up the guitar she kept in his sitting room and sat on his sofa. Within an hour she had written the music, and then she played the song for him.

"This is just what it needs, Little One. Thank you," Patrick smiled and hugged her. Just then, twelve-year-old Eric called her to dinner. "We'll do this tomorrow, okay? You eat and get some sleep tonight. I'll be back tomorrow."

Angilia kissed him and said, "I love you, Uncle Patrick."

After breakfast the next morning, Angilia kissed Matthew, Prince Eric, Patrick, and Eric. "I'm going to work in the recording studio this morning. I'll be done soon."

"Don't you ever stop, Mommy?" Prince Eric asked with a smile. Angilia smiled in return as she entered the elevator.

Angilia got everything prepared and tuned her guitar. "I'm ready, Uncle Patrick," she said, and he manifested within seconds. She giggled. "Are you ready?"

"Yeah. Let's do this." Patrick recorded a take, and Angilia played it back. "Well? Are we good to go?" he asked.

"Yes, we are. This is absolutely perfect, Uncle Patrick. I'll get this on the web site today, and expand the distribution as soon as possible. It may be more than a week before I can get back to this, but I will do it as soon as possible."

"Don't worry about that. You've got your 40th Jubilee starting tomorrow. Plus it's a double birthday tomorrow. That's far more important, Little One. I'll pop back in tomorrow, though. I'm attending the church service with you, if that's okay."

"Of course it's okay. It's always okay, Uncle Patrick. My grandsons are officially teenagers tomorrow. Thirteen. They are wonderful young men. I love them so much."

"I know. I do, too. So does Eric," Patrick said softly with a smile.

"Tell Daddy I love him," Angilia said as Patrick kissed her cheek and disappeared. Angilia smiled, and before lunch Patrick's song was available on her web site.

Destiny

The sun shines so bright this morning,

Taunting me with its cheer

When I can't feel it deep inside.

So I'll put on my veneer

And continue to hide this fear.

I never let them see

The angst, the turmoil I keep

Hidden deep within me,

This persistent and gnawing pain

That I don't want to know,

Though it remains my constant friend.

Friend? No. It is my foe.

I can't bear this any longer.

When will this misery end?

I know the answer in my heart.

Today I'll meet my friend.

They say I have a destiny.

Today I hope mine sets me free.

§§§§

"Good morning, and welcome to a very special day. I am Beatrice Maple, and this is November 17, 2069, the first day of Her Majesty Queen Angilia's 40th Jubilee. As is tradition, the Jubilee begins with a National Service of Thanksgiving in Christ Church Valmondois. The service will be broadcast live across the globe. Large screens are placed in parks across Valdavia, and the service will be relayed into every Valdavian church.

"This promises to be a joyous week filled with events to honor Queen Angilia. Forty years ago today, on his 75th birthday, King Eric proclaimed his daughter, Princess Consort Angilia, the Queen de Valdavia. Angilia was born to become the first hereditary Queen in Valdavia's history. However, His Majesty was inspired by King David of Israel, who proclaimed his son Solomon as his co-monarch.

"King David's son Solomon reigned for 40 years, the first three jointly with his father, which is yet another magnificent parallel between King Eric and Queen Angilia. The Royal Family is arriving at the church, so we commence our live coverage of the Service of Thanksgiving now."

Prince Eric drove the car, and he waved to the well-wishers across from the church when he stepped out. Matthew was assisted by his grandson Eric, and Angilia by her grandson Patrick. Billy, Shannon, Yvonne, and Leigh then emerged. People screamed when Patrick manifested, wearing one of his old navy suits, and took his niece's arm. Angilia smiled up at him, kissed his cheek, and said, "Thank you for coming, Uncle Patrick."

"Are you kidding? I wouldn't miss this for anything."

The family waved to everyone before they entered the church. Inside, parishioners bowed their heads as Angilia passed, a sign of reverence that her grandsons noticed with smiles. People loved their grandmother so much. That was evident when Angilia greeted her friends. William hugged her and told her he loved her. Nicole hugged her and, with tears in her eyes, said, "You are truly amazing, Angilia. I am so happy that you are my friend. I love you."

"I love you, Nicole. Thank you for everything."

Scott hugged Angilia, remembering the 16-year-old girl they had asked to become the COC sponsor. How much had happened in the 57 years since then. He smiled and told her he loved her. Darlene burst into tears when Angilia hugged her, not caring that potentially everyone in the world saw her. "Oh, Angilia. I can't believe it's been 40 years. Where has the time gone? Gosh, I love you. I am so beyond happy that you're my friend. I love you."

"I love you, Darlene. I hope those are happy tears," Angilia said with a giggle. Darlene nodded while she cried, and Scott put his arm around her.

Soon, the service began, and Reverend Olson came to the pulpit. "We gather on this beautiful Sunday for the National Service of Thanksgiving for the life and reign of Her Majesty Queen Angilia on the occasion of her 40th Jubilee. Let us pray." Everyone stood and bowed their heads. "Dear God, We thank you for the life of Queen Angilia. Long before she became our Queen, she was your servant. She has lived her life in obedience to you. That has remained ever consistent in the 40 years of her reign. Queen Angilia is a blessing to us, to Valdavia, and to the world. May she be granted many years to follow in our service and yours, oh merciful God. In this your sacred name we pray. Amen." The congregation repeated the Amen and took their seats.

Teenaged Eric stood and walked to the pulpit. "King David wrote Psalm 5:2, which speaks to the power in Grandmother's prayers. *Hearken unto the voice of my cry, my King, and my God: for unto thee will I pray.*" I love you, Grandmother."

Patrick gave his brother a fist bump and walked to the pulpit. "King David wrote Psalm 9:1, which is how Grandmother lives her life. *I will praise thee, O Lord, with all my whole heart; I will shew forth all thy marvelous works.*' I love you bunches, Grandmother."

Prince Eric smiled and patted his sons' shoulders before he went to the pulpit. "My mother knows that she will see God again in Heaven someday. King David believed that, too, as he wrote in Psalm 17:25. *'As for me, I will behold thy face in righteousness: I shall be satisfied, when I awake, with thy likeness.'* I pray that that day is many long years in the future. I love you, Mommy." Prince Eric walked to Angilia and bent to kiss her cheek.

"I love you, Eric."

Uncle Patrick gently squeezed her shoulder and went to the pulpit. "*'And, lo, the angel of the Lord came upon them, and the glory of the Lord shone round about them: and they were sore afraid.'* You have heard my brother and my niece recite that every Christmas. Luke 2:9. I chose this verse, because I know what the shepherds felt when the angel of God came to them. An angel of God came to me. My niece Angilia. I'm sure you know the story of my death. Angilia was my Spirit Guide when I died. She came to me when I died.

"I saw the angel of God when I died. I was not afraid. I was not terrified. Not anymore. But I understand what Luke means here. Those who were present when the angel of God appeared were so shocked, stunned by the glorious appearance of the angel. They had never beheld a being so magnificent.

"God sent the angel to the shepherds to tell them about Jesus' birth. That was the greatest news, and they received that news from the splendid angel of God. Wow! I can only image what that was like. Well, actually, I don't have to imagine. God sent the most beautiful angel to me when I died. That angel took me to Heaven, where I began my eternal life. Talk about wow!

"Heaven is beyond wow. Heaven is the only perfect place that exists. Words really can't describe its beauty and wonders. But Angilia, my niece, took me there, and I have to tell you that I have never had a more mind-blowing experience. I have never been happier than since my death, which I gotta say totally turned my thoughts upside down. I really feared what would happen after my death, but when Angilia appeared, the fear disappeared.

"Angilia is an angel among you. She lives and works on God's behalf. You see that every day. You feel that every day. She is living proof of God's existence. Angilia really is touched by God. We are all touched by an angel. I am so grateful to God for Angilia. To say I love her is just a scratch on the surface."

§§§§§

After lunch, everyone congregated in the sitting room for the birthday party. Patrick returned, much to his great-grandnephews' delight. This year, just the family and the four friends who lived in the palace attended, making for a much more intimate celebration. "I love our friends, but I'm glad it's just us this year. Today is too special, like it belongs just to us," young Eric said. "Does that make sense?"

"Yes, it does, Eric. I love our friends, too, I really do. But I'm happy it's just us. Today is very special. I was eight years old when Mommy became Queen. I was so happy both days that I thought I would burst," Prince Eric said with a smile.

"Both days?" young Eric asked.

"Yes. Forty years ago today was your great-grandfather's 75th birthday, the day he proclaimed his daughter the Queen. Your grandmother was coronated on her birthday the following January 3. That was such a magical, beautiful day. She looked like an angel, you know, the angels in paintings. She is an angel, of course. Just to watch the ceremonies, it was extraordinary," Prince Eric recalled.

"I've seen the coronation portraits, Dad. Grandmother did look like an angel. I like that you talked about her being an angel of God this morning, Uncle Patrick," young Patrick smiled.

"Yeah. She's pretty amazing," Patrick said.

"Yes, she is," Matthew agreed and kissed her.

"Speaking of Uncle Patrick, I remember that woman trying to drag him from the carriage. That was pretty scary," Prince Eric said.

"It sure was," Matthew smiled. "Mom fainted against Dad in their carriage behind ours. Thank goodness you couldn't be mauled by her."

"What happened?" young Eric and Patrick wanted to know. Everyone told them exactly what happened, and their eyes grew huge as they listened. "Gosh, that does sound scary," young Eric shivered.

"Nah. She was just one woman. She couldn't have done anything even if I were human. Gosh, that day really was wonderful. So is today, guys. My two favorite great-grandnephews are teenagers now," Patrick said and hugged them. "Why don't you have your cake now? It'll be the perfect desert." Patrick winked at them, and they giggled.

"Okay. We asked for a chocolate cake with strawberry icing," young Patrick said with a smile for his grandmother.

"Daddy's favorite cake. Thank you, Patrick and Eric." Angilia kissed them. Uncle Patrick put his hands on her shoulders while they cheered the boys as they blew out the candles. Yvonne cut and served the cake, except to Patrick of course, and everyone sat on the sofas and chairs. The stories and laughter lasted for over two hours.

Angilia stood and kissed her husband, grandsons, son, and uncle. "I need to go upstairs. You all keep enjoying yourselves. I love you."

"I love you, too, Grandmother," young Patrick said.

"I love you, Grandmother," young Eric told her.

"I love you, my Angilia," Matthew smiled at her.

Angilia smiled and blew him a kiss. She took the elevator to the third floor. She walked into the suite she shared with Matthew and looked around. She took a sheet of stationery and a pen from her desk and wrote *I love you A*. She walked into their bedroom and placed it on Matthew's side of the bed. She picked up Angel Bear and walked across the hall to her father's suite.

Nothing had been changed or moved. She traced her finger over the 2065 diary that still laid atop his desk as if he were going to write in it that night. "Oh, Daddy, I love you so much," Angilia said, and looked around his sitting room once more. She felt too tired to go any further, so she sat on her father's sofa while she clutched Angel Bear.

"Hey, I need to do something. I'll be back," Prince Eric said at that moment. He ran upstairs, and looked in his parents' suite for his mother. No one was there. He ran to Uncle Patrick's suite. No one was there, either. "Grandfather's," he suddenly whispered and ran to his Grandfather's suite. He stopped when he saw his mother sitting on the sofa there, holding the bear that Uncle Patrick had given her.

He slowly walked to the sofa and sat beside her. "Mommy?" he barely whispered.

Angilia looked up into his eyes and smiled. "I love you, Eric. You are such a remarkable man."

"No, Mommy," he said as tears filled his eyes.

"I have something for you," she said and pulled the pendant from under her dress and over her head. She held it in her hands for a moment, kissed it, and placed it around her son's neck. "You wear this for the rest of your life, my dear. Give this to Eric just as I am giving it to you." Angilia kissed Prince Eric's cheek.

"I'm not ready for this, Mommy. No."

"I know, Eric, but it's time for me to go."

"I don't want you to go. Please don't go," he cried. Suddenly, warmth surrounded them as Uncle Patrick manifested beside Angilia. "No, Uncle Patrick! You can't take her! No!"

"Look at the pendant, Eric," Angilia softly said. Prince Eric shook his head, crying, pushing the truth away. "Look."

Prince Eric finally lifted the pendant and looked at the heart-stopping scene of his grandparents together. He gasped when he saw his mother, in a long white dress, run to them in a joyous embrace. He stared at the pendant while his brain registered what he saw. "Mommy? Is this what I think it is?"

"Yes, darling. It's Heaven," Angilia said with a smile.

"Oh, Mommy, I don't want you to go. I know you want to be with Grandfather and Grandmother, I do, but I want you here with me," Prince Eric cried while he hugged his mother as if that would keep her there.

"I know, Eric. I know. It's time, though. I have to go. Tell Dad, Eric, and Patrick how much I love them." Prince Eric nodded, still holding his mother. Angilia softly said, "I love you, Eric," and kissed his cheek. She looked at Patrick. "Are you my Spirit Guide, Uncle Patrick?"

"Yeah. I have the honor of taking you home to your parents."

"I'm ready," Angilia said. Prince Eric cried uncontrollably when his mother died in his arms at that moment. He felt her hand on his cheek, and he looked up.

Her manifested soul stood with Uncle Patrick's. She wore the long white dress from the pendant. "Mommy?" Angilia nodded, kissed his cheek, and walked away with Uncle Patrick.

Angilia and Patrick climbed the invisible staircase to Heaven, the one they had climbed in 1977. Patrick escorted her to an exquisite field of flowers, the same one she had seen in the pendant. "You're home, Little One," he said.

Angilia beamed and ran to her parents. She, Eric, and Marisol hugged. She kissed Marisol's cheek and said, "Mommy! Oh, Mommy I love you! I love you, Mommy!"

"I so love you, mi hermosa hija Angilia," Marisol told her beloved daughter for the very first time.

Angilia turned to her father, clasped his arms, kissed his cheek, and joyfully exclaimed, "Oh, my magnificent Daddy, I love you so!"

Eric pulled her close, kissed the top of her head, and said, "I love you, my beautiful daughter Angilia."

Sheilah R. Craft is an English professor, writer, blogger, poet, artist, ardent genealogist, and book lover. Born and raised in the Midwestern United States, Sheilah was born surrounded by a close family—including several educators—books, and animals. She began reading and writing very early, and has published short stories, articles, and poems. She was literally born a writer. Her series of novels centered on the lives of one family dynasty and spanning more than two centuries began in the fall of 2012 with the first volume, <u>Heart-Glow</u>. The second volume, <u>First Love Never Dies</u>, was published in the spring of 2013. <u>Heart Eternal</u> is the third volume in the series. Four more volumes are planned.

Web Site and Exclusive Content

Please visit the companion web site, which contains additional information, pictures, and exclusive features. Those who purchase this book have access to specific password protected content on the web site. To access the exclusive content, please visit *Heart-Glow: A Novel* at **http://www.heartglownovel.org**

On the password protected pages, when prompted for the password, please enter **heartglowcraft16***

BOOKS BY SHEILAH R CRAFT

Published by STARLIGHT Books:

HEART-GLOW: A NOVEL

FIRST LOVE NEVER DIES: HEART-GLOW
VOLUME II

HEART ETERNAL: HEART-GLOW VOLUME III

MARY MAGDALENE: A MYSTERY PLAY

Published by Little Butterfly:

THE QUEST FOR PERFECTION: SHELLEY AND
THE POET-HERO

A DAY WITH TEDDY BEAR